Thomas

The Freemason's Monitor

SALZWASSER
VERLAG

Thomas Smith Webb

The Freemason's Monitor

Reprint of the original, first published in 1859.

1st Edition 2023 | ISBN: 978-3-37513-642-0

Verlag (Publisher): Salzwasser Verlag GmbH, Zeilweg 44, 60439 Frankfurt, Deutschland
Vertretungsberechtigt (Authorized to represent): E. Roepke, Zeilweg 44, 60439 Frankfurt, Deutschland
Druck (Print): Books on Demand GmbH, In de Tarpen 42, 22848 Norderstedt, Deutschland

THE
FREEMASON'S MONITOR,

OR

ILLUSTRATIONS OF MASONRY,

BY

THOMAS SMITH WEBB.

WITH COMMENTS AND COPIOUS NOTES UPON THE HISTORY, USAGE AND JURISPRUDENCE OF SYMBOLICAL MASONRY, TOGETHER WITH AN APPENDIX, EMBRACING

A SYNOPSIS OF MASONIC LAW,

FORMS, ODES AND CHRONOLOGICAL TABLES,

BY ROB MORRIS,

GRAND MASTER,

AUTHOR OF "CODE OF MASONIC LAW," ETC., ETC., AND COMPILER OF THE UNIVERSAL MASONIC LIBRARY.

Tomb of Webb, Providence, R. I.

CINCINNATI:

MOORE, WILSTACH, KEYS & CO.,

25 WEST FOURTH STREET,

1859.

J
P
F
T

TO

JOSEPH DRAPER,

OF

CINCINNATI, OHIO,

A FREEMASON OF LONG AND VALUED SERVICE,

A CITIZEN OF STERLING AND ACKNOWLEDGED MERIT,

A FRIEND WITH A HAND AND HEART THAT NEVER SLACKEN
IN WELL-WISHING AND WELL-DOING,

This Annotated Edition

OF

THE FREEMASONS' MONITOR

IS RESPECTFULLY AND FRATERNALLY

DEDICATED.

PREFACE.

In undertaking to edit this republication of the Freemason's Monitor, it is but justice to myself to say that the work has been long in contemplation; the notes, etc., for the most part, were long since prepared. As far back as 1852, I had an edition of the Monitor, embracing the Symbolical Degrees, nearly ready for the press. In all my teachings as a Masonic Lecturer, I have urged that whatever merits the fifteen or twenty Handbooks in use among us possessed over this, or one another, it was merely for their pictorial embellishments; the monitorial and really essential parts being but copies of this, with unimportant additions. I have never thought their dissemination, to the exclusion of Webb's Monitor, the true policy of the Craft.

To Mr. John Sherer I have now transferred the materials so long collected and elaborated, and would cordially recommend this laudable èffort of his to the Fraternity at large. His labors in the science of Masonic Symbology are well known at home and abroad. His large and elegant Carpets, approved and indorsed by the highest intelligence of our Order, are suspended in every Lodge and Chapter, and it is reasonably anticipated that THE FREEMASON'S MONITOR will be accepted by the Craft at large as the best accompaniment to them.

The first edition of the FREEMASON'S MONITOR was issued at Albany, N. Y., in 1797. In the preface the author declares that the work was chiefly intended for Freemasons, but is equally calculated to explain the nature and design of the institution to persons seeking Masonic information, from whatever motives. He admits that it is chiefly taken from the *Illustrations of Masonry* of William Preston; the principal changes being a reduction of the number of Sections, in the original *six*, *four* and *twelve* respectively, but in this work *three*, *two* and *three*. He conceived that the MONITOR embraced Masonic information not otherwise accessible in a single volume, and that Masonic bodies would find it a useful assistant and monitor. This hope has been amply fulfilled. The plan of the MONITOR is so lucid, and the working of the Degrees, by due attention to the various sections, so practical, that its publication, aided, as it was, for twenty-two years by Webb's personal teachings, and by those of his disciples, Gleason, Cushman, Cross, Barney, Fowle, Vinton, etc., who more or less accurately followed their master's steps, produced an admirable uniformity in the American rituals.

In this edition the phraseology of that of 1816 and subsequent issues has been followed, correcting typographical errors and improving the punctuation. Mr. Webb altered and amended the MONITOR in each successive edition from 1797 to 1816; after that time the text was unchanged. Hence the propriety of adopting the latter as a standard.

A few Scripture passages incorrectly quoted have been set right; a full copy of the Ancient Charges inserted, instead of the garbled one formerly used; and the headings of the pages improved. With these few exceptions, the reader will see the MONITOR as Webb himself perfected it and left it.

The omission of the Degrees and Orders of The Ancient and Accepted Rite was a matter of course. Webb, so far as is known, was not in possession of those Degrees, and could only give an imperfect sketch of their history and rituals from other authors equally in the dark. They are grossly, even ridiculously, incorrect; and the space occupied by them has been devoted here to a better purpose. The publication of exact and elegant rituals of this philosophical Rite by Pike, Lafon and Carson, renders it the less important that I should present one here.

In relation to the insertion of Masonic emblems illustrating the unwritten work of Masonry, it is known that Webb did not approve of them. In none of his ten or fifteen editions are any illustrations used, although English and French authors had adopted them before his day. Mr. Cross, whose "Masonic Chart" appeared about the time of Mr. Webb's death (1819,) and who is altogether indebted to the MONITOR for any thing valuable in his book, ventured to follow foreign authors in the use of emblems, and thereby made a work which became popular beyond precedent. Although the older Masons, Webb's pupils, opposed it as an innovation, the popular mind seized it as a valuable auxiliary in the study of esoteric Masonry; and it has maintained its place in the bookstores for forty years. Other ritualists, Tannehill, C. W.

Moore, Cornelius Moore, Gray, Macoy, Mackey, Davis, Dove, Stewart, etc., followed the plan thus made popular by Cross; and now no Handbook of Masonry is welcome without emblems. One improvement, which Mr. Sherer claims to have originated, has been adopted in this volume, viz: placing the emblems in juxtaposition with the corresponding letter-press.

If, as is fondly hoped, the establishment of Masonic Schools of Instruction, teaching nothing but the "Webb Work," should be crowned with general success, an important feature in them must be a uniform text-book. The FREEMASON'S MONITOR must of course possess the only claim to that position.

In the Appendix, with Odes, Forms, etc., will be found a practical synopsis of Masonic Law. This, as will be seen, has been prepared with great labor, and is the first work of the sort ever published. I can but anticipate its favorable reception, remembering the general and incessant call that has been made for a work of the kind. Its place in the MONITOR gives it an extrinsic value on the score of convenience.

In conclusion, but few will deny that the practical merits of THE FREEMASON'S MONITOR are enhanced by judicious notes and comment; sixty-two years having passed since the first edition appeared, and great progress having been made by the Fraternity in matters of Masonic science. The fact that Mr. Webb himself so often changed and improved the work until a short time previous to his death, implies that, had he lived to a period subsequent to the great Morgan excitement, he would have thought it necessary, as I have done, to add something more to the MONITOR than illustrations of working the Degrees. Having adopted his views, so far as I possessed them, in the selection and arrangement of my notes comment and synopsis, I feel a pleasing confidence that the present edition will be generally acceptable to his disciples and admirers.

ROB MORRIS.

LOUISVILLE, February, 1859.

INDEX.

FREEMASON'S MONITOR.

CHAPTER I.

ORIGIN OF MASONRY AND ITS GENERAL ADVANTAGES.*

FROM the commencement of the world, we may trace the foundation of Masonry.† Ever since symmetry began, and harmony displayed her charms, our Order has had a being. During many ages, and in many different countries, it has flourished. In the dark periods of antiquity, when literature was in a low state, and the rude manners of our forefathers withheld from them that knowledge we now so amply share, Masonry diffused its influence. This science unveiled, arts arose, civilization took place, and the progress of knowledge and philosophy gradually dispelled the gloom of ignorance and barbarism. Government being settled, authority was given to laws, and the assemblies of the fraternity acquired the patronage of the great and the good, while the tenets of the profession were attended with unbounded utility.

For ample proof of the *antiquity* of Masonry, that necessary foundation of its *universality* and *unchangeability*, see the writings of George Oliver, D. D., whose investigations under this head embrace the entire range of history, ancient and modern. A belief in the *antiquity* of Ma-

* The larger type is the *text*, as found in the Monitor; the paragraphs interspersed in smaller type are Mr. Morris's *comments* and *notes*.

† Masonry and Geometry are sometimes used as synonymous terms.

sonry is the first requisite of a good teacher. Upon this all the legends of the Order are based. The dignity of the Institution depends mainly upon its age, and to disguise its gray hairs is to expose it to a contemptuous comparison with every society of modern date.

Masonry is a science confined to no particular country, but diffused over the whole terrestrial globe. Wherever arts flourish, there it flourishes too. Add to this, that by secret and inviolable signs, carefully preserved among the fraternity throughout the world, Masonry becomes a universal language. Hence many advantages are gained: the distant Chinese, the wild Arab, and the American savage, will embrace a brother Briton, Franc or German; and will know, that beside the common ties of humanity, there is still a stronger obligation to induce him to kind and friendly offices. The spirit of the fulminating priest will be tamed; and a moral brother, though of a different persuasion, engage his esteem. Thus, through the influence of Masonry, which is reconcileable to the best policy, all those disputes, which embitter life, and sour the tempers of men, are avoided; while the common good, the general design of the Craft is zealously pursued.

In the United States there are at this time (1858) 36 Grand Lodges, viz: Alabama, Arkansas, California, Connecticut, Delaware, District of Columbia, Florida, Georgia, Illinois, Indiana, Iowa, Kansas, Kentucky, Louisiana, Maine, Maryland, Massachusetts, Michigan, Minnesota, Mississippi, Missouri, Nebraska, New Hampshire, New Jersey, New York, North Carolina, Ohio, Oregon, Pennsylvania, Rhode Island, South Carolina, Tennessee, Texas, Vermont, Virginia, Wisconsin. The aggregate number of Subordinate Lodges working under these is about 4500, having a membership in gross of 160,000 Master Masons. It is demonstrable that the United States has more Lodges and Masons than the whole of the world besides.

"Lo what a goodly heritage,
The Lord *to us* hath given!"

Each symbolic degree has at least one sign that is universal. The tokens and words, there is reason to believe, are universal.

The every-day experience of the Masonic reader will justify this exhibit of the influence of Masonic principles upon the brotherhood.

From this view of the system, its utility must be sufficiently obvious. The universal principles of the art unite men of the most opposite tenets, of the most distant countries, and of the most contradictory opinions, in one indissoluble bond of affection, so that in every nation a Mason finds a friend, and in every climate a home.

This paragraph demands some modification. "The most opposite tenets," and "the most contradictory opinions," must be harmonized on the broad basis of *The Ancient Charges* of Masonry, else Freemasonry as such could not exist. The belief and trust in one God, and in a Divine Revelation; and obedience to the Ten Commandments of Sinai, are essentials, opposed to which nothing "opposite" nor "contradictory" can be tolerated. No man was more strenuous in maintaining this view of Masonic conformity in practice than Webb himself.

CHAPTER II.

THE GOVERNMENT OF THE FRATERNITY EXPLAINED.

The mode of government observed by the fraternity will best explain the importance, and give the truest idea of the nature and design, of the Masonic system.

There are several classes of Masons, under different appellations. The privileges of these classes are distinct, and particular means are adopted to preserve those privileges to the just and meritorious of each class.

In general practice there is no Masonic discipline, as such, beyond the third degree. It is in the symbolic Lodge, which consists of only three degrees, that every Mason is initiated, passed and raised, affiliated, or demitted, tried, punished, restored or acquitted, enlightened, relieved or interred. Masonic edifices are underlaid and dedicated only by the symbolic Lodge. The honor of the fraternity is maintained, its actual standing is presented before the world, its awards and punishments published, only by the symbolic Lodge. It would comport better with the real purposes of Masonry, if more attention were paid to this department and less to the so called higher degrees.

Honor and probity are recommendations to the *first* class; in which the practice of virtue is enforced, and the duties of morality inculcated, while the mind is prepared for regular and social converse in the principles of knowledge and philosophy.

Diligence, assiduity and application are qualifications for the *second* class; in which an accurate elucidation of science, both in theory and practice, is given. Here human reason is cultivated by a due exertion of the rational and intellectual powers and faculties; nice and difficult theories are explained; new discoveries produced, and those already known beautifully embellished.

It is for this class that zealous men, during the past one hundred years, have provided such ample means of Masonic instruction. The publication of *The Universal Masonic Library*, embracing 53 distinct works, in 30 volumes, upon the History, Philosophy and Jurisprudence of Freemasonry, has left nothing wanting that can enlighten and perfect the aspiring Fellow-craft.

The *third* class is composed of those whom truth and fidelity have distinguished; who, when assaulted by threats and violence, after solicitation and persuasion have failed, have evinced their firmness and integrity in preserving inviolate the mysteries of the Order.

The government of the Lodge, the dispensing of its charities, and the selection of materials for its increase, are left by general usage in the United States, to the Masons of the *third* class, as before remarked.

The *fourth* class consists of those who have perseveringly studied the scientific branches of the art, and exhibited proof of their skill and acquirements, and who have consequently obtained the honor of this degree, as a reward of merit.

Hence the appellation "*the more honorable degree*" of Mark Master, as seen in the Diplomas and Certificates of Royal Arch Masonry. This and the subsequent degrees are comparatively modern.

The *fifth* class consists of those who, having acquired a proficiency of knowledge to become teachers, have been elected to preside over regularly constituted bodies of Masons.

The *sixth* class consists of those who, having discharged the duties of the chair with honor and reputation, are acknowledged and recorded as *Most Excellent Masters.*

The *seventh* class consists of a select few whom years and experience have improved, and whom merit and abilities have entitled to preferment. With this class the ancient landmarks of the Order are preserved; and from them we learn and practice the necessary and instructive lessons, which at once dignify the art, and qualify its professors to illustrate its excellence and utility.

This is the established mode of the Masonic government, when the rules of the system are observed. By this judicious arrangement, true friendship is cultivated among different ranks and degrees of men, hospitality promoted, industry rewarded, and ingenuity encouraged.

This is according to the *American System.* In other countries the degree of Royal Arch is communicated without the intermediate degrees of Mark Master and Most Excellent Master. All the degrees of the Chapter here named are intensely *Americanized.*

CHAPTER III.

THE IMPORTANCE OF THE SECRETS OF MASONRY DEMONSTRATED.

If the secrets of Masonry are replete with such advantages to mankind, it may be asked, Why are they not divulged for the general good of society? To which it may be answered; Were the privileges of Masonry to be indiscriminately bestowed, the design of the institution would be subverted; and, being familiar, like many other important matters, would soon lose their value, and sink into disregard.

A better reason than this is that we as Masons have received them under a binding pledge to preserve them as secrets from the world and can not, short of the most horrible falsehood, violate our covenant. This is well understood by the community at large, who stamped the seal of perjury so deeply into the forehead of those who in the last generation pretended to expose our mysteries to the world, that but few of them ever recovered from the disgrace.

It is a weakness in human nature, that men are generally more charmed with novelty, than the real worth or intrinsic value of things. Novelty influences all our actions and determinations. What is new, or difficult in the acquisition, however trifling or insignificant, readily captivates the imagination, and ensures a temporary admiration; while what is familiar, or easily obtained, however noble and eminent for its utility, is sure to be disregarded by the giddy and unthinking.

Did the particular secrets or peculiar forms prevalent among Masons constitute the *essence* of the art, it might be alleged that our amusements were trifling, and our ceremonies superficial. But this is not the case. Having their use, they are preserved; and from the recollection of the lessons they inculcate, the well-informed Mason derives instruction. Drawing them to a near inspection, he views them through a proper medium; adverts to the circumstances which gave them rise; dwells upon the tenets they convey; and, finding them replete with useful information, adopts them as keys to the privileges of his art, and prizes them as sacred. Thus convinced of their propriety, he estimates the value from their utility.

The "particular secrets or peculiar forms" taught by Webb up to the period of his death as the Rituals of Freemasonry are yet gloriously preserved by many of the old Masons of New England and elsewhere. The writer has received them from various persons in Massachusetts, Rhode Island, Vermont, etc., and has found them in the main, uniform and consistent. The changes made by Masonic lecturers subsequently to 1819, have not been for the better.

Many persons are deluded by their vague supposition that

our mysteries are merely nominal; that the practices established among us are frivolous; and that our ceremonies might be adopted, or waived, at pleasure. On this false foundation, we have found them hurrying through all the degrees, without adverting to the propriety of one step they pursue, or possessing a single qualification requisite for advancement. Passing through the usual formalities, they have accepted offices, and assumed the government of Lodges, equally unacquainted with the rules of the institution they pretended to support, or the nature of the trust reposed in them. The consequence is obvious; wherever such practices have been allowed, anarchy and confusion have ensued, and the substance has been lost in the shadow.

This grievous fault, as common at the present day as in 1797, is chargeable upon the Masters of Lodges and can not justly be imputed to the candidates themselves. If the blind lead the blind what other result can be expected!

Were the brethren who preside over Lodges properly instructed previous to their appointment, and regularly apprised of the importance of their respective offices, a general reformation would speedily take place. This would evince the propriety of our mode of government, and lead men to acknowledge, that our honors were deservedly conferred. The ancient consequence of the Order would be restored, and the reputation of the society preserved.

A careful study of the ancient laws of the Institution develops seventeen main principles, or landmarks which the intelligent officer of the Lodge may well commit to memory. They are as follows: 1, The Masonic landmarks are unchangeable, and imperative. 2, Masonry is a system teaching, symbolically, piety, morality, science, charity, and self-discipline. 3, The law of God is the rule and limit of Masonry. 4, The Civil law, so far as it accords with the Divine, is obligatory upon Masons. 5, The Masonic Lodge, and the Masonic institution, are one and indivisible. 6, Masonic qualifications regard the mental, moral, and physical nature of man. 7, Personal worth and merit are the basis of official worth and merit. 8, The official duties of Masonry are esoteric. 9, The selection of Masonic material, and the general labors of the Masonic Craft are exoteric. 10, The honors of Masonry are the gratitude of the Craft, and the approval of God. 11, Masonic promotion, both official and private, is by grades. 12, The Grand Master may have a deputy. 13, The head of the Lodge is the Master duly elected by the Craft. 14, The medium of communication between the head and the body of the Lodge, is the Wardens duly elected by the Craft. 15, Obedience to the Master and Wardens is obligatory upon the members. 16, Secresy is an indispensable element of Masonry. 17, The Grand Lodge is supreme in its sphere of jurisdiction, and controls both the Subordinate Lodges and individual Masons, but always subject to the ancient landmarks.

Such conduct alone can support our character. Unless prudent actions shall distinguish our title to the honors of Masonry, and regular deportment display the influence and utility of our rules, the world in general will not easily be led to reconcile our proceedings with the tenets of our profession.

CHAPTER IV.

GENERAL REMARKS.

Masonry is an art equally useful and extensive. In every art there is a mystery, which requires a gradual progression of knowledge to arrive at any degree of perfection in it. Without much instruction, and more exercise, no man can be skillful in any art: in like manner, without an assiduous application to the various subjects treated of in the different lectures of Masonry, no person can be sufficiently acquainted with its true value.

This sentiment is a severe rebuke upon those who declaim against all written publications as innovations, and denounce *the study* of Masonry as an unlawful thing. Without *much* instruction, and *more* exercise, no person will appreciate the wisdom, strength, and beauty of Freemasonry.

It must not, however, be inferred from this remark, that

persons who labor under the disadvantages of a confined education, or whose sphere of life requires a more intense application to business or study, are to be discouraged in their endeavors to gain a knowledge of Masonry.

The peculiarly difficult manner in which the essential secrets of Masonry are necessarily communicated to the American brethren, renders it a matter of time as well as labor, to acquire them. No such auxiliaries as go to the acquisition of other sciences are permitted here; frequent rehearsals impressing retentive memories, form the only road to this learning. It is not strange, therefore, that we have so few proficients.

To qualify an individual to enjoy the benefits of the society at large, or to partake of its privileges, it is not absolutely necessary that he should be acquainted with all the intricate parts of the science. These are only intended for the diligent and assiduous Mason, who may have leisure and opportunity to indulge such pursuits.

Though some are more able than others, some more eminent, some more useful, yet all, in their different spheres, may prove advantageous to the community. As the nature of every man's profession will not admit of that leisure which is necessary to qualify him to become an expert Mason, it is highly proper that the official duties of a Lodge should be executed by persons whose education and situation in life enable them to become adepts; as it must be allowed, that all who accept offices, and exercise authority, should be properly qualified to discharge the task assigned them, with honor to themselves, and credit to their sundry stations.

CHAPTER V.

THE CEREMONY OF OPENING AND CLOSING A LODGE.

In all regular assemblies of men, who are convened for wise and useful purposes, the commencement and conclusion of business are accompanied with some form. In every country of the world the practice prevails, and is deemed essential. From the most remote periods of antiquity it may be traced, and the refined improvements of modern times have not totally abolished it.

Ceremonies, when simply considered, it is true, are little more than visionary delusions; but their effects are sometimes important. When they impress awe and reverence on the mind, and engage the attention by external attraction, to solemn rites, they are interesting objects. These purposes are effected by judicious ceremonies, when regularly conducted and properly arranged. On this ground they have received the sanction of the wisest men in all ages, and consequently could not escape the notice of Masons. To begin well, is the most likely means to end well; and it is judiciously remarked, that when order and method are neglected at the beginning, they will be seldom found to take place at the end.

At every stated meeting, the Lodge should be thoroughly instructed in the ceremony of opening, as this embraces the whole art of preserving the essential secresy of the Craft, the duties and stations of officers, the appeal to Deity for grace and strength, and the unchangeable means of Masonic recognition.

The ceremony of opening and closing a Lodge with solemnity and decorum, is, therefore, universally admitted among Masons; and though the mode in some Lodges may vary, and in every degree *must* vary, still a uniformity in the general practice prevails in every Lodge; and the variation is solely occasioned by a want of method, which a little application might easily remove.

In the numerous Lodges I have visited, I have found the variation to consist chiefly in the different *amount* of ceremony and lecture rehearsed. In some the ceremony is deprived of all its vitality, in others it is made full and explicit, while the great mass of Lodges vary between these extremes.

To conduct this ceremony with propriety ought to be the peculiar study of every Mason, especially of those who have the honor to rule in our assemblies. To persons who are thus dignified, every eye is naturally directed for propriety of conduct and behavior; and from them, other brethren, who are less informed, will naturally expect to derive an example worthy of imitation.

It is comparatively easy *to confer a degree*, but few can open and close a Lodge with dignity and propriety. Years of study and experience go to make one proficient in this desirable art.

From a share in this ceremony no Mason can be exempted. It is a general concern, in which all must assist. This is the first request of the Master, and the prelude to all business. No sooner has it been signified, than every officer repairs to his station, and the brethren rank according to their degrees. The intent of the meeting becomes the sole object of attention, and the mind is insensibly drawn from those indiscriminate subjects of conversation which are apt to intrude on our less serious moments.

This effect accomplished, our care is directed to the external avenues of the Lodge, and the proper officers, whose province it is to discharge that duty, execute their trust with fidelity, and by certain mystic forms, of no recent date, intimate that we may safely proceed. To detect impostors among ourselves, an adherence to order in the character of Masons ensues, and the Lodge is either opened or closed in solemn form.

By the general usage in the United States this order is reversed. The Lodge is first congregated, then *purged*, then *tyled*. This seems to me the more consistent method.

At opening the Lodge, two purposes are wisely effected: the Master is reminded of the dignity of his character, and the brethren of the homage and veneration due from them in their sundry stations. These are not the only advantages resulting from a due observance of this ceremony; a reverential awe for the Deity is inculcated, and the eye fixed on that object, from whose radiant beams light only can be derived. Here we are taught to adore the God of heaven, and to supplicate his protection on our well-meant endeavors. The Master assumes his government in due form, and under him his Wardens; who accept their trust, after the customary salutations. The brethren then, with one accord, unite in duty and respect, and the ceremony concludes.

This is a beautiful synopsis of the form and purposes of the opening ceremony.

At closing the Lodge, a similar form takes place. Here the less important duties of Masonry are not passed over unobserved. The necessary degree of subordination in the government of a Lodge is peculiarly marked, while the proper tribute of gratitude is offered up to the beneficent Author of life, and his blessing invoked and extended to the whole fraternity. Each brother faithfully locks up the treasure he has acquired, in his own secret repositary; and, pleased with his reward, retires to enjoy and disseminate, among the private circle of his brethren, the fruits of his labor and industry in the Lodge.

The work of the Lodge in each degree is a portion of *the secrets* of Masonry.

These are faint outlines of a ceremony which universally prevails among Masons in every country, and distinguishes all their meetings. It is arranged as a general section in every degree, and takes the lead in all our illustrations.

The best usage at *stated* meetings is to open the three Lodges in regular order, commencing with the lowest. No abbreviating or slurring over the ceremonies should be allowed, but every response given and every ceremony performed with plodding exactness. The *closing* may be more brief.

At *called* meetings those Lodges only are opened in which the business of the meeting is to be performed.

Charge used at Opening a Lodge.

"Behold! how good and how pleasant it is for brethren to dwell together in unity!

"It is like the precious ointment upon the head, that ran down upon the beard, even Aaron's beard, that went down to the skirts of his garments:

"As the dew of Hermon, and as the dew that descended upon the mountains of Zion; for there the Lord commanded the blessing, even life for evermore."

An Invocation at Closing the Lodge.

May the blessing of Heaven rest upon us, and all regular Masons! may brotherly love prevail, and every moral and social virtue cement us! *Amen. So mote it be.*

No Lodge can be regularly opened or closed without religious services of some sort. The general usage is for the Master to call upon brethren gifted in prayer to make supplication to the Divine Throne. In very many Lodges, opening and closing Odes are likewise sung. See Appendix.

CHAPTER VI.

CHARGES AND REGULATIONS FOR THE CONDUCT AND BEHAVIOR OF MASONS.

A rehearsal of the Ancient Charges properly succeeds the opening, and precedes the closing, of a Lodge. This was the constant practice of our ancient brethren, and ought never to be neglected in our regular assemblies. A recapitulation of our duty can not be disagreeable to those who are acquainted with it; and to those who know it not, should any such be, it must be highly proper to recommend it.

The Synopsis of the *Ancient Charges*, introduced here by Webb, is so abbreviated and imperfect that it is thought better to insert the whole, unabridged. All questions upon Masonic Law must be referred, as a last resort, to these *Ancient Charges*. A mere skeleton of a document, not in itself very lengthy, does not therefore answer the purpose Webb had in view, nor would it serve as a standard, so necessary in this inquiring age, for the settlement of the numerous mooted questions that arise in the workings of every Lodge.

THE

ANCIENT CHARGES OF MASONRY.

FIRST PUBLISHED IN 1723 UNDER THE AUTHORITY OF THE

GRAND LODGE OF ENGLAND.

CHAPTER I.

CONCERNING GOD AND RELIGION.

A Mason is obliged, by his tenure, to obey the moral law, and if he rightly understands the art, he will never become a stupid Atheist nor an irreligious Libertine.

But though in ancient times, Masons were charged in every country to be of the Religion of that country or nation, whatever it was, yet it is now thought more expedient only to oblige them to that Religion in which all men agree, leaving their particular opinions to themselves; that is, to be good and true, or men of honor and honesty, by whatever denominations or persuasions they may be distinguished: whereby Masonry becomes the center of union, and the means of conciliating true friendship among persons that must have remained at a perpetual distance.

CHAPTER II.

OF THE CIVIL MAGISTRATE, SUPREME AND SUBORDINATE.

A Mason is a peaceable subject to the civil powers, wherever he resides or works, and is never to be concerned in plots or conspiracies against the peace and welfare of the nation, nor to behave himself undutifully to inferior magistrates. For as Masonry hath always been injured by war, bloodshed and confusion, so ancient kings and princes have been much disposed to encourage the Craftsmen, because of their peaceableness and loyalty, whereby they practically answered the cavils of their adversaries, and promoted the honor of the fraternity who ever flourished in times of peace. So that if a Brother should be a rebel against the State, he is not to be countenanced in his rebellion, however he may be pitied as an unhappy man; and if convicted of no other crime, though the loyal Brotherhood must and ought to disown his rebellion and give no umbrage or ground of political jealousy to the government for the time being, they can not expel him from the Lodge, and his relation to it remains indefeasible.

CHAPTER III.

OF LODGES.

A Lodge is a place where Masons assemble and work; hence that Assembly, or duly-organized Society of Masons, is called a Lodge, and every Brother ought to belong to one, and to be subject to its by-laws and the general regulations. It is either particular or general, and will be best understood by attending it, and by the Regulations of the General or Grand Lodge hereunto annexed.* In ancient times, no Master or Fellow could be absent from it, especially when warned to appear at it, without incurring a severe censure, until it appeared to the Master and Wardens, that pure necessity hindered him.

The persons admitted members of a Lodge must be good and true men, free born, and of mature and discreet age, no

* Alluding to the Constitution of the Grand Lodge of England which is not given in this volume.

bondmen, no woman, no immoral or scandalous men, but of good report.

CHAPTER IV.

OF MASTERS, WARDENS, FELLOWS AND APPRENTICES.

All preferment among Masons is grounded upon real worth and personal merit only; that so the lord may be well served, the brethren not put to shame, nor the Royal Craft despised. Therefore no Mason or Warden is chosen by seniority but for his merit. It is impossible to describe these things in writing, and every Brother must attend in his place and learn them in a way peculiar to this fraternity. Only candidates may know that no Master should take an Apprentice unless he has sufficient employment for him, and unless he be a perfect youth, having no maim or defect in his body that may render him incapable of learning the art, of serving his Master's Lord, and of being made a Brother, and then a Fellow-craft in due time, even after he has served such a term of years as the custom of the country directs, and that he should be descended of honest parents: That so, when otherwise qualified he may arrive to the honor of being the Warden, and then the Master of the Lodge, the Grand Warden and at length the Grand Master of all the Lodges, according to his merit.

No Brother can be a Warden until he has passed the part of a Fellow-craft; nor a Master until he has acted as a Warden; nor Grand Warden until he has been Master of a Lodge; nor Grand Master unless he has been a Fellow-craft before his election, who is also to be nobly born, or a gentleman of the best fashion, or some eminent scholar, or some curious architect, or other artist, descended of honest parents, and who is of singular great merit in the opinion of the Lodges.

And for the better and easier and more honorable discharge of his office, the Grand Master has a power to choose his own

Deputy Grand Master who must be then or must have been formerly, the Master of a particular Lodge, and has the privilege of acting whatever the Grand Master, his principal, should act, unless the principal be present or interpose his authority by a letter.

These rulers and governors, supreme and subordinate, of the Ancient Lodge, are to be obeyed in their respective stations by all the brethren, according to the old Charges and Regulations, with all humility, reverence, love, and alacrity.

CHAPTER V.

OF THE MANAGEMENT OF THE CRAFT IN WORKING.

All Masons should work honestly on working days, that they may live creditably on holy days; and the time appointed by the law of the land, or confirmed by custom, shall be observed.

The most expert of the Fellow craftsmen, shall be chosen or appointed the Master or Overseer of the lord's work, who is to be called Master by those that work under him.

The Craftsmen are to avoid all ill language, and to call each other no disobliging names, but Brother or Fellow; and to behave themselves courteously within and without the Lodge.

The Master, knowing himself to be able of cunning, shall undertake the lord's work as reasonably as possible, and truly dispend his goods as if they were his own, nor to give more wages to any Brother or Apprentice than he really may deserve.

Both the Master and the Masons, receiving their wages justly, shall be faithful to the lord, and honestly finish their work whether task or journey; nor put the work to task, that hath been accustomed to journey.

None shall discover envy at the prosperity of a Brother, nor supplant him, or put him out of his work, if he be capable to finish the same; for no man can finish another's work so much to the lord's profit, unless he be thoroughly acquainted with the designs and drafts of him that began it.

When a Fellow-craftsman is chosen Warden of the work, under the Master, he shall be true both to Master and Fellows, and shall carefully oversee the work in the Master's absence to the lord's profit: and his brethren shall obey him.

All Masons employed shall meekly receive their wages without murmuring or mutiny, and not desert the Master till the work is finished.

A younger Brother shall be instructed in working, to prevent spoiling the materials for want of judgment, and for increasing and continuing of brotherly love. All the tools used in working shall be approved by the Grand Lodge.

No laborer shall be employed in the proper work of Masonry; nor shall Freemasons work with those that are not free, without an urgent necessity; nor shall they teach laborers, unaccepted Masons, as they should teach Brother or Fellow.

CHAPTER VI.

OF BEHAVIOR, VIZ: IN THE LODGE WHILE CONSTITUTED.

You are not to hold private committees or separate conversation without leave from the Master, nor to talk of any thing impertinent or unseemly, or interrupt the Master or Wardens, or any Brother speaking to the Master; nor behave yourself hilariously or jestingly while the Lodge is engaged in what is serious and solemn, nor use any unbecoming language upon any pretense whatever, but to pay due reverence to your Master, Wardens and Fellows, and put them to worship.

If any complaint is brought, the Brother found guilty shall stand to the award and determination of the Lodge, who are the proper and competent judges of all such controversies (unless you carry it by appeal to the Grand Lodge), and to whom they ought to be referred, unless a lord's work be hindered the mean while; in which case a particular reference may be made. But you must never go to law about what concerneth Masonry, without absolute necessity, apparent to the Lodge.

After the Lodge is over and the Brethren not gone.

You may enjoy yourselves with innocent mirth, treating one another according to ability, but avoiding all excess, or forcing any Brother to eat or drink beyond his inclination, or hindering him going when his occasions call him, or doing or saying any thing offensive, or that may forbid an easy and free conversation; for that would blast our harmony and defeat our laudable purposes. Therefore, no private piques or quarrels must be brought within the door of the Lodge, far less any quarrels about religion, or nations, or State policy, we being only as Masons of the catholic religion above mentioned. We are also of all nations, tongues, kindreds and languages, and are resolved against all politics as what never yet conduced to the welfare of the Lodge, and never will. This charge has been always strictly enjoined and observed; but especially ever since the Reformation in Britain, or the dissent and secession of these nations from the communion of Rome.

When Brethren meet without Strangers, but not in a Lodge formed.

You are to salute one another in a courteous manner, as you will be instructed, calling each other Brother, freely giving mutual instruction, as shall be thought expedient, without being overseen or overheard, and without encroaching upon each other, or derogating from that respect which is due to any Brother were he not a Mason. For though all Masons are as brethren upon the same level, yet Masonry takes no honor from a man that he had before,—nay, rather it adds to his honor, especially if he has deserved well of the Brotherhood, who must give honor to whom it is due, and avoid ill-manners.

In presence of Strangers, not Masons.

You shall be cautious in your words and carriage, that the most penetrating stranger shall not be able to discover or find out what is not proper to be intimated; and sometimes you shall divert a discourse, and manage it prudently, for the honor of the worshipful fraternity.

At Home and in your Neighborhood.

You are to act as becomes a moral and wise man: particularly not to let your family, friends and neighbors know the concerns of the Lodge, etc., but wisely to consult your own honor, and that of the ancient Brotherhood, for reasons not to be mentioned here. You must also consult your health, by not continuing together too late, or too long from home after Lodge hours are past, and by avoiding of gluttony or drunkenness, that your families be not neglected or injured, nor you disabled from working.

Toward a strange Brother.

You are cautiously to examine him in such a method as prudence shall direct you, that you may not be imposed upon by an ignorant false pretender, whom you are to reject with contempt and derision, and beware of giving him any hints of knowledge. But if you discover him to be a true and genuine Brother, you are to respect him accordingly; and if he is in want, you must relieve him if you can, or else direct him how he may be relieved. You must employ him some days, or else recommend him to be employed. But you are not charged to do beyond your ability, only to prefer a poor Brother, that is a good man and true, before any other poor people in the same circumstances.

Finally, all these charges you are to observe, and also those that shall be communicated to you in another way; cultivating *Brotherly Love*, the foundation and cap-stone, the cement and glory of the ancient fraternity, avoiding all wrangling and quarreling, all slander and backbiting, not permitting others to slander any honest Brother, but defending his character, and doing him all good offices as far as is consistent with your honor and safety, and no further. And if any of them do you injury, you must apply to your own or his Lodge, and from thence you may appeal to the Grand Lodge at the quarterly Communication, and from thence to the annual Grand Lodge, as has been the ancient laudable conduct of our forefathers in every nation; never taking a legal course, but when the case can not be otherwise decided, and patiently listening to the honest and friendly advice of Master and Fellows, when they would prevent your going to law with strangers, or would excite you to put a speedy period to all lawsuits, that so you may mind the affair of Masonry with the more alacrity and success. But with respect to Brothers or Fellows at law, the Master and brethren should kindly offer their mediation, and if that submission is impracticable, they must however carry on their process or lawsuit without wrath and rancor, not in the common way, saying or doing nothing which may hinder *Brotherly Love* and good offices to be renewed and continued; that all may see the benign influence of Masonry, as all true Masons *have done* from the beginning of the world, and *will do* to the end of time. *Amen. So mote it be.*

In addition to this ancient and most valuable document, the reader is referred to Records of the tenth century (*Code*, p. 18), the fourteenth century (Ibid. pp. 21 and 27), the fifteenth century (Ibid. p. 29); the seventeenth century (Ibid. p. 35, republished in this volume under head of "Charges to a Past Master"), and of the eighteenth century (Ibid. p. 47). The Constitutions of the thirty-six American Grand Lodges form useful subjects of study. (For that of New York see Ibid. p. 64.) The standard form of by-laws in very general use is worthy of notice in the same connection (Ibid. p. 91). Nothing will so readily form the ripe Mason as the study of these ancient and standard documents.

CHAPTER VII.

PRE-REQUISITES FOR A CANDIDATE.

By a late regulation, adopted by most of the Grand Lodges in America, no candidate for the mysteries of Masonry can be initiated without having been proposed at a previous meeting of the Lodge; in order that no one may be introduced without due inquiry relative to his character and qualifications.

This is so far from being a *late regulation* that it is a portion of the oldest Masonic statutes ever brought to America: viz., in 1773, at the establishment of the first Lodge in Boston, Massachusetts. It formed a part, at that time, of the Constitutions of the Grand Lodge of England, as follows: "RULE V. No man can be made or admitted a member of a particular Lodge, without previous notice, one month before, given to the said Lodge in order to make due inquiry into the reputation and capacity of the candidate; unless by the Dispensation aforesaid." This being a fundamental law of Masonry, it was not a regulation that could be "adopted by most of the Grand Lodges in America." See, also, the Installation Service of the Master of a Lodge, Charge xiv.

All applications for initiation should be made by petition in writing, signed by the applicant, giving an account of his age, quality, occupation, and place of residence, and that he is desirous of being admitted a member of the fraternity; which petition should be kept on file by the Secretary.

Form of a Petition to be presented by a Candidate for Initiation.

"To the Worshipful Master, Wardens, and Brethren of ——— Lodge, of Free and Accepted Masons:

"The petition of the subscriber respectfully showeth, that having long entertained a favorable opinion of your ancient institution, he is desirous of being admitted a member thereof, if found worthy.

To this is properly added the words, "If admitted he pledges himself to a cheerful obedience to all the requirements of the Institution."

"His place of residence is ——; his age —— years; his occupation ——.

[Signed] "A. B."

After this petition is read, the candidate must be proposed in form, by a member of the Lodge, and the proposition seconded by another member; a committee is then appointed to make inquiry relative to his character and qualifications.

The only exception to this rule is found in Virginia, where no examining committees are appointed.

The qualifications of candidates are of three classes: *mental*, *moral*, and *physical*.

Mentally, each must possess a sound intellect, and a good memory, so as quickly to appreciate, thoroughly to comprehend, and faithfully to retain the instructions to be communicated to him.

Morally, he must be of good report before all men, obedient to the laws of God, keeping his passions under subjection, industrious, economical, and a good citizen.

Physically, he must have the parts and members of a man, without any serious maim or defect. All the Masonic means of recognition he must be able Masonically to *receive*, and Masonically to *communicate*.

Declaration to be assented to by a Candidate, in an adjoining apartment, previous to Initiation.

"Do you seriously declare, upon your honor, before these gentlemen,* that, unbiased by friends, and uninfluenced by mercenary motives, you freely and voluntarily offer yourself a candidate for the mysteries of Masonry?" I do.

"Do you seriously declare, upon your honor, before these gentlemen, that you are prompted to solicit the privileges of Masonry by a favorable opinion conceived of the institution,

* The Stewards of the Lodge are usually present. If not, then a Committee of Preparation.

a desire of knowledge, and a sincere wish of being serviceable to your fellow-creatures?" I do.

"Do you seriously declare, upon your honor, before these gentlemen, that you will cheerfully conform to all the ancient established usages and customs of the fraternity?" I do.

A *clear ballot* must be had before the candidate is notified to appear in the "adjoining apartment." The only exception to this is in South Carolina, where it requires two black balls to reject.

The usage in balloting is by balls, and in a manner so secret that no one is informed how another voted. If one black ball only is found in the box, a second ballot is immediately had to correct a possible mistake; the black ball appearing the second time, the candidate is declared rejected, nor can he apply to the Lodge again until after a period (usually twelve months) designated in the standard regulations of the Grand Lodge having jurisdiction. More than one black ball ensures a peremptory rejection.

The same rule of balloting is applicable to petitions for affiliation and advancement.

There is no Grand Lodge which at present authorizes an addition to these declarations. A few private Lodges append a pledge, to the effect that the applicant believes in a state of future rewards and punishments, that he conceives the Holy Scriptures to be of Divine import, etc. All this, however, is irregular and un-Masonic.

After the above declarations are made, and reported to the Master, he makes it known to the Lodge, in manner following, viz:

"BRETHREN,—At the request of Mr. A. B., he has been proposed and accepted in regular form; I therefore recommend him as a proper candidate for the mysteries of Masonry, and worthy to partake of the privileges of the fraternity; and, in consequence of a declaration of his intentions, voluntarily made, I believe he will cheerfully conform to the rules of the Order."

If there are then no objections made, the candidate is introduced in due form.

τῳ κρουοντι ανοιγησεται

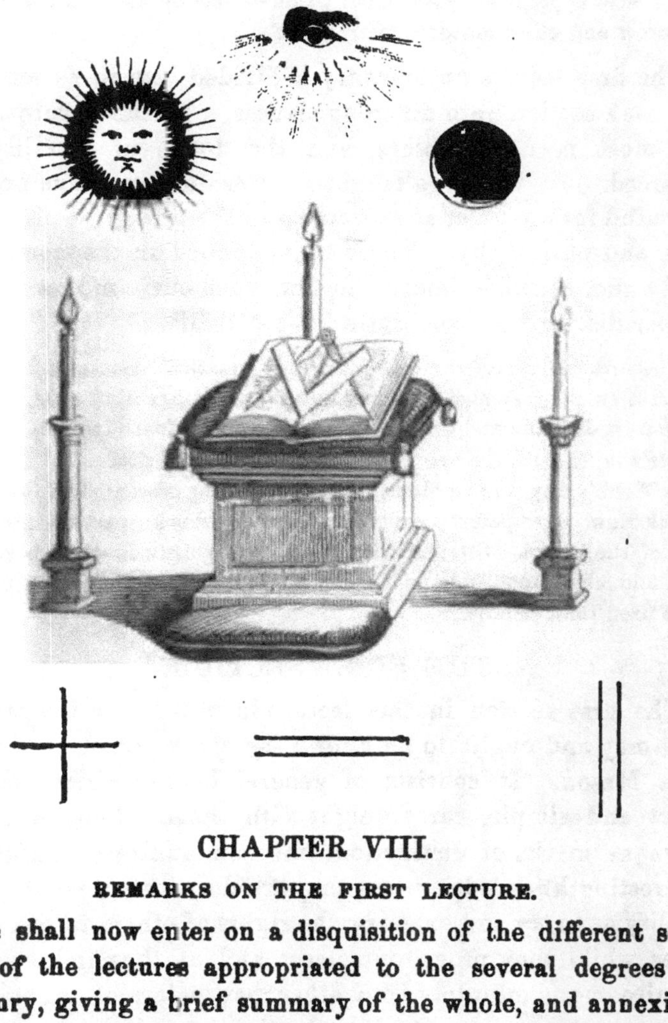

CHAPTER VIII.

REMARKS ON THE FIRST LECTURE.

We shall now enter on a disquisition of the different sections of the lectures appropriated to the several degrees of Masonry, giving a brief summary of the whole, and annexing to every remark the particulars to which the section alludes. By these means the industrious Mason will be instructed in the regular arrangement of the sections in each lecture, and be enabled with more ease to acquire a knowledge of the art.

The whole of these lectures, as taught by Webb, are yet extant, and would most appropriately accompany this volume by the mouth of Grand Lecturers and other Masonic instructors.

The first lecture on Masonry is divided into three sections, and each section into different clauses. Virtue is painted in the most beautiful colors, and the duties of morality are enforced. In it we are taught such useful lessons as prepare the mind for a regular advancement in the principles of knowledge and philosophy. These are imprinted on the memory by lively and sensible images, to influence our conduct in the proper discharge of the duties of social life.

These *images* relate to the chaste and beautiful drama of Masonry, wherein emblem, symbol, and ceremonial, are elegantly combined with the purest doctrine and the most venerable tradition, to impress the candidate's mind with the grace and sublimity of the Rite.

In Webb's day, the emblems, instead of being presented in the Monitor as now, were painted upon canvas, and formed a part of the hangings of the Lodge. Oftener they were merely drawn with chalk, charcoal, and clay, upon the floor, for temporary use. The same designs were used then as now.

THE FIRST SECTION.

The first section in this lecture is suited to all capacities, and may and ought to be known by every person who ranks as a Mason. It consists of general heads, which, though short and simple, carry weight with them. They not only serve as marks of distinction, but communicate useful and interesting knowledge, when they are duly investigated. They qualify us to try and examine the rights of others to our privileges, while they prove ourselves; and, as they induce us to inquire more minutely into other particulars of greater importance, they serve as an introduction to subjects more amply explained in the following sections.

The examination of a visiting Brother is made particularly minute and thorough upon this degree.

A Prayer used at the Initiation of a Candidate.

Vouchsafe thine aid, Almighty Father of the Universe, to this, our present convention; and grant that this candidate for Masonry may dedicate and devote his life to thy service, and become a true and faithful Brother among us! Endue him with a competency of thy divine wisdom, that by the secrets of our art, he may be better enabled to display the beauties of Brotherly Love, Relief and Truth, to the honor of thy holy name. *Amen. So mote it be.*

All the prayers introduced into this work may be considered as models or forms to be enlarged upon or abbreviated, or others substituted in their places, at the Master's will and pleasure.

It is a duty incumbent on every Master of a Lodge, before the ceremony of initiation takes place, to inform the candidate of the purpose and design of the institution; to explain the nature of his solemn engagements; and, in a manner peculiar to Masons alone, to require his cheerful acquiescence to the duties of morality and virtue, and all the sacred tenets of the Order.

This important regulation has been of latter years generally neglected. The usage, however, is gaining ground again.

Toward the close of the section is explained that peculiar ensign of Masonry, the *lamb-skin*, or *white leather apron*, which is an emblem of innocence, and the badge of a Mason; more ancient than the Golden Fleece or Roman Eagle; more honorable than the Star and Garter, or any other order that could be conferred upon the candidate at the time of his initiation, or at any time thereafter, by king, prince, potentate, or any other person, except he be a Mason; and which every one ought to wear with equal pleasure to himself, and honor to the fraternity.

The Masonic apron of the symbolic degrees should be cut with *right angles* throughout.

This section closes with an explanation of the *working tools* and implements of an Entered Apprentice, which are, the *Twenty-four inch Gauge*, and the *Common Gavel.*

These should be a part of the furniture or equipments of the Lodge. The following is the correct form of the Gavel:

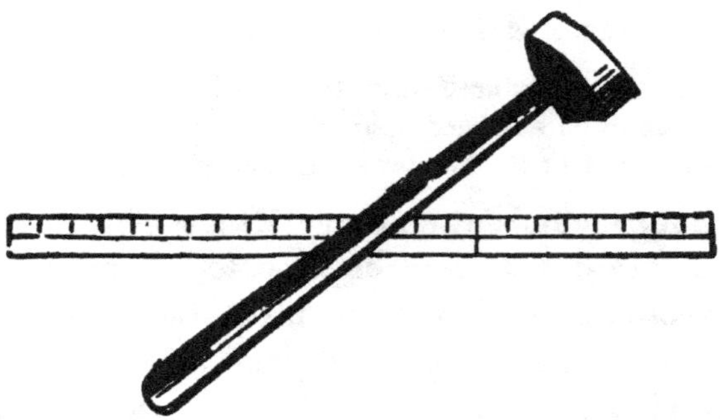

The *Twenty-four inch Gauge* is an instrument made use of by operative masons, to measure and lay out their work; but we, as free and accepted Masons are taught to make use of it for the more noble and glorious purpose of dividing our time. It being divided into twenty-four equal parts, is emblematical of the twenty-four hours of the day, which we are taught to divide into *three* equal parts, whereby we find eight hours for the service of God and a distressed worthy Brother; eight hours for our usual avocations; and eight for refreshment and sleep.*

*"The most effectual expedient employed by Alfred the Great, for the encouragement of learning, was his own example, and the constant assiduity with which he employed himself in the pursuit of knowledge. He usually divided his time into three equal portions: one was employed in sleep, and the refection of his body; another in the dispatch of business; and a third in study and devotion."—*Hume's History of England.*

The *Common Gavel* is an instrument made use of by operative masons, to break off the corners of rough stones, the better to fit them for the builder's use; but we, as free and accepted Masons, are taught to make use of it for the more noble and glorious purpose of divesting our minds and consciences of all the vices and superfluities of life, thereby fitting our bodies, as living stones, for that spiritual building, that house not made with hands, eternal in the heavens.

THE SECOND SECTION.

The second section rationally accounts for the origin of our hieroglyphical instruction, and convinces us of the advantages which will ever accompany a faithful observance of our duty; it maintains, beyond the power of contradiction, the propriety of our rites, while it demonstrates to the most skeptical and hesitating mind, their excellence and utility; it illustrates, at the same time, certain particulars, of which our ignorance might lead us into error, and which, as Masons, we are indispensably bound to know.

It is not enough to instruct the initiate in the forms through which he has passed; this were but child-like and trivial. The antiquity, origin and meaning of those forms is that which alone can recommend them to the intellectual mind. In this, and not in mere expertness or dramatic effect, lies the forte of a skillful Master.

To make a daily progress in the art is our constant duty, and expressly required by our general laws. What end can be more noble, than the pursuit of virtue? what motive more alluring, than the practice of justice? or what instruction more beneficial, than an accurate elucidation of symbolical mysteries which tend to embellish and adorn the mind? Every thing that strikes the eye, more immediately engages the attention, and imprints on the memory serious and solemn truths; hence Masons, universally adopting this method of inculcating the tenets of their Order by typical figures and allegorical emblems, prevent their mysteries from descending into the familiar reach of inattentive and unprepared novices, from whom they might not receive due veneration.

Our records inform us, that the usages and customs of Masons have ever corresponded with those of the Egyptian philosophers, to which they bear a near affinity. Unwilling to expose their mysteries to vulgar eyes, they concealed their particular tenets, and principles of polity, under hieroglyphical figures; and expressed their notions of government by signs and symbols, which they communicated to their Magi alone, and who were bound by oath not to reveal them. The Pythagorean system seems to have been established on a similar plan, and many orders of a more recent date. Masonry, however, is not only the most ancient, but the most moral institution that ever subsisted; every character, figure and emblem, depicted in a Lodge, has a moral tendency, and inculcates the practice of virtue.

It must not be supposed that all the ancient emblems and symbols of Masonry are given in this or any other Manual. Many have fallen into disuse; some are too closely allied to the essential secrets of Masonry to be published with impunity; some are too elaborate for a mere Handbook like this.

THE BADGE OF A MASON.

Every candidate, at his initiation, is presented with a lambskin or white leather apron.

By the Old Regulations, No. VII., "Every Brother at his making is decently to clothe the Lodge, that is, all the Brethren present." By this was meant the presentation of white gloves and aprons. But the usage with us has become obsolete.

The *Lamb* has in all ages been deemed an emblem of *innocence;* he, therefore, who wears the lamb-skin as a badge of Masonry, is thereby continually reminded of that purity of life and conduct, which is essentially necessary to his gaining admission into the Celestial Lodge above, where the Supreme Architect of the Universe presides.

THE THIRD SECTION.

The third section explains the nature and principles of our constitution, and teaches us to discharge with propriety the duties of our respective stations. Here, too, we receive instruction relative to the *form*, *supports*, *covering*, *furniture*, *ornaments*, *lights* and *jewels* of a Lodge, how it should be situated, and to whom dedicated. A proper attention is also paid to our ancient and venerable patrons.

From east to West, Freemasonry extends, and between the north and south, in every clime and nation, are Masons to be found.

Modern investigations prove this assertion to be well founded. Every civilized land has its Lodges; every nation possessing the spark of liberty and religion, its trestle-board of Masonic secrets.

Our institution is said to be supported by *Wisdom*, *Strength* and *Beauty;* because it is necessary that there should be *wisdom* to contrive, *strength* to support, and *beauty* to adorn all great and important undertakings. Its dimensions are unlimited, and its *covering* no less than the canopy of heaven. To this object the Mason's mind is continually directed, and thither he hopes at last to arrive, by the aid of the theological

ladder, which Jacob in his vision saw ascending from earth to heaven; the three *principal rounds* of which are denominated *Faith*, *Hope* and *Charity*; and which admonish us to have faith in God, hope in immortality, and charity to all mankind.

Every well governed Lodge is *furnished* with the *Holy Bible*, the *Square*, and the *Compass*; the *Bible* points out the path that leads to happiness and is dedicated to *God*; the *Square* teaches us to regulate our conduct by the principles of morality and virtue, and is dedicated to the *Master*; the *Compass* teaches us to limit our desires in every station, and is dedicated to the *Craft*.

The Bible is dedicated to the service of God, because it is the inestimable gift of God to man; the Square to the Master, because, being the proper Masonic emblem of his office, it is constantly to remind him of the duty he owes to the Lodge over which he is appointed to preside; and the Compass to the Craft, because by a due attention to its use, they are taught to regulate their desires, and keep their passions within due bounds.

The *ornamental* parts of a Lodge, displayed in this section, are, the *Mosaic pavement*, the *Indented tessel*, and the *Blazing star*. The *Mosaic pavement* is a representation of the ground floor of king Solomon's temple; the *Indented tessel*, that beautiful tesselated border, or skirting, which surrounded it; and the *Blazing star*, in the center, is commemorative of the star which appeared, to guide the wise men of the east to the place of our Savior's nativity. The *Mosaic pavement* is emblematic of human life, checkered with good and evil; the *Beautiful border* which urrounds it, those blessings a d comforts which surround us, and which we hope to obtain by a faithful reliance on Divine Providence, which is hieroglyphically represented by the *Blazing star* in the center.

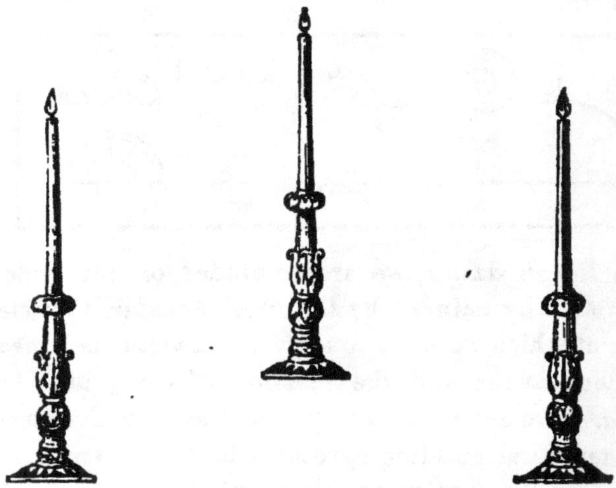

The *Movable* and *Immovable* jewels also claim our attention in this section.

By the general usage the square, level and plumb are styled the *immovable* jewels, and this is in accordance with Webb's private instructions.

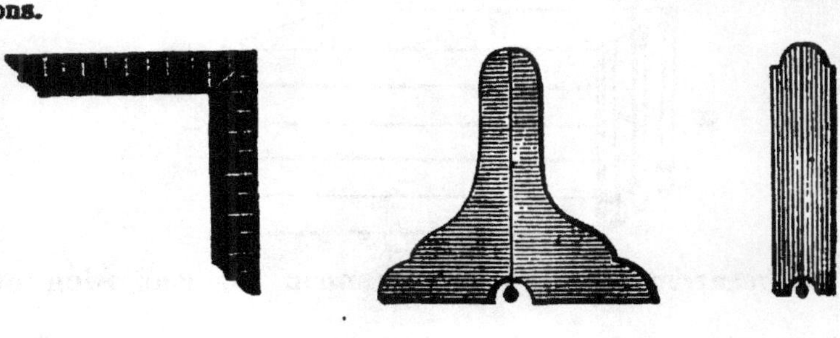

The *Rough ashlar* is a stone as taken from the quarry in its rude and natural state.

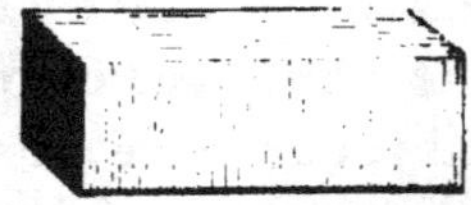

The *Perfect ashlar* is a stone made ready by the hands of the workman to be adjusted by the tools of the Fellow-craft.

The *Trestle-board* is for the master workman to draw his designs upon.

By the *Rough ashlar*, we are reminded of our rude and imperfect state by nature; by the *Perfect ashlar*, that state of perfection at which we hope to arrive, by a virtuous education, our own endeavors, and the blessing of God; and by the *Trestle-board*, we are reminded, that as the operative workman erects his temporal building agreeably to the rules and designs laid down by the master on his trestle-board, so should we, both operative and speculative, endeavor to erect our spiritual building agreeably to the rules and designs laid down by the Supreme Architect of the Universe, in the book of life, which is our spiritual trestle-board.

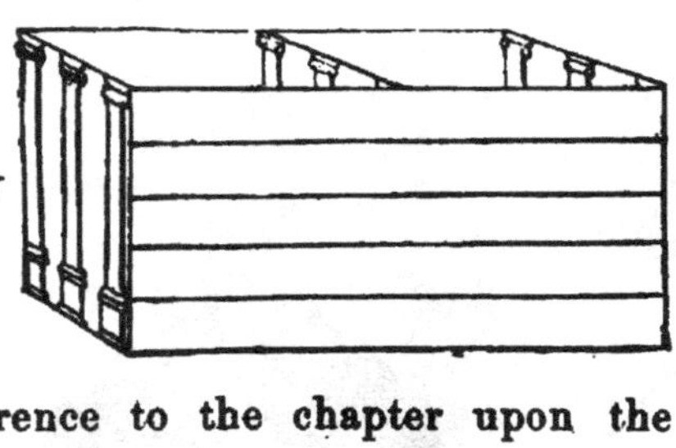

By a recurrence to the chapter upon the dedication of

Lodges, it will be perceived, that although our ancient brethren dedicated their Lodges to king Solomon, yet Masons professing Christianity dedicate theirs to St. John the Baptist, and St. John the Evangelist, who were eminent patrons of Masonry; and since their time there is represented in every regular and well governed Lodge, a certain *Point within a Circle;* the *Point* representing an individual brother, the *Circle* representing the boundary line of his duty to God and man, beyond which he is never to suffer his passions, prejudices or interests to betray him on any occasion. This *Circle* is embordered by two perpendicular parallel lines, representing St. John the Baptist and St. John the Evangelist; who were perfect parallels, in Christianity as well as Masonry; and upon the vertex rests the book of Holy Scriptures, which point out the whole duty of man. In going round this circle, we necessarily touch upon these two lines, as well as upon the Holy Scriptures; and while a Mason keeps himself thus circumscribed, it is impossible that he should materially err.

This section, though the last in rank, is not the least considerable in importance. It strengthens those which precede, and enforces, in the most engaging manner, a due regard to character and behavior, in public as well as in private life; in the Lodge, as well as in the general commerce of society.

It forcibly inculcates the most instructive lessons. *Brotherly love*, *Relief*, and *Truth*, are themes on which we here expatiate.

OF BROTHERLY LOVE.

By the exercise of brotherly love, we are taught to regar l the whole human species as one family, the high and low, the rich and poor; who, as created by one Almighty Parent, and inhabitants of the same planet, are to aid, support and protect each other. On this principle, Masonry unites men of every country, sect, and opinion, and conciliates true friendship among those who might otherwise have remained at a perpetual distance.

OF RELIEF.

To relieve the distressed, is a duty incumbent on all men; but particularly on Masons, who are linked together by an indissoluble chain of sincere affection. To soothe the unhappy, to sympathize with their misfortunes, to compassionate their miseries, and to restore peace to their troubled minds, is the grand aim we have in view. On this basis we form our friendships, and establish our connections.

OF TRUTH.

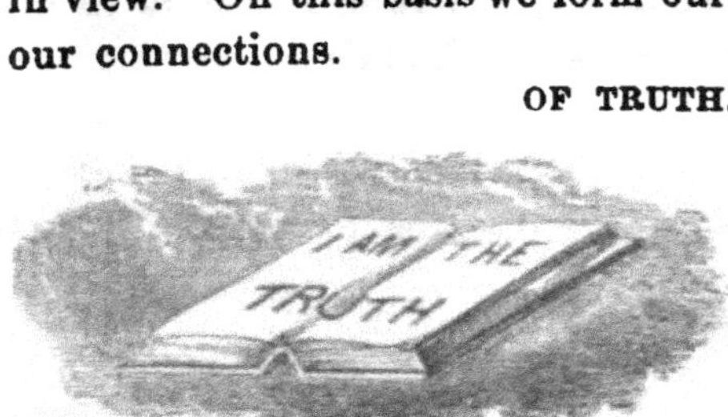

Truth is a divine attribute, and the foundation of every virtue. To be good and true, is the first lesson we are taught in Masonry. On this theme we contemplate, and by its dictates endeavor to regulate our conduct. Hence, while influenced by this principle, hypocrisy and deceit are unknown among us, sincerity and plain dealing distinguish us, and the heart and tongue join in promoting each other's welfare, and rejoicing in each other's prosperity.

To this illustration succeeds an explanation of the four cardinal virtues—*temperance*, *fortitude*, *prudence and justice*.

This order of arranging the cardinal virtues while it is the oldest in Masonic use, is also the most convenient. They are found, however, in the Apocryphal Books of the *wisdom of Solomon*, *Ch.* 8, *V.* 7, in the order of Temperance, Prudence, Justice and Fortitude.

OF TEMPERANCE.

Temperance is that due restraint upon our affections and passions, which renders the body tame and governable, and frees the mind from the allurements of vice. This virtue should be the constant practice of every Mason, as he is thereby taught to avoid excess, or contracting any licentious or vicious habit, the indulgence of which might lead him to disclose some of those valuable secrets, which he has promised to conceal and never reveal, and which would consequently subject him to the contempt and detestation of all good Masons.

* * * * * * * * * *

It will be seen that there is no injunction that would authorize the votaries of Masonry to make it a *total abstinence Temperance Society*, as some have attempted to do.

OF FORTITUDE.

Fortitude is that noble and steady purpose of the mind, whereby we are enabled to undergo any pain, peril or danger, when prudentially deemed expedient. This virtue is equally distant from rashness and cowardice; and, like the former, should be deeply impressed upon the mind of every Mason, as a safeguard or security against any illegal attack that may be made, by force or otherwise, to extort from him any of those secrets with which he has been so solemnly entrusted: and which was emblematically represented upon his first admission into the Lodge.

* * * * * * * * * *

OF PRUDENCE.

Prudence teaches us to regulate our lives and actions agreeably to the dictates of reason, and is that habit by which we wisely judge, and prudentially determine, on all things relative to our present, as well as to our future happiness. This virtue should be the peculiar characteristic of every Mason, not only for the government of his conduct while in the Lodge, but also when abroad in the world: it should be particularly attended to in all strange and mixed companies, never to let fall the least sign, token or word, whereby the secrets of Masonry might be unlawfully obtained.

* * * * * * * * * *

OF JUSTICE.

Justice is that standard, or boundary, of right, which enables us to render to every man his just due, without distinction. This virtue is not only consistent with Divine and human laws, but is the very cement and support of civil society; and, as justice in a great measure constitutes the real good man, so should it be the invariable practice of every Mason never to deviate from the minutest principles thereof.

* * * * * * * * * *

The illustration of these virtues is accompanied with some general observations peculiar to Masons.

The illustration of *Masonic Service*, viz.: freedom, fervency and zeal was a part of Webb's system of lectures.

* * * * * * * * * *

Such is the arrangement of the different sections in the first lecture, which, with the forms adopted at the opening and closing of a Lodge, comprehends the whole of the first degree of Masonry. This plan has the advantage of regularity to recommend it, the support of precedent and authority, and the sanction and respect which flow from antiquity. The whole is a regular system of morality, conceived in a strain of interesting allegory, which must unfold its beauties to the candid and industrious inquirer.

For closing Odes in this Degree see the Appendix.

Charge at Initiation into the First Degree.

BROTHER,—As you are now introduced into the first principles of Masonry, I congratulate you on being accepted into this ancient and honorable Order; ancient, as having subsisted from time immemorial; and honorable, as tending, in every particular, so to render all men who will be conformable to its precepts. No institution was ever raised on a better principle, or more solid foundation; nor were ever more excellent rules and useful maxims laid down, than are inculcated in the several Masonic lectures. The greatest and best of men in all ages have been encouragers and promoters of the art, and have never deemed it derogatory from their dignity to level themselves with the fraternity, extend their privileges, and patronize their assemblies.

There are three great duties, which, as a Mason, you are charged to inculcate—to God, your neighbor, and yourself. To God, in never mentioning his name, but with that reverential awe which is due from a creature to his Creator; to implore his aid in all your laudable undertakings, and to esteem him as the chief good: to your neighbor, in acting upon the square, and doing unto him as you wish he should do unto you: and to yourself, in avoiding all irregularity and intemperance, which may impair your faculties, or debase the dignity of your profession. A zealous attachment to these duties will insure public and private esteem.

In the State, you are to be a quiet and peaceful subject, true to your government, and just to your country; you are not to countenance disloyalty or rebellion, but patiently submit to legal authority, and conform with cheerfulness to the government of the country in which you live.

In your outward demeanor be particularly careful to avoid censure or reproach. Let not interest, favor, or prejudice, bias your integrity, or influence you to be guilty of a dishonorable action. Although your frequent appearance at our regular meetings is earnestly solicited, yet it is not meant that Masonry should interfere with your necessary vocations; for these are on no account to be neglected: neither are you to suffer your zeal for the institution to lead you into argument with those who, through ignorance, may ridicule it. At your leisure hours, that you may improve in Masonic knowledge, you are to converse with well informed brethren, who will be always as ready to give, as you will be ready to receive instruction.

Finally; keep sacred and inviolable the mysteries of the Order, as these are to distinguish you from the rest of the community, and mark your consequence among Masons. If, in the circle of your acquaintance, you find a person desirous of being initiated into Masonry, be particularly attentive not to recommend him, unless you are convinced he will conform to our rules; that the honor, glory, and reputation of the institution may be firmly established, and the world at large convinced of its good effects.

As the materials for the increase of the Lodge are examined and passed upon in the *Master's Lodge* only, this injunction can only be prospectively necessary here. The rules of examining materials, however, are entirely exoteric, and may be understood as readily by an Entered Apprentice as a Master Mason. See the *Ancient Charges*, Chapters III. and IV.

In the first edition, or that of 1797, this Charge at Initiation contains various injunctions subsequently omitted. A few of these are deemed worthy of introduction here. "Above all, practice benevolence and charity, for by these virtues Masons have been distinguished in every age and country. The inconceivable pleasure of contributing toward the relief of our fellow-creatures, is truly experienced by persons of a humane disposition, who are naturally excited by sympathy to extend their aid in alleviation of the miseries of others. This encourages the generous Mason to distribute his bounty with cheerfulness. Supposing himself in the situation of an unhappy sufferer, he listens to his complaints with attention, bewails his misfortunes, and speedily relieves his distress."

"The next object of your attention is our excellent Constitutions. These contain the history of Masonry, from the earliest periods, and the laws and charges by which the brethren have been long governed."

CHAPTER IX.

REMARKS ON THE SECOND DEGREE.

Masonry is a progressive science, and is divided into different classes or degrees, for the more regular advancement in the knowledge of its mysteries. According to the progress we make, we limit or extend our inquiries; and in proportion to our capacity, we attain to a less or greater degree of perfection.

No person on any consideration or under any emergency should be allowed to advance from the Checkered Pavement to the Middle Chamber until he is proficient in the ceremony and lecture of the degree he has taken. A *fair* proficiency consists in memorizing the first two Sections of the Lecture, but a *thorough* proficiency in committing the three Sections to memory, learning to open and close the Lodge and confer the

degree of Entered Apprentice. Were this required, our Lodges would soon abound in well-informed Craftsmen fit for the Master's use

By general usage an interval of one month or more, is required between the first and second degrees.

Masonry includes within its circle almost every branch of polite learning. Under the veil of its mysteries is comprehended a regular system of science. Many of its illustrations, to the confined genius, may appear unimportant; but the man of more enlarged faculties will perceive them to be, in the highest degree, useful and interesting. To please the accomplished scholar, and ingenious artist, Masonry is wisely planned; and, in the investigation of its latent doctrines, the philosopher and mathematician may experience equal delight and satisfaction.

To exhaust the various subjects of which it treats, would transcend the powers of the brightest genius; still, however, nearer approaches to perfection may be made, and the man of wisdom will not check the progress of his abilities, though the task he attempts may at first seem insurmountable. Perseverance and application remove each difficulty as it occurs; every step he advances, new pleasures open to his view, and instruction of the noblest kind attends his researches. In the diligent pursuit of knowledge, the intellectual faculties are employed in promoting the glory of God, and the good of man.

The first degree is well calculated to enforce the duties of *morality*, and imprint on the memory the noblest principles which can adorn the human mind. It is, therefore, the best introduction to the second degree, which not only extends the same plan, but comprehends a more diffusive system of *knowledge*.

A convenient formula for this is thus given: in the *First* Degree we are taught Morality, in the *Second* Science, in the *Third* Religion. The instruction to the Entered Apprentice is directed to the *heart;* to the Fellow-craft to the *intellect;* to the Master Mason to the *soul.*

Here practice and theory join, in qualifying the industrious Mason to share the pleasures which an advancement in the art must necessarily afford. Listening with attention to the wise opinion of experience' Craftsmen on important subjects, he gradually familiarizes his mind to useful instruction, and is soon enabled to investigate truths of the utmost concern in the general transactions of life.

From this system proceeds a rational amusement; while the mental powers are fully employed, the judgment is properly exercised. A spirit of emulation prevails; and all are induced to vie who shall most excel in promoting the valuable rules of the institution.

Appropriate Odes for opening the Lodge of Fellow-crafts are given in the Appendix.

THE FIRST SECTION.

The first section of the second degree accurately elucidates the mode of introduction into that particular class; and instructs the diligent Craftsman how to proceed in the proper arrangement of the ceremonies used on the occasion. It qualifies him to judge of their importance, and convinces him of the necessity of strictly adhering to every established usage of the Order. Here he is entrusted with particular tests, to enable him to prove his title to the privileges of this degree, while satisfactory reasons are given for their origin. Many duties, which cement in the firmest union well informed brethren, are illustrated in this section; and an opportunity is given to make such advances in Masonry, as will always distinguish the abilities of those who have arrived at preferment. The knowledge of this section is absolutely necessary for all Craftsmen; and as it recapitulates the ceremony of initiation, and contains many other important particulars, no officer or member of a Lodge should be unacquainted with it.

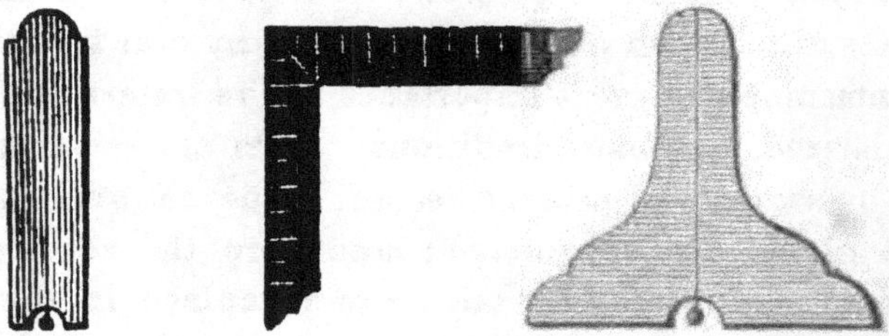

The PLUMB, SQUARE, and LEVEL, those noble and useful implements of a Fellow-craft; are here introduced and moralized, and serve as a constant admonition to the practice of virtue and morality.

The *Plumb* is an instrument made use of by *operative* masons, to raise perpendiculars, the *Square*, to square their work, and the *Level*, to lay horizontals ; but we, as Free and Accepted Masons, are taught to make use of them for more noble and glorious purposes: the *Plumb* admonishes us to walk uprightly in our several stations before God and man, squaring our actions by the *Square* of virtue, and remembering that we are traveling upon the *Level* of time, to "that undiscovered country, from whose bourne no traveler returns."

See the Appendix for Ode, "*The Emblems of the Craft*," in which a practical application of these emblems is made.

THE SECOND SECTION.

The second section of this degree has recourse to the origin of the institution, and views Masonry under two denominations, *operative* and *speculative*. These are separately considered, and the principles on which both are founded, particularly explained. Their affinity is pointed out by allegorical figures, and typical representations. The period stipulated for rewarding merit is fixed, and the inimitable moral to which that circumstance alludes is explained. The creation of the world is described, and many particulars recited, all of which have been carefully preserved among Masons, and transmitted from one age to another, by oral tradition.

Circumstances of great importance to the fraternity are here particularized, and many traditional tenets and customs confirmed by sacred and profane record. The celestial and terrestrial globes are considered; and here the accomplished gentleman may display his talents to advantage in the elucidation of the *Orders of Architecture*, the *Senses* of human nature, and the liberal *Arts and Sciences*, which are severally classed in a regular arrangement. In short, this section contains a store of valuable knowledge, founded on reason and sacred record, both entertaining and instructive.

It is not desirable, in this portion of the Masonic Lecture, that any set forms of words should be employed. The Brother whose duty it is to moralize upon the Winding Stairway, is expected to draw upon his intellectual resources to their fullest extent. Large accessions to this part of Masonry may be derived from "The Historical Landmarks of Masonry" (U. M. L. Vol. XI. and XII.).

Masonry is considered under two denominations; *Operative* and *Speculative*.

OPERATIVE MASONRY.

By *Operative Masonry* we allude to a proper application of the useful rules of architecture, whence a structure will derive figure, strength and beauty, and whence will result a due proportion, and a just correspondence in all its parts. It furnishes us with dwellings, and convenient shelter from the vicissitudes and inclemencies of seasons; and while it displays the effects of human wisdom, as well in the choice, as in the arrangement, of the sundry materials of which an edifice is composed, it demonstrates that a fund of science and industry is implanted in man for the best, most salutary and beneficent purposes.

SPECULATIVE MASONRY.

By *Speculative Masonry*, we learn to subdue the passions, act upon the square, keep a tongue of good report, maintain secresy, and practice charity. It is so far interwoven with religion, as to lay us under obligations to pay that rational homage to the Deity, which at once constitutes our duty and our happiness. It leads the contemplative to view with reverence and admiration the glorious works of the creation, and inspires him with the most exalted ideas of the perfections of his Divine Creator.

In six days God created the heavens and the earth, and rested upon the seventh day; the seventh, therefore, our ancient brethren consecrated as a day of rest from their labors, thereby enjoying frequent opportunities to contemplate the glorious works of the creation, and to adore their great Creator.

The doctrine of the spheres is included in the science of astronomy, and particularly considered in this section.

* * * * * * * * * * *

OF THE GLOBES.

The globes are two artificial spherical bodies on the convex surface of which are represented the countries, seas, and various parts of the earth, the face of the heavens, the planetary revolutions, and other particulars.

The sphere, with the parts of the earth delineated on its surface, is called the *terrestrial* globe; and that with the constellations, and other heavenly bodies, the *celestial* globe.

THE USE OF THE GLOBES.

Their principal use, beside serving as maps to distinguish the outward parts of the earth, and the situation of the fixed stars, is to illustrate and explain the phenomena arising from the annual revolution, and the diurnal rotation, of the earth round its own axis. They are the noblest instruments for

improving the mind, and giving it the most distinct idea of any problem or proposition, as well as enabling it to solve the same. Contemplating these bodies, we are inspired with a due reverence for the Deity and his works, and are induced to encourage the studies of astronomy, geography, navigation, and the arts dependent on them, by which society has been so much benefited.

The orders of architecture come under consideration in this section; a brief description of them may therefore not be improper.

OF ORDER IN ARCHITECTURE.

By order in architecture, is meant a system of all the members, proportions and ornaments of columns and pilasters; or, it is a regular arrangement of the projecting parts of a building, which, united with those of a column, form a beautiful, perfect and complete whole.

OF ITS ANTIQUITY.

From the first formation of society, order in architecture may be traced. When the rigor of seasons obliged men to contrive shelter from the inclemency of the weather, we learn that they first planted trees on end, and then laid others across, to support a covering. The bands which connected those tree at the top and bottom, are said to have given rise to the idea of the base and capital of pillars; and from this simple hint originally proceeded the more improved art of architecture.

The five orders are thus classed: the Tuscan, Doric, Ionic, Corinthian, and Composite.

THE TUSCAN.

It is the most simple and solid of the five orders. It was invented in Tuscany, whence it derived its name. Its column is seven diameters high; and its capital, base and entablature have but few moldings. The simplicity of the construction of this column renders it eligible where ornament would be superfluous.

THE DORIC,

Which is plain and natural, is the most ancient, and was invented by the Greeks. Its column is eight diameters high, and has seldom any ornaments on base or capital, except moldings; though the frieze is distinguished by triglyphs and metopes, and triglyphs compose the ornaments of the frieze. The solid composition of this order gives it a preference in structures where strength and a noble simplicity are chiefly required.

The Doric is the best proportioned of all the orders. The several parts of which it is composed are founded on the natural position of solid bodies. In its first invention it was more simple than in its present state. In after times, when it began to be adorned, it gained the name of Doric; for when it was constructed in its primitive and simple form, the name of Tuscan was conferred on it. Hence the Tuscan precedes the Doric in rank, on account of its resemblance to that pillar in its original state.

THE IONIC

Bears a kind of mean proportion between the more solid and delicate orders. Its column is nine diameters high; its capital is adorned with volutes, and its cornice has dentals. There is both delicacy and ingenuity displayed in this pillar; the invention of which is attributed to the Ionians, as the famous temple of Diana at Ephesus was of this order. It is said to have been formed after the model of an agreeable young woman, of an elegant shape, dressed in her hair; as a contrast to the Doric order, which was formed after that of a strong, robust man.

THE CORINTHIAN,

The richest of the five orders, is deemed a masterpiece of art. Its column is ten diameters high, and its capital is adorned with two rows of leaves, and eight volutes, which sustains the abacus. The frieze is ornamented with curious devices, the cornice with dentals and modillions. This order is used in stately and superb structures.

OF THE INVENTION OF THIS ORDER.

It was invented at Corinth, by Callimachus, who is said to have taken the hint of the capital of this pillar from the following remarkable circumstances. Accidentally passing by the tomb of a young lady, he perceived a basket of toys, covered with a tile, placed over an acanthus root, having been left there by her nurse. As the branches grew up, they encompassed the basket, till, arriving at the tile, they met with an obstruction, and bent downward. Callimachus, struck with the object, set about imitating the figure; the vase of the capital he made to represent the basket; the abacus the tile; and the volutes the bending leaves.

THE COMPOSITE

Is compounded of the other orders, and was contrived by the Romans. Its capital has the two rows of leaves of the Corinthian, and the volutes of the Ionic. Its column has the quarter-round as the Tuscan and Doric order, is ten diameters high, and its cornice has dentals, or simple modillions. This pillar is generally found in buildings where strength, elegance and beauty are displayed.

OF THE INVENTION OF ORDER IN ARCHITECTURE.

The ancient and original orders of architecture, revered by Masons, are no more than three, the Doric, Ionic, and Cor-

INTHIAN, which were invented by the Greeks. To these the Romans have added two: the Tuscan, which they made plainer than the Doric; and the Composite, which was more ornamental, if not more beautiful, than the Corinthian. The first three orders alone, however, shew invention and particular character, and essentially differ from each other: the two others having nothing but what is borrowed, and differ only accidentally: the Tuscan is the Doric in its earliest state; and the Composite is the Corinthian enriched with the Ionic. To the Greeks, therefore, and not to the Romans, we are indebted for what is great, judicious and distinct in architecture.

OF THE FIVE SENSES OF HUMAN NATURE.

An analysis of the human faculties is next given in this section, in which the five external senses particularly claim attention: these are, hearing, seeing, feeling, smelling and tasting.

HEARING

Is that sense by which we distinguish sounds, and are capable of enjoying all the agreeable charms of music. By it we are enabled to enjoy the pleasures of society, and reciprocally to communicate to each other our thoughts and intentions, our purposes and desires; while thus our reason is capable of exerting its utmost power and energy.

The wise and beneficent Author of Nature intended, by the formation of this sense, that we should be social creatures, and receive the greatest and most important part of our knowledge by the information of others. For these purposes we are endowed with hearing, that, by a proper exertion of our natural powers, our happiness may be complete.

SEEING

Is that sense by which we distinguish objects, and in an instant of time, without change of place or situation, view armies in battle array, figures of the most stately structures, and all the agreeable variety displayed in the landscape of nature. By this sense we find our way in the pathless ocean, traverse the globe of earth, determine its figure and dimensions, and delineate any region or quarter of it. By it we measure the planetary orbs, and make new discoveries in the sphere of the fixed stars. Nay, more: by it we perceive the tempers and dispositions, the passions and affections, of our fellow creatures, when they wish most to conceal them; so that though the tongue may be taught to lie and dissemble, the countenance would display hypocrisy to the discerning eye. In fine, the rays of light which administer to this sense, are the most astonishing parts of the animated creation, and render the eye a peculiar object of admiration.

Of all the faculties, sight is the noblest. The structure of the eye, and its appurtenances, evinces the admirable contrivance of nature for performing all its various external and internal motions; while the variety displayed in the eyes of different animals, suited to their several ways of life, clearly demonstrates this organ to be the masterpiece of nature's work.

FEELING

Is that sense by which we distinguish the different qualities of bodies; such as heat and cold, hardness and softness, roughness and smoothness, figure, solidity, motion, and extension.

These three senses, HEARING, SEEING, and FEELING, are deemed peculiarly essential among Masons.

* * * * * *

SMELLING

Is that sense by which we distinguish odors, the various kinds of which convey different impressions to the mind. Animal and vegetable bodies, and indeed most other bodies, while exposed to the air, continually send forth effluvia of vast subtilty, as well in the state of life and growth, as in the state of fermentation and putrefaction. These effluvia, being drawn into the nostrils along with the air, are the means by which all bodies are smelled. Hence it is evident, that there is a manifest appearance of design in the great Creator's having planted the organ of smell in the inside of that canal, through which the air continually passes in respiration.

TASTING

Enables us to make a proper distinction in the choice of our food. The organ of this sense guards the entrance of the alimentary canal, as that of smelling guards the entrance of the canal for respiration. From the situation of both these organs, it is plain that they were intended by nature to distinguish wholesome food from that which is nauseous. Every thing that enters into the stomach must undergo the scrutiny of tasting; and by it we are capable of discerning the changes which the same body undergoes in the different compositions of art, cookery, chemistry, pharmacy, etc.

Smelling and tasting are inseparably connected, and it is by the unnatural kind of life men commonly lead in society, that these senses are rendered less fit to perform their natural offices.

On the mind all our knowledge must depend; what, therefore, can be a more proper subject for the investigation of Masons? By anatomical dissection and observation, we become acquainted with the body; but it is by the anatomy of the mind alone we discover its powers and principles.

To sum up the whole of this transcendent measure of God's bounty to man, we shall add, that memory, imagination, taste, reasoning, moral perception, and all the active powers of the soul, present a vast and boundless field for philosophical disquisition, which far exceed human inquiry, and are peculiar mysteries, known only to nature, and to nature's God, to whom we and all are indebted for creation, preservation, and every blessing we enjoy.

OF THE SEVEN LIBERAL ARTS AND SCIENCES.

The seven liberal ARTS and SCIENCES are next illustrated in this section: it may not, therefore, be improper to insert here a short explanation of them.

The *full* explanation, with their Masonic applications, are conveyed in the lectures of the enlightened Master, whose mind is stored with knowledge, and whose experience has shown him the readiest method of directing it.

GRAMMAR.

Grammar teaches the proper arrangement of words, according to the idiom or dialect of any particular people; and that excellency of pronunciation, which enables us to speak or write a language with accuracy, agreeably to reason and correct usage.

RHETORIC.

Rhetoric teaches us to speak copiously and fluently on any subject, not merely with propriety alone, but with all the advantages of force and elegance; wisely contriving to captivate the hearer by strength of argument and beauty of expression, whether it be to entreat and exhort, to admonish or applaud.

LOGIC.

Logic teaches us to guide our reason discretionally in the general knowledge of things, and directs our inquiries after truth. It consists of a regular train of argument, whence we infer, deduce, and conclude, according to certain premises laid down, admitted, or granted; and in it are employed the faculties of conceiving, judging, reasoning, and disposing; all of which are naturally led on from one gradation to another, till the point in question is finally determined.

ARITHMETIC.

Arithmetic teaches the powers and properties of numbers, which is variously effected, by letters, tables, figures and instruments. By this art, reasons and demonstrations are given, for finding out any certain number, whose relation or affinity to another is already known or discovered.

GEOMETRY.

Geometry treats of the powers and properties of magnitudes in general, where length, breadth, and thickness, are considered, from a *point* to a *line*, from a line to a *superficies*, and from a superficies to a *solid*.

A *point* is a dimensionless figure; or an indivisible part of space.

A *line* is a point continued, and a figure of one capacity, namely, *length*.

A *superficies* is a figure of two dimensions, namely, *length* and *breadth*.

A *solid* is a figure of three dimensions, namely, *length*, *breadth*, and *thickness*.

OF THE ADVANTAGES OF GEOMETRY.

By this science, the architect is enabled to construct his plans, and execute his designs; the general to arrange his soldiers; the engineer to mark out ground for encampments; the geographer to give us the dimensions of the world, and all things therein contained, to delineate the extent of seas, and specify the divisions of empires, kingdoms and provinces. By it, also, the astronomer is enabled to make his observations, and to fix the duration of times and seasons, years and cycles. In fine, geometry is the foundation of architecture, and the root of the mathematics.

MUSIC.

Music teaches the art of forming concords, so as to compose delightful harmony, by a mathematical and proportional arrangement of acute, grave and mixed sounds. This art, by a series of experiments, is reduced to a demonstrative science, with respect to tones, and the intervals of sound. It inquires into the nature of concords and discords, and enables us to find out the proportion between them by numbers.

ASTRONOMY.

Astronomy is that divine art, by which we are taught to read the wisdom, strength and beauty of the Almighty Creator, in those sacred pages, the celestial hemisphere. Assisted by astronomy, we can observe the motions, measure the distances, comprehend the magnitudes, and calculate the periods and eclipses, of the heavenly bodies. By it we learn the use of the globes, the system of the world, and the preliminary law of nature. While we are employed in the study of this science, we must perceive unparalleled instances of wisdom and goodness, and, through the whole creation, trace the glorious Author by his works.

* * * * *

OF THE MORAL ADVANTAGES OF GEOMETRY.

From this theme we proceed to illustrate the moral advantages of Geometry; a subject on which the following observations may not be unacceptable:*

Geometry, the first and noblest of sciences, is the basis on which the superstructure of Masonry is erected. By geometry, we may curiously trace nature, through her various windings, to her most concealed recesses. By it, we discover the power, the wisdom, and the goodness of the Grand Artificer of the Universe, and view with delight the proportions which connect this vast machine. By it we discover how the planets move in their different orbits, and demonstrate their various revolutions. By it we account for the return of seasons, and the variety of scenes which each season displays to the discerning eye. Numberless worlds are around us, all framed by the same Divine artist, which roll through the vast expanse, and are all conducted by the same unerring law of nature.

A survey of nature, and the observations of her beautiful proportions, first determined man to imitate the Divine plan, and study symmetry and order. This gave rise to societies, and birth to every useful art. The architect began to design, and the plans which he laid down, being improved by experience and time, have produced works which are the admiration of every age.

The lapse of time, the ruthless hand of ignorance, and the devastations of war, have laid waste and destroyed many valuable monuments of antiquity, on which the utmost exertions of human genius have been employed. Even the Temple of Solomon, so spacious and magnificent, and constructed by so many celebrated artists, escaped not the unsparing ravages of barbarous force. Freemasonry, notwithstanding, has still survived. The *attentive ear* receives the sound from the *instructive tongue*, and the mysteries of Masonry are safely lodged in the repository of *faithful breasts*. Tools and implements of architecture are selected by the fraternity, to imprint on the memory wise and serious truths; and thus, through a succession of ages, are transmitted unimpaired the excellent tenets of our institution.

*   *   *   *   *   *

Thus end the two sections of the second lecture, which, with the ceremony used at opening and closing the Lodge, comprehend the whole of the second degree of Masonry. This lecture contains a regular system of science, demonstrated on the clearest principles, and established on the firmest foundation.

For closing Odes suitable to this Degree, see the Appendix.

CHARGE AT INITIATION INTO THE SECOND DEGREE.

BROTHER:—Being advanced to the second degree of Masonry, we congratulate you on your preferment. The internal, and not the external qualifications of a man, are what Masonry regards. As you increase in knowledge, you will improve in social intercourse.

It is unnecessary to recapitulate the duties which as a Mason you are bound to discharge; or enlarge on the necessity of a strict adherence to them, as your own experience must have established their value.

Our laws and regulations you are strenuously to support; and be always ready to assist in seeing them duly executed. You are not to palliate, or aggravate, the offenses of your brethren; but, in the decision of every trespass against our rules, you are to judge with candor, admonish with friendship, and reprehend with justice.

The decision of all cases of discipline is left by general usage to *Masters'* Lodges alone.

The study of the liberal arts, that valuable branch of education which tends so effectually to polish and adorn the mind, is earnestly recommended to your consideration; especially the science of geometry, which is established as the basis of our art. Geometry, or Masonry, originally synonymous terms, being of a divine and moral nature, is enriched with the most useful knowledge; while it proves the wonderful properties of nature, it demonstrates the more important truths of morality.

Your past behavior and regular deportment have merited the honor which we have now conferred; and in your new character it is expected that you will conform to the principles of the Order, by steadily persevering in the practice of every commendable virtue.

Such is the nature of your engagements as a Fellow-craft, and to these duties you are bound by the most sacred ties.

In the first edition, that of 1797, the following injunctions were added: "All regular signs and summonses, given and received, you are duly to honor and punctually to obey, inasmuch as they consist with our professed principles. You are to supply the wants and relieve the necessities of your brethren to the utmost of your power and ability, and on no account are you to wrong them or to see them wronged, but apprise them of approaching danger, and view their interests as inseparable from your own."

"In our private assemblies, as a Craftsman, you may offer your sentiments and opinions on such subjects as are regularly introduced in the Lecture. By this privilege you may improve your intellectual powers, qualify yourself to become a useful member of society, and like a skillful Brother strive to excel in every thing that is good and great."

CHAPTER X.

REMARKS ON THE THIRD DEGREE.

From this class the rulers of regular bodies of Masons, in the first three degrees, are selected; as it is only from those who are capable of giving instruction, that we can properly expect to receive it. The lecture of this degree, considered separately from the duties and ceremonies appertaining to the degree of Presiding or Past Master, is divided into three sections.

For appropriate odes to the opening of the Lodge of Master Masons, see Appendix.

No person should be allowed to advance from the Middle Chamber to the Holy of Holies until he is proficient in the last degree. A *fair* proficiency consists in committing the first section of the lecture, but a *thorough* proficiency in committing the whole to memory, learning to open and close the Lodge, and to confer the degree of Fellow-craft.

By general usage an interval of one month or more is required between the second and third degrees.

THE FIRST SECTION.

The ceremony of initiation into the third degree is particularly specified in this branch of the lecture, and here many other useful instructions are given.

Such is the importance of this section, that we may safely declare, that the person who is unacquainted with it, is illy qualified to act as a ruler or governor of the work.

The following passage of Scripture is introduced during the ceremonies:

ECCLESIASTES, xii: 1—7.

"Remember now thy Creator in the days of thy youth, while the evil days come not, nor the years draw nigh, when thou shalt say, I have no pleasure in them; while the sun, or the light, or the moon, or the stars, be not darkened, nor the clouds return after the rain: in the day when the keepers of the house shall tremble, and the strong men shall bow themselves, and the grinders cease because they are few, and those that look out of the windows be darkened, and the doors shall be shut in the streets, when the sound of the grinding is low, and he shall rise up at the voice of the bird, and all the daughters of music shall be brought low; also when they shall be afraid of that which is high, and fears shall be in the way, and the almond tree shall flourish, and the grasshopper shall be a burden, and desire shall fail: because man goeth to his long home, and the mourners go about the streets: or ever the silver cord be loosed, or the golden bowl be broken, or the pitcher be broken at the fountain, or the wheel broken at the cistern. Then shall the dust return to the earth as it was: and the spirit shall return unto God who gave it."

FRIENDSHIP. MORALITY. BROTHERLY LOVE.

The *working tools* of a Master Mason, which are illustrated in this section, are all the implements of Masonry indiscriminately, but more especially the *trowel.*

The TROWEL is an instrument made use of by operative masons, to spread the cement which unites a building into one common mass; but we, as Free and Accepted Masons, are taught to make use of it for the more noble and glorious purpose of spreading the cement of *Brotherly love* and affection; that cement which unites us into one sacred band, or society of friends and brothers, among whom no contention should ever exist, but that noble contention, or rather emulation, of who best can work, or best agree.

THE SECOND SECTION.

This section recites the historical traditions of the Order, and presents to view a finished picture, of the utmost consequence to the fraternity. It exemplifies an instance of virtue, fortitude, and integrity, seldom equaled, and never excelled, in the history of man.

PRAYER AT RAISING A BROTHER TO THE SUBLIME DEGREE OF A MASTER MASON.

Thou, O God! knowest our down-sitting and our up-rising, and understandest our thoughts afar off. Shield and defend us from the evil intentions of our enemies, and support us under the trials and afflictions we are destined to endure, while traveling through this vale of tears. Man that is born of a woman, is of few days and full of trouble. He cometh forth as a flower, and is cut down; he fleeth also as a shadow, and continueth not. Seeing his days are determined, the number of his months are with thee, thou hast appointed his bounds that he can not pass; turn from him that he may rest, till he shall accomplish his day. For there is hope of a tree, if it be cut down, that it will sprout again, and that the tender branch thereof will not cease. But man dieth and wasteth away; yea, man giveth up the ghost, and where is he? As the waters fail from the sea, and the flood decayeth and drieth up, so man lieth down, and riseth not up till the heavens shall be no more. Yet, O Lord! have compassion on the children of thy creation, administer them comfort in time of trouble, and save them with an everlasting salvation. *Amen.* So mote it be.

This prayer is an adaptation from the XIV. Chapter of Job.

The Temple, unfinished, is an emblem of all mortal felicity, and of every human acquisition. Perfection is reserved for the immortal Temple above.

THE THIRD SECTION.

The third section illustrates certain hieroglyphical emblems, and inculcates many useful lessons, to extend knowledge, and promote virtue.

In this branch of the lecture, many particulars relative to King Solomon's Temple are considered.

The construction of this grand edifice was attended with two remarkable circumstances. From Josephus we learn, that although seven years were occupied in building it, yet during the whole term it rained not in the day time, that the workmen might not be obstructed in their labor: and from the sacred history it appears that there was neither the sound of the hammer, nor ax, nor any tool of iron, heard in the house, while it was building.

This famous fabric was supported by fourteen hundred and fifty-three columns, and two thousand nine hundred and six pilasters; all hewn from the finest Parian marble. There were employed in its building, three Grand Masters; three thousand and three hundred masters, or overseers of the work; eighty thousand Fellow-crafts; and seventy thousand

Entered Apprentices, or bearers of burdens. All these were classed and arranged in such a manner by the wisdom of Solomon, that neither envy, discord, nor confusion were suffered to interrupt that universal peace and tranquillity, which pervaded the world at this important period.*

7{1/6

5{2/3

3

THE POT OF INCENSE

Is an emblem of a pure heart, which is always an acceptable sacrifice to the Deity; and, as this glows with fervent heat, so should our hearts continually glow with gratitude to the great and beneficent Author of our existence for the manifold blessings and comforts we enjoy.

THE BEE-HIVE

Is an emblem of industry, and recommends the practice of that virtue to all created beings, from the highest seraph in heaven, to the lowest reptile in the dust. It teaches us, that as we came into the world rational and intelligent beings,

*For ample particulars relative to this Sacred Edifice, see the *Universal Masonic Library*, volumes xi., xii., and others.

so we should ever be industrious ones; never sitting down contented while our fellow-creatures around us are in want, when it is in our power to relieve them, without inconvenience to ourselves.

When we take a survey of nature, we view man, in his infancy, more helpless and indigent than the brutal creation; he lies languishing for days, months and years, totally incapable of providing sustenance for himself, of guarding against the attack of the wild beasts of the field, or sheltering himself from the inclemencies of the weather.

It might have pleased the great Creator of heaven and earth to have made man independent of all other beings; but, as dependence is one of the strongest bonds of society, mankind were made dependent on each other for protection and security, as they thereby enjoy better opportunities of fulfilling the duties of reciprocal love and friendship. Thus was man formed for social and active life, the noblest part of the work of God; and he that will so demean himself as not to be endeavoring to add to the common stock of knowledge and understanding, may be deemed a *drone* in the *hive* of nature, a useless member of society, and unworthy of our protection as Masons.

THE BOOK OF CONSTITUTIONS, GUARDED BY THE TYLER'S SWORD,

Reminds us that we should be ever watchful and guarded, in our thoughts, words and actions, particularly when before the enemies of Masonry; ever bearing in remembrance those truly Masonic virtues, *silence* and *circumspection*.

THE SWORD, POINTING TO A NAKED HEART,

Demonstrates that justice will sooner or later overtake us; and although our thoughts, words, and actions, may be hidden from the eyes of man, yet that

ALL-SEEING EYE,

Whom the SUN, MOON, and STARS obey, and under whose watchful care even COMETS perform their stupendous revolutions, pervades the inmost recesses of the human heart, and will reward us according to our merits.

THE ANCHOR AND ARK

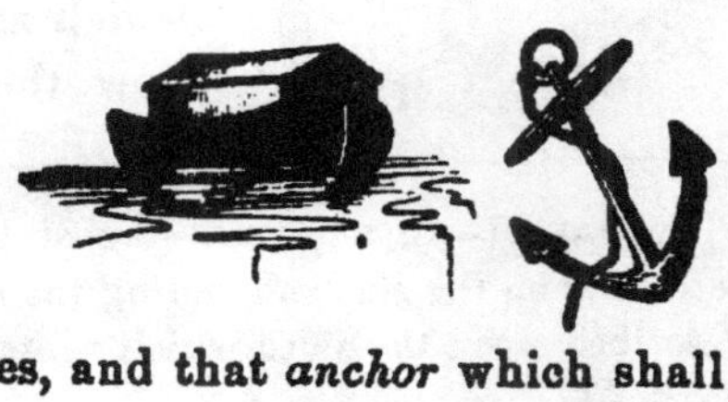

Are emblems of a well-grounded *hope*, and a well-spent life. They are emblematical of that divine *ark* which safely wafts us over this tempestuous sea of troubles, and that *anchor* which shall

safely moor us in a peaceful harbor, where the wicked cease from troubling, and the weary shall find rest.

THE FORTY-SEVENTH PROBLEM OF EUCLID.*

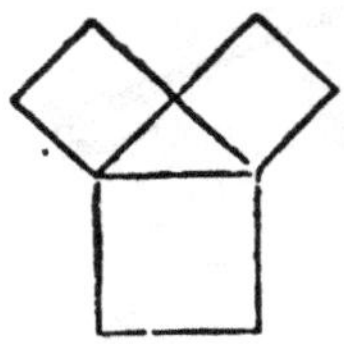

This was an invention of our ancient friend and Brother, the great Pythagoras, who, in his travels through Asia, Africa, and Europe, was initiated into several orders of priesthood, and raised to the sublime degree of a Master Mason. This wise philosopher enriched his mind abundantly in a general knowledge of things, and more especially in Geometry or Masonry; on this subject he drew out many problems and theorems, and among the most distinguished, he erected this, which in the joy of his heart he called *Eureka*, in the Grecian language signifying, *I have found it;* and upon the discovery of which, he is said to have sacrificed a hecatomb.

The historical truth of this statement is not clearly established.

It teaches Masons to be general lovers of the arts and sciences.

THE HOUR-GLASS

Is an emblem of human life. Behold! how swiftly the sands run, and how rapidly our lives are drawing to a close. We can not without astonishment behold the little particles which are contained in this machine, how they pass away almost imper-

---

* [THEOREM.]—In any right-angled triangle, the square which is described upon the side subtending the right-angle, is equal to the squares described upon the sides which contain the right-angle.—*Euclid, lib.* 1; *Prop.* 47.

ceptibly, and yet, to our surprise, in the short space of an hour they are all exhausted. Thus wastes man! to-day, he puts forth the tender leaves of hope; to-morrow, blossoms, and bears his blushing honors thick upon him; the next day comes a frost, which nips the shoot, and when he thinks his greatness is still aspiring, he falls, like autumn leaves, to enrich our mother earth.

THE SCYTHE

Is an emblem of time, which cuts the brittle thread of life, and launches us into eternity. Behold! what havoc the scythe of time makes among the human race; if by chance he should escape the numerous evils incident to childhood and youth, and with health and vigor arrive to the years of manhood, yet withal we must soon be cut down by the all-devouring scythe of time, and be gathered into the land where our fathers have gone before us.

THE THREE STEPS,

Usually delineated upon the Master's Carpet, are emblematical of the three principal stages of human life, viz.: youth, manhood, and age. In youth, as Entered Apprentices, we ought industriously to occupy our minds in the attainment of useful knowledge; in manhood, as Fellow-crafts, we should apply our knowledge to the discharge of our respective duties to God, our neighbors, and ourselves; that so in age, as Master Masons, we may enjoy the happy reflections consequent on a well-spent life, and die in the hope of a glorious immortality.

For appropriate Odes to close Masters' Lodge, see Appendix.

CHARGE AT INITIATION INTO THE THIRD DEGREE.

BROTHER:—Your zeal for the institution of Masonry, the progress you have made in the mystery, and your conformity to our regulations, have pointed you out as a proper object of our favor and esteem.

You are now bound by duty, honor and gratitude, to be faithful to your trust; to support the dignity of your character on every occasion; and to enforce, by precept and example, obedience to the tenets of the Order.

In the character of a Master Mason, you are authorized to correct the errors and irregularities of your uninformed brethren, and to guard them against a breach of fidelity. To preserve the reputation of the fraternity unsullied, must be your constant care; and for this purpose it is your province to recommend to your inferiors, obedience and submission; to your equals, courtesy and affability, to your superiors, kindness and condescension. Universal benevolence you are always to inculcate; and, by the regularity of your own behavior, afford the best example for the conduct of others less informed. The ancient landmarks of the Order, entrusted to your care, you are carefully to preserve; and never suffer them to be infringed, or countenance a deviation from the established usages and customs of the fraternity.

Your virtue, honor and reputation are concerned in supporting with dignity the character you now bear. Let no motive, therefore, make you swerve from your duty, violate your vows, or betray your trust; but be true and faithful, and imitate the example of that celebrated artist whom you this evening represent. Thus you will render yourself deserving of the honor which we have conferred, and merit the confidence that we have reposed.

THE
CAPITULAR DEGREES:

CONSISTING OF

THE MARK MASTER,

THE MOST EXCELLENT MASTER,

AND

THE ROYAL ARCH.

COMPOSING

THE SECOND ORDER IN MASONRY.

The Capitular Degrees are conferred in a Body styled *a Chapter*. The ballot is taken in the last or Royal Arch Degree; the same rules of balloting are observed as in a Lodge. All discipline exercised by the Lodge, such as suspension and expulsion, is indorsed by the Chapter without question; in addition to which it has a discipline of its own for offenses against its own regulations.

Not less than nine can open, work, or close a Chapter, and this is independent of the Tyler.

The whole system of Capitular Masonry as practiced in United States was organized in the latter part of the 18th century.

THE DEGREE

OF

MARK MASTER.

Mark Master.

CHAPTER XI.

REMARKS ON THE FOURTH, OR MARK MASTER'S DEGREE.

This degree of Masonry was not less useful in its original institution, nor are its effects less beneficial to mankind, than those which precede it.

By the influence of this degree, each operative mason, at the erection of the Temple of Solomon, was known and distinguished by the Senior Grand Warden.

By its effects the disorder and confusion that might otherwise have attended so immense an undertaking was completely prevented; and not only the craftsmen themselves, who were eighty thousand in number, but every part of their workmanship, was discriminated with the greatest nicety, and the utmost facility. If defects were found, by the help of this degree the overseers were enabled without difficulty to ascertain who was the faulty workman: so that deficiencies might be remedied, without injuring the credit, or diminishing the reward, of the industrious and faithful of the craft.

CHARGE TO BE READ AT OPENING THE LODGE.

"Wherefore, brethren, lay aside all malice, and guile, and hypocrisies, and envies, and all evil speakings:

"If so be ye have tasted that the Lord is gracious: To whom coming as unto a living stone, disallowed indeed of men, but chosen of God, and precious, ye also, as lively stones, are built up a spiritual house, an holy priesthood, to offer up spiritual sacrifices acceptable to God.

"Wherefore, also, it is contained in the Scriptures, Behold, I lay in Zion, for a foundation, a tried stone, a precious corner-stone, a sure foundation; he that believeth shall not make haste to pass it over. Unto you, therefore, which believe, it is an honor; and even to them which be disobedient, the stone which the builders disallowed, the same is made the head of the corner.

"Brethren, this is the will of God, that with well-doing ye put to silence the ignorance of foolish men. As free, and not using your liberty for a cloak of maliciousness, but as the servants of God. Honor all men, love the brotherhood, fear God."

The regular officers of a Mark Master's Lodge are, 1. Right Worshipful Master; 2, Worshipful Senior Warden; 3, Worshipful Junior Warden; 4, Master Overseer; 5, Senior Overseer; 6, Junior Overseer; 7, Senior Deacon; 8, Junior Deacon.

Although the antiquity of this degree can not be demonstrated, and its origin is obscure, yet for beauty of ceremonial, impressiveness of principles, and the readiness with which the degree is made available in practice between Brother and Brother, there is no other which excels it.

REMARKS ON THE FOURTH LECTURE.

THE FIRST SECTION.

The first section explains the manner of convocating and opening a Mark Master's Lodge. It teaches the stations and duties of the respective officers, and recapitulates the mystic ceremony of introducing a candidate.

In this section is exemplified the regularity and good order that were observed by the craftsmen on Mount Libanus, and in the plains and quarries of Zeredatha, and it ends with a beautiful display of the manner in which one of the principal events originated, which characterizes this degree.

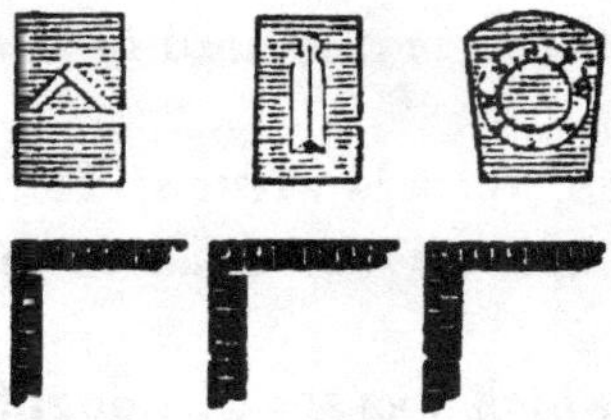

THE SECOND SECTION.

In the second section the Mark Master is particularly instructed in the origin and history of this degree, and the indispensable obligations he is under to stretch forth his assisting hand to the relief of an indigent and worthy brother, to a certain and specified extent.

The progress made in architecture, particularly in the reign of Solomon, is remarked; the numbers of artists employed in the building the Temple of Jerusalem, and the privileges they enjoyed, are specified; the mode of rewarding merit, and of punishing the guilty, are pointed out; and the marks of distinction which were conferred on our ancient brethren, as the rewards of excellence, are named.

In the course of the lecture, the following texts of Scripture are introduced and explained, viz.:

To him that overcometh will I give to eat of the hidden manna, and will give him a *white stone*, and in the stone a *new name* written, which no man knoweth saving him that receiveth it.—*Rev. John* ii: 17.

And we will cut wood out of Lebanon, as much as thou shalt need; and we will bring it to thee in floats by sea to Joppa, and thou shalt carry it up to Jerusalem.—2 *Chron.* ii: 16.

The stone which the builders refused, is become the head stone of the corner.—*Psalm* cxviii: 22.

Did ye never read in the Scriptures, The stone which the builders rejected, is become the head of the corner?—*Matth.* xxi: 42.

And have ye not read this Scripture, The stone which the builders rejected, is become the head of the corner?—*Mark* xii: 10.

What is this, then, that is written, The stone which the builders rejected, is become the head of the corner?—*Luke* xx: 17.

This is the stone which was set at nought of you builders, which is become the head of the corner.—*Acts* iv: 11.

He that hath *an ear* to hear, let him hear.—*Rev.* iii: 13.

Then he brought me back the way of the gate of the outward sanctuary, which looketh toward the east, and it was shut. Then said the Lord unto me, This gate shall be shut, it shall not be opened, and no man shall enter in by it; because the Lord, the God of Israel, hath entered in by it, therefore it shall be shut. It is for the prince; the prince he shall sit in it to eat bread before the Lord: he shall enter by the way of the porch of that gate, and shall go out by the way of the same. And the Lord said unto me, Son of man, *mark well*, and behold with thine eyes, and hear with thine ears, all that I say unto thee concerning all the ordinances of the House of the Lord, and all the laws thereof; and *mark well* the entering in of the house, with every going forth of the sanctuary.—*Ezekiel* xliv: 1–3, 5.

The *working tools* of a Mark Master are the *Chisel* and *Mallet*.

The *Chisel* morally demonstrates the advantages of Discipline and Education. The mind, like the diamond in its original state, is rude and unpolished; but, as the effect of the chisel on the external coat soon presents to view the latent beauties of the diamond, so education discovers the latent virtues of the mind, and draws them forth to range the large field of matter and space, to display the summit of human knowledge, our duty to God and to man.

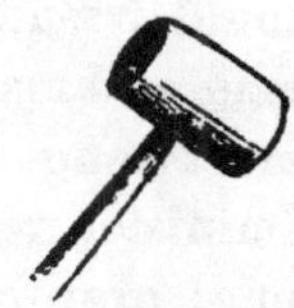

The *Mallet* morally teaches to correct irregularities, and to reduce man to a proper level; so that, by quiet deportment, he may, in the school of discipline, learn to be content. What the mallet is to the workman, enlightened reason is to the passions: it curbs ambition, it depresses envy, it moderates anger, and it encourages good dispositions; whence arises, among good Masons, that comely order,

> "Which nothing earthly gives, or can destroy—
> The soul's calm sunshine, and the heart-felt joy."

CHARGE TO BE DELIVERED WHEN A CANDIDATE IS ADVANCED TO THE FOURTH DEGREE.

BROTHER:—I congratulate you on having been thought worthy of being promoted to this honorable degree of Masonry. Permit me to impress it on your mind, that your assiduity should ever be commensurate with your duties, which become more and more extensive as you advance in Masonry.

The situation to which you are now promoted will draw upon you not only the scrutinizing eyes of the world at large, but those also of your brethren, on whom this degree of Masonry has not been conferred; all will be justified in expecting your conduct and behavior to be such as may with safety be imitated.

In the honorable character of Mark Master, it is more particularly your duty to endeavor to let your conduct in the Lodge and among your brethren, be such as may stand the test of the Grand Overseer's square, that you may not, like the unfinished and imperfect work of the negligent and unfaithful of former times, be rejected and thrown aside, as unfit for that spiritual building, that house not made with hands, eternal in the heavens.

While such is your conduct, should misfortunes assail you,

should friends forsake you, should envy traduce your good name, and malice persecute you; yet may you have confidence, that among Mark Masters, you will find friends who will administer relief to your distresses, and comfort your afflictions; ever bearing in mind, as a consolation under all the frowns of fortune, and as an encouragement to hope for better prospects, that *the stone which the builders rejected*, possessing merits to them unknown, *became the chief stone of the corner.*

Previous to closing the Lodge, the following Parable is recited:

"For the kingdom of Heaven is like unto a man that is an householder, which went out early in the morning to hire laborers into his vineyard. And when he had agreed with the laborers for a penny a day, he sent them into his vineyard. And he went out about the third hour, and saw others standing idle in the market-place, and said unto them, Go ye also into the vineyard, and whatsoever is right I will give you. And they went their way. Again he went out about the sixth and ninth hour and did likewise. And about the eleventh hour, he went out, and found others standing idle, and saith unto them, Why stand ye here all the day idle? They say unto him, Because no man hath hired us. He saith unto them, Go ye also into the vineyard, and whatsoever is right, that shall ye receive. So when even was come, the lord of the vineyard saith unto his steward, Call the laborers, and give them their hire, beginning from the last unto the first. And when they came that were hired about the eleventh hour, they received every man a penny. But when the first came, they supposed that they should have received more, and they likewise received every man a penny. And when they had received it, they murmured against the good man of the house, saying, These last have wrought but one hour, and thou hast made them equal unto us, which have borne the burden and heat of the day. But he answered one of them, and said, Friend, I do thee no wrong: didst not thou agree with me for a penny? Take that thine is, and go thy way; I will give unto this last even as unto thee. Is it not lawful for me to do what I will with mine own? Is thine eye evil because I am good? So the last shall be first, and the first last: for many be called, but few chosen."—*Matth.* xx: 1–16.

The ceremony of closing a Lodge in this degree, when properly conducted, is peculiarly interesting. It assists in strengthening the social affections; it teaches us the duty we owe to our brethren in particular, and the whole family of mankind in general, by ascribing praise to the meritorious, and dispensing rewards to the diligent and industrious.

MARK MASTERS' ODE.

ADAPTED AND ARRANGED BY BRO. JAS. J. TAYLOR.

3 Hiram, the widow's son,
Sent unto Solomon
Our great key-stone;
On it appears the name
Which raises high the fame
Of all to whom the same
Is truly known.

4 Now to the westward move,
Where, full of strength and love,
Hiram doth stand;
But if impostors are
Mixed with the worthy there,
Cau'ion them to beware
Ot the right hand.

—CEREMONIES.—

5 Now to the praise of those
Who triumph'd o'er the foes
Of Mason's art;
To the praiseworthy three,
Who founded this degr-e,
May all their virtues be
Deep in our hearts.

THE DEGREE

OF

PAST MASTER.

Past Master.

CHAPTER XII.

OBSERVATIONS ON THE DEGREE OF PRESENT OR PAST MASTER.

This degree should be carefully studied, and well understood, by every Master of a Lodge. It treats of the government of our society, and the disposition of our rulers; and illustrates their requisite qualifications. It includes the ceremony of opening and closing Lodges in the several preceding degrees; and also the forms of installation and consecration, in the Grand Lodge, as well as private Lodges. It comprehends the ceremonies at laying the foundation stones of public buildings, and also at dedications and at funerals, by a variety of particulars explanatory of those ceremonies.

In Masonic strictness this degree should be given to none, save those who are regularly elected to govern a Symbolical Lodge. The deviation from this rule, in favor of Royal Arch Masonry, has not been to the credit of the degree, nor to the advantage of the Craft.

No person should be allowed to take the degree of Past Master, at least until he has made himself thoroughly proficient in the three degrees of Symbolical Masonry, is able to open and close the Lodges, confer the degrees with dramatic effectiveness, and give the lectures of each from memory.

The regular officers of a Past Masters' Lodge, correspond exactly with a Lodge of Master Masons. The titles are *Right Worshipful Master; Worshipful Senior and Worshipful Junior Warden.*

REMARKS ON THE FIFTH LECTURE.

THE FIRST SECTION.

OF THE MANNER OF CONSTITUTING A LODGE OF MASTER MASONS.

Any number of Master Masons, not under seven, desirous of forming a new Lodge, must apply, by petition, to the Grand Lodge of the State in which they reside.*.

This petition, being signed by at least seven regular Masons, and recommended by a Lodge, or Lodges, adjacent to the place where the new Lodge is to be holden, is delivered to the Grand Secretary, who lays it before the Grand Lodge.

If the petition meets the approbation of the Grand Lodge, they generally order a Dispensation to be issued,† which is signed by the Grand, or Deputy Grand Master, and authorizes the petitioners to assemble as a *legal* Lodge, for a certain specified term of time.

The usage is, that all Dispensations terminate on the first day of the subsequent Grand Annual Communication of the Grand Lodge.

In some jurisdictions, the Grand and Deputy Grand Masters, respectively, are invested with authority to grant dispensations, at pleasure, during the recess of the Grand Lodge; in others, they are never issued without the special direction of the Grand Lodge.

Lodges working under dispensations are considered merely as agents of the Grand Lodge; their presiding officers are not entitled to the rank of Past Masters; their officers are not privileged with a vote or voice in the Grand Lodge; they can not change their officers without the special approbation and appointment of the Grand Lodge; and in case of the cessation of such Lodges, their funds, jewels, and other property accu-

---

* For *Form of Petition* see Appendix.

† For *Form of Dispensation* see Appendix.

mulated by initiations into the several degrees, become the property of the Grand Lodge, and must be delivered over to the Grand Treasurer.

When Lodges, that are at first instituted by dispensation, have passed a proper term of probation, they make application to the Grand Lodge for a charter of constitution.* If this be obtained, they are then confirmed in the possession of their property, and possess all the rights and privileges of regularly constituted Lodges, as long as they conform to the constitutions of Masonry.

The forfeiture of a Charter, however, works a total forfeiture of all property, real or personal, which was in its possession at the period of its demise.

After a charter is granted by the Grand Lodge, the Grand Master appoints a day and hour for constituting and consecrating the new Lodge, and for installing its Master, Wardens, and other officers.

If the Grand Master, in person, attends the ceremony, the Lodge is said to be constituted in *ample form;* if the Deputy Grand Master only, it is said to be constituted in *due form;* but if the power of performing the ceremony is vested in a Subordinate Lodge, it is said to be constituted in *form.*

When charters of constitution are granted for places where the distance is so great as to render it inconvenient for the Grand officers to attend, the Grand Master, or his Deputy, issues a written instrument under his hand and private seal, to some worthy Present or Past Master, with full power to congregate, constitute and install the petitioners.

For *form* *Dispensation* to install officers, see Appendix.

CEREMONY OF CONSTITUTION AND CONSECRATION.

On the day and hour appointed, the Grand Master and his

* For *Form of Charter, or Warrant,* see Appendix.

officers meet in a convenient room, near to that in which the Lodge to be constituted is assembled, and open the Grand Lodge in the three degrees of Masonry.

The officers of the new Lodge are to be examined by the Deputy Grand Master, after which they return to their Lodge.

The new Lodge then sends a messenger to the Grand Master with the following message, viz.:

"MOST WORSHIPFUL:—The officers and brethren of........ Lodge, who are now assembled at......... have instructed me to inform you, that the Most Worshipful Grand Lodge [or Grand Master] was pleased to grant them a letter of Dispensation, bearing date the ... day of ......, in the year ...., authorizing them to form and open a Lodge of Free and Accepted Masons, in the town of............; that since that period they have regularly assembled, and conducted the business of Masonry according to the best of their abilities; that their proceedings having received the approbation of the M. W. Grand Lodge, they have obtained a charter of constitution, and are desirous that their Lodge should be consecrated, and their officers installed, agreeably to the ancient usages and customs of the Craft; for which purpose they are now met, and await the pleasure of the Most Worshipful Grand Master."

He then returns to his Lodge, who prepare for the reception of the Grand Lodge. When notice is given that they are prepared, the Grand Lodge walk in procession to their hall. When the Grand Master enters, the grand honors are given by the new Lodge; the officers of which resign their seats to the Grand Officers, and take their several stations on the left.

These are the *private* Grand Honors which can not be described here.

The necessary cautions are then given, and all, excepting Masters and Past Masters of Lodges, are requested to retire until the Master of the new Lodge is placed in the Chair of

Solomon. He is then bound to the faithful performance of his trust, and invested with the characteristics of the Chair.

The usage has been to throw around this a ceremony of marked dramatic effect. At the Triennial Convention of the General Grand Royal Arch Chapter, 1856, it was *recommended* that this be omitted; but the advice has not been generally acceptable, and the usage is mostly continued as before.

Upon due notice, the Grand Marshal reconducts the brethren into the hall, and all take their places, except the members of the new Lodge, who form a procession on one side of the hall, to salute their Master. As they advance, the Grand Master addresses them, "*Brethren, behold your Master!*" As they pass, they make the proper salutation; and when they have all passed, he joins them, and takes his appropriate station.

A grand procession is then formed, in the following order, viz.:

Tyler, with a drawn sword.
Two Stewards, with White Rods.
Entered Apprentices.
Fellow Crafts.
Master Masons.
Stewards.
Junior Deacons.
Senior Deacons.
Secretaries.
Treasurers.
Past Wardens.
Junior Wardens.
Senior Wardens.
Past Masters.
Royal Arch Masons.
Knights Templar.
Masters of Lodges.

The New Lodge.

Tyler, with a Drawn Sword.
Stewards, with White Rods.

Entered Apprentices.
Fellow Crafts.
Master Masons.
Deacons.
Secretary and Treasurer.
Two Brethren, carrying the Lodge.*
Junior and Senior Wardens.
The Holy Writings carried by the Oldest
Member, not in Office.
The Master.
Music.

The Grand Lodge.

Grand Tyler, with a Drawn Sword.
Grand Stewards, with White Rods.
A Brother, carrying a Golden Vessel of Corn.†
Two Brethren, carrying Silver Vessels, one of
Wine, the other of Oil.
Grand Secretaries.
Grand Treasurers.
A Burning Taper, borne by a Past Master.
A Past Master, bearing the Holy Writings.
Square and Compass, supported by two Stewards, with Rods.
Two Burning Tapers, borne by the two Past Masters.
Clergy and Orator.
The Tuscan and Composite Orders.
The Doric, Ionic and Corinthian Orders.
Past Grand Wardens.
Past Deputy Grand Masters.
Past Grand Masters.
The Globes.
Junior and Senior Grand Wardens.
Right Worshipful Deputy Grand Master.
The Master of the Oldest Lodge, carrying the
Book of Constitutions.
The M. W. Grand Master.
The Grand Deacons, on a line seven feet apart, on the right
and left of the Grand Master, with Black Rods.

---

* Flooring. † Wheat.

Grand Sword Bearer, with a Drawn Sword.
Two Stewards, with White Rods.

The whole procession moves on to the church or house where the services are to be performed. When the front of the procession arrives at the door, they halt, open to the right and left, and face inward, while the Grand Master, and others in succession, pass through and enter the house.

A platform is erected in front of the pulpit, and provided with seats for the accommodation of the Grand Officers.

The bible, square and compass, and book of constitutions, are placed upon a table, in front of the Grand Master; the *lodge* is placed in the center, upon the platform, covered with white satin or linen, and encompassed by the three tapers, and the vessels of corn, wine and oil.

A piece of music is performed, and the public services commence with prayer. An oration, or sermon, upon the design and principles of the institution, is then delivered by the Grand Chaplain, or some one appointed for that purpose, which is succeeded by a piece of music.

The Grand Marshal then directs the officers and members of the new Lodge to form in front of the Grand Master. The Deputy Grand Master addresses the Grand Master, as follows:

"MOST WORSHIPFUL:—A number of brethren, duly instructed in the mysteries of Masonry, having assembled together, at stated periods, for some time past, by virtue of a dispensation granted them for that purpose, do now desire to be *constituted* into a *regular Lodge*, agreeably to the ancient usages and customs of the fraternity."

Their Secretary then delivers the dispensation and records to the Master elect, who presents them to the Grand Master.

The Grand Master examines the records, and if they are found correct, proclaims,

"The records appear to be properly entered, and are approved. Upon due deliberation, the Grand Lodge have granted the brethren of this new Lodge a Charter, confirming them in the rights and privileges of a *regular constituted Lodge;* which the Grand Secretary will now read."

After the Charter is read, the Grand Master then says:

"We shall now proceed, according to ancient usage, to constitute these brethren into a regular Lodge."

Whereupon the several officers of the new Lodge deliver up their jewels and badges to *their* Master, who presents them with his own, to the Deputy Grand Master, and he to the Grand Master.

The Deputy Grand Master now presents the Master elect of the new Lodge to the Grand Master, saying:

"MOST WORSHIPFUL:—I present you Brother * * * * * whom the members of the Lodge now to be constituted have chosen for their Master."

The Grand Master asks them if they remain satisfied with their choice. (*They bow in token of assent.*)

The Master then presents, severally, his Wardens, and other officers, naming them and their respective offices. The Grand Master asks the brethren if they remain satisfied with each and all of them. (*They bow as before.*)

The officers and members of the new Lodge then form in the broad aisle, in front of the Grand Master; and the business of consecration commences with solemn music.

CEREMONY OF CONSECRATION.

The Grand Master, attended by the Grand officers and the Grand Chaplain, form themselves in order, round the Lodge, which is then uncovered. All devoutly kneeling, the first clause of the consecration prayer is rehearsed, as follows, viz.:

"Great Architect of the Universe! Maker and Ruler of all Worlds! deign, from thy celestial Temple, from realms of light and glory, to bless us in all the purposes of our present assembly!

"We humbly invoke Thee to give us, at this and at all times, *wisdom* in all our doings, *strength* of mind in all our difficulties, and the *beauty* of harmony in all our communications!

"Permit us, O thou Author of Light and Life, great source of Love and Happiness, to erect this Lodge, and now solemnly to *consecrate* it to the honor of Thy glory!

"Glory be to God on high."

[*Response by the Brethren.*]—"As it was in the beginning, is now, and ever shall be! Amen."

During the response, the Deputy Grand Master, and Grand Wardens, take the vessels of corn, wine, and oil, and sprinkle the elements of consecration upon the Lodge.

[*The Grand Chaplain then continues.*]

"Grant, O Lord our God, that those who are now about to be invested with the government of this Lodge, may be endued with wisdom to instruct their brethren in all their duties. May *brotherly love*, *relief* and *truth*, always prevail among the members of this Lodge; and may this bond of union continue to strengthen the Lodges throughout the world!

"Bless all our brethren, wherever dispersed: and grant speedy relief to all who are either oppressed or distressed.

"We affectionately commend to Thee all the members of Thy whole family. May they increase in the knowledge of Thee, and in the love of each other.

"Finally: May we finish all our work here below with thine approbation; and then have our transition from this earthly abode to Thy Heavenly Temple above, there to enjoy light, glory and bliss, ineffable and eternal!

"Glory be to God on high!"

[*Response by the Brethren.*]—"As it was in the beginning, s now, and ever shall be! Amen! so mote it be! Amen!"

Then succeeds solemn music, while the Lodge is covered. The Grand Chaplain then DEDICATES the Lodge, in the following terms:

"To the memory of HOLY SAINT JOHN, we dedicate this Lodge. May every Brother revere his character and imitate his virtues.

"Glory be to God on high!"

[*Response.*]—"As it was in the beginning, is now, and ever shall be, world without end. Amen! so mote it be! Amen!"

A piece of music is then performed, while the Brethren of the new Lodge advance in procession to salute the Grand Lodge, with their hands crossed upon their breasts, and bowing as they pass. They then take their places, and stand as they were.

The Grand Master then rises, and constitutes the new Lodge in the form following:

"In the name of the Most Worshipful Grand Lodge, I now constitute and form you, my good brethren, into a Lodge of Free and Accepted Masons. From henceforth I empower you to act as a regular Lodge, constituted in conformity to the rites of our Order, and the charges of our ancient and honorable fraternity; and may the Supreme Architect of the Universe prosper, direct and counsel you in all your doings."

[*Response by all the brethren.*]—"So mote it be!"

The ceremony of installation then succeeds.

The *Installation Covenant* must be taken by every officer, whether elected or appointed. This is of course taken in the Lodge, open in either degree; but the installation itself may be, and often is, performed in public.

No person can be legally installed Master of a Lodge until he has received the degree (or order) of Past Master. In Virginia, by modern usage, even a Warden elect must have this degree before he can be installed.

THE SECOND SECTION.

CEREMONY OF INSTALLATION.

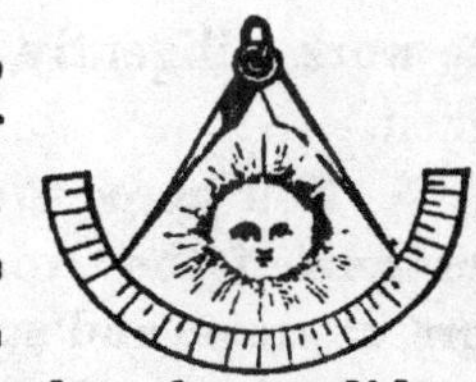

The Grand Master* asks his Deputy, "Whether he has examined the Master nominated in the Warrant, and finds him well skilled in the noble science and the royal art." The Deputy, answering in the affirmative,† by the Grand Master's order, takes the candidate from among his fellows, and presents him at the pedestal, saying, "Most Worshipful Grand Master, I present my worthy Brother, A B, to be installed Master of this new Lodge. I find him to be of good morals, and of great skill, true and trusty; and as he is a lover of the whole fraternity, wheresoever dispersed over the face of the earth, I doubt not that he will discharge his duty with fidelity."

The Grand Master then addresses him:

"BROTHER:—Previous to your investiture, it is necessary that you should signify your assent to those ancient charges and regulations which point out the duty of a Master of a Lodge."

The Grand Master then reads, or orders to be read, a summary of the ancient charges to the Master elect, as follows, viz.:

1. You agree to be a good man and true, and strictly to obey the moral law.

2. You agree to be a peaceable subject, and cheerfully to conform to the laws of the country in which you reside.

---

*In this, and other similar instances, where the Grand Master is specified in acting, may be understood *any Master* who performs the ceremony.

†A private examination is understood to precede the installation of every officer.

3. You promise not to be concerned in plots and conspiracies against government, but patiently to submit to the decisions of the supreme legislature.

4. You agree to pay a proper respect to the civil magistrate, to work diligently, live creditably, and act honorably by all men.

5. You agree to hold in veneration the original rulers and patrons of the Order of Masonry, and their regular successors, supreme and subordinate, according to their stations; and to submit to the awards and resolutions of your brethren when convened, in every case consistent with the constitutions of the Order.

6. You agree to avoid private piques and quarrels, and to guard against intemperance and excess.

7. You agree to be cautious in carriage and behavior, courteous to your brethren, and faithful to your Lodge.

8. You promise to respect genuine brethren, and to discountenance impostors, and all dissenters from the original plan of Masonry.

9. You agree to promote the general good of society, to cultivate the social virtues, and to propagate the knowledge of the art.

10. You promise to pay homage to the Grand Master for the time being, and to his officers when duly installed; and strictly to conform to every edict of the Grand Lodge, or General Assembly of Masons, that is not subversive of the principles and ground-work of Masonry.

11. You admit that it is not in the power of any man, or body of men, to make innovations in the body of Masonry.

12. You promise a regular attendance on the committees and communications of the Grand Lodge, on receiving proper notice, and to pay attention to all the duties of Masonry, on convenient occasions.

13. You admit that no new Lodge shall be formed without

permission of the Grand Lodge; and that no countenance be given to any irregular Lodge or to any person clandestinely initiated therein, being contrary to the Ancient charges of the Order.

14. You admit that no person can be regularly made a Mason in, or admitted a member of, any regular Lodge, without previous notice, and due inquiry into his character.

15. You agree that no visitors shall be received into your Lodge without due examination, and producing proper vouchers of their having been initiated in a regular Lodge.*

---

* As the curious reader may wish to know the ancient charges that were used on this occasion, we shall here insert them verbatim, as they are contained in a MS. in possession of the Lodge of Antiquity, in London, written in the reign of James the Second.

" * * * And furthermore, at diverse assemblies, have been put and ordained diverse crafties by the best advice of magistrates and fellowes.

"Every man that is a Mason take good heed to these charges, wee pray, that if any man find himselfe guilty of any of these charges, that he may amend himselfe, or principally for dread of God you that be charged to take good heed that you keepe all these charges well, for it is a great evill for a man to forsweare himselfe upon a book.

"The first charge is, That yee shall be true men to God and the Holy Church, and to use no error or heresie by your understanding and by wise men's teaching.

"Also, secondly, yee shall be true one to another; that is to say, every mason of the craft that is mason allowed, yee shall doe to him as yee would be done unto yourselfe.

"Thirdly. And yee shall keepe truely all the counsell that ought to be kept in the way of masonhood, and all the counsell of the lodge or of the chamber. Allso that yee shall bee no thiefe, nor thieves to your knowledge free: that yee shall be true to the king, lord or master that yee serve, and truely to see and work for his advantage.

"Fourthly. Yee shall call all masons your fellowes, or your brethren, and no other names.

"Fifthly. Yee shall not take your fellowe's wife in villainy, nor deflower his daughter or servant, nor put him to no disworship.

These are the regulations of Free and Accepted Masons.

The Grand Master then addresses the Master elect in the following manner: "Do you submit to these charges, and promise to support these regulations, as Masters have done in

---

"Sixthly. Yee shall truely pay for your meat or drinke, wheresoever yee goe to table or boarde. Allso, yee shall doe no villainy there whereby the craft or science may be slandered.

"These shall be the charges general to every true mason, both master and fellowes.

"Now will I rehearse other charges single for masons allowed or accepted.

"First. That no mason take on him no lorde's worke, nor any other man's, unless he know himselfe well able to perform the worke, so that the craft have no slander.

"Secondly. Allso that no master take worke but that he take reasonable pay for itt; so that the lord may be truely served and the master to live honestly, and to pay his fellowes truly. And that no master or fellow supplant others of their worke; that is to say, that if he hath taken a worke, or else stand master of any worke, that he shall not put him out, unless he be unable of cunning to make an end of his worke. And no master or fellow shall take an apprentice for less than seven years. And that the apprentice be free born, and of limbs whole as a man ought to be, and no bastard. And that no master or fellow take no allowance to be made mason without the assent of his fellowes, at the least six or seven.

"Thirdly. That he that be made be able in all degrees; that is, freeborn, of a good kindred, true, and no bondsman, and that he have his right limbs as a man ought to have.

"Fourthly. That a master take no apprentice without he have occupation to occupy two or three fellowes at the least.

"Fifthly. That no master or fellow put away any lorde's worke to task that ought to be journey worke.

"Sixthly. That every master give pay to his fellowes and servants as they may desurve, soe that he be not defamed with false workeing. And that none slander another behind his backe, to make him loose his good name.

"Seventhly. That no fellow in the house or abroad answer another ungodly or reproveable without a cause.

all ages before you?" The new Master having signified his cordial submission as before, the Grand Master thus addresses him:

"Brother A B, in consequence of your cheerful conformity to the charges and regulations of the Order, you are now to be installed Master of this new Lodge, in full confidence of your care, skill and capacity to govern the same."

"Eighthly. That every master mason doe reverence his elder; and that a mason be no common plaier at the cards, dice or hazeard, nor at any other unlawfull plaies, through which the science and craft may be dishonored or slandered.

"Ninthly. That no fellow goe into the town by night, except he have a fellow with him, who may bear him record that he was in an honest place.

"Tenthly. That every master and fellow shall come to the assemblie, if it be within fifty miles of him, if he have any warning. And if he have trespassed against the craft, to abide the award of masters and fellowes.

"Eleventhly. That every master mason and fellow that hath trespassed against the craft shall stand to the correction of other masters and fellowes to make him accord; and if they cannot accord, to go to the common law.

"Twelfthly. That no master or fellow make not a mould stone, square nor rule to no lower, nor let no lower worke within their lodge nor without, to mould stone.

"Thirteenthly. That every mason receive and cherish strange fellowes when they come over the countrie, and set them on worke if they will worke, as the manner is; that is to say, if the mason have any mould stone in his place, he shall give him a mould stone, and sett him on worke: and if he have none, the mason shall refresh him with money unto the next lodge.

"Fourteenthly. That every mason shall truely serve his master for his pay.

"Fifteenthly. That every master shall truely make an end of his worke, taske or journey, whethersoe it be.

"These be all the charges and covenants that ought to be read at the instalment of master or making of a freemason or freemasons. The Almighty God of Jacob, who ever have you and me in his keeping, bless us now and ever. Amen."

The new Master is then regularly invested with the insignia of his office, and the furniture and implements of his Lodge.

The various implements of the profession are emblematical of our conduct in life, and upon this occasion carefully enumerated.

"The *Holy Writings*, that great light in Masonry, will guide you to all truth; it will direct your paths to the temple of happines, and point out to you the whole duty of man.

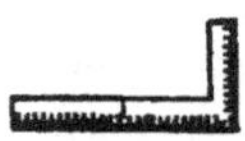

"The *Square* teaches to regulate our actions by rule and line, and to harmonize our conduct by the principles of morality and virtue.

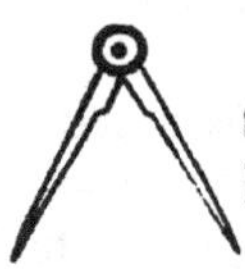

"The *Compass* teaches to limit our desires in every station, that, rising to eminence by merit, we may live respected, and die regretted.

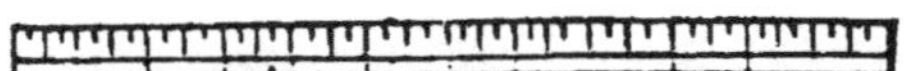

"The *Rule* directs that we should punctually observe our duty; press forward in the path of virtue, and, neither inclining to the right nor to the left, in all our actions have *eternity* in view.

"The *Line* teaches the criterion of moral rectitude, to avoid dissimulation in conversation and action, and to direct our steps to the path which leads to *immortality*.

"The *Book of Constitutions* you are to search at all times. Cause it to be read in your Lodge, that none may pretend ignorance of the excellent precepts it enjoins.

"Lastly, you receive in charge the *By-Laws* of your Lodge, which you are to see carefully and punctually executed."

The jewels of the officers of the new Lodge being then returned to the Master, he delivers them, respectively, to the several officers of the Grand Lodge, according to their rank.

The subordinate officers of the new Lodge are then invested with their jewels, by the Grand Officers of corresponding rank; and are by them, severally in turn, conducted to the Grand Master, who delivers each of them a short charge, as follows, viz.:

THE SENIOR WARDEN.

"Brother C D, you are appointed Senior Warden of this new Lodge, and are now invested with the ensign of your office.

The introduction of the word "appointed" here—which in practice is usually rendered "elected"—may be traced to two circumstances. 1. In the first organization of the Lodge, the officers are usually *appointed* by the Grand Lodge; and 2d. In former times, the Wardens were *appointed* by the Master.

"The *Level* demonstrates that we are descended from the same stock, partake of the same nature, and share the same hope; and though distinctions among men are necessary to preserve subordination, yet no eminence of station should make us forget that we are brethren; for he who is placed on the lowest spoke of fortune's wheel, may be entitled to our regard; because a time will come, and the wisest knows not how soon, when all distinctions, but that of goodness, shall cease; and death, the grand leveler of human greatness, reduce us to the same state.

"Your regular attendance on our stated meetings is essentially necessary; in the absence of the Master you are to govern this Lodge: in his presence you are to assist him in the government of it. I firmly rely on your knowledge of Masonry, and attachment to the Lodge, for the faithful discharge of the duties of this important trust—*Look well to the West!*"

THE JUNIOR WARDEN.

"Brother E F, you are appointed Junior Warden of this new Lodge; and are now invested with the badge of your office.

"The *Plumb* admonishes us to walk uprightly in our several stations, to hold the scale of justice in equal poise, to observe the just medium between intemperance and pleasure, and to make our passions and prejudices coincide with the line of our duty.

"To you, with such assistance as may be necessary, is entrusted the examination of visitors, and the reception of candidates.

This is not now the general usage in the American Lodges; for the former, a special committee is usually appointed; for the latter the stewards are designated, or, in their absence, a special committee.

"To you is also committed the superintendence of the Craft during the hours of refreshment.

This sentence expresses the prime duty, care and responsibility of the Junior Warden, "to take charge of the brethren while at refreshment," i. e. between the meetings of the Lodge.

"It is therefore indispensably necessary, that you should not only be temperate and discreet, in the indulgence of your own inclinations, but carefully observe that none of the Craft be suffered to convert the purposes of refreshment into intemperance and excess.

"Your regular and punctual attendance is particularly requested; and I have no doubt that you will faithfully execute the duty which you owe to your present appointment.—*Look well to the South!*"

THE TREASURER.

"Brother G H, you are appointed Treasurer of this new Lodge. It is your duty to receive all moneys from the hands of the Secretary, keep just and regular accounts of the same, and pay them out at the Worshipful Master's will and pleasure, with the consent of the Lodge. I trust, your regard for the fraternity will prompt you to the faithful discharge of the duties of your office."

THE SECRETARY.

"Brother I K, you are appointed Secretary of this new Lodge. It is your duty to observe the Worshipful Master's will and pleasure, to record the proceedings of the Lodge, to receive all moneys, and pay them into the hands of the Treasurer.

"Your good inclination to Masonry and this Lodge, I hope, will induce you to discharge your office with fidelity, and by so doing, you will merit the esteem and applause of your brethren."

THE SENIOR AND JUNIOR DEACONS.

"Brothers L M and N O, you are appointed Deacons of this new Lodge. It is your province to attend on the Master and Wardens, and to act as their proxies in the active duties of the Lodge; such as the reception of candidates into the different degrees of Masonry; the introduction and accommodation of visitors, and in the immediate practice of our rites. These columns, as badges of your office, I entrust to your care, not doubting your vigilance and attention."

The *badge* or *jewel* of the Deacons' offices is, by common usage, changed, as may be seen in the cut. But in many Lodges other emblems are worn, such as the Winged Mercury, the Triangles, the Stone-Cutters' Hammer, etc. There is little uniformity in this respect.

THE STEWARDS.

"Brothers P Q and R S, you are appointed Stewards of thi new Lodge. The duties of your office are, to assist in the collection of dues and subscriptions, to keep an account of the Lodge expenses, to see that the tables are properly furnished at refreshment, and that every brother is suitably provided for; and generally to assist the Deacons and other officers in performing their respective duties. Your regular and early attendance will afford the best proof of your zeal and attachment to the Lodge."

THE TYLER

Is then appointed, and receives the instrument of his office, with a short charge on the occasion.

The Grand Master then addresses the officers and members of the new Lodge as follows:

CHARGE UPON THE INSTALLATION OF THE OFFICERS OF A LODGE.

"WORSHIPFUL MASTER:—The Grand Lodge having committed to your care the superintendence and government of the brethren who are to compose this new Lodge, you can not be insensible of the obligations which devolve on you, as their head; nor of your responsibility for the faithful discharge of the important duties annexed to your appointment.

"The honor, reputation and usefulness of your Lodge will materially depend on the skill and assiduity with which you manage its concerns; while the happiness of its members will be generally promoted, in proportion to the zeal and ability with which you propagate the genuine principles of our institution.

"For a pattern of imitation, consider the great luminary of nature, which, rising in the *East*, regularly diffuses light and luster to all within its circle. In like manner it is your province to spread and communicate light and instruction to the brethren of your Lodge. Forcibly impress upon them the dignity and high importance of Masonry; and seriously admonish them never to disgrace it. Charge them to practice *out* of the Lodge, those duties which they have been taught *in* it; and by amiable, discreet and virtuous conduct, to convince mankind of the goodness of the institution; so that when any one is said to be a member of it, the world may know that he is one to whom the burdened heart may pour out its sorrows; to whom distress may prefer its suit; whose hand is guided by justice, and his heart expanded by benevolence. In short, by a diligent observance of the By-Laws of your Lodge, the Constitutions of Masonry, and, above all, the Holy Scriptures, which are given as a rule and guide to your faith, you will be enabled to acquit yourself with honor and reputation, and lay up a *crown of rejoicing*, which shall continue when time shall be no more."

"BROTHER SENIOR AND JUNIOR WARDENS:—You are too well acquainted with the principles of Masonry to warrant any distrust that you will be found wanting in the discharge of your respective duties. Suffice it to mention, that what you have seen praiseworthy in others, you should carefully imitate; and what in them may have appeared defective, you should in yourselves amend. You should be examples of good order and regularity; for it is only by a due regard to the laws in your own conduct, that you can expect obedience to them from others. You are assiduously to assist the Master in the discharge of his trust; diffusing light and imparting knowledge to all whom he shall place under your care. In the absence of the Master you will succeed to higher duties; your acquirements must, therefore, be such, as that the Craft may never suffer for want of proper instruction. From the spirit which you have hitherto evinced, I entertain no doubt that your future conduct will be such as to merit the applause of your brethren, and the testimony of a good conscience."

"BRETHREN OF .... LODGE:—Such is the nature of our constitution, that as some must of necessity rule and teach, so others must of course learn to submit and obey. Humility in both is an essential duty. The officers who are appointed to govern your Lodge, are sufficiently conversant with the rules of propriety, and the laws of the institution, to avoid exceeding the powers with which they are intrusted; and you are of too generous dispositions to envy their preferment. I therefore trust that you will have but one aim, to please each other, and unite in the grand design of being happy, and communicating happiness.

"Finally, my brethren, as this association has been formed and perfected in so much unanimity and concord, in which we greatly rejoice, so may it long continue. May you long enjoy every satisfaction and delight, which disinterested friendship can afford. May kindness and brotherly affection distinguish your conduct as men and as Masons. Within your peaceful walls, may your children's children celebrate with joy and gratitude the transactions of this auspicious solemnity. And may *the tenets of our profession* be transmitted through your Lodge, pure and unimpaired, from generation to generation."

The Grand Marshal then proclaims the new Lodge, in the following manner, viz.:

"In the name of the Most Worshipful Grand Lodge of the State of ...., I proclaim this new Lodge, by the name of .... Lodge, duly constituted."

This proclamation is made thrice, and each time followed with a flourish of drums or trumpets.

The Grand Chaplain then makes the concluding prayer, which ends the public ceremonies.

The grand procession is then formed in the same order as before, and returns to the hall.

The Grand Master, Deputy Grand Master, and Grand Wardens, being seated, all but Master Masons are caused to retire, and the procession continues round the hall, which upon passing the several Grand officers, pays them due homage, by the usual congratulations and honors, in the different degrees, commencing with the lowest. During the procession (which passes three times round the Lodge) the following song is sung, which concludes the ceremony of installation:

INSTALLATION ODE.

AIR.—ITALIAN HYMN. Adapted and arranged by BRO. JAS. B. TAYLOR.

2 Great fabrics still arise,
And grace the azure skies;
Great are thy schemes;
Thy noble orders are
Matchless, beyond compare;
No art with thee can share.
Thou art divine!

3 Hiram, the architect,
Did all the Craft direct
How they should build.
Solomon, Israel's king,
Did mighty blessings bring.
Which gave us cause to sing,
Hail, royal art!

The Lodge is then closed with the usual solemnities in the different degrees, by the Grand Master and his officers.

This is the usual ceremony observed by regular Masons at the constitution of a new Lodge, which the Grand Master may abridge or extend at pleasure; but the material points are on no account to be omitted. The same ceremony and charges attend every succeeding installation of new officers.

Officers re-elected to office without an intermission of time, need not be re-installed.

THE THIRD SECTION.

CEREMONY OBSERVED AT LAYING THE FOUNDATION STONE OF PUBLIC STRUCTURES.

This ceremony is conducted by the Grand Master and his officers, assisted by the members of the Grand Lodge, and such officers and members of private Lodges, as can conveniently attend. The chief magistrate, and other civil officers of the place where the building is to be erected, also generally attend on the occasion.

At the time appointed, the Grand Lodge is convened in some suitable place, approved by the Grand Master. A band of martial music is provided, and the brethren appear in the insignia of the Order, and with white gloves and Aprons. The Lodge is opened by the Grand Master, and the rules for regulating the procession to and from the place where the ceremony is to be performed, are read by the Grand Secretary. The necessary cautions are then given from the Chair, and the Lodge is adjourned: after which the procession sets out in the following order:

PROCESSION AT LAYING CORNER-STONES.

Two Tylers, with drawn swords.

Tyler of the oldest Lodge, with sword.

Two Stewards of the oldest Lodge.

Entered Apprentices.

Marshal.

Fellow Crafts.
Master Masons.
Stewards.
Junior Deacons.
Senior Deacons.
Secretaries.
Treasurers.
Past Wardens.
Junior Wardens.
Senior Wardens.
Past Masters.
Royal Arch Masons.
Knights Templar.
Masters.
Music.
Grand Tyler, with a Drawn Sword.
Grand Stewards, with White Rods.
A Brother, with a Golden Vessel containing Corn.
Two Brethren, with Silver Vessels, one containing Wine, and the other Oil.
Principal Architect, with Square, Level and Plumb.
Grand Secretary and Treasurer.
Bible, Square and Compass, carried by a Master of a Lodge, supported by two Stewards.
Grand Chaplain.
The Five Orders.
Past Grand Wardens.
Past Deputy Grand Masters.
Past Grand Masters.
Chief Magistrate of the place.
Two Large Lights, borne by two Masters of Lodges.
Grand Wardens.
One Large Light, borne by a Master of a Lodge.
Deputy Grand Master.
Master of the Oldest Lodge, bearing the Book of Constitutions, on a Velvet Cushion.
Grand Deacons, with Black Rods, on a line seven feet apart.
GRAND MASTER.
Grand Sword Bearer, with a Drawn Sword.
Two Stewards, with White Rods.

A triumphal arch is usually erected at the place where the ceremony is to be performed.

The procession passes through the arch, and the brethren repairing to their stands, the Grand Master and his officers take their places on a temporary platform, covered with carpet. An ode on Masonry is sung. The Grand Master commands silence, and the necessary preparations are made for laying the stone, on which is engraved the year of Masonry, the name and titles of the Grand Master, etc., etc.

The stone is raised up, by means of an engine erected for that purpose, and the Grand Chaplain or orator repeats a short prayer. The Grand Treasurer then, by the Grand Master's command, places under the stone various sorts of coin and medals of the present age. Solemn music is introduced, and the stone let down into its place. The principal Architect then presents the working tools to the Grand Master, who applies the *plumb*, *square* and *level* to the stone, in their proper positions, and pronounces it to be "WELL FORMED, TRUE AND TRUSTY."

The golden and silver vessels are next brought to the table, and delivered, the former to the Deputy Grand Master, and the latter to the Grand Wardens, who successively present them to the Grand Master; and he, according to ancient ceremony, pours the corn, the wine and the oil which they contain, on the stone, saying,

"May the all-bounteous Author of Nature bless the inhabitants of this place with all the necessaries, conveniences and comforts of life; assist in the erection and completion of this building; protect the workmen against every accident, and long preserve this structure from decay; and grant to us all, in needed supply, the CORN of *nourishment*, the WINE of *refreshment*, and the OIL of *joy*."

"Amen! so mote it be! Amen!"

He then strikes the stone thrice with the mallet, and the *public* honors of Masonry are given.

The Grand Master then delivers over to the Architect the various implements of architecture, entrusting him with the superintendence and direction of the work; after which he re-ascends the platform, and an oration suitable to the occasion is delivered. A voluntary collection is made for the workmen, and the sum collected is placed upon the stone by the Grand Treasurer. A song in honor of Masonry concludes the ceremony, after which the procession returns to the place whence it set out, and the Lodge is closed.

THE FOURTH SECTION.

CEREMONY OBSERVED AT THE DEDICATION OF MASONS' HALLS.

See *Preston's Illustrations* (U. M. L. Vol. 3), for a detailed account of the dedication of a Masonic Hall, in England.

On the day appointed for the celebration of the ceremony of dedication, the Grand Master and his officers, accompanied by the members of the Grand Lodge, meet in a convenient room near to the place where the ceremony is to be performed, and the Grand Lodge is opened in ample form in the first three degrees of Masonry.

Commencing with the *lowest.*

The Master of the Lodge to which the hall to be dedicated belongs, being present, rises, and addresses the Grand Master, as follows;

"MOST WORSHIPFUL:—The brethren of .... Lodge, being animated with a desire of promoting the honor and interest of the Craft, have, at great pains and expense, erected a Masonic hall, for their convenience and accommodation. They are now desirous that the same should be examined by the M. W. Grand Lodge; and if it should meet their approbation, that it should be solemnly dedicated to Masonic purposes, agreeably to ancient form."

The Grand Master then directs the Grand Secretary to read the order of procession, which is delivered over to the Grand Marshal; and a general charge respecting propriety of behavior, is given by the Deputy Grand Master.

A grand procession is then formed in the order laid down in the first section. The whole moves forward to the hall which is to be dedicated, and upon the arrival of the front of the procession at the door, they halt, open to the right and left, and face inward; while the Grand Master, and others in succession, pass through and enter. The music continues while the procession marches three times round the hall.

The Lodge is then placed in the center; and the Grand Master having taken the chair, under a canopy of state, the Grand officers, and the Masters and Wardens of the Lodges, repair to the places previously prepared for their reception: the three lights, and the gold and silver pitchers, with corn, wine and oil, are placed round the Lodge, at the head of which stands the pedestal, with the Bible open, and the Square and Compass laid thereon, with the Constitution-roll, on a crimson velvet cushion.* Matters being thus disposed, an anthem is sung, and an exordium on Masonry given: after which the Architect addresses the Grand Master, as follows:

"MOST WORSHIPFUL:—Having been entrusted with the superintendence and management of the workmen employed in the construction of this edifice; and having, according to the best of my ability, accomplished the task assigned me; I now return my thanks for the honor of this appointment, and beg leave to surrender up the implements which were committed to my care when the foundation of this fabric was laid; humbly hoping, that the exertions which have been

---

* For an appropriate Anthem see Appendix.

made on this occasion, will be crowned with your approbation, and that of the Most Worshipful Grand Lodge."

To which the Grand Master makes the following reply:

"BROTHER ARCHITECT:—The skill and fidelity displayed in the execution of the trust reposed in you, at the commencement of this undertaking, have secured the entire approbation of the Grand Lodge; and they sincerely pray, that this edifice may continue a lasting monument of the taste, spirit, and liberality of its founders."

An ode in honor of Masonry is sung, accompanied with instrumental music.

The Deputy Grand Master then rises, and says:

"MOST WORSHIPFUL:—The hall in which we are now assembled, and the plan upon which it has been constructed, having met with your approbation, it is the desire of the fraternity that it should be now dedicated, according to ancient form and usage."

Whereupon the Grand Master requests all to retire but such as are Master Masons. A procession is then formed in the following order, viz.:

Grand Sword Bearer.
A Past Master, with a Light.
A Past Master, with Bible, Square and Compass, on a Velvet Cushion.
Two Past Masters, each with a Light.
Grand Secretary and Treasurer, with Emblems.
Grand Junior Warden, with Pitcher of Corn.
Grand Senior Warden, with Pitcher of Wine.
Deputy Grand Master, with Pitcher of Oil.
Grand Master.
Two Stewards, with Rods.

All the other brethren keep their places, and assist in performing an ode, which continues during the procession, excepting only at the intervals of dedication. The Lodge is uncovered, and the first procession being made round it, the Junior Grand Warden presents the pitcher of corn to the Grand Master, who pours it out upon the Lodge, at the same time pronouncing, "In the name of the great Jehovah, to whom be all honor and glory, I do solemnly dedicate this hall to MASONRY." *The grand honors are given.*

The following is a description of the Public Grand Honors: The arms are crossed over the breast, the left arm uppermost. The palms are then struck smartly together, over the head, the eyes glancing upward. Lastly, the hands are brought down, open, and struck upon the thighs (see *Mackey's Lexicon*); thus the Grand Honors are given in full. This is to be repeated three times.

The second procession is then made round the Lodge, and Grand Senior Warden presents the pitcher of wine to the Grand Master, who sprinkles it upon the Lodge, at the same time saying, "In the name of the holy Saint John, I do solemnly dedicate this hall to VIRTUE." *The grand honors are twice repeated.*

The third procession is then made round the Lodge, and the Deputy Grand Master presents the pitcher of oil to the Grand Master, who sprinkles it upon the Lodge, saying, "In the name of the whole Fraternity, I do solemnly dedicate this hall to UNIVERSAL BENEVOLENCE." *The grand honors are thrice repeated.*

A solemn invocation is made to Heaven, by the Grand Chaplain, and an anthem sung; after which the Lodge is covered, and the Grand Master retires to his chair. An oration is then delivered, and the ceremonies conclude with music. The Grand Lodge is then closed in ample form, in the several degrees.

Commencing with the *highest.* The more frequent usage is, to close the three Lodges by a single order.

THE FIFTH SECTION.

THE CEREMONY USED AT FUNERALS, ACCORDING TO ANCIENT CUSTOM; WITH THE SERVICE USED ON THE OCCASION.

No Mason can be interred with the formalities of the Order, unless it be by his own special request, communicated to the Master of the Lodge of which he died a member, foreigners and sojourners excepted; nor unless he has been advanced to the third degree of Masonry; and from this restriction there can be no exception. Fellow-crafts, or Apprentices, are not entitled to funeral obsequies, nor to attend the Masonic procession on such occasion.

This rule has been, until lately, shamefully violated, by the admission of Fellow-crafts, and even Entered Apprentices into the ranks.

The Master of a Lodge, having received notice of a Master Mason's death, and of his request to be interred with the ceremonies of the Order, fixes the day and hour for the funeral, and issues his command to summon the Lodge.

A custom prevails in many Lodges of keeping a "Book of Memory," in which those who desire Masonic honors after death record their wishes. It is worthy of general adoption.

He may invite as many Lodges as he thinks proper, and the members of those Lodges may accompany their officers in form; but the whole ceremony must be under the direction of the Master of the Lodge to which the deceased belonged, and he and his officers must be duly honored, and cheerfully obeyed on the occasion.* But in case the deceased was not a member of either of the attending Lodges, the procession and ceremony must be under the direction of the Master of the oldest Lodge.

---

* Except when the Grand or Deputy Grand Master is present and exercises his authority.

All the brethren who walk in procession should observe, as much as possible, an uniformity in their dress. Decent mourning, with white stockings, gloves, and aprons, is most suitable.

THE FUNERAL SERVICE.

The brethren being assembled at the Lodge room (or some other convenient place), the presiding Master opens the Lodge, in the third degree, with the usual forms; and having stated the purpose of the meeting, the service begins:

Master. "What man is he that liveth, and shall not see death? shall he deliver his soul from the hand of the grave?"

Response. "Man walketh in a vain shadow; he heapeth up riches, and can not tell who shall gather them."

Master. "When he dieth, he shall carry nothing away; his glory shall not descend after him."

Response. "Naked he came into the world, and naked he must return."

Master. "The Lord gave, and the Lord hath taken away; blessed be the name of the Lord!"

The grand honors are then given, and certain forms used, which can not be here explained.

The Master then taking the SACRED ROLL in his hand, says,

This is simply a sheet of parchment or paper.

"Let us die the death of the righteous, and let our last end be like his."

The brethren answer,

"God is our God for ever and ever; he will be our guide even unto death!"

The Master then records the name and age of the deceased upon the roll, and says,

"Almighty Father! into thy hands we commend the soul of our loving brother."

The brethren answer three times (giving the grand honors each time),

"The will of God is accomplished! Amen! so mote it be."

The Master then deposits the roll in the archives, and repeats the following prayer:

"Most glorious God! author of all good, and giver of all mercy! pour down thy blessings upon us, and strengthen our solemn engagements with the ties of sincere affection! May the present instance of mortality remind us of our approaching fate, and draw our attention toward Thee, the only refuge in time of need! that when the awful moment shall arrive, that we are about to quit this transitory scene, the enlivening prospect of Thy mercy may dispel the gloom of death; and after our departure hence in peace and in Thy favor, we may be received into Thine everlasting kingdom, to enjoy, in union with the souls of our departed friends, the just reward of a pious and virtuous life. *Amen.*"

A procession is then formed, which moves to the house of the deceased, and from thence to the place of interment. The different Lodges rank according to seniority, excepting that the Lodge, of which the deceased was a member, walks nearest the corpse. Each Lodge forms one division, and the following order is observed:

ORDER OF PROCESSION AT A FUNERAL.

Tyler, with a Drawn Sword.

Stewards, with white Rods.

Musicians (if they are Masons, otherwise they follow the Tyler).

Master Masons.

Senior and Junior Deacons.

Secretary and Treasurer.

Senior and Junior Wardens.

Past Masters.

The Holy Writings, on a Cushion covered with Black Cloth, carried by the oldest member of the Lodge.

The Master.

Clergy.

The

with the insignia

and two

Pall Bearers.

Body,

placed thereon,

Swords crossed.

Pall Bearers.

The brethren are not to desert their ranks, or change places, but keep in their different departments. When the procession arrives at the church-yard, the members of the Lodge form a circle round the grave, and the clergyman and officers of the acting Lodge taking their station at the head of the grave, and the mourners at the foot, the service is resumed, and the following exhortation given:

"Here we view a striking instance of the uncertainty of life, and the vanity of all human pursuits. The last offices paid to the dead are only useful as lectures to the living: from them we are to derive instruction, and consider every solemnity of this kind as a summons to prepare for our approaching dissolution.

"Notwithstanding the various mementoes of mortality with which we daily meet, notwithstanding death has established his empire over all the works of nature, yet, through some unaccountable infatuation, we forget that we are born to die. We go on from one design to another, add hope to hope, and lay out plans for the employment of many years, till we are suddenly alarmed with the approach of death, when we least expect him, and at an hour which we probably conclude to be the meridian of our existence.

"What are all the externals of majesty, the pride of wealth, or charms of beauty, when nature has paid her just debt? Fix your eyes on the last scene, and view life stript of her ornaments, and exposed in her natural meanness; you will then be convinced of the futility of those empty delusions. In the grave, all fallacies are detected, all ranks are leveled, and all distinctions are done away.

"While we drop the sympathetic tear over the grave of our deceased friend, let charity incline us to throw a veil over his foibles, whatever they may have been, and not withhold from his memory the praise that his virtues may have claimed. Suffer the apologies of human nature to plead in his behalf. Perfection on earth has never been attained; the wisest, as well as the best of men, have erred.

"Let the present example excite our most serious thoughts, and strengthen our resolutions of amendment. As life is uncertain, and all earthly pursuits are vain, let us no longer postpone the important concern of preparing for eternity; but embrace the happy moment, while time and opportunity offer, to provide against the great change, when all the pleasures of this world shall cease to delight, and the reflections of a virtuous life yield the only comfort and consolation. Thus our expectations will not be frustrated, nor we hurried unprepared into the presence of an all-wise and powerful Judge, to whom the secrets of all hearts are known.

"Let us, while in this state of existence, support with propriety the character of our profession, advert to the nature of our solemn ties, and pursue with assiduity the sacred tenets of our Order: Then, with becoming reverence, let us supplicate the Divine grace, to ensure the favor of that eternal Being, whose goodness and power know no bound; that when the awful moment arrives, be it soon or late, we may be enabled to prosecute our journey, without dread or apprehension, to that far distant country whence no traveler returns."

The following invocations are then made by the Master:

Master. May we be true and faithful; and may we live and die in love!

Answer. So mote it be.

Master. May we profess what is good, and always act agreeably to our profession!

Answer. So mote it be.

Master. May the Lord bless us, and prosper us; and may all our good intentions be crowned with success!

Answer. So mote it be.

Master. Glory be to God on high! on earth peace! good will toward men!

Answer. So mote it be, now, from henceforth, and forevermore.

The brethren then move in procession round the place of interment, and severally drop a sprig of evergreen into the grave, accompanied with the usual honors.

The Master then concludes the ceremony at the grave, in the following words:

"From time immemorial it has been a custom among the fraternity of Free and Accepted Masons, at the request of a Brother, to accompany his corpse to the place of interment, and there to deposit his remains with the usual formalities.

"In conformity to this usage, and at the special request of our deceased Brother, whose memory we revere, and whose loss we now deplore, we have assembled in the character of Masons, to resign his body to the earth whence it came, and to offer up to his memory, before the world, the last tribute of our affection; thereby demonstrating the sincerity of our past esteem, and our steady attachment to the principles of the Order.

"The great Creator having been pleased, out of his mercy, to remove our Brother from the cares and troubles of a transitory existence, to a state of eternal duration, and thereby to weaken the chain by which we are united, man to man; may we, who survive him, anticipate our approaching fate, and be more strongly cemented in the ties of union and friendship; that, during the short space allotted to our present existence, we may wisely and usefully employ our time; and, in the reciprocal intercourse of kind and friendly acts, mutually promote the welfare and happiness of each other.

"Unto the grave we resign the body of our deceased friend, there to remain until the general resurrection; in favorable expectation that his immortal soul may then partake of joys which have been prepared for the righteous from the beginning of the world. And may Almighty God, of his infinite goodness, at the grand tribunal of unbiased justice, extend his mercy toward him, and all of us, and crown our hope with everlasting bliss in the expanded realms of a boundless eternity! This we beg, for the honor of his name; to whom be glory, now and for ever. *Amen.*"

Thus the service ends, and the procession returns in form to the place whence it set out, where the necessary duties are complied with, and the business of Masonry is renewed. The insignia and ornaments of the deceased, if an officer of the Lodge, are returned to the Master, with the usual ceremonies, after which the charges for regulating the conduct of the brethren are rehearsed, and the Lodge is closed in the third degree.

NOTES.—If the Past or Present Grand Master should join the procession of a private Lodge, or a Deputy Grand Master, or a Grand Warden, a proper attention is to be paid to them. They take place after the Master of the Lodge. Two Deacons with black rods, are appointed by the Master to attend a Grand Warden; and when the Grand Master is present, or Deputy Grand Master, the Book of Constitutions is borne before him, a Sword Bearer follows him, and the Deacons, with black rods, are placed on his right and left, at an angular distance of seven feet.

Marshals are to walk, or ride, on the left of the procession.

On entering public buildings, the Bible, Square and Compass, Book of Constitutions, etc., are placed before the Grand Master. The Grand Marshal and Grand Deacons keep near him.

THE DEGREE

OF

MOST EXCELLENT MASTER.

Most Excellent Master.

CHAPTER XIII.

REMARKS ON THE SIXTH, OR MOST EXCELLENT MASTER'S DEGREE.

None but the meritorious and praiseworthy; none but those who through diligence and industry have advanced far toward perfection; none but those who have been seated in the *Oriental Chair*, by the unanimous suffrages of their brethren, can be admitted to this degree of Masonry.

The regular officers of a Most Excellent Master's Lodge are two:
1. Most Excellent Master. 2. Most Excellent Senior Warden.

In its original establishment, when the Temple of Jerusalem was finished, and the fraternity celebrated the cap-stone with great joy, it is demonstrable that none but those who had proved themselves to be complete masters of their profession were admitted to this honor; and indeed the duties incumbent on every Mason who is accepted and acknowledged as a Most Excellent Master, are such as render it indispensable that he should have a perfect knowledge of all the preceding degrees.

One of the following passages of Scripture is rehearsed at opening, accompanied by solemn ceremonies:

The earth is the Lord's, and the fullness thereof; the world, and they that dwell therein. For he hath founded it upon the seas, and established it upon the floods. Who shall ascend into the hill of the Lord? and who shall stand in his holy place? He that hath clean hands, and a pure heart; who hath not lifted up his soul unto vanity, nor sworn deceitfully. He shall receive the blessing from the Lord, and righteousness from the God of his salvation. This is the generation of them that seek him, that seek thy face, O Jacob. Selah. Lift up your heads, O ye gates, and be ye lifted up, ye everlasting doors, and the King of Glory shall come in. Who is this King of Glory? The Lord, strong and mighty, the Lord, mighty in battle. Lift up your heads, O ye gates, even lift them up, ye everlasting doors, and the King of Glory shall come in. Who is this King of Glory? The Lord of Hosts, he is the King of Glory. Selah.—*Psalm* xxiv.

I was glad when they said unto me, Let us go into the house of the Lord. Our feet shall stand within thy gates, O Jerusalem. Jerusalem is builded as a city that is compact together; whither the tribes go up, the tribes of the Lord, unto the testimony of Israel, to give thanks unto the name of the Lord. For there are set thrones of judgment, the thrones of the house of David.

Pray for the peace of Jerusalem; they shall prosper that love thee. Peace be within thy walls, and prosperity within thy palaces. For my brethren and companions' sakes, I will now say, Peace be within thee. Because of the house of the Lord our God, I will seek thy good.—*Psalm* cxxii.

In the original editions the following Ode occurs in the Appendix. It is set in this place for the greater convenience of use.

MOST EXCELLENT MASTERS' ODE.

AIR—"ALL HAIL TO THE MORNING." ARRANGED BY BRO. JAS. B. TAYLOR.

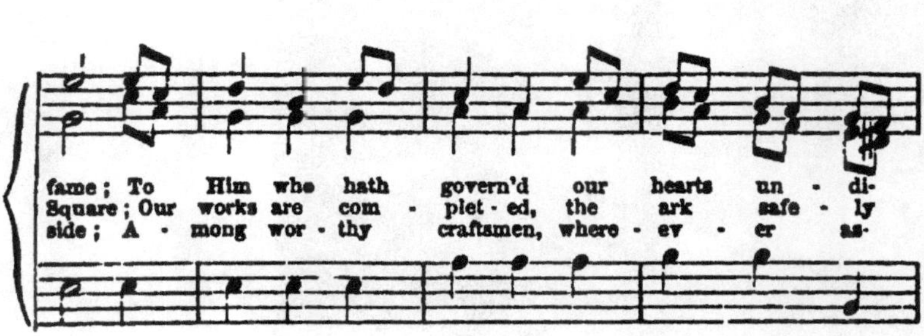

4. Almighty Jehovah!
  Descend now and fill
This Lodge with thy glory,
  Our hearts with good will!
Preside at our meetings,
  Assist us to find
True pleasure in teaching
  Good-will to mankind.

Thy *Wisdom* inspired the great institution,
  Thy *Strength* shall support it, till Nature expire;
And when the creation shall fall into ruin,
  Its *Beauty* shall rise, through the midst of the fire.

Passages of Scripture from 2 Chron. vi: are also introduced with solemn ceremonies.

The whole of this chapter, or extracts from it, is used by the Master at discretion. As every Lodge is provided with a copy of the Holy Scriptures as an essential part of its furniture, we have thought proper to omit the lengthy passages, and use the space for other matter not so easily available to the Craft.

Now, when Solomon had made an end of praying, the fire came down from heaven, and consumed the burnt-offering and the sacrifices; and the glory of the Lord filled the house. And the priests could not enter into the house of the Lord, because the glory of the Lord had filled the Lord's house.

And when all the children of Israel saw how the fire came down, and the glory of the Lord upon the house, they bowed themselves with their faces to the ground upon the pavement, and worshiped, and praised the Lord, saying, For he is good; for his mercy endureth forever.—2. *Chr.* vii: 1–4.

CHARGE TO BE DELIVERED TO A BROTHER WHO IS ACCEPTED AND ACKNOWLEDGED AS A MOST EXCELLENT MASTER.

BROTHER:—Your admittance to this degree of Masonry, is a proof of the good opinion the brethren of this Lodge entertain of your Masonic abilities. Let this consideration induce you to be careful of forfeiting, by misconduct or inattention to our rules, that esteem which has raised you to the rank you now possess.

"It is one of your great duties, as a Most Excellent Master, to dispense light and truth to the uninformed Mason; and I need not remind you of the impossibility of complying with this obligation without possessing an accurate acquaintance with the lectures of each degree.

"If you are not already completely conversant in all the degrees heretofore conferred on you, remember, that an indulgence, prompted by a belief that you will apply yourself with double diligence to make yourself so, has induced the brethren to accept you.

"Let it therefore be your unremitting study to acquire such a degree of knowledge and information as shall enable you to discharge with propriety the various duties incumbent on you, and to preserve unsullied the title now conferred upon you of a Most Excellent Master."

THE DEGREE

OF

ROYAL ARCH MASON.

Royal Arch Mason.

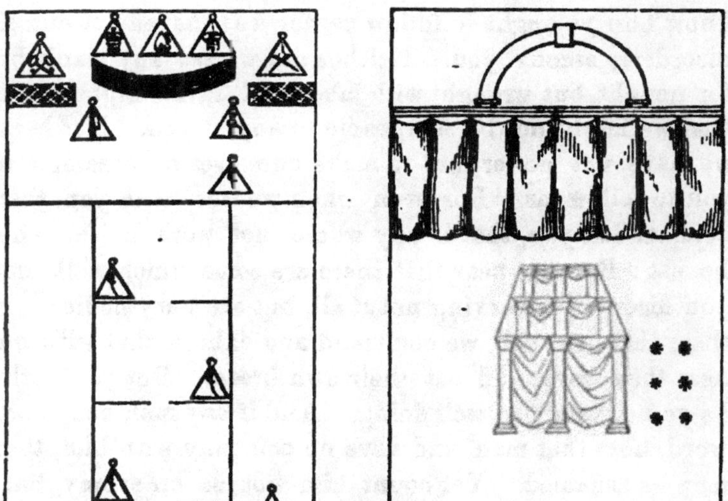

CHAPTER XIV.

OBSERVATIONS ON THE SEVENTH, OR DEGREE OF ROYAL ARCH MASON.

This degree is indescribably more august, sublime, and important, than all which precede it; and it is the summit and perfection of Ancient Masonry. It impresses on our minds a belief of the being and existence of a Supreme Deity, without beginning of days or end of years: and reminds us of the reverence due to his holy name.

This degree brings to light many essentials of the Craft, which were for the space of four hundred and seventy years buried in darkness; and without a knowledge of which the Masonic character can not be complete.

The following passage of Scripture is read at the opening:

Now we command you, brethren, that ye withdraw yourselves from every brother that walketh disorderly, and not after the tradition which ye received of us. For yourselves know how ye ought to follow us, for we behaved not ourselves disorderly among you. Neither did we eat any man's bread for nought, but wrought with labor and travail night and day, that we might not be chargeable to any of you. Not because we have not power, but to make ourselves an ensample unto you to follow us. For even when we were with you, this we commanded you, that if any would not work, neither should he eat: For we hear that there are some which walk among you disorderly, working not at all, but are busy-bodies. Now them that are such, we command and exhort, that with quietness they work, and eat their own bread. But ye, brethren, be ye not weary in well doing. And if any man obey not our word, note that man, and have no company with him, that he may be ashamed. Yet count him not as an enemy, but admonish him as a brother. Now the Lord of peace himself give you peace always, by all means. The salutations of Paul, with mine own hand; which is the token: so I write.—2. *Thes.* iii: 6–17.

OBSERVATIONS ON THE SEVENTH LECTURE.

The lecture of this degree is divided into two sections, and should be well understood by every Royal Arch Mason. Upon an accurate acquaintance with it, will depend his usefulness at our assemblies; and without it, he will be unqualified to perform the duties of the various stations in which his services may be required by the Chapter.

THE FIRST SECTION.

The first section opens to our view a large field for contemplation and study. It furnishes us with many interesting particulars relative to the state of the fraternity, during and since the reign of King Solomon; and illustrates the causes and consequences of some very important events which occurred during his reign.

This section explains the mode of government in this class of Masons: it designates the appellation, number, and situation, of the several officers; and points out the purposes and duties of their respective stations.

THE SECOND SECTION.

This section contains much valuable historical information, and proves, beyond the power of contradiction, and in the most striking colors, that prosperity and happiness are ever the ultimate consequences of virtue and justice, while disgrace and ruin invariably follow the practices of vice and immorality.

A proper arrangement of the following charges, etc., is essentially necessary to be observed in every Chapter; and their application should be familiar to every Royal Arch Mason.

I will bring the blind by a way that they knew not; I will lead them in paths that they have not known; I will make darkness light before them, and crooked things straight: These things will I do unto them, and will not forsake them. —*Isaiah,* xlii., 16.

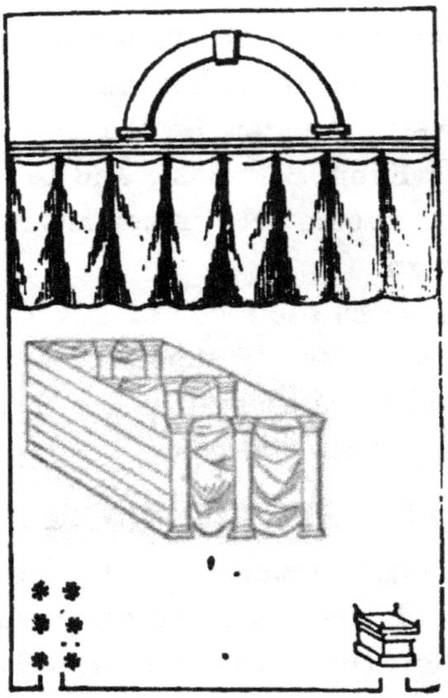

PRAYER REHEARSED DURING THE CEREMONY OF EXALTATION TO THE DEGREE OF ROYAL ARCH MASON.

"Supreme Architect of Universal Nature, who, by thine almighty word, didst speak into being the stupendous Arch of Heaven, and for the instruction and pleasure of thy rational creatures, didst adorn us with greater and lesser lights; thereby magnifying Thy power, and endearing Thy goodness unto the sons of men: we humbly adore and worship thine unspeakable perfection. We bless Thee that when man had fallen from his innocence and his happiness, Thou didst still leave unto him the powers of reasoning, and capacity of improvement and of pleasure. We thank Thee that amid the pains and calamities of our present state, so many means of refreshment and satisfaction are reserved unto us, while traveling the *rugged path of life.* Especially would we at this time render Thee our thanksgiving and praise for the institution, as members of which we are at this time assembled, and for all the pleasures we have derived from it. We thank Thee that the few here assembled before Thee, have been favored with new inducements, and laid under new and stronger obligations, to virtue and holiness. May these obligation, O blessed Father, have their full effect upon us. Teach us, we pray Thee, the true reverence of Thy great, mighty and terrible name. Inspire us with a firm and unshaken resolution in our virtuous pursuits. Give us grace diligently to search Thy word in the Book of Nature, wherein the duties of our high vocation are inculcated with divine authority. May the solemnity of the ceremonies of our institution be duly impressed on our minds, and have a lasting and happy effect upon our lives. Oh Thou who didst aforetime appear unto Thy servant Moses *in a flame of fire out of the midst of a bush*, enkindle, we beseech Thee, in each of our hearts, a flame of devotion to Thee, of love to each other, and of charity to all mankind. May all Thy *miracles and mighty works* fill us with the dread, and Thy goodness impress us with the love, of Thy holy name. May *holiness to the Lord* be engraven on all our thoughts, words and actions. May the incense of piety ascend continually unto Thee from the *altar* of our hearts, and burn, day and night, as a sacrifice of a sweet smelling savor, well-pleasing unto Thee. And since sin has destroyed within us the *first temple* of purity and innocence, may Thy heavenly grace guide and assist us in rebuilding a *second temple* of reformation, and may the glory of this latter house be greater than the glory of the former. *Amen.*"

Now Moses kept the flock of Jethro his father-in-law, the priest of Midian; and he led the flock to the backside of the desert, and came to the mountain of God, even to Horeb. And the angel of the Lord appeared unto him in a flame of fire out of the midst of a bush: and he looked, and, behold, the bush burned with fire, and the bush was not consumed. And Moses said, I will now turn aside, and see this great sight, why the bush is not burned. And when the Lord saw that he turned aside to see, God called unto him out of the midst of the bush, and said, Moses, Moses! And he said, Here am I. And he said, Draw not nigh hither: put off thy shoes from off thy feet, for the place whereon thou standest is holy ground. Moreover he said, I am the God of thy father, the God of Abraham, the God of Isaac, and the God of Jacob. And Moses hid his face, for he was afraid to look upon God. —*Exodus* iii: 1–6.

Zedekiah was one-and-twenty years old when he began to reign, and reigned eleven years in Jerusalem. And he did that which was evil in the sight of the Lord his God, and humbled not himself before Jeremiah the prophet, speaking from the mouth of the Lord. And he also rebelled against King Nebuchadnezzar, and stiffened his neck, and hardened his heart from turning unto the Lord God of Israel.

Moreover all the chiefs of the priests and the people transgressed very much, after all the abominations of the heathen, and polluted the house of the Lord, which he had hallowed in Jerusalem. And the Lord God of their fathers sent to them by his messengers; because he had compassion on his people, and on his dwelling-place. But they mocked the messengers of God, and despised his words, and misused his prophets, until the wrath of the Lord arose against his people, till there was no remedy. Therefore he brought upon them the king of the Chaldees, who slew their young men with the sword, in the house of their sanctuary, and had no compassion upon young men or maiden, old men, or him that stooped for age: he gave them all into his hand. And all the vessels of the house of God, great and small, and the treasures of the house of the Lord, and the treasures of the king, and of his princes; all these he brought to Babylon. And they burnt the house of God, and brake down the wall of Jerusalem, and burnt all the palaces thereof with fire, and destroyed all the goodly vessels thereof. And them that had escaped from the sword, carried he away to Babylon: where they were servants to him and his sons, until the reign of the kingdom of Persia.—2 *Chron.* xxxvi: 11–20.

Now in the first year of Cyrus, king of Persia, the Lord stirred up the spirit of Cyrus, king of Persia, that he made a proclamation throughout all his kingdom, and put it also in writing, saying, Thus saith Cyrus, king of Persia, The Lord God of Heaven hath given me all the kingdoms of the earth, and he hath charged me to build him an house at Jerusalem, which is in Judah.

PROCLAMATION OF CYRUS.

WHO IS THERE AMONG YOU OF ALL HIS PEOPLE? HIS GOD BE WITH HIM, AND LET HIM GO UP TO JERUSALEM WHICH IS IN JUDAH, AND BUILD THE HOUSE OF THE LORD GOD OF ISRAEL, HE IS THE GOD, WHICH IS IN JERUSALEM.—*Ezra* i: 1–3.

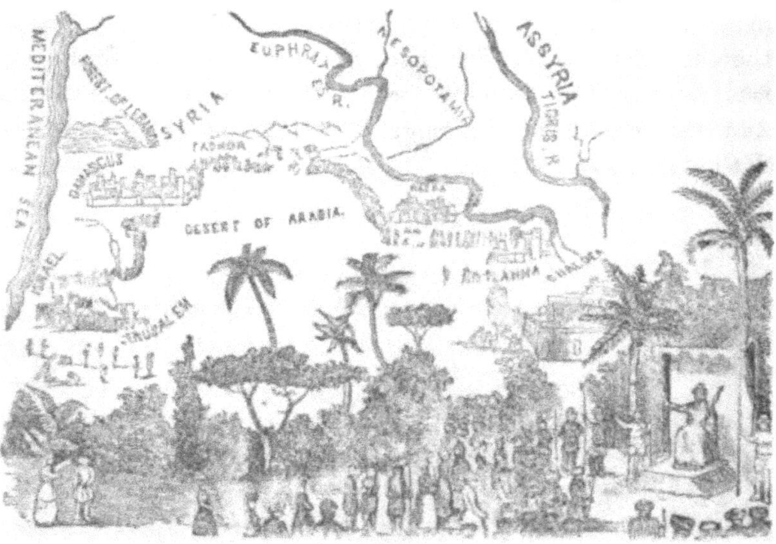

And Moses said unto God, Behold, when I come unto the children of Israel, and shall say unto them, The God of your fathers hath sent me unto you; and they shall say to me, What is his name? what shall I say unto them?

And God said unto Moses, I AM THAT I AM: And thus shalt thou say unto the children of Israel, I AM hath sent me unto you.—*Exodus*, iii: 13–14.

Lord, I cry unto Thee: make haste unto me: give ear unto my voice. Let my prayer be set forth before Thee as incense, and the lifting up of my hands as the evening sacrifice. Set a watch, O Lord, before my mouth; keep the door of my lips. Incline not my heart to any evil thing, to practice wicked works with men that work iniquity. Let the righteous smite me, it shall be a kindness; and let him reprove me, it shall be an excellent oil. Mine eyes are unto Thee, O God the Lord: in Thee is my trust; leave not my soul destitute. Keep me from the snares which they have laid for me, and the gins of the workers of iniquity. Let the wicked fall into their own nets, whilst that I withal escape.—*Psalm*, cxli.

I cried unto the Lord with my voice; with my voice unto the Lord did I make my supplication. I poured out my complaint before him: I showed before him my trouble. When my spirit was overwhelmed within me, then Thou knewest my path: in the way wherein I walked have they privily laid a snare for me. I looked on my right hand, and beheld, but there was no man that would know me: refuge failed me: no man cared for my soul. I cried unto Thee, O Lord: I said, Thou art my refuge, and my portion in the land of the living. Attend unto my cry; for I am brought very low: deliver me from my persecutors; for they are stronger than I. Bring my soul out of darkness, that I may praise Thy name.—*Psalm* cxlii.

Hear my prayer, O Lord; give ear to my supplications: in Thy faithfulness answer me, and in Thy righteousness. And enter not into judgment with Thy servant: for in Thy sight shall no man living be justified. For the enemy hath persecuted my soul; he hath smitten my life down to the ground: he hath made me to dwell in darkness. Therefore is my spirit overwhelmed with me: my heart within me is desolate. Hear me speedily, O Lord; my spirit faileth: hide not Thy face from me, lest I be like unto them that go down into the pit. Cause me to hear Thy loving kindness in the morning; for in Thee do I trust: cause me to know the way wherein I should walk; for I lift up my soul unto Thee. Teach me to do Thy will; for Thou art my God: bring my soul out of trouble, and of Thy mercy cut off mine enemies, for I am Thy servant.—*Psalm* cxliii.

And Moses answered and said, But behold, they will not believe me, nor hearken unto my voice: for they will say, The Lord hath not appeared unto thee. And the Lord said unto him, What is that in thine hand? And he said, A rod. And he said, Cast it on the ground; and he cast it on the ground, and it became a serpent; and Moses fled from before it. And the Lord said unto Moses, Put forth thine hand, and take it by the tail. And he put forth his hand and caught it, and it became a rod in his hand. That they may believe that the Lord God of your fathers, the God of Abraham, the God of Isaac, and the God of Jacob, hath appeared unto thee.

And the Lord said furthermore unto him, Put now thine hand into thy bosom; and he put his hand into his bosom: and when he took it out, behold, his hand was leprous as snow. And He said, Put thine hand into thy bosom again: and he put his hand into his bosom again, and plucked it out of his bosom, and, behold, it was turned again as his other flesh. And it shall come to pass, if they will not believe thee, neither hearken to the voice of the first sign, that they will believe the voice of the latter sign.

And it shall come to pass, if they will not believe also these two signs, neither hearken unto thy voice, that thou shalt take of the water of the river, and pour it upon the dry land: and the water which thou takest out of the river, shall become blood upon the dry land.—*Exodus*, iv: 1–10.

In the seventh month, in the one-and-twentieth day of the month, came the word of the Lord by the prophet Haggai, saying, Speak now to Zerubbabel the son of Shealtiel, governor of Judah, and to Joshua the son of Josedech, the high priest, and to the residue of the people, saying, Who is left among you that saw this house in her first glory? and how do ye see it now? is it not in your eyes in comparison of it as nothing? Yet now be strong, O Zerubbabel, and be strong, O Joshua, son of Josedech the high priest, and be strong all ye people of the land, and work; for I am with you, according to the word which I covenanted with you when ye came out of Egypt, so my spirit remaineth among you: fear ye not. For thus saith the Lord of hosts, Yet once, it is a little while, and I will shake the heavens, and the earth, and the sea, and the dry land: and I will shake all nations, and the desire of all nations shall come, and I will fill this house with glory. The silver is mine, and the gold is mine. The glory of this latter house shall be greater than of the former, and in this place will I give peace.

In that day will I take thee, O Zerubbabel, my servant, the son of Shealtiel, saith the Lord, and will make thee as a signet: for I have chosen thee.—*Haggai* ii: 1–9, 23.

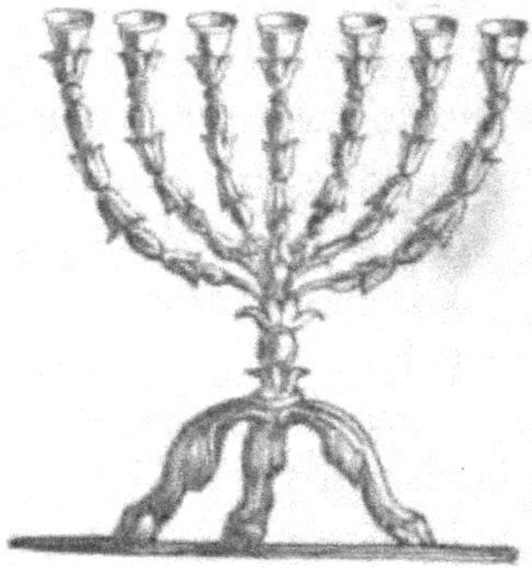

This is the word of the Lord unto Zerubbabel, saying, Not by might nor power, but by my spirit. Who art thou, O great mountain? before Zerubbabel thou shalt become a plain, and he shall bring forth the head stone thereof with shouting, crying Grace, grace, unto it. Moreover the word of the Lord came unto me, saying, The hands of Zerubbabel have laid the foundation of this house, his hands shall also finish it; and thou shalt know that the Lord of Hosts hath sent me unto you. For who hath despised the day of small things? for they shall rejoice, and shall see the plummet in the hands of Zerubbabel with those seven.—*Zachariah* iv: 6–10.

In the beginning was the Word, and the Word was with God, and the Word was God. The same was in the beginning with God. All things were made by him; and without him was not any thing made that was made. In him was life, and the life was the light of men. And the light shineth in darkness, and the darkness comprehendeth it not.—*John* i: 1–5.

And it came to pass when Moses had made an end of writing the words of this law in a book, until they were finished, that Moses commanded the Levites which bare the ark of the covenant of the Lord, saying, Take this book of the law, and put it in the side of the ark of the covenant of the Lord your God, that it may be there for a witness against thee.—*Deut.* xxxi: 24–26.

And thou shalt put the Mercy Seat above, upon the ark; and in the ark thou shalt put the testimony that I shall give thee.—*Exodus* xxv: 21.

And Moses said, This is the thing which the Lord commandeth, Fill an omer of the manna, to be kept for your generations: that they may see the bread wherewith I have fed you in the wilderness, when I brought you forth from the land of Egypt. And Moses said unto Aaron, Take a pot and put an omer full of manna therein, and lay it up before the

Lord, to be kept for your generations. As the Lord commanded Moses, so Aaron laid it up before the testimony to be kept.—*Exodus* xvi: 32–34.

And the Lord said unto Moses, Bring Aaron's rod again before the testimony, to be kept for a token.—*Numbers* xvii: 10.

For there was a tabernacle made; the first, wherein was the candlestick, and the table, and the shewbread; which is called The Sanctuary. And after the vails, the tabernacle, which is called The Holiest of all; which had a golden censer, and the ark of the covenant overlaid round about with gold, wherein was the golden pot that had manna, and Aaron's rod that budded, and the tables of the covenant; and over it the cherubims of glory, shadowing the mercy seat; of which we can not now speak particularly.—*Hebrews* ix: 2–5.

In that day will I raise up the tabernacle of David that is fallen, and close up the breaches thereof, and I will raise up his ruins, and I will build it as in the days of old.—*Amos* ix: 11.

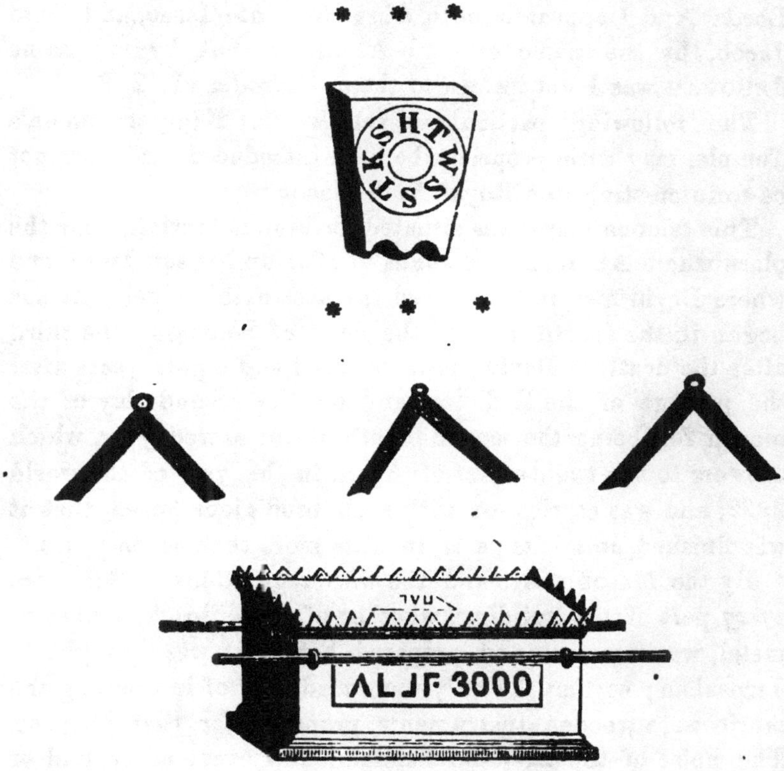

HTWSSTKS
3000

And God spake unto Moses, and said unto him, I am the Lord: And I appeared unto Abraham, unto Isaac, and unto Jacob, by the name of God Almighty, but by my name JEHOVAH was I not known to them.—*Exodus* vi: 2, 3.

The following particulars, relative to King Solomon's Temple, may with propriety be here introduced, and can not be uninteresting to a Royal Arch Mason:

This famous fabric was situated on Mount Moriah, near the place where Abraham was about to offer up his son Isaac, and where David met and appeased the destroying angel. It was begun in the fourth year of the reign of Solomon; the third after the death of David; four hundred and eighty years after the passage of the Red Sea, and on the second day of the month Zif, being the second month of the sacred year, which answers to the twenty-first of April, in the year of the world 2992, and was carried on with such prodigious speed, that it was finished, in all its parts, in little more than seven years.

By the Masonic art, and the wise regulations of Solomon, every part of the building, whether of stone, brick, timber or metal, was wrought and prepared before it was brought to Jerusalem; so that the only tools made use of in erecting the fabric were wooden instruments prepared for that purpose. The noise of the axe, the hammer, and every other tool of metal, was confined to the forests of Lebanon, where the timber was procured, and to Mount Libanus, and the plains and quarries of Zeredatha, where the stones were raised, squared, marked and numbered; that nothing might be heard among the Masons at Jerusalem, but harmony and peace.

In the year of the world 3029, King Solomon died, and was succeeded by his son Rehoboam, who, immediately after the death of his father, went down to Shechem, where the chiefs of the people were met together to proclaim him king.

When Jeroboam, the son of Nebat, who was in Egypt, whither he had fled from the presence of Solomon, and whose ambition had long aspired to the throne, heard of the death of the king, he hastened to return from Egypt, to put himself at the head of the discontented tribes, and lead them on to rebellion. He accordingly assembled them together, and came to King Rehoboam, and spake to him after this manner:

Thy father made our yoke grievous; now, therefore, ease thou somewhat the grievous servitude of thy father, and his heavy yoke that he put upon us, and we will serve thee. And he said unto them, Come again unto me after three days. And the people departed. And King Rehoboam took counsel with the old men that had stood before Solomon his father while he yet lived, saying, What counsel give ye me, to return answer to this people? And they spake unto him, saying, If thou be kind to this people, and please them, and speak good words to them, they will be thy servants for ever. But he forsook the counsel which the old men gave him, and took counsel with the young men that were brought up with him, that stood before him. And he said unto them, What advice give ye, that we may return answer to this people, which have spoken to me, saying, Ease somewhat the yoke that thy father did put upon us? And the young men that were brought up with him spake unto him, saying, Thus shalt thou answer the people that spake unto thee, saying, Thy father made our yoke heavy, but make thou it somewhat lighter for us; thus shalt thou say unto them, My little finger shall be thicker than my father's loins. For, whereas my father put a heavy yoke upon you, I will put more to your yoke: my father chastised you with whips, but I will chastise you with scorpions. So Jeroboam and all the people came to Rehoboam on the third day, as the king bade, saying, come again to me on the third day. And the king answered them roughly; and King Rehoboam forsook the counsel of the old men; and answered them after the advice of the young men, saying, My father made your yoke heavy, but I will add thereto; my father chastised you with whips, but I will chastise you with scorpions. And when all Israel saw that the king would not hearken unto them, the people answered the king, saying, What portion have we in David? and we have none inheritance in the son of Jesse: every man to your tents, O Israel: and now, David, see to thine own house. So all Israel went to their tents.—2 *Chron.* x.

But as for the children of Israel that dwelt in the cities of Judah and Benjamin, Rehoboam reigned over them.

In this manner were the tribes of Israel divided, and under two distinct governments, for two hundred and fifty-four years, when the ten revolted tribes, having become weak and degenerated, by following the wickedness and idolatry of the kings who governed them, fell a prey to Salmanezer, king of Assyria, who in the reign of Hoshea, king of Israel, besieged the city of Samaria, laid their country waste, and utterly extirpated their government. Such was the wretched fate of a people who disdained subjection to the laws of the house of David, and whose impiety and effeminacy ended in their destruction.

After a series of changes and events, of which an account may be found in the history of the Temple, Nebuchadnezzar, king of Babylon, with his forces, took possession of Jerusalem, and having made captive Jehoiachim the king of Judah, elevated his uncle Zedekiah to the throne, after binding him by a solemn oath, neither to make innovations in the government, nor to take part with the Egyptians in their wars against Babylon.

At the end of eight years Zedekiah violated his oath to Nebuchadnezzar, by forming a treaty offensive and defensive with the Egyptians; thinking that jointly they could subdue the king of Babylon. Nebuchadnezzar immediately marched, and ravaged Zedekiah's country, seized his castle and fortress, and proceeded to the siege of Jerusalem. Pharaoh, learning how Zedekiah was pressed, advanced to his relief, with a view of raising the siege. Nebuchadnezzar, having intimation thereof, would not wait his approach, but proceeded to give him battle, and in one contest drove him out of Syria. This circumstance suspended the siege.

In the ninth year of Zedekiah's reign, the king of Babylon again besieged Jerusalem, with a large army, and for a year and a half exerted all his strength to conquer it; but the city did not yield, though enfeebled by famine and pestilence.

In the eleventh year the siege went on vigorously; the Babylonians completed their works, having raised towers all round the city, so as to drive the invaded party from its walls. The place, though a prey to plague and famine, was obstinately defended during the space of a year and a half. But at length, want of provisions and forces compelled its surrender, and it was accordingly delivered, at midnight, to the officers of Nebuchadnezzar.

Zedekiah, seeing the troops enter the Temple, absconded by a narrow pass to the desert, with his officers and friends: but advice of his escape being given to the Babylonians, they pursued them early in the morning, and surrounded them near Jericho, where they were bound, and carried before the king, who ordered his wives and children to be put to death in his sight; and then ordered Zedekiah's eyes to be put out, and himself conducted in chains to Babylon.

After this victory, Nebuchadnezzar dispatched his principal officer, Nebuzaradan, to Jerusalem, to ransack and burn both palace and Temple, to raze the city to the ground, and conduct the captive inhabitants to Babylon; this order he accordingly executed. Among the captives were the following persons of eminence: Seraiah, the High Priest; Zephaniah, next in rank; the secretary to the king; three principal keepers of the Temple; seven of the king's chosen friends, and other persons of distinction.

In the seventieth year of the captivity of the Jews, and the first of the reign of Cyrus, king of Persia, he issued his famous edict, purporting that the God adored by the Israelites was the eternal Being through whose bounty he enjoyed the regal dignity, and that he had found himself honorably mentioned by the prophets of ancient date, as the person who should cause Jerusalem to be rebuilt, and restore the Hebrews to their former state of grandeur and independency; he, therefore, gave orders for the release of the captives, with his permission to return to their own native country, to rebuild the city, and the house of the Lord.

The principal people of the tribes of Judah and Benjamin, with the priests and Levites, immediately departed for Jerusalem and commenced the undertaking; but many of the Jews determined to remain in Babylon rather than relinquish the possessions they had obtained in that city.

CHARGE TO A NEWLY EXALTED COMPANION.

"WORTHY COMPANION:—By the consent and assistance of the members of this Chapter, you are now exalted to the sublime and honorable degree of a Royal Arch Mason.

"Having attained this degree, you have arrived at the summit and perfection of ancient Masonry; and are consequently entitled to a full explanation of the mysteries of the Order.

"The rites and mysteries developed in this degree have been handed down through a chosen few, unchanged by time, and uncontrolled by prejudice; and we expect and trust, they will be regarded by you with the same veneration, and transmitted with the same scrupulous purity to your successors.

"No one can reflect on the ceremonies of gaining admission into this place, without being forcibly struck with the important lessons which they teach.

"Here we are necessarily led to contemplate with gratitude "nd admiration the sacred source from whence all earthly comforts flow; here we find additional inducements to continue steadfast and immovable in the discharge of our respective duties; and here we are bound, by the most solemn ties, to promote each others' welfare and correct each others' failings, by advice, admonition and reproof.

"As it is our most earnest desire, and a duty we owe to our Companions of this Order, that the admission of every candidate into this Chapter should be attended by the approbation of the most scrutinizing eye, we hope always to possess the satisfaction of finding none among us, but such as will promote to the utmost of their power the great end of our institution. By paying due attention to this determination, we expect you will never recommend any candidate to this Chapter, whose abilities, and knowledge of the foregoing degrees, you can not freely vouch for, and whom you do not firmly and confidently believe, will fully conform to the principles of our Order, and fulfill the obligations of a Royal Arch Mason. While such are our members, we may expect to be united in one object, without lukewarmness, inattention or neglect; and that zeal, fidelity, and affection, will be the distinguishing characteristics of our society, and that satisfaction, harmony and peace be enjoyed at our meetings, which no other society can afford."

CLOSING.

The Chapter is closed with solemn ceremonies; and the following prayer is rehearsed, by the Most Excellent High Priest:

"By the *Wisdom* of the Supreme High Priest may we be directed, by his *Strength* may we be enabled, and by the *Beauty* of virtue may we be incited, to perform the obligations here enjoined on us; to keep inviolably the mysteries here unfolded to us; and invariably to practise all those duties *out of* the Chapter, which are inculcated *in* it."

Response: So mote it be. Amen.

After these observations, little more can be wanted to encourage the zealous Mason to persevere in his researches. Whoever has traced the Art in regular progression from the commencement of the first to the conclusion of the seventh degree, according to the plan here laid down, will have amassed an ample store of useful learning: and must reflect with pleasure on the good effects of his past diligence and attention; while, by applying the whole to the general advantage of society, he will observe method in the proper distribution of what he has acquired, secure to himself the veneration of Masons, and the approbation of all good men.

THE ORDER

OF

HIGH PRIESTHOOD.

This Order, when conferred with solemn ceremony, as in Ohio and Kentucky, is truly grand and imposing; but in general it is only communicated in a convocation of three or more Past High Priests, and without ceremony. This is in accordance with a common practice in the *Ancient and Accepted Rite*, from which the Order was chiefly borrowed.

High Priesthood.

CHAPTER XV.

OBSERVATIONS ON THE ORDER OF HIGH PRIESTHOOD.

THIS Order appertains to the office of High Priest of a Royal Arch Chapter, and no one can be legally entitled to receive it until he has been elected to sustain that office in some regular Chapter of Royal Arch Masons.

The following passages of Scripture are made use of during the ceremonies appertaining to this Order, viz.:

And they took Lot, Abram's brother's son, who dwelt in Sodom, and his goods, and departed. And there came one that had escaped, and told Abram the Hebrew; for he dwelt in the plain of Mamre the Amorite, brother of Eschol, and brother of Aner: and these were confederate with Abram. And when Abram heard that his brother was taken captive, he armed his trained servants, born in his own house, three hundred and eighteen, and pursued them unto Dan. And he divided himself against them, he and his servants, by night, and smote them, and pursued them unto Hobah, which is on the left hand of Damascus. And he brought back all the goods, and also brought again his brother Lot, and his goods, and the women also, and the people. And the king of Sodom went out to meet him (after his return from the slaughter of Chedorlaomer, and of the kings that were with him), at the valley of Shevah, which is the king's dale. And Melchisedek, king of Salem, brought forth bread and wine: and he was the priest of the most high God. And he blessed him, and said, Blessed be Abram of the most high God, possessor of heaven and earth: and blesssed be the most high God, which hath delivered thine enemies into thy hand. And he gave him tithes of all. And the king of Sodom said unto Abraham, Give me the persons, and take the goods to thyself. And Abram said to the king of Sodom, I have lifted up mine hand unto the Lord, the most high God, the possessor of heaven and earth, that I will not take from a thread even to a shoe-latchet, and that I will not take any thing that is thine, lest thou shouldest say, I have made Abram rich: Save only that which the young men have eaten, and the portion of the men which went with me, Aner, Eschol, and Mamre; let them take their portion.—*Genesis* xiv: 12–24.

And the Lord spake unto Moses, saying, "Speak unto Aaron, and unto his sons, saying, On this wise ye shall bless the children of Israel, saying unto them, The Lord bless thee, and keep thee; the Lord make his face shine upon thee, and be gracious unto thee; the Lord lift up his countenance upon thee, and give thee peace.—*Numbers* vi: 22–26.

For this Melchisedek, king of Salem, priest of the most high God, who met Abraham returning from the slaughter of the kings, and blessed him; to whom also Abraham gave a tenth part of all; (first being, by interpretation, King of Righteousness, and after that also King of Salem, which is, King of Peace; without father, without mother, without descent, having neither beginning of days nor end of life, but made like unto the Son of God); abideth a priest continually. Now consider how great this man was, unto whom even the patriarch Abraham gave the tenth of the spoils. And verily they that are of the sons of Levi, who receive the office of the priesthood, have a commandment to take tithes of the people according to the law, that is, of their brethren, though they come out of the loins of Abraham.—*Heb.* vii: 1–5.

For he testifieth, Thou art a priest for ever, after the order of Melchisedek.

And inasmuch as not without an oath he was made priest.

For those priests (*under the Levitical law*) were made without an oath; but this with an oath, by him that said unto him, The Lord sware, and will not repent, Thou art a Priest for ever, after the order of Melchisedek.—*Heb.* vii: 17–21.

CEREMONIES AND CHARGES UPON CONSTITUTING AND DEDICATING A ROYAL ARCH CHAPTER AND INSTALLING ITS OFFICERS.

In the original editions there is a historical account of Royal Arch Masonry of 25 pages inserted here, which seems to us unsuited to the place, and unnecessarily cumbersome to the volume. It is therefore omitted.

I. The Grand officers will meet at a convenient place, and open.

II. The subordinate Chapter will meet in the outer courts of their hall, and form an avenue for the reception of the Grand officers.

III. When formed, they will dispatch a committee to the place where the Grand officers are assembled, to inform the Grand Marshal that the chapter is prepared to receive them; the Grand Marshal will announce the same to the Grand officers, and introduce the Committee.

IV. The Grand officers will move in procession, conducted by the Committee, to the hall of the Chapter.

When the Grand High Priest enters, the Grand Chapter will give *the Grand Honors*.

V. When the Grand officers have passed through the avenue they countermarch in the rear of the left-hand line and face to the left. In the meantime the Chapter will form rank entire and face to the front. The officers of the Chapter then file off and form a front rank, two paces in advance of their members.

VI. The Grand Secretary will then call over the names of the officers elect; and the Grand High Priest will ask whether they accept their respective offices. If they answer in the affirmative, he then asks the members whether they remain satisfied with their choice. If they answer in the affirmative, he directs their officers to approach the sacred volume, and become qualified for installation, according to ancient usage and custom.

VII. The Grand Marshal will then form the whole in procession, and they will march through the *veils* into the inner apartment, where they will surround the altar, which is previously furnished and prepared in *ample form* for the occasion.

VIII. All present will then kneel, and the following prayer will be recited:

PRAYER.

"Almighty and Supreme High Priest of heaven and earth! Who is there in heaven but thee, and who upon earth can stand in competition with thee? Thy OMNISCIENT mind brings all things in review, past, present and to come: thine OMNIPOTENT arm directs the movements of the vast creation; thine OMNIPRESENT eye pervades the secret recesses of every heart; thy boundless *beneficence* supplies us with every comfort and enjoyment; and thine unspeakable *perfections* and *glory* surpass the understandings of the children of men! Our Father, who art in heaven, we invoke thy benediction upon the purposes of our present assembly. Let this Chapter be established to thine honor: let its officers be endowed with wisdom to discern, and fidelity to pursue, its truest interests: let its members be ever mindful of the duty they owe to their GOD; the obedience they owe to their superiors; the love they owe to their equals, and the good will they owe to all mankind. Let this Chapter be consecrated to thy glory, and its members ever exemplify their love to GOD by their beneficence to man. Glory be to GOD on high."

Response—"Amen. So mote it be."

All the Companions except the High Priests and Past High Priests, are then desired to withdraw, while the new High Priest is solemnly bound to the performance of his duties; and after the performance of other necessary ceremonies, not proper to be written, they are permitted to return.

IX. The whole then repair to their appropriate stations.

NOTE.—Those paragraphs which are inclosed within brackets apply exclusively to cases where *new Chapters* are constituted, and their officers installed for the first time. The rest apply equally to such cases and to annual installations.

X. An Anthem or Ode is to be performed.

XI. An Oration or Address is to be delivered.

XII. An Ode or piece of Music.

[XIII. The Deputy Grand High Priest then rises and informs the Grand High Priest, that "a number of Companions, duly instructed in the sublime mysteries, being desirous of promoting the honor, and propagating the principles of the Art, have applied to the Grand Chapter for a warrant to constitute a new Chapter of Royal Arch Masons, which, having obtained, they are now assembled for the purpose of being constituted, and having their officers installed in due and ancient form."]

[XIV. The Grand Marshal will then form the officers and members of the new Chapter in front of the Grand officers; after which, the Grand High Priest directs the Grand Secretary to read the warrant.]

[XV. The Grand High Priest then rises and says: "By virtue of the high powers in me vested, I do form you, my respected Companions, into a regular Chapter of Royal Arch Masons. From henceforth you are authorized and empowered to open and hold a Lodge of Mark Masters, Past Masters, and Most Excellent Masters, and a Chapter of Royal Arch Masons; and to do and perform all such things as thereunto may appertain; conforming, in all your doings, to the General Grand Royal Arch Constitution, and the general regulations of the State Grand Chapter. And may the God of your fathers be with you, guide and direct you in all your doings."]

[XVI. The Public Grand Honors will then be given by the officers and members of the new Chapter while passing in review in front of the Grand officers.]

[XVII. The furniture, clothing, jewels, implements, utensils, etc., belonging to the Chapter (having been previously placed in the center, in front of the Grand officers, covered), are now uncovered, and the new Chapter is dedicated in due and ancient form, as is well described in the Most Excellent Master's Degree.]

INSTALLATION.

XVIII. The Deputy Grand High Priest will then present the first officer of the new Chapter to the Grand High Priest, saying,

"MOST EXCELLENT GRAND HIGH PRIEST:—I present you my worthy Companion . . . ., nominated in the warrant, to be installed High Priest of this new Chapter. I find him to be skillful in the royal Art, and attentive to the moral precepts of our forefathers, and have therefore no doubt but he will discharge the duties of his office with fidelity."

The Grand High Priest then addresses him as follows:

"MOST EXCELLENT COMPANION:—I feel much satisfaction in performing my duty on the present occasion, by installing you into the office of High Priest of this new Chapter. It is an office highly honorable to all those

who diligently perform the important duties annexed to it. Your reputed Masonic knowledge, however, precludes the necessity of a particular enumeration of those duties. I shall, therefore, only observe, that by a frequent recurrence to the Constitution, and General regulations, and constant practice of the several sublime lectures and charges, you will be best able to fulfill them; and I am confident that the Companions who are chosen to preside with you, will give strength to your endeavors, and support your exertions. I shall now propose certain questions to you, relative to the duties of your office, and to which I must request your unequivocal answer:

"1. Do you solemnly promise that you will redouble your endeavors to correct the vices, purify the morals, and promote the happiness of those of your Companions, who have attained this sublime degree?

"2. That you will never suffer your Chapter to be opened, unless there be present nine regular Royal Arch Masons?

"3. That you will never suffer either more or less than three brethren to be exalted in your Chapter at one and the same time?

This rule in practice is relaxed, and technically observed by admitting one and sometimes two Companions as substitutes, where the necessity of the case seems to demand it.

"4. That you will not exalt any one to this degree, who has not shown a charitable and humane disposition; or who has not made a considerable proficiency in the foregoing degrees?

"5. That you will promote the general good of our Order, and, on all proper occasions, be ready to give and receive instructions, and particularly from the General and State Grand officers?

"6. That, to the utmost of your power, you will preserve the solemnities of our ceremonies, and behave, in open Chapter, with the most profound respect and reverence, as an example to your Companions?

"7. That you will not acknowledge or have intercourse with any Chapter that does not work under a constitutional warrant or dispensation?

"8. That you will not admit any visitor into your Chapter, who has not been exalted in a Chapter legally constituted, without his being first formally healed?

"9. That you will observe and support such by-laws as may be made by your Chapter, in conformity to the General Grand Royal Arch Constitution, and the general regulations of the Grand Chapter?

"10. That you pay due respect and obedience to the instructions of the General and State Grand officers, particularly relating to the several lectures and charges, and will resign the Chair to them, severally, when they may visit your Chapter?

"11. That you will support and observe the General Grand Royal Arch Constitution, and the general regulations of the Grand Royal Arch Chapter, under whose authority you act?

"Do you submit to all these things, and do you promise to observe and practice them faithfully?"

These questions being answered in the affirmative, the Companions all kneel, and the Grand Chaplain repeats the following or some other suitable prayer:

"Most Holy and glorious LORD GOD, the Great High Priest of heaven and earth! we approach thee with reverence, and implore thy blessings on the Companion appointed to preside over this new assembly, and now prostrate before thee; fill his heart with fear, that his tongue and actions may pronounce thy glory. Make him steadfast in thy service; grant him firmness of mind; animate his heart, and strengthen his endeavors; may he teach thy judgments and thy laws; and may the incense he shall put before thee, upon thine altar, prove an acceptable sacrifice unto thee. Bless him, O LORD, and bless the work of his hands. Accept us, in mercy; hear thou from heaven, thy dwelling-place, and forgive our transgressions. Glory be to God the Father: as it was in the beginning," etc.

Response.—"So mote it be."

XIX. The Grand High Priest will then cause the High Priest elect to be invested with his clothing, badges, etc.; after which he will address him as follows:

"COMPANION:—In consequence of your cheerful acquiescence with the charges, which you have heard recited, you are qualified for installation as the High Priest of this Royal Arch Chapter; and it is incumbent upon me, upon this occasion, to point out some of the particulars appertaining to your office, duty and dignity.

"All legally constituted bodies of Royal Arch Masons are called Chapters: as regular bodies of Masons of all other degrees are called Lodges. Every Chapter ought to assemble for work at least once in every three months, and must consist of a High Priest, King, Scribe, Captain of the Host, Principal Sojourner, Royal Arch Captain, Three Masters of the Veils, Secretary, Treasurer, and as many members as may be found convenient for working to advantage. The officers of the Chapter officiate in the Lodges holden for conferring the preparatory degrees according to rank, as follows:

The High Priest as Master.
The King as Senior Warden.
The Scribe as Junior Warden.
The Captain of the Host as Marshal, or Master of Ceremonies.
The Principal Sojourner as Senior Deacon.
The Royal Arch Captain as Junior Deacon.
The Master of the First Veil as Junior Overseer.
The Master of the Second Veil as Senior Overseer.
The Master of the Third Veil as Master Overseer.
The Secretary, Treasurer, and Tyler as officers of corresponding rank.

The High Priest of every Chapter has it in special charge to see that the By-Laws of his Chapter, as well as the Grand Royal Arch Constitution and the Regulations of the Grand Chapter, are well observed; that all the officers of his Chapter perform the duties of their respective offices faithfully, and are examples of diligence and industry to their companions; that true and accurate records of all the proceedings of the Chapter are kept by the Secretary; that the Treasurer keeps and renders exact and just accounts of all the moneys and other property belonging to the Chapter; that the regular returns be made annually to the Grand Chapter; and that the annual dues to the Grand Chapter be regularly and punctually paid. He has the right and authority of calling his Chapter together at pleasure upon any emergency or occurrence which, in his judgment, may require their meeting. It is his privilege and duty, together with the King and Scribe, to attend the meetings of the Grand Chapter, either in person or by proxy; and the well-being of the institution requires that his duty should on no occasion be omitted."

"The office of High Priest is a station highly honorable to all those who diligently perform the important duties annexed to it. By a frequent recurrence to the Constitution and general regulations, and a constant practice of the several sublime lectures and charges, you will be best enabled to fulfill those duties; and I am confident that the Companions, who are chosen to preside with you, will give strength to your endeavors, and support to your exertions.

"Let the *mitre*, with which you are invested, remind you of the dignity of the office you sustain, and its inscription impress upon your mind a sense of your dependence upon GOD; that perfection is not given unto man upon earth, and that *perfect holiness belongeth alone unto the Lord.*

"The *breast-plate* with which you are decorated, in imitation of that upon which were engraven the names of the twelve tribes, and worn by the High Priest of Israel, is to teach you that you are always to bear in mind your responsibility to the laws and ordinances of the institution, and that the honor and interests of your Chapter and its members, should be always *near your heart.*

"The *various colors* of the *Robes* you wear, are emblematical of every grace and virtue which can adorn and beautify the human mind; each of which will be briefly illustrated in the course of the charges to be delivered to your subordinate officers.

"You will now take charge of your officers, standing upon their right, and present them severally in succession to the Deputy Grand High Priest, by whom they will be presented to me for installation."

XX. The High Priest of the Chapter will then present his second officer to the Deputy Grand High Priest, who will present him to the Grand High Priest, in the words of the Constitution. The Grand High Priest will ask him whether he has attended to the ancient charges and regulations before recited to his superior officer; if he answers in the affirmative, he is asked whether he fully and freely assents to the same; if he answers in the affirmative, the Grand High Priest directs his Deputy to invest him with his clothing, etc., and then addresses him as follows, viz.:

CHARGE TO THE SECOND OFFICER OR KING.

"COMPANION:—The important station to which you are elected in this Chapter, requires from you exemplary conduct; its duties demand your most assiduous attention; you are to second and support your chief in all the requirements of his office; and should casualties at any time prevent his attendance, you are to succeed him in the performance of his duties. Your badge (the *Level, surmounted by a Crown*) should remind you, that although you are the representative of a king, and exalted by office above your companions, yet that you remain upon a level with them, as respects your duty to GOD, to your neighbor, and to yourself; that you are equally bound with them to be obedient to the laws and ordinances of the institution, to be charitable, humane and just, and to seek every occasion of doing good.

"Your office teaches a striking lesson of humility. The

institutions of political society teach us to consider the king as the chief of created beings, and that the first duty of his subjects is to obey *his* mandates; but the institutions of our sublime degrees, by placing the King in a situation subordinate to the High Priest, teach us that our duty to GOD is paramount to all other duties, and should ever claim the priority of our obedience to man; and that, however strongly we may be bound to obey the laws of civil society, yet that those laws, to be just, should never intermeddle with matters of conscience, nor dictate articles of faith.

"The *Scarlet Robe*, an emblem of imperial dignity, should remind you of the paternal concern you should ever feel for the welfare of your Chapter, and the *ardent zeal* with which you should endeavor to promote its prosperity.

"In presenting to you the *Crown*, which is an emblem of royalty, I would remind you that, to reign sovereign in the hearts and affections of men, must be far more grateful to a generous and benevolent mind, than to rule over their lives and fortunes; and that to enable you to enjoy this pre-eminence with honor and satisfaction, you must subject your own passions and prejudices to the dominion of reason and charity.

"You are entitled to the second seat in the council of your companions. Let the bright example of your illustrious predecessor in the Grand Council at Jerusalem, stimulate you to the faithful discharge of your duties; and when the King of kings shall summon you into his immediate presence, from his hand may you receive a *crown of glory*, which shall never fade away."

XXI. The King will then retire to the line of officers, and the Scribe will be presented in the manner before mentioned. After his investiture, the Grand High Priest will address him as follows, viz.:

CHARGE TO THE THIRD OFFICER, OR SCRIBE.

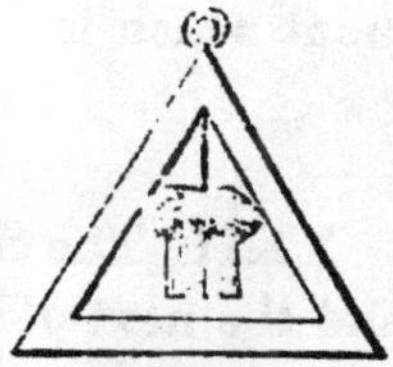

"COMPANION:—The office of Scribe, to which you are elected, is very important and respectable. In the absence of your superior officers, you are bound to succeed them and perform their duties. The purposes of the institution ought never to suffer for want of intelligence in its proper officers; you will therefore perceive the necessity there is of your possessing such qualifications as will enable you to accomplish those duties which are incumbent upon you, in your appropriate station, as well as those which may occasionally devolve on you by the absence of your superiors.

"The *Purple Robe*, with which you are invested, is an emblem of *union*, and is calculated to remind you that the harmony and unanimity of the Chapter should be your constant aim; and to this end you are studiously to avoid all occasions of giving offense, or countenancing any thing that may create divisions or dissensions. You are, by all the means in your power, to endeavor to establish a permanent union and good understanding among all orders and degrees of Masonry; and, as the glorious sun, at its meridian hight, dispels the mist and clouds which obscure the horizon, so may your exertions tend to dissipate the gloom of jealousy and discord whenever they may appear.

"Your badge (a *Plumb-rule, surmounted by the Turban*) is an emblem of rectitude and vigilance; and while you stand as a watchman upon the tower, to guard your companions against the approach of those enemies of human felicity, *intemperance* and *excess*, let this faithful monitor ever remind you to walk uprightly in your station; admonishing and animating your companions to fidelity and industry while at labor, and to temperance and moderation while at refreshment. And when the great Watchman of Israel, whose eye never slumbers nor sleeps, shall relieve you from your post on earth, may he permit you, in heaven, to participate in that food and refreshment which is

> 'Such as the saints in glory love,
> And such as angels eat.'"

XXII. The Scribe will then retire to the line of officers, and the next officer be presented as before.

CHARGE TO THE FOURTH OFFICER, OR CAPTAIN OF THE HOST.

"COMPANION:—The office with which you are entrusted is of high importance, and demands your most zealous consideration. The preservation of the most essential traits of our ancient customs, usages and landmarks, are within your province; and it is indispensably necessary that the part assigned to you, in the immediate practice of our rites and ceremonies, should be perfectly understood and correctly administered. He that brings the blind by a way that they knew not, and leads them in paths that they have not known, should always be well qualified to make darkness light before them and crooked things straight.

"Your office corresponds with that of *Marshal*, or Master of Ceremonies. You are to superintend all processions of your Chapter, when moving as a distinct body, either in public or private; and as the world can only judge of our private discipline by our public deportment, you will be careful that the utmost order and decorum be observed on all such occasions."

XXIII. He will then retire to the line of officers, and the next officer will be presented.

CHARGE TO THE FIFTH OFFICER, OR PRINCIPAL SOJOURNER.

"COMPANION:—The office confided to you, though subordinate in degree, is equal in importance to any in the Chapter, that of your chief alone excepted. Your office corresponds with that of *Senior Deacon*, in the preparatory degrees. Among the duties required of you, the preparation and introduction of candidates are not the least. As in our intercourse with the world, experience teaches that first impressions are often the most durable, and the most difficult to eradicate; so it is of great importance, in all cases, that those impressions should be correct and just; hence it is essential that the officer, who sustains the station assigned to you should possess a thorough knowledge of his various duties; and that he should execute them with a promptitude and propriety of deportment that shall give them their proper effect.

"Your *robe of office* is an emblem of humility; and teaches that, in the prosecution of a laudable undertaking, we should never decline taking any part that may be assigned us, although it may be the most difficult or dangerous.

"The *rose-colored tesselated border*, adorning the robe, is an emblem of ardor and perseverance, and signifies, that when we have engaged in a virtuous course, notwithstanding all the impediments, hardships and trials we may be destined to encounter, we should endure them all with fortitude, and ardently persevere unto the end; resting assured of receiving, at the termination of our labors, a noble and glorious reward. The *White Banner* entrusted to your care is emblematical of that purity of life and rectitude of conduct which should distinguish every one that passes the white veil of the sanctuary. Your past exertions will be considered as a pledge o your future assiduity in the faithful discharge of your duties."

XXIV. He will then retire to the line of officers, and the next officer is presented.

CHARGE TO THE SIXTH OFFICER, OR ROYAL ARCH CAPTAIN.

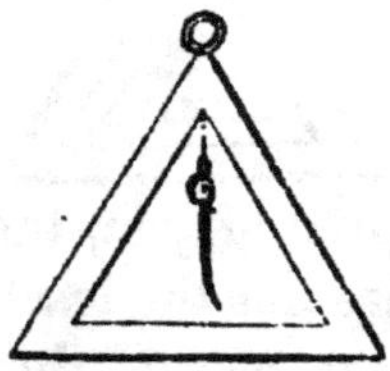

"COMPANION:—The well-known duties of your station require but little elucidation. Your office in the preparatory degrees corresponds with that of *Junior Deacon.** It is your particular province, conjointly with the Captain of the Host, to attend the examination of all visitors, and to take care that none are permitted to enter the Chapter but such as have *traveled the rugged path* of trial, and evinced their title to our favor and friendship. You will be attentive to obey the commands of your chief and always near at hand to execute them.

"I give it to you strongly in charge, never to suffer any one to pass your post without the *Signet of Truth.* I present you the badge of your office, in expectation of your performing your duties with intelligence, assiduity and propriety."

XXV. He then retires, and the three Grand Masters of the Veils are presented together.

CHARGE TO THE MASTER OF THE THIRD VEIL.

"COMPANION:—I present you with the *Scarlet Banner*, which is the ensign of your office, and with a sword to protect and defend the same. The rich and beautiful color of your banner is emblematical of *fervency* and *fidelity;* it is the appropriate color of the Royal Arch degree. It admonishes us that we should be fervent in the exercise of our devotions to GOD, and faithful in our endeavors to promote the happiness of man."

* In this place as in a preceding page it is "Senior" Deacon. This is opposed to theory and practice and we change it.

CHARGE TO THE MASTER OF THE SECOND VEIL.

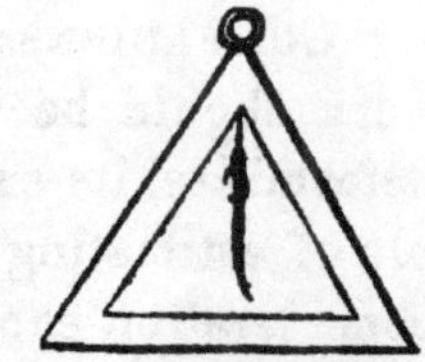

"COMPANION:—I invest you with the *Purple Banner*, which is the ensign of your office, and arm you with a sword, to enable you to maintain its honor. The color of your banner is produced by a combination of two distinct colors, namely, *blue* and *scarlet;* the former of which is the characteristic color of the *symbolic* or *first three degrees of Masonry*, and the latter that of the *Royal Arch degree.* It is an emblem of *union*, and is the characteristic color of the intermediate degrees. It admonishes us to cultivate and improve that spirit of union and harmony, between the brethren of the symbolic degrees, and the companions of the sublime degrees, which should ever distinguish the members of a society founded upon the principles of everlasting truth and universal philanthropy."

CHARGE TO THE MASTER OF THE FIRST VEIL.

"COMPANION:—I invest you with the *Blue Banner*, which is the ensign of your office, and a sword for its defense and protection. The color of your banner is one of the most durable and beautiful in nature. It is the appropriate color adopted and worn by our ancient brethren of the three symbolic degrees, and is the *peculiar characteristic* of an institution which has stood the test of ages, and which is as much distinguished by the durability of its materials or principles, as by the beauty of its superstructure. It is an emblem of universal benevolence; and instructs us that in the mind of a Mason this virtue should be as expansive as the blue arch of heaven itself."

CHARGE TO THE THREE MASTERS OF THE VEILS, AS OVERSEERS.

"COMPANIONS:—Those who are placed as overseers of any work should be well qualified to judge of its beauties and deformities, its excellencies and defects; they should be capable of estimating the former and amending the latter. This consideration should induce you to cultivate and improve all those qualifications with which you are already endowed, as well as to persevere in your endeavors to acquire those in which you may be in any wise deficient. Let the various *colors* of the *banners* committed to your charge, admonish you to the exercise of the several virtues of which they are emblematic; and you are to enjoin the practice of those virtues upon all who shall present themselves, or the *work* of their hands *for your inspection*. Let no work receive your approbation but such as is calculated to adorn and strengthen the Masonic edifice. Be industrious and faithful in practicing and disseminating a knowledge of the *true and perfect work*, which alone can stand the test of the *Grand Overseer's square*, in the great day of trial and retribution. Then, although every *rod* should become a *serpent*, and every serpent an enemy to this institution, yet shall their utmost exertions to destroy its reputation, or sap its foundation, become as impotent as the *leprous hand*, or as *water spilled upon the ground*, which can not be gathered up again."

XXVI. They then retire, and the Secretary is presented.

CHARGE TO THE SECRETARY.

"COMPANION:—I with pleasure invest you with your badge as Secretary of this Chapter. The qualities which should recommend a Secretary are, *promptitude* in issuing notifications and orders of his superior officers; *punctuality* in attending the meetings of the Chapter; *correctness* in recording their proceedings; *judgment* in discriminating between what is proper and what is improper to be committed to writing; *regularity* in making his annual returns to the Grand Chapter; *integrity* in accounting for all moneys that may pass through his hands; and *fidelity* in paying the same over into the hands of the Treasurer. The possession of these good qualities, I presume, has designated you a suitable candidate for this important office; and I can not entertain a doubt that you will discharge its duties beneficially to the Chapter, and honorably to yourself. And when you shall have completed the record of your transactions here below, and finished the term of your probation, may you be admitted into the celestial Grand Chapter of saints and angels, and find your name *recorded* in the *book of life eternal.*"

XXVII. He then retires, and the Treasurer is presented.

CHARGE TO THE TREASURER.

"COMPANION:—You are elected Treasurer of this Chapter, and I have the pleasure of investing you with the badge of your office. The qualities which should recommend a Treasurer, are *accuracy* and *fidelity;* accuracy in keeping a fair and minute account of all receipts and disbursements; fidelity in carefully preserving all the property and funds of the Chapter, that may be placed in his hands, and rendering a just account of the same, whenever he is called upon for that purpose. I presume that your respect for the institution, your attachment to the interests of your Chapter, and your regard for a good name, which is better than precious ointment, will prompt you to the faithful discharge of the duties of your office."

XXVIII. He then retires, and the Stewards are presented.

CHARGE TO THE STEWARDS.

"COMPANIONS:—You being elected Stewards of this Chapter, I with pleasure invest you with the badges of your office. It is your province to see that every necessary preparation is made for the convenience and accommodation of the Chapter, previous to the time appointed for meeting. You are to see that the clothing, implements and furniture of each degree, respectively, are properly disposed and in suitable array for use, whenever they may be required, and that they are secured, and proper care taken of them, when the business of the Chapter is over. You are to see that necessary refreshments are provided, and that all your companions, and particularly visitors, are suitably accommodated and supplied. You are to be frugal and prudent in your disbursements, and to be careful that no extravagance or waste is committed in your department: and when you have faithfully fulfilled your stewardship here below, may you receive from heaven the happy greeting of 'Well done, good and faithful servants.'"

XXIX. They then retire, and the Tyler is presented.

CHARGE TO THE TYLER.

"COMPANION:—You are appointed Tyler of this Chapter, and I invest you with this implement of your office. As the sword is placed in the hands of the Tyler, to enable him effectually to guard against the approach of *cowans and eavesdroppers*, and suffer none to pass or repass but such as are duly qualified; so it should morally serve as a constant admonition to us to set a guard at the entrance of our thoughts, to place a watch at the door of our lips; to post a sentinel at the avenue of our actions; thereby excluding every unqualified and unworthy thought, word, and deed; and preserving consciences void of offense toward GOD and toward man.

As the first application from visitors for admission into the Chapter is generally made to the Tyler at the door, your station will often present you to the observation of strangers; it is, therefore, essentially necessary that he who sustains the office with which you are intrusted, should be a man of good morals, steady habits, strict discipline, temperate, affable, and discreet. I trust that a just regard for the honor and reputation of the institution will ever induce you to perform, with fidelity, the trust reposed in you; and when the door of this earthly tabernacle shall be closed, may you find an abundant entrance through the gates into the temple and city of our GOD.

XXX. He will then retire, and then follows an

ADDRESS TO THE HIGH PRIEST.

"M. E. COMPANION:—Having been honored with the free suffrages of the members of this Chapter, you are elected to the most important office which is within their power to bestow. This expression of their esteem and respect should draw from you corresponding sensations; and your demeanor should be such as to repay the honor they have so conspicuously conferred upon you, by an honorable and faithful discharge of the duties of your office.

"The station you are called to fill is important, not only as it respects the correct practice of our rites and ceremonies, and the internal economy of the Chapter over which you preside; but the public reputation of the institution will be generally found to rise or fall according to the skill, fidelity, and discretion with which its concerns are managed, and in proportion as the characters and conduct of its principal officers are estimable or censurable.

"You have accepted a trust, to which is attached a weight of responsibility that will require all your efforts to discharge, honorably to yourself and satisfactorily to the Chapter. You are to see that your officers are capable and faithful in the exercises of their offices. Should they lack ability you are expected to supply their defects; you are to watch carefully the progress of their performances, and to see that the long-established customs of the institution suffer no derangement in their hands.

"You are to have a careful eye over the general conduct of the Chapter; see that due order and subordination are observed on all occasions; that the members are properly instructed; that due solemnity be observed in the practice of our rites; that no improper levity be permitted at any time, but more especially at the *introduction of strangers among the workmen.* In fine, you are to be an example to your officers and members which they need not hesitate to follow; thus securing to yourself the favor of heaven and the applause of your brethren and companions."

ADDRESS TO THE OFFICERS GENERALLY.

"COMPANIONS IN OFFICE:—Precept and example should ever advance with an equal pace. Those moral duties which you are required to teach unto others, you should never neglect to practice yourselves.

"Do you desire that the demeanor of your equals and inferiors toward you should be marked with deference and respect? Be sure that you omit no opportunity of furnishing them with examples in your own conduct toward your superiors. Do you desire to obtain instruction from those who are more wise or better informed than yourselves? Be sure that you are always ready to impart of your knowledge to those within your sphere, who stand in need of and are entitled to receive it. Do you desire distinction among your companions? Be sure that your claims to preferment are founded upon superior attainments; let no ambitious passion be suffered to induce you to envy or supplant a companion who may be considered as better qualified for promotion than yourselves; but rather let a laudable emulation induce you to strive to excel each other in improvement and discipline; ever remembering, that he who *faithfully performs his duty*, ever in a subordinate or private station, is as justly entitled to esteem and respect, as he who is invested with supreme authority."

ADDRESS TO THE CHAPTER AT LARGE.

"COMPANIONS:—The exercise and management of the sublime degrees of Masonry in your Chapter hitherto, are so highly appreciated, and the good reputation of the Chapter so well established, that I must presume these considerations alone, were there no others of greater magnitude, would be sufficient to induce you to preserve and perpetuate this valuable and honorable character. But when to this is added the pleasure which every philanthropic heart must feel in doing good, in promoting good order, in diffusing light and knowledge, in cultivating Masonic and Christian charity, which are the great objects of this sublime institution, I can not doubt that your future conduct, and that of your successors, will be calculated still to increase the luster of your justly esteemed reputation.

"May your *Chapter* become *beautiful* as the TEMPLE, *peaceful* as the ARK, and *sacred* as its *most holy place*. May your oblations of *piety* and *praise* be *grateful* as the INCENSE; your love *warm* as its *flame*, and your charity diffusive as its fragrance. May your hearts be *pure* as the ALTAR, and your conduct *acceptable* as the OFFERING.

"May the exercise of your CHARITY be as constant as the returning wants of the distressed *widow* and the helpless *orphan.* May the approbation of Heaven be your encouragement, and the testimony of a good conscience your support; may you be endowed with every good and perfect gift, while *traveling the thorny path of life*, and finally *admitted within the veil* of heaven, to the full enjoyment of life eternal."

Amen. So mote it be.

XXXI. The officers and members of the Chapter will then pass in review in front of the Grand officers, and pay them the customary salutation as they pass.

XXXII. The Grand Marshal will then make proclamation as follows, viz.: "In the name of the M. E. Grand High Priest, I do proclaim this Chapter, by the name of ———, to be regularly constituted, and its officers duly installed."

XXXIII. The officers of the Chapter will then take their stations upon the left of the Grand officers respectively, and the members will be seated until the Grand officers retire.

XXXIV. The ceremonies conclude with an Ode, or appropriate piece of music.

XXXV. When the Grand officers retire, the Chapter will form an avenue for them to pass through, and salute them with the Grand honors. They will be attended as far as the door of their apartment, by the committee who introduced them.

XXXVI. The two bodies then separately close their respective Chapters.

THE

CRYPTIC DEGREES:

CONSISTING OF

THE ROYAL MASTER,

AND

SELECT MASTER,

COMPOSING

THE THIRD ORDER IN MASONRY.

19

The Cryptic Degrees are conferred in a Body styled *a Council.* The ballot is taken in the Second or Select Masters' Degree; the same rules of balloting are observed as in the preceding degrees. All discipline exercised by the Lodge or Chapter, such as suspension or expulsion, is indorsed by the Council without question; in addition to which, it has a discipline of its own for offenses against its own regulations.

Not less than nine nor more than twenty-seven can open, work, or close a Council. If a larger number than twenty-seven is present, they take no part in the proceedings.

The whole system of Cryptic Masonry is confined to the United States alone, and was borrowed about the year 1815, from the *Ancient and Accepted Rite.*

THE DEGREE

OF

ROYAL MASTER.

Royal Master.

CHAPTER XVI.

ROYAL MASTER'S DEGREE.

The Monitor containing nothing relative to the degrees of Royal and Select Master, we draw our illustration from Cross's Chart.

This degree can not legally be conferred on any but Royal Arch Masons, who have taken all the preceding degrees; and it is preparatory to that of the Select Master. Although it is short, yet it contains some valuable information, and is intimately connected with the degree of Select Master. It also enables us with ease and facility to examine the privileges of others to this degree; while, at the same time, it proves ourselves.

The following passages of Scripture, etc., are considered to be appropriate to this degree:

And Solomon made all the vessels that pertained unto the house of the Lord: the altar of gold, and the table of gold, whereupon the shew-bread was; and the candlesticks of pure gold; five on the right side, and five on the left, before the oracle; with the flowers, and the lamps, and the tongs of gold; and the bowls, and the snuffers, and the basons, and the spoons, and the censers, of pure gold; and the hinges of gold, both for the doors of the inner house, the most holy place, and for the doors of the house, to wit, of the Temple. So Hiram made an end of doing all the work, that he had made King Solomon, for the house of the Lord.—1 *Kings* vii: 48–50, 40.

And behold I come quickly; and my reward is with me, to give every man according as his work shall be. I am Alpha and Omega, the beginning and the end, the first and the last. Blessed are they that do his commandments, that they may have a right to the tree of life, and may enter in through the gates of the city.—*Rev.* xxii: 12–14.

And he set the cherubims within the inner house; and they stretched forth the wings of the cherubims, so that the wing of the one touched the one wall; and the wing of the other cherub touched the other wall; and their wings touched one another in the midst of the house.—1 *Kings* vi: 27.

The Ark, called the glory of Israel, which was seated in the middle of the holy place, under the wings of the cherubim, was a small chest, or coffer, three feet nine inches long, two feet three inches wide, and three feet three inches high. It was made of wood, excepting only the mercy seat, but overlaid with gold both inside and out. It had a ledge of gold surrounding it at the top, into which the cover, called the mercy seat, was let in. The mercy seat was of solid gold, the thickness of a hand's breadth: at the two ends of it were two cherubims, looking inward, toward each other, with their wings expanded; which embracing the whole circumference of the mercy seat, they met on each side, in the middle; all of which, the Rabbins say, was made out of the same mass, without any soldering of parts.

Here the Shekinah, or Divine Presence, rested, and was visible in the appearance of a cloud over it. From hence the Bathkoll issued, and gave answers when God was consulted. And hence it is, that God is said, in the Scripture, to dwell between the cherubim; that is, between the cherubim on the mercy seat, because there was the seat or throne of the visible appearance of his glory among them.

THE DEGREE

OF

SELECT MASTER.

Select Master.

CHAPTER XVII.

SELECT MASTER'S DEGREE.

THIS degree is the summit and perfection of ancient Masonry; and without which the history of the Royal Arch degree can not be complete. It rationally accounts for the concealment and preservation of those essentials of the Craft, which were brought to light at the erection of the second Temple, and which lay concealed from the Masonic eye four hundred and seventy years.

Many particulars relative to those few who, for their superior skill, were selected to complete an important part of King Solomon's Temple, are explained.

And here, too, is exemplified an instance of *justice* and *mercy*, by our ancient patron, toward one of the Craft, who was led to disobey his commands, by an over *zealous* attachment for the institution. It ends with a description of a particular circumstance, which characterizes the degree.

The following Psalm is read at opening:

His foundation is in the holy mountains. The Lord loveth the gates of Zion more than all the dwellings of Jacob. Glorious things are spoken of thee, O city of God. Selah. I will make mention of Rahab and Babylon, to them that know me. Behold Philistia, and Tyre, with Ethiopia; this man was born there. And of Zion it shall be said, This and that man was born in her: and the Highest himself shall establish her. The Lord shall count, when he writeth up the people, that this man was born there. Selah. As well the singers, as the players on instruments, shall be there: all my springs are in thee.—*Psalm* lxxxvii.

The following passages of Scripture are introduced and explained:

So King Solomon was king over all Israel. Azariah, the son of Nathan, was over the officers; and Zabud, the Son of Nathan, was principal officer, and the king's friend; and Ahishar was over the household; and Adoniram, the son of Abda, was over the tribute.—1 *Kings*, iv: 1, 5, 6.

And the king commanded, and they brought great stones, costly stones, and hewed stones, to lay the foundation of the house. And Solomon's builders and Hiram's builders did hew them, and the stone-squarers: so they prepared timber and stones to build the house.—1 *Kings*, v: 17, 18.

And King Solomon sent and fetched Hiram out of Tyre. He was a widow's son, of the tribe of Naphthali: and his father was a man of Tyre, a worker of brass; and he was filled with wisdom and understanding, and cunning, to work all works in brass.—1 *Kings*, viii: 13, 14.

The ancients of Gebal, and the wise men thereof, were in thee thy calkers: all the ships of the sea, with their mariners, were in thee, to occupy thy merchandise.—*Ezekiel*, xxvii: 9.

And it came to pass, when Moses had made an end of writing the words of this law in a book, until they were finished, that Moses commanded the Levites, which bore the ark of the covenant of the Lord, saying, Take this book of the law, and put it in the side of the ark of the covenant of the

Lord your God, that it may be there for a witness against thee.—*Deuteronomy*, xxxi : 24–26.

And Moses said unto Aaron, Take a pot, and put an omer full of manna therein, and lay it up before the Lord, to be kept for your generations. As the Lord commanded Moses, so Aaron laid it up before the testimony to be kept.—*Exodus*, xvi : 33, 34.

And the Lord said unto Moses, Bring Aaron's rod again before the testimony, to be kept for a token.—*Numbers*, xvii : 10.

And when Moses was gone into the tabernacle of the congregation, to speak with him, then he heard the voice of one speaking unto him from off the mercy seat, that was upon the ark of the testimony, from between the two cherubims: and he spake unto him.—*Numbers*, vii : 89.

And look that thou make them after their pattern, which was shewed thee in the mount.—*Exod.*, xxv : 40.

CHARGE TO A SELECT MASTER.

COMPANION:—Having attained to this degree, you have passed the *circle of perfection* in ancient Masonry. In the capacity of Select Master, you must be sensible that your obligations are increased in proportion to your privileges. Let it be your constant care to prove yourself worthy of the confidence reposed in you, and of the high honor conferred on you, in admitting you to this Select degree. Let uprightness and integrity attend your steps; let *justice* and *mercy* mark your conduct; let *fervency* and *zeal* stimulate you in the discharge of the various duties incumbent on you; but suffer not an idle or impertinent *curiosity* to lead you astray, or betray you into danger. Be *deaf* to every insinuation which would have a tendency to weaken your resolution, or tempt you to an act of *disobedience*. Be voluntarily *dumb* and *blind*, when the exercise of those faculties would endanger the peace of your mind or the probity of your conduct; and let *silence* and *secresy*, those cardinal virtues of a Select Master, on all necessary occasions, be scrupulously observed. By a steady adherence to the important instructions contained in this degree, you will merit the approbation of the select number with whom you are associated, and will enjoy the high satisfaction of having acted well your part in the important enterprise in which you are engaged; and after having *wrought your regular hours*, may you be admitted to participate in all the privileges of a *Select Master*.

There is a ceremony of Constituting Councils of Royal and Select Masters and Installing officers, but as we can not use it without violating copy right we omit it.

THE

CHIVALRIC DEGREES:

CONSISTING OF

THE KNIGHTS OF THE RED CROSS,

KNIGHTS TEMPLAR,

AND

KNIGHTS OF MALTA,

COMPOSING

THE FOURTH ORDER IN MASONRY.

THE ORDER

OF

KNIGHTS OF THE RED CROSS.

Knights of the Red Cross.

CHAPTER XVIII.

OBSERVATIONS ON THE ORDERS OF KNIGHTHOOD.

As several Orders of Knighthood are conferred, both in Europe and America, reputedly under the sanction of Masonic assemblies, it may be expected that some notice will be taken of them in this work. It may be necessary to premise that the Orders of Knighthood compose no part of the system of Freemasonry. They are in comparison to it, societies of but yesterday, and all of them fall short of the excellence, harmony, universality, and utility of the noble institution.

The design of this part of the work will be to collect together such observations from Scripture and history as are deemed applicable to the several orders; and as in America, they are only conferred as honorary degrees, it is possible that this may be the means of producing a uniformity in their application and use.

OF THE ORDER OF KNIGHTS OF THE RED CROSS.

The incidents upon which this Order is founded, occurred in the reign of Darius, king of Persia. It is more immediately connected with symbolic Masonry, than any other Order of Knighthood. Their meetings are called *Councils;* their sashes are decorated with a *Sword* and *Trowel*, and trimmed with red and green.

The following passages of Scripture are considered by Knights of this order, as applicable to their institution, and are occasionally rehearsed in their Councils.

"Now in the second year of their coming into the house

of God at Jerusalem, in the second month, began Zerubbabel, the son of Shealtiel, and Jeshua, the son of Jozadak, and the remnant of their brethren the priests and Levites, and all they that were come out of the captivity unto Jerusalem: and appointed the Levites, from twenty years old and upward, to set forward the work of the house of the Lord. Then stood Jeshua, with his sons and his brethren, Kadmiel and his sons, the sons of Judah, together, to set forward the workmen in the house of God; the sons of Henadad, with their sons and their brethren the Levites. And when the builders laid the foundation of the Temple of the Lord, they set the priests in their apparel with trumpets, and the Levites, the sons of Asaph, with cymbals, to praise the Lord, after the ordinance of David king of Israel. And they sung together by course, in praising and giving thanks unto the Lord; because he is good, for his mercy endureth forever toward Israel. And all the people shouted with a great shout when they praised the Lord, because the foundation of the house of the Lord was laid.—*Ezra*, iii. 8–11.

Now when the adversaries of Judah and Benjamin heard that the children of the captivity builded the Temple unto the Lord God of Israel, then they came to Zerubbabel, and to the chief of the fathers, and said unto them, Let us build with you; for we seek your God as ye do; and we do sacrifice unto him, since the days of Esar-Haddon king of Assur, which brought us up hither. But Zerubbabel, and Jeshua, and the rest of the chief of the fathers of Israel, said unto them, Ye have nothing to do with us to build an house unto our God; but we ourselves together will build unto the Lord God of Israel, as King Cyrus, the king of Persia, hath commanded us. Then the people of the land weakened the hands of the people of Judah, and troubled them in building; and hired counselors against them, to frustrate their purpose, all the days of Cyrus king of Persia, even until the reign of Darius king of Persia. And in the reign of Ahasuerus, in the beginning of his reign, wrote they unto him an accusation against the inhabitants of Judah and Jerusalem. And in the days of Artaxerxes wrote Bishlam, Mithredah, Tabeel, and the rest of their companions, unto Artaxerxes king of Persia; and the writing of the letter was written in the Syrian tongue, and interpreted in the Syrian tongue; Rehum the chancelor, and Shimshai the scribe, wrote a letter against Jerusalem to Artaxerxes the king, in this sort: This is the copy of the letter that they sent unto him, even unto Artaxerxes the king: Thy servants, the men on this side the river, and at such a time. Be it known unto the king, that the Jews, which came up from thee to us, are come unto Jerusalem, building the rebellious and the bad city, and have set up the walls thereof, and joined the foundations. Be it known now unto the king, that if this city be builded, and the walls set up again, then will they not pay toll, tribute, and custom, and so thou shalt endamage the revenue of the kings. Now, because we have maintenance from the king's palace, and it was not meet for us to see the king's dishonor; therefore have we sent and certified the king. That search may be made in the book of the records of thy fathers: so shalt thou find in the book of the records, and know, that this city is a rebellious city, and hurtful unto kings and provinces, and that they have moved sedition within the same of old time; for which cause was this city destroyed. We certify the king, that if this city be builded again, and the walls thereof set up, by this means thou shalt have no portion on this side the river. Then sent the king an answer unto Rehum the chancelor, and to Shimshai the scribe, and to the rest of their companions that dwell in Samaria, and unto the rest beyond the river, Peace, and at such a time. The letter which ye sent unto us hath been plainly read before me. And I commanded, and search hath been made, and it is found, that this city of old time hath made insurrection against kings, and that rebellion and sedition have been made therein. There have been mighty kings also over Jerusalem, which have ruled over all countries beyond the river; and toll, tribute, and custom, was paid unto them. Give ye now commandment to cause these men to cease, and that this city be not builded, until another commandment shall be given from me. Take heed now that ye fail not to do this: why should damage grow to the hurt of the kings? Now, when the copy of King Artaxerxes' letter was read before Rehum, and Shimshai the scribe, and their companions, they went up in haste to Jerusalem, unto the Jews, and made them cease by force and power. Then ceased the work of the house of God, which is at Jerusalem. So it ceased unto the second year of the reign of Darius, king of Persia.—*Ezra*, iv.

Josephus informs us that Darius, while he was yet a private man, made a vow to God, that if ever he came to the throne, he would send all the holy vessels that were at Babylon, back again to Jerusalem; and it happened about the time of his accession, that Zerubbabel, who was a captain or prince of the Jewish captives, came from Jerusalem, to Darius, as well to solicit his protection against their adversaries on the other side of the river, as to watch a suitable opportunity of endeavoring to persuade the king to fulfill his promise. He had long been known to Darius as a man of great judgment and understanding, and was therefore taken into the king's confidence, and put into a particular trust, with two other great officers, as his constant attendants.

Darius, in the first year of his reign, gave a splendid and magnificent entertainment to the princes and nobility, and after they had retired, finding himself unable to sleep, he fell into a discourse with his three favorite officers, to whom he proposed certain questions, telling them, at the same time, that he who should give him the most reasonable and satisfactory answer should be clothed in purple, drink in a golden cup, wear a silken tiara, and a golden chain about his neck.

He then proposed this question: Which is greatest, the strength of *wine*, of the *king*, of *women*, or of *truth?* To this the first answered, *wine* is the strongest; the second, that the *king* was strongest; and the third (who was Zerubbabel) that *women* were stronger, but above all things TRUTH beareth the victory.

On the following day the king assembled together the princes and nobility, to hear the question debated; and having placed himself upon the royal seat of judgment, he called upon them to make a public defense of their several opinions: whereupon the first began upon the strength of wine, as follows:

"O ye princes and rulers, how exceeding strong is wine! it causeth all men to err that drink it: it maketh the mind of the king and the beggar to be all one; of the bondman and the freeman; of the poor man and of the rich; it turneth, also, every thought into jollity and mirth, so that a man remembereth neither sorrow nor debt; it changeth and elevateth the spirits, and enliveneth the heavy hearts of the miserable. It maketh a man forget his brethren, and draw his sword against his best friends. O ye princes and rulers, is not wine the strongest, that forceth us to do these things?"

Then began the second upon the power of kings, and spoke as follows: "It is beyond dispute, O princes and rulers, that God has made man master of all things under the sun; to command them, to make use of them, and apply them to his service as he pleases: but whereas men have only dominion over other sublunary creatures, kings have an authority even over men themselves, and a right of ruling them by will and pleasure. Now, he that is master of those who are masters of all things else, hath no earthly thing above him."

Then began Zerubbabel upon the power of women and of truth, and spoke as follows: "O princes and rulers, the force of wine is not to be denied; neither is that of kings, that unites so many men in one common bond of allegiance; but the super-eminency of *women* is yet above all this; for *kings* are but the gifts of women, and they are, also, the mothers of those that cultivate our *vineyards*. Women have the power to make us abandon our very country and relations, and many times to forget the best friends we have in the world, and forsaking all other comforts to live and die with them. But when all is said, neither they, nor wine, nor kings, are comparable to the almighty force of *truth*. As for all other things, they are mortal and transient, but truth alone is unchangeable and everlasting; the benefits we receive from it are subject to no variations or vicissitudes of time and fortune. In her judgment is no unrighteousness, and she is the strength, wisdom, power, and majesty of all ages. Blessed be the God of truth."

When Zerubbabel had finished speaking, the princes and rulers cried out: "Great is truth, and mighty above all things."

Then, said the king to Zerubbabel, "Ask what thou wilt, and I will give it thee, because thou art found wisest among thy companions."

Then said he to Darius, "O king, remember thy vow, which thou hast vowed, to build Jerusalem in the day when thou shouldest come to thy kingdom, and to restore the holy vessels which were taken away out of Jerusalem. Thou hast also vowed to build up the temple, which was burned when Judah was made desolate by the Chaldees. And now, O king, this is that I desire of thee, that thou make good the vow, the performance whereof with thine own mouth thou hast vowed to the King of Heaven."

Then Darius the king stood up and embraced him, and

gave him passports and letters to his governors and officers, that they should safely convey both him and those who should go with him, to Jerusalem; and that they should not be delayed or hindered from building the city and the temple, until they should be finished. He also restored all the holy vessels remaining in his possession, that had been taken from Jerusalem, when the children of Israel were carried away captive to Babylon, and reserved by Cyrus.

"But it came to pass, that when Sanballat, and Tobiah, and the Arabians, and the Ammonites, and the Ashdodites, heard that the walls of Jerusalem were made up, and that the breaches began to be stopped, then they were very wroth, and conspired all of them together to come and to fight against Jerusalem, and to hinder it. Nevertheless we made our prayer unto our God, and set a watch against them day and night because of them. And Judah said, The strength of the bearers of burdens is decayed, and there is much rubbish; so that we are not able to build the wall. And our adversaries said, They shall not know, neither see, till we come in the midst among them, and slay them, and cause the work to cease. And it came to pass, that when the Jews which dwelt by them came, they said unto us ten times, From all places whence ye shall return unto us they will be upon you.

"Therefore set I in the lower places behind the wall, and on the higher places, I even set the people after their families, with their swords, their spears, and their bows. And I looked, and rose up, and said unto the nobles, and to the rulers, and to the rest of the people, Be not ye afraid of them: remember the Lord which is great and terrible, and fight for your brethren, your sons, and your daughters, your wives, and your houses. And it came to pass, when our enemies heard that it was known unto us, and God had brough ir counsel to nought, that we returned all of us to the wall, every one unto his work. And it came to pass from that time forth, that the half of my servants wrought in the work, and the other half of them held both the spears, the shields, and the bows, and the habergeons; and the rulers were behind all the house of Judah. They which builded on the wall, and they that bare burdens, with those that laded, every one with one of his hands wrought in the work, and with the other hand held a weapon. For the builders, every one had his sword girded by his side, and so builded. And he that sounded the trumpet was by me.

"And I said unto the nobles, and to the rulers, and to the rest of the people, The work is great and large, and we are separated upon the wall, one far from another. In what place therefore ye hear the sound of the trumpet, resort ye thither unto us: our God shall fight for us."

"Then the prophets, Haggai the prophet and Zechariah the son of Iddo, prophesied unto the Jews that were in Judah and Jerusalem, in the name of the God of Israel, even unto them. Then rose up Zerubbabel, the son of Shealthiel, and Jeshua the son of Josadak, and began to build the house of God which is at Jerusalem: and with them were the prophets of God helping them. At the same time came to them Tatnai, governor on this side the river, and Shethar-boznai, and their companions, and said thus unto them: Who hath commanded you to build this house, and to make up this wall? Then said we unto them after this manner: What are the names of the men that make this building? But the eye of their God was upon the elders of the Jews, that they could not cause them to cease, till the matter came to Darius; and then they returned answer by letter concerning this matter. The copy of the letter that Tatnai, governor on this side the river, and Shethar-boznai, and his companions the Apharsachites, which were on this side the river, sent unto Darius the king: They sent a letter unto him, wherein was written: Unto Darius the king, all peace. Be it known unto the king, that we went into the province of Judea, to the house of the great God, which is builded with great stones, and timber is laid in the walls, and this work goeth fast on, and prospereth in their hands. Then asked we those elders, and said unto them thus: Who commanded you to build this house, and to make up these walls? We asked their names also, to certify thee, that we might write the names of the men that were the chief of them. And thus they returned us answer, saying, We are the servants of the God of heaven and earth, and build the house that was builded these many years ago, which a great king of Israel builded and set up. But after that our fathers had provoked the God of heaven unto wrath, he gave them into the hand of Nebuchadnezzar the king of Babylon, the Chaldean, who destroyed this house, and carried the people away into Babylon. But in the first year of Cyrus the king of Babylon, the same king Cyrus made a decree to build this house of God. And the vessels also of gold and silver of the house of God, which Nebuchadnezzar took out of the temple that was in Jerusalem, and brought them into the temple of Babylon, those did Cyrus the king take out of the temple at Babylon, and they were delivered unto one whose name was Sheshbazzar, whom he made governor; and said unto him, Take these vessels, go, carry them into the temple that is in Jerusalem, and let the house of God be builded in his place. Then came the same Sheshbazzar, and laid the foundation of the house of God which is in Jerusalem: and since that time even until now hath it been in building, and yet it is not finished. Now, therefore, if it seem good to the king, let there be search made in the king's treasure-house, which is there at Babylon, whether it be so, that a decree was made of Cyrus the king to build this house of God at Jerusalem, and let the king send his pleasure to us concerning this matter."—*Ezra* v.

"Then Darius the king made a decree, and search was made

in the house of the rolls, where the treasures were laid up in Babylon. And there was found at Achmetha, in the palace that is in the province of the Medes, a roll, and therein was a record thus written: In the first year of Cyrus the king, the same Cyrus the king made a decree concerning the house of God at Jerusalem, Let the house be builded, the place where they offered sacrifice, and let the foundations thereof be strongly laid; the hight thereof threescore cubits; and the breadth thereof threescore cubits; with three rows of great stones, and a row of new timber: and let the expenses be given out of the king's house. And also let the golden and silver vessels of the house of God, which Nebuchadnezzar took forth out of the temple which is at Jerusalem and brought unto Babylon, be restored, and brought again unto the temple which is at Jerusalem, every one to his place, and place them in the house of God. Now, therefore, Tatnai, governor beyond the river, Shethar-boznai, and your companions the Apharsachites, which are beyond the river, be ye far from thence; let the work of this house of God alone, let the governor of the Jews, and the elders of the Jews, build this house of God in his place. Moreover, I make a decree what ye shall do to the elders of these Jews, for the building of this house of God; that of the king's goods, even of the tribute beyond the river, forthwith expenses be given unto these men that they be not hindered. And that which they have need of, both young bullocks, and rams, and lambs, for the burnt-offerings of the God of Heaven; wheat, salt, wine, and oil, according to the appointment of the priests which are at Jerusalem, let it be given them day by day without fail; that they may offer sacrifices of sweet savors unto the God of Heaven, and pray for the life of the king and of his sons. Also I have made a decree, that whosoever shall alter this word, let the timber be pulled down from his house, and, being set up, let him be hanged thereon; and let his house be made a dunghill for this. And the God that hath caused his name to dwell there, destroy all kings and people that shall put to their hand to alter and to destroy this house of God which is at Jerusalem. I Darius have made a decree; let it be done with speed. Then Tatnai, governor on this side the river, Shethar-boznai, and their companions, according to that which Darius the king had sent, so they did speedily. And the elders of the Jews builded, and they prospered through the prophesying of Haggai the prophet, and Zechariah the son of Iddo; and they builded, and finished it, according to the commandment of the God of Israel, and according to the commandment of Cyrus, and Darius, and Artaxerxes king of Persia. And this house was finished on the third day of the month Adar, which was in the sixth year of the reign of Darius the king," and in the year of the world 3489.—*Ezra* vi.

THE ORDER

OF

KNIGHTS TEMPLAR.

Knights Templar.

CHAPTER XIX.

OBSERVATIONS ON THE ORDERS OF KNIGHTS TEMPLAR, AND KNIGHTS OF MALTA.

According to the Abbe de Vertot, the Order of Knights of Malta, who were originally called Hospitallers of St. John of Jerusalem, took its rise about the year 1099; from which time to the year 1118, their whole employment was works of charity, and taking care of the sick.

Some time after the establishment of this Order, nine gentlemen of whose names two only remain on record, viz. : Hugho de Paganis and Godfrey Adelman formed a society to guard and protect the Christian pilgrims who traveled from abroad to visit the holy Sepulcher.

These men were encouraged by the Abbot of Jerusalem, who assigned them and their companions a place of retreat in a Christian church, called the Church of the Holy Temple, from which they were called Templars, and not from the temple of Jerusalem, that having been destroyed by Titus Vespasian, 982 years before the society of Templars was instituted.

The society increased rapidly, and was much respected ; but had neither habit, order, or mark of distinction, for the space of nine years, when Pope Honorius II., at the request of Stephen, Patriarch of Jerusalem, laid down a rule and manner of life for them; and ordained that they should be clothed in white; to which garment Pope Eugenius III. added a red cross, to be worn on the breast, which they promised by a solemn oath to observe forever.

Incited by the example of the *Knights Templar*, about the year 1118, the *Hospitallers* also took up the profession of arms, in addition to their original charitable profession; occupying themselves at one time in attending upon the sick, and at others in acts of hostility against the Turks and Saracens. At this time they took the name of *Knights* Hospitallers.

Both Orders flourished and increased daily; but that of the Templars, though the younger of the two, having from its original establishment been wholly employed in the profession of arms, was by many esteemed to be the most honorable; and therefore many noblemen, princes, and persons of the highest distinction, who thought the service of tending the sick too servile an employment, entered themselves among the *Knights Templar*, in preference to the other Order.

Both Orders, for years, generally took the field together, and, as well by themselves as in conjunction with the troops of the Crusades, won many battles, and performed prodigies of valor. The emulation, however, which subsisted between them often occasioned warm disputes, which rose to such a hight as produced frequent skirmishes between detached parties of the two Orders. This occasioned the Pope and the respective Grand Masters to interfere; who in a great measure suppressed these quarrels; but the Knights of the different Orders ever afterward continued to view each other with jealous eyes.

Some time after these difficulties were thus partially suppressed, the Turks assembled a great force and drove the whole of the Christians out of Palestine. The last fortress they had possession of was that of St. John d'Acre. This was long and bravely defended by the Knights Templar against their besiegers. The Turks, however, at last forced three hundred Knights, being all that remained of the garrison, to take refuge in a strong tower, to which also the women fled for safety. The Turks hereupon set about undermining it, which they in a short time so effectually accomplished, that the Knights saw, in case they held out any longer, they must inevitably perish. They therefore capitulated, stipulating, among other things, that the honor of their women should not be violated. Upon this, the tower being opened, the Turks marched in; but, in total breach of the terms of capitulation, they immediately began to offer violence to the women. The enraged Knights instantly drew their swords, hewed in pieces all the Turks who had entered, shut the gates against those who remained without, and resigned themselves to inevitable death, which they soon met with, by the tower being undermined and thrown down upon their heads.

After this defeat, the two Orders found an asylum in the island of Cyprus; from whence, after some time, the Knights Templar, finding their number so diminished as to leave no hopes of effecting any thing toward the recovery of the holy land, without new Crusades (which the Christian princes did not seem inclined to set on foot), returned to their different commanders in the various parts of Christendom.

From this time the Orders separated; the Knights Hospitallers remained a while at Cyprus, from whence they afterward went to Rhodes, and thence to Malta; which name they then assumed. The Knights Templar dispersed themselves throughout all Europe, but still enjoyed princely revenues, and were extremely wealthy.

Vertot says, that Pope Boniface VIII. having engaged in a warm dispute with Philip, king of France, the two Orders, as had too frequently happened before, took opposite sides. The Knights of Malta declared in favor of King Philip, while the Knights Templar espoused the cause of the Pope. This conduct, Philip, partly from a revengeful disposition, and partly from the hope of getting possession of the vast wealth of the Knights, never could forgive ; but formed, thenceforward, the design of suppressing the Order, whenever a proper opportunity should offer. This, however, did not occur, until after the decease of Pope Boniface.

Immediately on the death of that pontiff, the Cardinals assembled to elect his successor; but party disputes ran so high in the conclave, that there seemed no probability of again filling the papal chair very speedily. At length, through the intrigues and machinations of the friends of Philip, the Cardinals were all brought to consent to the election of any priest that he should recommend to them.

This was the darling object the monarch had in view: this being accomplished, he immediately sent for the Archbishop of Bordeaux, whose ambition he knew had no bounds, and who would hesitate at nothing to gratify it; and communicated to him the power he had received of nominating a person to the papal chair, and promising he should be the person, on his engaging to perform six conditions. The Archbishop greedily snatched at the bait, and immediately took an oath on the sacrament to the faithful performance of the conditions. Philip then laid open to him five of the conditions, but reserved the sixth until after the Archbishop's coronation as Pope; which soon took place in consequence of the recommendation of the king to the conclave; and the new Pope took upon himself the name of Clement V.

Vertot goes on to say, that a Templar and a citizen of Beziers, having been apprehended for some crime, and committed together to a dungeon, for want of a priest confessed to each other; that the citizen, having heard the Templar's confession, in order to save his own life, accused the Order to King Philip; charging them, on the authority of what his fellow prisoner had told him, with idolatry, sodomy, robbery and murder; adding that the Knights Templar being secretly Mohammedans, each Knight, on his admission in the Order, was obliged to renounce Jesus Christ, and to spit on the cross in token of his abhorrence of it. Philip, on hearing these accusations, pardoned the citizen, and disclosed to the Pope his sixth condition, which was the suppression of the Order of Knights Templar.

Not only every Knight Templar must know to a certainty the absolute falsehood of these charges, but every unprejudiced reader of Vertot's history must also perceive that the whole of their accusation was the product of Philip's own brain, in order to accomplish his long-wished-for object of suppressing the Order, and getting possession of their vast riches in his dominions. It is therefore, evident that the story of the Templar's confession was all a forgery, and that the citizen was no other than a tool of Philip, who, to insure his own pardon, was prevailed on to make oath of such a confession having been made to him by the Templar.

The historian proceeds to say, that in consequence of this accusation, the Knights Templar in France, and other parts of the Pope's dominions, were imprisoned by his order, and put to the most exquisite tortures, to make them confess themselves guilty. They, however, bore these tortures with the most heroic fortitude, persisting to the last in asserting their own innocence, and that of their Order.

In addition to these proceedings, Pope Clement, in the year 1312, issued his bull for the annihilation of the Order of Knights Templar, which he caused to be published throughout every country in Christendom. He at the same time gave their possessions to the Knights of Malta, which appropriation of the Templar's estates was assented to by most of the sovereigns in Europe; and there is now extant among the English statutes, an act of parliament, whereby, after setting forth that the Order of Templars has been suppressed, their possessions in England are confirmed to the Knights of St. John.

Vertot, however, further says, that in Germany, the historians of that nation relate, that Pope Clement having sent his bull for abolishing the Order, to the Archbishop of Metey, for him to enforce, that prelate summoned all his clergy together, that the publication might be made with greater solemnity; and that they were suddenly surprised by the entry of Wallgruffor Count Sauvage, one of the principals of the Order, attended by twenty other Templars, armed, and in their regular habits.

The Count declared he was not come to do violence to any body, but having heard of the bull against his Order, came to insist that the appeal which they made from that decree to the next council, and the successor of Clement, should be received, read and published. This he pressed so warmly, that the Archbishop, not thinking it proper to refuse men whom he saw armed, complied. He sent the appeal afterward to the Pope, who ordered him to have it examined in a council of his province. Accordingly, a synod was called, and after a lengthy trial, and various formalities which were then observed, the Templars of that province were declared innocent of the crimes charged upon them.

Although the Templars were thus declared innocent, it does not appear that either their possessions or their government, as a distinct order was restored; but that their estates in the German Empire were divided between the Knights of Malta and the Teutonic Knights; to the first of which Orders, many Knights Templar afterward joined themselves. This appears altogether probable from the following circumstances, viz.: It is unquestionable, that the habit of the Knights Templar was originally *white;* but we now observe they distinguish themselves by the same color as the Knights of Malta, viz.: *black;* which change can not be accounted for in any other way than by a union with the Knights of that Order.

MANUAL.

The throne is situated in the east; above is suspended the arms of the Grand Patron, between a banner of the emblems of the Order, and another of the arms of the Grand Master.

On the right of the throne the Deputy Grand Master, and Past Grand Master; or in Subordinate Encampments the Past Grand Commander.

On the left the Grand Prelate and Grand Chancelor.

The Grand Treasurer on the right, and the Grand Register on the left in front.

The Knights, who are entitled to seats above the standards, are so arranged as that there shall be an equal number on each side the throne.

Over the stall of each is a banner of arms or emblems. Next on each side is a standard-bearer, with a banner of sky-blue silk, on which is a cross of Malta in silver, with the motto, *The will of God.*

Next below the standards two experts, one bearing a spear and a shield, and the other a battle-axe. Next to them the sword-bearer, and cross-bearer; then the Knights not in office, concluding with the two stewards, each with his staff.

In the south-west the Senior Warden; in the north-west the Junior Warden.

In the west, between the Warden, a stall for the initiate, supported by the Master of Ceremonies and a herald.

APRONS.

White, with a black border; or black, with a white border. The flap, black, and a skull and cross bones embroidered in silver thereon.

DRESS.

A full suit of black, with a rapier and military hat; a broad black on the right shoulder; across the body to the left side, ornamented with a silver star opposite to the left breast, having seven points.

The Grand Master or Commander, a star of nine points; in the center of the star a cross and serpent of gold, surrounded by a circle, on which is engraved, or enameled, *In Hoc Signo Vinces.*

The following passages of Scripture are occasionally rehearsed in encampments of Knights Templar.

"James, a servant of God and of the Lord Jesus Christ, to the twelve tribes which are scattered abroad, greeting. My brethren, count it all joy when you fall into divers temptations; knowing this, that the trying of your faith worketh patience. But let patience have her perfect work, that ye may be perfect and entire, wanting nothing. If any of you lack wisdom let him ask of God, that giveth to all men liberally, and upbraideth not; and it shall be given him. But let him ask in faith, nothing wavering; for he that wavereth is like a wave of the sea, driven with the wind, and tossed. For let not that man think that he shall receive any thing of the Lord. A double minded man is unstable in all his ways. Let the brother of low degree rejoice in that he is exalted. If any man among you seem to be religious, and bridleth not his tongue, but deceiveth his own heart, that man's religion is vain. Pure religion, and undefiled before God and the Father, is this, To visit the fatherless and widows in their affliction, and to keep himself unspotted from the world."

EXHORTATION.

1. Let the brother of low degree rejoice in that he is exalted.

2. Come unto me all ye that labor and are heavy laden, and I will give you rest.

3. Christ suffered for us, leaving us an example that we should follow his steps.

4. For we were as sheep going astray, but now are we returned to the shepherd and bishop of our souls.

5. If our brother or sister be naked, and destitute of daily food, and one of you say, Depart in peace, be ye warmed and filled, and ye give them not of those things which are needful for the body, what doth it profit?

6. To do good and to communicate forget not, for with such sacrifices God is well pleased.

7. May he who is able send you forth into the world thoroughly furnished for every good work, keep you from falling into vice and error, improve, strengthen, establish and perfect you.

Then one of the twelve, called Judas Iscariot, went unto the chief priests, and said unto them, What will ye give me, and I will deliver him unto you? And they covenanted with him for thirty pieces of silver. And from that time he sought opportunity to betray him. Now, the first day of the feast of unleavened bread, the disciples came to Jesus, saying unto him, Where wilt thou that we prepare for thee to eat the passover? And he said, Go into the city to such a man, and say unto him, The master saith, My time is at hand; I will keep the passover at thy house with my disciples. And the disciples did as Jesus had appointed them. And they made ready the passover. Now when the even was come, he sat down with the twelve. And as they did eat, he said, Verily I say unto you, that one of you shall betray me. And they were exceeding sorrowful, and began every one of them to say unto him, Lord, is it I? Add he answered and said, He that dippeth his hand with me in the dish, the same shall betray me. The son of man goeth, as it is written of him; but wo unto that man by whom the son of man is betrayed!

It had been good for that man if he had not been born. Then Judas, which betrayed him, answered and said, Master, is it I? He said unto him, Thou hast said.—*Matt.* xxvi: 14–25.

Then cometh Jesus with them unto a place called Gethsemane, and saith unto the disciples, Sit ye here, while I go and pray yonder. And he took with him Peter and the two sons of Zebedee, and began to be sorrowful and very heavy. Then saith he unto them, My soul is exceeding sorrowful, even unto death: tarry ye here, and watch with me. And he went a little further, and fell on his face, and prayed, saying, O my Father, if it be possible, let this cup pass from me; nevertheless, not as I will, but as thou wilt. And he cometh unto the disciples, and findeth them asleep, and saith unto Peter, What! could ye not watch with me one hour? Watch and pray, that ye enter not into temptation: the spirit indeed is willing, but the flesh is weak. He went away again the second time, and prayed, saying, O my Father, if this cup may not pass away from me, except I drink it, thy will be done. And he came and found them asleep again; for their eyes were heavy. And he left them, and went away again, and prayed the third time, saying the same words. Then cometh he to his disciples, and saith unto them, Sleep on now, and take your rest: behold, the hour is at hand, and the son of man is betrayed into the hands of sinners. Rise, let us be going: behold, he is at hand that doth betray me. And while he yet spake, lo, Judas, one of the twelve, came, and with him a great multitude, with swords and staves, from the chief priests and elders of the people. Now he that betrayed him gave them a sign, saying, Whomsoever I shall kiss, that same is he: hold him fast. And forthwith he came to Jesus, and said, Hail Master; and kissed him.—*Matt.* xxvi: 36–49.

When Pilate saw that he could prevail nothing, but that rather a tumult was made, he took water, and washed his hands before the multitude, saying, I am innocent of the blood of this just person; see ye to it. Then answered all the people and said, His blood be upon us, and our children. Then released he Barabbas unto them: and when he had scourged Jesus, he delivered him to be crucified. Then the soldiers of the governor took Jesus into the common hall, and gathered unto him the whole band of soldiers. And they stripped him, and put on him a scarlet robe. And when they had platted a crown of thorns they put it upon his head, and a reed in his right hand; and they bowed the knee before him, and mocked him, saying, Hail, king of the Jews! And they spit upon him, and took the reed and smote him on the head. And after that they had mocked him, they took the robe off from him, and put his own raiment on him, and led him away to crucify him. And as they came out they found a man of Cyrene, Simon by name: him they compelled to bear his cross. And when they were come unto a place called Golgotha, that is to say, A place of a scull, they gave him vinegar to drink, mingled with gall; and when he had tasted thereof he would not drink. And they crucified him, and parted his garments, casting lots: that it might be fulfilled which was spoken by the prophet, They parted my garments among them, and upon my vesture did they cast lots. And, sitting down, they watched him there; and set up over his head his accusation written, THIS IS JESUS THE KING OF THE JEWS.—*Matt.* xxvii: 24–38.

OLD HUNDRED L. M.

2. Break off your tears, ye saints, and tell
   How high our great deliv'rer reigns;
Sing how he spoil'd the hosts of hell,
   And led the monster, Death, in chains.

3. Say, "live for ever glorious King,
   Born to redeem, and strong to save,"
Then ask—"O Death! where is thy sting?"
   "And where's thy victory?" boasting grave.

And in those days Peter stood up in the midst of the disciples, and said, (the number of the names together were about an hundred and twenty,) men and brethren, this Scripture must needs have been fulfilled, which the Holy Ghost by the mouth of David, spake before concerning Judas, which was guide to them that took Jesus. For he was numbered with us, and had obtained part of this ministry. Now this man purchased a field with the reward of iniquity; and falling headlong he burst asunder in the midst, and all his bowels gushed out. And it was known unto all the dwellers at Jerusalem; insomuch as that field is called in their proper tongue, Aceldama, that is to say, The field of blood. For it is written in the book of Psalms, Let his habitation be desolate, and let no man dwell therein: and his bishopric let another take. Wherefore, of these men which have companied with us all the time, that the Lord Jesus went in and out among us, beginning from the baptism of John, unto that same day that he was taken up from us, must one be ordained to be a witness with us of his resurrection. And they appointed two, Joseph, called Barsabas, who was surnamed Justus, and Matthias. And they prayed, and said, Thou, Lord, which knowest the hearts of all men, shew whether of these two thou hast chosen, that he may take part of this ministry and apostleship, from which Judas by transgression fell, that he might go to his own place. And they gave forth their lots; and the lot fell upon Matthias; and he was numbered with the eleven apostles.—*Acts* i:15–26.

Finally my brethren, be strong in the Lord, and in the power of his might.

Put on the *whole armor* of God, that ye may be able to stand against the wiles of the devil.

For we wrestle not against flesh and blood, but against principalities and powers, against the rulers of the darkness of the world, against spiritual wickedness in high places.

Wherefore, take unto you the whole armor of God, that ye may be able to withstand in the evil day, and having done all, *to stand.*

Stand therefore having your loins girt about with truth;

And having on the breast-plate of righteousness;

And your feet shod with the preparation of the Gospel of peace;

Above all taking the shield of faith, wherewith you shall be able to quench the fiery darts of the wicked;

And take the helmet of Salvation, and the sword of the Spirit, which is the word of God.—*Eph.* vi. 10–17.

THE ORDER

OF

KNIGHTS OF MALTA.

Knights of Malta.

CHAPTER XX.

KNIGHTS OF MALTA.

THE following passages of Scripture are occasionally rehearsed in encampments of Knights of Malta.

And when they were escaped, then they knew that the island was called Melita. And the barbarous people shewed us no little kindness; for they kindled a fire, and received us every one, because of the present rain, and because of the cold. And when Paul had gathered a bundle of sticks, and laid them on the fire, there came a viper out of the heat, and fastened on his hand. And when the barbarians saw the venomous beast hang on his hand, they said among themselves, No doubt this man is a murderer, whom, though he hath escaped the sea, yet vengeance suffereth not to live. And he shook off the beast into the fire, and felt no harm. Howbeit they looked when he should have swollen, or fallen down dead suddenly; but after they had looked a great while, and saw no harm come to him, they changed their minds, and said that he was a god.—*Acts* xxviii: 1–6.

And Pilate wrote a title, and put it on the cross. And the writing was, JESUS OF NAZARETH, THE KING OF THE JEWS.—*St. John* xix: 19.

But Thomas, one of the twelve, called Didymus, was not with them when Jesus came. The other disciples, therefore, said unto him, We have seen the Lord. But he said unto them, Except I shall see in his hands the print of the nails, and put my finger into the print of the nails, and thrust my hand into his side, I will not believe. And after eight days, again his disciples were within, and Thomas with them. Then came Jesus, the doors being shut, and stood in the midst, and said, Peace be unto you. Then saith he to Thomas, Reach hither thy finger, and behold my hands; and reach hither thy hand, and thrust it into my side; and be not faithless, but believing. And Thomas answered and said unto him, My Lord and my God.—*John* xx: 24–28.

CHARGE TO A NEWLY CREATED SIR KNIGHT TEMPLAR AND KNIGHT OF MALTA.

This charge is from a later author; there was none in the Monitor. It is taken from Cross.

SIR KNIGHT:—Having passed through the several degrees and honorary distinctions of our ancient and honorable institution—in your admission to the tesselated Masonic ground floor—your ascent into the middle chamber—your entrance to the unfinished *sanctum sanctorum*—your regularly passing the several gates of the temple—induction to the *oriental chair*, witnessing the completion and dedication of that superb model of excellence, the *Temple*, which has immortalized the names of our ancient Grand Masters, and the justly celebrated craftsmen:—Having wrought in the ruins of the first Temple, and from its sacred *Royal Arch* brought to light incalculable treasures and advantages to the Craft—Having duly studied into the way and manner of their concealment; also having been engaged in the hazardous enterprise of traversing an enemy's dominions, and there convincing a foreign prince that *truth* is great and will prevail—therefore you are now admitted to a participation of those labors which are to effect the erection of a Temple more glorious than the first, even that beauteous Temple of *Holiness and Innocence*, whose pillars are *Charity*, *Mercy* and *Justice*, the foundation of which is in the breast of every one, who has tasted that the Lord is gracious; to whom coming as unto a living *stone*, disallowed indeed of men, but chosen of God and precious, even that hope which is an anchor to the soul both sure and steadfast, that demonstrates the existence of the soul, and animates us with the certainty of a glorious immortality.

And now, Sir Knight, we bid you welcome to all those rights and privileges, even to that disinterested friendship, and unbounded hospitality which ever has, and we hope and trust ever will continue to adorn, distinguish, and characterize this noble Order.

It will henceforth become your duty as well as inclination, to assist, protect, and befriend, the weary way-worn traveler who finds the hights of fortune inaccessible, and the thorny paths of life broken, adverse, and forlorn; to succor, defend, and protect *innocence*, the *distressed*, and *helpless*, ever standing forth as a champion to espouse the cause of the *Christian Religion*.

You are to inculcate, enforce, and practice *virtue;* and amid all the temptations which surround you, never to be drawn aside from the path of duty, or forgetful of those due guards and pass-words which are necessary to be had in perpetual remembrance; and while one hand is wielding the sure defense for your Companion in danger, let the other grasp the mystic Trowel, and widely diffuse the genuine cement of Brotherly Love and Friendship.

Should calumny assail the character of a Brother Sir Knight, recollect that you are to step forth and vindicate his good name, and assist him on all necessary occasions. Should assailants ever attempt your honor, interest, or happiness, remember, also, at the same time, you have the counsel and support of your brethren, whose mystic words, combining the virtues of Faith, Hope, and Charity, with *Justice*, *Fortitude* and *Mercy*, will leap from their scabbards in defense of your just rights, and insure you a glorious triumph over all your enemies.

On this occasion permit me, Sir Knight, to remind you of our mutual engagements, our reciprocal ties; for whatever may be your situation or rank in life, on close examination, you will find those in similar stations, who have dignified themselves and been useful to mankind. Whether, therefore, you are placed upon the highest pinnacle of worldly grandeur, and distinctly seen to glitter from afar; or glide more securely in the humble vale of obscurity, unnoticed save by a few; it matters not, for a few rolling suns will close the scene, when nought but holiness will serve as a sure pass-word to gain admission into that REST prepared from the foundation of the world. You are therefore called upon to discharge all your duties with fidelity and patience, whether in the *field*, in the *Senate*, on the *Bench*, at the *Bar*, or at the *Holy Altar*.

If you see a Brother bending under the cross of adversity and disappointment, look not idly on, neither pass by on the other side, but fly to his relief. If he be deceived, tell him the *Truth;* if he be calumniated, vindicate his cause; for, although in some instances, he may have erred, still recollect that indiscretion in him should never destroy humanity in you.

Finally, Sir Knights, as *memento mori* is deeply engraved on all sublunary enjoyments, let us ever be found in the habiliments of righteousness, traversing the straight path of rectitude, virtue, and true holiness; so that having discharged our duty here below, performed the *pilgrimage of life*, burst the *bands of mortality*, passed over the *Jordan of death*, and safely landed on the broad shore of eternity—there, in the presence of myriads of attending angels, we may be greeted as brethren, and received into the widely extended arms of the blessed EMANUEL, and for ever made to participate in his Heavenly Kingdom.

There is no form of constituting Encampments and installing officers in the Monitor, and we can not use those in other authors without a violation of copyright.

A PRACTICAL SYNOPSIS

OF

MASONIC LAW AND USAGE.

FOR GENERAL USE

BY ROB MORRIS,

MASONIC AUTHOR AND LECTURER

PREFATORY REMARKS.

"THE system of Masonic law has little of the republican or democratic spirit about it. All its greater principles (well termed in Masonic parlance *landmarks*) and most of the minor details of its governmental polity, are provided to our hands as they were provided to our fathers' hands ages since, in the traditions and publications of the Order. Of all the wretched theories into which even some learned in the economy of Masonic government have been misled, none probably have been more pernicious in their results than that assumption which places the original and sole authority of Masonic government *in the consent of the governed.* This error strikes a blow at the very base of the structure on which all government and order rests among men, *the inviolable sanctity of law.* It substitutes popular caprice for the authority of antiquity, and, perhaps, it is not too much to add, in view of the high and mighty purposes for which the Masonic institution was originally set up, *the authority of God.* It writes upon the sand of the wave-washed sea-shore the laws which ought to be carved in the rock of eternal justice."*

Under these impressions, I have devoted my attention in this work, less to the local and ephemeral legislation of modern Grand Lodges than to those fragments of Masonic law, ancient and universal, which remain to us in the "Constitutions," "Charges," etc., happily reserved from the ravages of time. In these there is space enough to set up the posts and pillars of the Masonic structure, and to erect an edifice which shall be recognized by the intelligent eyes of Masons every where, and shall stand until the last great purpose for

* Altered from a passage in a late Discourse upon "Reverence for Law," by Rev. J. P. Safford, D. D.

which the Institution was originally designed shall be accomplished. The authority for each of these Masonic decisions is derived directly or indirectly from the "Constitutions" and "Charges," accessible in these latter days to every seeker for Masonic light. It matters but little to the present writer whether they are found to agree with the local practices in all the thirty-six Grand Lodge jurisdictions of the United States or not.

But it matters much to the reader, earnestly bent upon pursuing the science of Masonry, according to ancient and universal principles, that he finds discrepancies, sometimes fundamental in their nature, in the usages of the Craft around him. It is not a little disheartening to the conscientious student of Masonry to discover that his covenant with the Grand Lodge, and his covenant with the Craft universal, are not identical. This has startled, discouraged, disgusted many a young and zealous Brother who, but for this, had attained to be a bright light in the Masonic Society.

The first duty of the reader of this Synopsis, is to obey the edicts of his Grand Lodge. Right or wrong, his very existence as a Mason hangs upon obedience to the powers immediately set above him. Failure in this must infallibly bring down *expulsion* which, as a Masonic death, ends all. Tho one unpardonable crime in a Mason is *contumacy*, or disobedience.

But Grand Lodges are easily swayed, and most easily swayed *in the right direction*. There are so many lights available at the present time—the argument irrefragible ("it is opposed to the Masonic Landmarks,") can be hurled from so many engines—from books, from periodicals, from intelligent lecturers, from large and increasing usage—that the zealous and learned Brother, conscientiously opposed to an innovation adopted by the Grand Lodge which governs him, has it almost in his own power to control that body and effect a change. My personal observations have given me numerous instances to confirm this most encouraging opinion and reduce it to a certainty.

Then let the ardent and unselfish Brother take courage. Perusing these "decisions" which, indeed, are not mine but those of thousands and of tens of thousands, let him compare them one by one with the ancient law to which I, in common with all the Craft, humbly bend, and if found accordant therewith, let him be the vehicle of their introduction into the practice of his own Grand Lodge. Let him be a co-laborer with those thousands and tens of thousands who are already enjoying some of the sweets of a victory, accomplished under the auspices of "time, patience, and perseverance," a band whose numbers are increasing day by day, and with whom "the only contention is that noble contention, or rather emulation, of who best can work and best agree."

To make the alphabet as nearly complete as possible, I have added a few topics, such as Adoption, etc., etc., which are not so directly connected with the Masonic system as some others, but which it is hoped the reader will find instructive.

In continuation of this Synopsis, the reader is advised to use the following works: Morris's Code of Masonic Law; Hubbard's Decisions of Masonic Questions; Mackey's Principles of Masonic Law; C. W. Moore's Decisions of Masonic Questions, as scattered through the volumes of The Freemason's Magazine, Boston; and Mackey's Lexicon of Freemasonry. Dr. George Oliver has recently published a work upon Masonic Jurisprudence, which I have not seen, but take it for granted it is of equal weight with his other valuable publications.

The reader's devoted Brother,

ROB MORRIS.

LOUISVILLE, KY., *January* 1, 1859.

TO

WORS. BRO. ALBERT G. HODGES,

OF

FRANKFORT, KENTUCKY;

A MASON WHOSE GRIP AND WORD HAVE LIFTED AND CHEERED ME IN MORE THAN ONE DESPONDING HOUR,

THIS SYNOPSIS OF

MASONIC LAW AND USAGE

IS

FRATERNALLY DEDICATED.

A PRACTICAL SYNOPSIS

OF

MASONIC LAW AND USAGE.

ADOPTION.

(See also Androgynous; Eastern Star; Females; Good Samaritan; Heroine of Jericho; Holy Virgin; Mason's Daughter.)

Adoptive Masonry is that system by which it is proposed to secure the attachment of females to the Masonic institution, and to afford them some means, however partial or imperfect, of recognizing and being recognized by Masons, when otherwise strangers. There are many orders or degrees of Adoptive Masonry in vogue.

The philosophy of Adoptive Masonry lies in this, that the worthy and distressed widow and orphan daughter of a Master Mason are entitled, by the very covenant of Symbolical Masonry, to the same measure of protection and relief as the Master Mason himself. It would seem to follow then that some means should be communicated to such females by which they may make their claims good and enjoy the valuable privileges to which their relationship entitles them.

The principal Orders or Degrees of Adoptive Masonry practiced in the United States are named in the parenthesis in the caption. The most popular and most consistent of them all is *The Eastern Star*, which is communicated under proper precautions to the wives, widows, sisters and daughters of worthy Master Masons.

There is no special privilege, however, inherent in any of these Orders of Adoptive Masonry; in none of them is it proposed to bring females nearer to Masonry, or to communicate any of its secrets to them; or to extend its benefits more abundantly to them. The sole design is, as before stated, to enable them to secure privileges already, by their relationship to Master Masons, their due, and thus induce them the more highly to prize a system from the inner mysteries of which they, from their very sex, are for ever debarred.

All the orders or degrees of Adoptive Masonry, like those of Capitular and Cryptic Masonry, are modern; none of them exceeding a century in age.

There is no general head or government to the orders of Adoptive Masonry. Every person who communicates them varies their ceremonies, obligations, etc., to his own taste; consequently, with the exception of one (*The Eastern Star*), they possess, at present, but little value as a means of recognition; being deficient in *universality*, the very essence of a Masonic system.

ADULTERY.

(See also Discipline; Females; Fornication.)

There is no offense in the Masonic code treated more severely than unlawful carnal connexion with the female relation of a Mason. It is considered well-nigh unpardonable. No degree of solicitation, however urgent on the part of the one; no circumstances of temptation, however great, on the part of the other; and no after repentance, however sincere, are admitted in plea. The penalty is *expulsion*, and the door of return to the Order closed for ever. Adultery or fornication with another party, however, stands upon the same footing as other offenses enumerated in the Decalogue.

AFFILIATION.

(See also Discipline; Non-affiliation; Withdrawals.)

The connection between the Master Mason and his Lodge, so vitally important to his Masonic usefulness and character, and so urgently enjoined in the "Ancient Charges," is denominated *affiliation*. It is a crying evil of the present day that thousands of brethren have been allowed to withdraw from the fold provided for them in the constitutions of Masonry, and to encumber its workings with almost insurmountable difficulties.

Affiliation with the Lodge should be encouraged by every

honorable means, and none should be allowed to withdraw from it save for the laudable purpose of uniting immediately with other Lodges. Non-affiliated Masons should not be encouraged in their condition of withdrawal; or allowed to visit the Lodge more than once or twice: or admitted under any circumstances into the public celebrations, festivals, funerals, etc., of the Order; or aided from the treasury of the Lodge; or buried with Masonic honors; or introduced to Masons as brothers.

It is lawful and proper to solicit non-affiliating Masons to unite with the Lodge.

The fees of affiliation should be set at a price merely nominal (say $1 or $2) to allure the non-affiliating Masons to return to the fold.

The following form of petition for affiliation is appropriate:

"To the Master, Wardens and Brethren of ——— Lodge, No. —— ——: The undersigned. a regular Master Mason, late a member of ——— Lodge, No. ——, at ——— ——, respectfully prays to become a member of your Lodge. If his petition is granted, he pledges himself to a cheerful acquiescence in the By-laws and regulations of the Lodge.

(Signed) —— ———.

Recommended by —— ———."

This paper, if accepted, should be carefully preserved by the Secretary and filed in the Archives of the Lodge.

A petition for affiliation, if accepted by the Lodge, is referred to a committee, who are permitted the term of one month to make suitable inquiries as to character, etc., and report their conclusions to the Lodge. A ballot is then spread, and by unanimous vote the applicant is admitted. If one or more black balls appear, the applicant is rejected.

The rejection of a petition for affiliation, like that of a petition for initiation, removes the subject beyond the control of the Lodge for a certain period, designated by the Grand Lodge. This is usually six or twelve months. In some jurisdictions no period is set, and then the petition can be renewed at every meeting, if thought proper.

The reception of an Entered Apprentice or Fellow-craft from another Lodge is not termed *affiliation*, although, like that, it demands an unanimous vote of the Lodge. It is rather to be considered in the light of *accepting unfinished work from another Lodge*, and involves the pledge, if the party is qualified and proves worthy, to advance him in due time.

None but Master Masons regularly affiliated can take any part in balloting, or in the government of the Lodge. Exceptions to this rule, however, may be found in the Canadian Lodges, and a portion of the Lodges in Kentucky; in which, strangely enough, Entered Apprentices and Fellow-crafts are allowed a ballot and a vote. Yet even there they are not deemed *affiliated* Masons, can not vote in the election of officers, share in the benefits of the Lodge treasury, visit the Grand Lodge, or receive Masonic burial.

For the system of Honorary Affiliation see *Honorary* and *Membership*.

ALMSGIVING.

(See Charity, etc.)

The bounties of Masons are due to all suffering creatures whom they may encounter, but more especially to Brother Masons. See the caption *Relief*, in the Entered Apprentice's Lecture.

ANDROGYNOUS.

(See also Adoption; Eastern Star; Good Samaritan: Heroine of Jericho; Holy Virgin; Mason's Daughter.

The theory of Androgynous or Adoptive Masonry is this,—to afford to certain classes of females, entitled by the Masonic constitutions to the protection and aid of the Order, some means whereby they may *know and be known* by Masons wherever met, and thus claim their privileges. As no female can lawfully be entrusted with the secrets of Symbolical Masonry, other means of recognition have been invented, the names of which appear in the caption.

That these orders or degrees of Androgynous Masonry have thus far failed in accomplishing so great and desirable a result, is no argument against their use; nor is the opposition which the whole system is encountering in certain quarters a matter of fundamental importance. This opposition is but trifling compared with that which Royal Arch Masonry, now so popular, encountered in the first fifty years of its establishment; and the friends of Adoptive Masonry are quite as numerous and influential as its opponents. While the fact remains that *there is an inherent privilege in females without the means of enjoying it*, attempts will continue to be made to remove the discrepancy.

Modern as Androgynous Masonry is, it is at least as old as Royal Arch or Capitular Masonry, and considerably older than other Masonic systems which are sharing largely in the favor of the Craft.

APPEAL.

(See Discipline.)

In all cases of Masonic discipline an appeal to the Grand Lodge may be taken against the action of the Lodge, either by the accused or by one of the members. In case of an appeal the Lodge, through its Secretary, must forward to the Grand Secretary a certified copy of all the evidence and papers used in the course of the trial. The original papers are to be filed in the archives of the Subordinate Lodge. The punishment of a Brother dates from the hour of his conviction; nor does the appeal in itself give him standing as a Mason. The Grand Lodge may restore him to Masonry, but until they do so his sentence is recorded against him. A restoration by the Grand Lodge does not imply a restoration to *membership*, but to the general (limited) privileges of a demitted Mason. A reversal of the whole proceedings and order for a new trial, however, restores the accused to membership, placing him exactly where he was before trial.

APPRENTICES.

(See also Crafts; Entered Apprentices; Materials; Religion.)

A Brother having been initiated regularly into the first degree of Masonry, is styled an *Apprentice* or *Entered Apprentice*. By the philosophy of the Masonic Institution, he is covenanted to preserve its secrets, and charged to be moral and charitable. It is necessary he should profess belief in Deity, before he can be initiated. The principal tenets expounded to him, are Brotherly Love, Relief and

Truth; the cardinal virtues are Temperance, Fortitude, Prudence and Justice. (See those captions in the Entered Apprentice's Lecture.) He is required to serve the Order, personified in its executive head, the Master, with Freedom, Fervency and Zeal.

An Apprentice is encouraged to visit his Lodge at every meeting, it being understood that it shall be opened in the first degree for his accommodation, but he is charged not to slight his necessary avocations for that purpose, as they are by no means to be neglected. An Apprentice can not travel as such, nor visit other Lodges than his own, except by special courtesy, and then avouched by some one who has set with him in his own. He is not allowed to enter into arguments with non-masons upon the topics of Masonry, but is encouraged to study to acquire a knowledge of the art by the assurance that he will find the brethren as ready to impart information, as he will be to receive it.

An Apprentice is not allowed the benefits of the Masonic treasury; nor to be interred with the honors of the Order. Neither can he take any part in the ceremonials of Masonic interment, the funeral Lodge and procession, being opened in *the third* degree only. The female relatives of an Apprentice have no claim as such to the protection and aid of the Fraternity. He has no vote in the proceedings of the Lodge, nor can he take any part in debate. An exception to the rule of voting, however, is found in the Canadian Lodges, and in some of the Lodges in Kentucky, wherein Apprentices are allowed a vote and voice in their own degree.

No dues are charged to Apprentices, nor are the dues, ordinary or extraordinary of the Lodge, exacted of them. The exception named above in Kentucky, applies however, to this rule.

An Apprentice may be tried upon regular charges for any offense against law, morals or good behavior, and punished accordingly. The trial in such a case will be had before a committee of the Lodge, the evidence, etc., being taken in presence of the accused, or it may be conducted in a Lodge of Entered Apprentices if preferred, but the final decision is had in the Masters' Lodge, where he can not enter. The offense of divulging Masonic secrets, is peculiarly heinous in an Apprentice.

An Apprentice changing his residence, and desiring to attach himself to a Lodge contiguous, may, by order of his former Lodge, have a certificate of his standing and good conduct, with a recommendation. (See *non-affiliation* for form of certificate.)

An Apprentice can not hold office in the Lodge, nor serve upon a committee, nor even fill an official station temporarily. He may (and ought) to peruse the books and periodicals in the Lodge library, thus qualifying himself by an acquaintance with the history, philosophy, and jurisprudence of Masonry, for after places of honor and usefulness.

No person can lawfully receive the degree of Entered Apprentice, save one who is mentally, morally, and physically *perfect*, according to the ancient Masonic meaning of the term. (See *Materials*.)

The theory of the First Degree is *Morality*.

ARCHIVES.

(See also Secretary.)

Every document of the least value, belonging to the Lodge, should be folded to a convenient size, uniform with the rest, indorsed on the back as to contents and date, placed in a bundle of the same department and year, and carefully preserved by the Secretary, in a locked receptacle. Of this sort are all petitions for initiation, membership or withdrawals; all letters from corresponding Lodges, or from the Grand Lodge, or from individuals upon Masonic or business subjects; all evidence taken under authority of the Lodge in trial; the blot copies of minutes as kept by the Secretary; all receipts given the Secretary by the Treasurer for moneys paid him, in accordance with his stated or extraordinary duties; and all the books and records of the Lodge.

The Secretary under the instructions of the Master, is the custodian or keeper of the Archives, and is responsible to the Lodge for the preservation of the same while in his charge, as well as for their faithful delivery to his successor when his term of service shall expire.

The Archives of a Lodge are often of great historical value, not only to Freemasons, but to those who compose the history of nations. For the purpose therefore, of securing them against conflagration and the assaults of thieves, a commodious iron closet should be at the command of the Secretary, in which they may be safely stored.

ASSEMBLAGES.

(See also Communications; Meetings.)

The stated Assemblages of Masons, that is those meetings required by the By-laws, and which Master Masons particularly, are regularly bound to attend, should not occur oftener than twice a month in town, or once a month in country Lodges. More frequent meetings are burdensome upon the feeble, the aged, and those immersed in business avocations; three classes of individuals in which the most useful members are sometimes found, and if persisted in, will eventually drive them from active participation in the work of the Lodge. Many a Lodge have been ruined in the attempt to maintain weekly meetings. There is little demand for more than monthly stated meetings. The collection of dues, passing upon accounts, examining questions of discipline, and receiving and acting upon petitions, which are about the only classes of business necessary to be performed in *stated* meetings, requires but a two hours' session monthly. Other matters, such as conferring degrees, interring the dead, instructing the brethren, etc., are best performed at *called* meetings, which may be made as frequent as a quorum of eight Masons with the Master or a Warden to preside, can be gathered together.

Informal assemblies of brethren result in no good, and should be discountenanced. They lead to cabals and caucuses, and speedily break down the perfect harmony, without which there can be no genuine Masonry. There is no Masonic business which can not be done "in a Lodge formed." The instruction of the younger brethren, and the dispensations of charity, do not come under this rule.

Assemblages for funeral purposes, if met within a reasonable distance of the Lodge, are controlled under the same rule; a Charter, a Master, the Wardens; a Secretary for recording, and an open Lodge being the essentials of all regular Masonic gatherings. But in the absence of a Lodge organization, or at a distance too great for such formality, a proper number of brethren, working in the spirit of seriousness and prudence may convene, and with the solemn rites of Masons, lay "dust to dust." In some jurisdictions, however, no public assemblage, not even for Masonic obsequies, can be held without a dispensation from an officer of the Grand Lodge.

ASSISTANCE.

(See Charity, etc.)

To help, aid and assist, a worthy distressed brother, his widow and orphan children, is as well a Masonic privilege, as a covenanted duty. Whatever derelictions of duty or shortcomings, are chargeable upon the Masonic brotherhood, this is not one, to neglect the sacred calls of charity. A lodge or an individual Mason, regularly accused of a spirit of parsimony, in refusing such an appeal, would meet with little countenance from his brethren.

BALLOTING.

(See Election; Voting.)

Voting by balls, counters, or slips, is styled *balloting.* It is one of the most serious acts of the Lodge, and should be performed under all the sanctities of the Masonic covenant. The three higher officers of the Lodge take joint possession of the ballot-box, and have special care that the result of the ballot is announced, while the Master sees that the views of the brethren who have voted are recorded correctly.

The ballot is strictly secret, it being a misdemeanor for any member to announce his intention before voting, or the manner of his voting after the ball is cast. Many and serious evils have resulted to Masonry from a neglect of this provision. The ballot-box should be so arranged as to compel the utmost secresy in dropping the balls, and a plan for collecting the balls should be adopted which will prevent too-inquisitive brethren (if such are present) from acquiring any knowledge beyond that of their own deposit.

Each member is responsible to his own conscience alone for the manner of his vote.

Each member must vote upon every question before the Lodge, unless excused by vote of the Lodge.

The ordinary usage, upon an application for initiation, is that when an applicant is rejected by *one ballot only*, a second ballot is taken without debate or delay. But if two or more black balls appear, the balloting ceases, and can *never* be resumed upon that application. A period specified in the Constitution of the Grand Lodge (usually twelve months) having elapsed, *a new application* may be presented by the same party, which takes the same direction as the former.

The ballot-box should be prepared with anxious reference to secresy. The ballots used may conveniently be arranged into *balls* and *cubes*, the former colored white, the latter black. The box should be lined with cloth.

BENEVOLENCE.

(See Charity, etc.)

This genial virtue is inculcated in Masonic lectures, and impressed by the Masonic ceremonial. Every Mason of fame and note has illustrated it in his walk and conversation, until the world has learned to consider Freemasonry as the most benevolent institution on earth.

BLASPHEMY.

(See Discipline.)

Among the highest offenses against the Masonic code, that of blasphemy, or avowed disrespect to the name of Deity, is ranked. The candidate having upon his first entrance into the Order declared *his trust* to be *in God*, blasphemy stamps him a hypocrite, or implies that his trust is removed; in either case he is a proper subject for Masonic discipline. The term "irreligious libertine," used in the Ancient Charges, implies an avowed scoffer at religion; such an one is forbidden in the Masonic covenants to be admitted to the Order.

There is no excuse for confirmed blasphemy, as there is no temptation alluring a person to commit it.

BY-LAWS.

(See Constitutions, Edicts, and Rules.)

That code of Masonic jurisprudence which, containing

many of the regulations of the Grand Lodge and of the ancient constitutions of Masonry, is extended to embrace all the minor details of government and discipline of a Subordinate Lodge, so far as they can be reduced to writing, is called the *By-laws.* These should be full, explicit, systematically arranged into Chapters and Sections, printed in convenient size, and tasteful to the eye, and afforded to the members and visitors in ample quantities.

The Lodge should adopt a form of By-laws only after careful and protracted examination and consideration. They should be submitted to the judgment of experienced Masons in other Lodges, and, once adopted, remain forever unchanged, save in local particulars. Obedience to the By-laws is enforced upon the members by the utmost sanctity of the Masonic covenant.

Until the Grand Lodge has examined and approved the By-laws of a Lodge, they are not to be considered as permanently adopted, and should not be published. A Lodge working Under Dispensation should not print its By-laws.

The topics which must be treated in a perfect form of By-laws are the following:

The Lodge; its title, warrant and meetings. *The Membership;* the members, their duties. *The Officers;* their election, installation and duties. *Petitions;* for initiation, membership, advancement, demit, diploma, charity, appeal. Action on petitions. *Financials;* fees, charity, wages, management of the funds. *Committees;* standing, special. *Discipline;* offenses, trials, penalties, appeals. *Amendments.*

It is not meant to imply, however, that no other topics are admissible. A practical exhibit of the constitution and edicts of the Grand Lodge and of the "Ancient Charges," or a collection of appropriate Masonic Songs, an approved form of Funeral Service, a catalogue of the officers and members of the Lodge since the period of its organization, and a condensed history of the Lodge itself, as exhibited in its own records, these are all appropriate to a place in, or as an appendix to the By-laws. A set of By-laws thus enlarged and dignified, reflects infinite credit upon the Lodge whose name they bear.

Several Grand Lodges, Kentucky being the first, have framed standard forms of By-laws, as models for the use of their Subordinates. This is praise-worthy. There is so little in the workings of one Lodge that differs from another, that nineteen-twentieths of the text of the By-laws in 4500 Lodges might be stereotyped, much to the advantage of the whole.

A code of By-laws well systematized, whatever be the amount of matter they contain, is convenient for use, and no complaint will ever arise as to their length or bulk. While on the contrary, a code "without form," as the majority are, is inconvenient for use, no matter how brief, and it will never command the respect of the members, or of the world.

It is the duty of the Stewards (or Tyler) to place a copy of the By-laws on every seat, prior to opening the Lodge. A copy should be presented to each newly initiated Brother. Lodges in correspondence with each other, should exchange copies of their By-laws respectively. A traveling Brother should carry a copy of the By-laws of the Lodge of which he is a member, to exhibit to examining Committees, at the doors of the various Lodges he may desire to visit.

Lodges should not legislate in their By-laws against any practice which is legalized by the laws of the State. The sale or moderate use of ardent spirits, the traffic in lottery tickets, enlisting in the army, etc., where legalized as above, should not be denounced by Masonic regulations. Neither must the By-laws of Lodges discriminate in regard to sectarian creeds and faith. To legislate against belief in Universalism, Mormonism, Spiritualism, etc., is not in the prerogative of Masonic Lodges, Grand or Subordinate.

An applicant for initiation, also a visitor, has a right to demand a perusal of the By-laws of the Lodge.

The following is a "Model Form of By-laws," prepared by the author of this Appendix, and first published in 1854. It is the earliest pattern of By-laws ever promulgated, and has been so often pronounced the best as to justify its insertion here entire.

By-Laws.

CHAPTER I.

THE LODGE.

Its Title, Warrant and Meetings.

SEC. 1.—*The Title of the Lodge.*

The title of this Lodge shall be ——— ——— No. ——.

SEC. 2.—*The Warrant of the Lodge.*

The Warrant of this Lodge is a charter granted on the —— day of ———, A. D. ——, A. L. ——, by the Most Worshipful Grand Lodge of ————————, to whose constitutional rules and edicts the most implicit respect and obedience shall ever be paid by its members. The jurisdiction of this Lodge extends on each side of it to a point equidistant to the nearest Lodges, respectively.

SEC. 3.—*The Meetings of the Lodge.*

The meetings of this Lodge shall be either stated, festival, or called. The *stated meetings* shall be held on the ——— ——— of each month. The hour of meeting from March 21st to September 22d, inclusive, shall be 7½ o'clock; and from September 22d to March 21st, at 6 o'clock, P. M. The hour of closing shall be 10 P. M. throughout the year.

The order of business, at every stated meeting of the Lodge, shall be as follows, subject, however, to be changed at any time, or temporarily dispensed with, at the discretion of the Lodge:

1st. Reading minutes of last stated, and all intervening meetings.

2d. Unfinished business.

3d. Reports of Committees.

4th. Balloting.

5th. Reception of petitions.

6th. Motions.

7th. Work.

All business of this Lodge must originate at stated meetings, except the burial of the dead and installations; all balloting on petitions for initiation, advancement or membership, and all appropriations of the funds of the Lodge, must be done at stated meetings.

No stated meetings can be called off beyond the day and night in which it was opened, and the Lodge must be regularly closed before the brethren disperse.

Degrees may be conferred at called meetings, provided the candidates have been duly elected at stated meetings.

Festival meetings, for the purpose of installation or social pleasure, shall be held on the anniversaries of the Saints John (St. John the Baptist, June 24th; St. John the Evangelist, December 27th), or the day before or the day after, at such hour as shall have been previously designated by vote of the Lodge.

Called meetings may be held at any time at the discretion of the Worshipful Master, by giving due notice to a reasonable number of the members for such purposes as may be strictly specified in the notice, and not incompatible with the laws and usages of Masonry. All meetings of this Lodge shall be held at the Masonic Hall, at ———, unless for funeral or other strictly emergent purposes the Worshipful Master direct otherwise.

No meeting of this Lodge, either stated, called or festival, can be held unless the charter is present and displayed in view of the members present; and none be declared open until after devout prayer to God.

This Lodge shall be represented at each Grand Communication of the Grand Lodge of ———, when practicable.

CHAPTER II.

THE MEMBERSHIP.

The Members and their Duties.

SEC. 1.—*Who are Members of this Lodge.*

The members of this Lodge are all who have been or may be initiated or elected to membership herein, and who have subscribed their names to these By-Laws, not having demitted or been excluded for unmasonic conduct.

SEC. 2.—*The Duties of the Members.*

The duties of the members of this Lodge are primarily divided into three classes—toward God, their neighbors and themselves.

Toward God—to respect the name, and exalt the honor of the Grand Master in Heaven, and ever to allude to him with that profound respect due from the creature to the Creator; likewise, to love, honor and obey the Holy Bible, the Word of God, as the only Masonic guide of faith and practice.

Toward their neighbors—to do unto others as in like circumstances they would have others do to them.

Toward themselves—to avoid all irregularity and intemperance which may impair their faculties or debase the dignity of their profession.

The duties of the members of this Lodge are secondarily divided into three classes—toward an individual Brother, this Lodge and the body of Masonry.

Toward an individual Brother—to aid him in the hour of difficulty; console him in the hour of grief; relieve him in distress; counsel him when astray; pray for him at all times; and to avoid every word and act that might injure him in person, character, purse, or feeling.

Toward this Lodge—to obey these By-Laws, and all other of its rules and edicts, as well in spirit as in letter; to uphold all its lawful interests, and extend the honor of its name throughout the Masonic world.

Toward the body of Masonry—to support the Constitution of the Grand Lodge of the State of ————, which is the conservator and ruler of the Order in this jurisdiction, and see that none of the ancient landmarks of Masonry are removed or overthrown.

The various "Charges" delivered monitorially to candidates in three symbolic degrees respectively, are hereby acknowledged to contain a correct summary of Masonic duties. Any violation of these rules, or neglect of the duties specified in this section, is an offense against Masonry.

CHAPTER III.

THE OFFICERS.

The Officers, their Election, Installation and Duties.

SEC. 1.—*The Officers of the Lodge.*

The officers of this Lodge shall be ranked and entitled as follows:

1. The Worshipful Master.
2. The Senior Warden.
3. The Junior Warden.
4. The Treasurer.
5. The Secretary.
6. The Senior Deacon.
7. Junior Deacon.
8. The Steward.
9. The Tyler.

All the officers of this Lodge, except the Deacons, are elective.

The offices of Steward and Tyler may be vested in one and the same individual, at the discretion of the Lodge.

SEC. 2.—*The Election of the Officers.*

The election of the officers of this Lodge is considered under three heads, to wit: The *time* of election, the *manner* of election, and the *eligibility* of electors.

The time of election shall be annual—that is to say on the ____________________, at such an hour as may have been designated at the stated meeting last preceding. But if for any reason the members prefer another day, the Lodge, by unanimous vote, may select the day before or the day after, at its discretion.

Each officer, duly elected and installed, shall hold his office until his successor is duly elected and installed.

The *manner of election and appointment* shall be as follows: When the day of election shall arrive, the presiding officer shall open this Lodge in the third degree of Masonry.

The Secretary shall then call over the roll of all the members of the Lodge (Master Masons) who are entitled to vote, beginning with the Worshipful Master, and continuing according to rank and seniority.

Nominations for the office of Worshipful Master shall then be made—the last Master, unless excused at his own request (or withdrawn), being always considered in nomination for re-election.

The roll of voters shall again be called, as before; and as each one's name is announced, the Senior Deacon shall carry the box to him and receive from him a written ballot.

When all the votes are thus collected, they shall be delivered to the presiding officer to count, who, after he has carefully ascertained the state of the vote, shall order the Secretary to proclaim the officer elected.

While the Senior Deacon is collecting the votes, and until the Secretary has made proclamation, as aforesaid, each member shall be silent and keep his seat. None can serve as Master until he has first served as Warden in this or some other legal Lodge.

After the office of Worshipful Master is filled, the vote shall be taken for Senior Warden, for Junior Warden, for Treasurer and for Secretary, according to the same rules and principles. Finally, the offices of Steward and Tyler shall be filled on the same plan, except that the individuals last occupying those stations shall not be considered in nomination for re-election, unless specially nominated for the occasion.

Immediately following the election of officers, as above described, the Worshipful Master elect shall appoint a Senior Deacon, and the Senior Warden elect shall appoint a Junior Deacon, who shall be proclaimed by the Secretary as the other officers.

All preferment among Masons is grounded upon real worth and personal merit only; therefore no Master or Warden shall be chosen by seniority, but for his merit.

A majority of all the votes cast shall be essential to a choice.

No member shall suffer another to know for whom his vote is cast.

No member present and entitled to vote shall be excused from that duty, save by permission of the Lodge, granted for good and sufficient reasons presented.

No officer, duly elected and installed, can resign his office during the term thereof, save by demitting.

The eligibility of electors.—Every Master Mason, a member of this Lodge, whose dues are paid up to the day of election, and who is not at the time of election under exclusion for unmasonic conduct, shall be eligible to vote and no others.

SEC. 3.—*The Installation of the Officers.*

The installation of the officers of this Lodge shall take place on December 27th, unless that day come on Sunday, or as soon as practicable after their election.

The last Past Master, when present, may install the Worshipful Master elect, who may then proceed to install the other officers.

The rules for installing shall be those set forth in the various Masonic Manuals, approved by the Grand Lodge of ————.

An officer, re-elected to the office in which he has just served one or more terms, need not be reinstalled therein.

SEC. 4.—*The Duties of the Officers.*

The duties of the officers of this Lodge are considered under eight heads, as follows:

The Worshipful Master.—In addition to those duties which appertain to every individual Mason, and those which are purely traditional, and therefore unwritten, the duties of the Worshipful Master are: 1. To open and preside over the Lodge when present, and to make all necessary provision for the faithful performance of those duties when absent. 2. To preserve the charter of the Lodge with unfailing care, and deliver it to his successor in office. 3. To see that these By-Laws, the Constitution of the Grand Lodge of ————, and the Ancient Constitutions of Freemasonry, be duly understood, respected and obeyed by the members. 4. To give Masonic instruction at every meeting of the Lodge. 5. To take command of the other officers, and claim of them at any time advice and assistance on any business relative to the Craft. 6. To represent this Lodge, in conjunction with the Senior and Junior Wardens, at all the Grand Communications of the Most Worshipful Grand Lodge of the State of —————. 7. To see that the proper officers collect and truly keep the moneys of the Lodge; to see that the furniture and other valuables are not wasted, damaged or lost; and, in the event that the charter of this Lodge should ever be forfeited or surrendered, to preserve these things subject to the order of the Grand Lodge. 8. To draw all orders upon the Treasurer, but not without the consent of the Lodge. 9. To act upon the Standing Committee of Charity. 10. To appoint all Committees except the Standing Committee of Charity. 11. To see that all unmasonic conduct that comes to his knowledge be faithfully dealt with according to the By-Laws of the Lodge and the general rules of Masonry. 12. To guarantee to every one charged with unmasonic conduct a fair trial, and an appeal to the Grand Lodge if demanded. 13. To preside at the burial services of deceased Master Masons, members of this Lodge. 14. To appoint the Senior Deacon. 15. To fill all vacant offices by *pro tem* appointments. 16. To convene the Lodge in called meetings, whenever there shall appear to him an emergent occasion. 17. To install his successor in office. 18. To see that worthy Brothers, visitors from other Lodges, have courteous attention and a welcome in this Lodge. 19. To give the casting vote at any time, in the event of a tie. 20. To appoint the standing Committee of Finance on the day of his installation. 21. To read and expound to the Lodge the proceedings of the Grand Lodge. 22. To decide all questions of order subject to an appeal to the Grand Lodge, or Grand Master.

The Senior Warden.—In addition to those duties which appertain to every individual Mason, and those which are purely traditional and therefore unwritten, the duties of the Senior Warden are: 1. To succeed to and exercise all the powers of the Worshipful Master in the event of his absence. 2. To represent the Lodge, in conjunction with the Worthy Master and Junior Warden, at all the Grand Communications of the Most Worshipful Grand Lodge of the State of —————. 3. To act on the Standing Committee of Charity.

4. To appoint the Junior Deacon. 5. To take charge of the Craft during the hours of labor.

The Junior Warden.—In addition to those duties which appertain to every individual Mason, and those which are purely traditional and therefore unwritten, the duties of the Junior Warden are: 1. To succeed to and exercise all the powers of the Worshipful Master in the absence of the two officers above him. 2. To represent the Lodge, in conjunction with the Worshipful Master and Senior Warden, at all the Grand Communications of the Most Worshipful Grand Lodge of the State of ————. 3. To act on the Standing Committee of Charity. 4. To take charge of the Craft during the hours of refreshment.

The Treasurer.—In addition to those duties which appertain to every individual Mason, the duties of the Treasurer are: 1. To receive all moneys from the hands of the Secretary. 2. To keep just and regular accounts of the same. 3. To pay them out at the Worshipful Master's will and pleasure, with the consent of the Lodge. 4. To prepare an official statement of his account with the Lodge, and deliver it to the Master on the ————.

The Treasurer shall promptly deliver to his successor in office all the funds of the Lodge, together with all the books, vouchers, etc., having any reference to the financial business of the Lodge.

The Secretary.—In addition to those duties which appertain to every individual Mason, the duties of the Secretary are: 1. To observe the Worshipful Master's will and pleasure. 2. To record the proceedings of the Lodge. 3. To receive all moneys. 4. And to pay them into the hands of the Treasurer. 5. To attend upon trials and meetings for taking evidence. 6. To furnish copies of all evidence taken on trials where an appeal to the Grand Lodge is demanded. 7. To furnish diplomas, demits, certificates, etc., duly signed and sealed, by order of the Lodge. 8. To prepare the annual reports for the Grand Lodge, and certificates of the representatives. 9. To notify the Grand Secretary promptly of all expulsions from this Lodge. 10. To keep a book of Masonic biography, for recording all important facts relative to the Masonic history of each member of this Lodge. 11. To keep a visitor's book. 12. To prepare a balance-sheet of all the accounts of the members, and a roll of all who are entitled to vote; likewise, an official statement of his own account with the Lodge, and deliver them to the Master on the day of his installation. 13. To preserve the seal of the Lodge with care, and deliver it to the Worshipful Master at the close of his term of service. The Secretary shall promptly deliver to his successor in office all the books, papers, vouchers, etc., in his possession, having any reference to the business of his office.

All petitions and documents of every character, handed to the Secretary, on the business of the Lodge, shall be labeled, filed for preservation, and kept in some safe and secure place, and only delivered up by order of the Lodge, according to the evident intention of these By-Laws.

The Senior Deacon.—In addition to those duties which appertain to every individual Mason, and those which are purely traditional and therefore unwritten, the duties of the Senior Deacon are: 1. To act as the proxy of the Worshipful Master, in the active duties of the Lodge. 2. To give fraternal attention to visiting Brethren. 3. To prepare and conduct candidates in the different degrees of Masonry.

The Senior Deacon is appointed by the Worshipful Master.

The Junior Deacon.—In addition to those duties which appertain to every individual Mason, and those which are purely traditional and therefore unwritten, the duties of the Junior Deacon are: 1. To act as the proxy of the Senior Warden in the active duties of the Lodge. 2. To have special care to the security of the Lodge.

The Junior Deacon is appointed by the Senior Warden.

The Steward.—In addition to those duties which appertain to every individual Mason, the duties of the Steward are: 1. To have in charge, subject to the direct orders of the Worshipful Master, the furniture, jewels, and other property of the Lodge. 2. To provide light, fuel and refreshments for the comfort of the Brethren. 3. To have special care to cleanliness in the hall and ante-rooms.

The office of Steward may be merged into that of Tyler, at the discretion of the Lodge.

The Tyler.—In addition to those duties which appertain to every individual Mason, the duties of the Tyler are: 1. To tyle the door, subject to the direct orders of the Worshipful

Master. 2. To serve notices, summonses, citations, etc., issued under authority of the Worshipful Master and the Lodge.

The duties of Steward and Tyler may be united in the office of Tyler at the discretion of the Lodge.

Supernumerary Officers.—The Lodge may at its discretion, appoint a Chaplain, a Marshal, a Physician, an Organist, and one or more Masters of Ceremonies, whose duties shall correspond with their titles.

Each officer of this Lodge shall be held personally responsible to the Worshipful Master, and, through him, to the Lodge and to the Grand Lodge, that his office be filled with dignity, honor and correctness, and that its various duties be performed without haughtiness or tyranny, but according to love, and in a diligent desire to exemplify the virtues and sublime morality of Freemasonry to the world.

Due respect and obedience shall be paid by the members of this Lodge to its various officers, according to their respective rank and station.

CHAPTER IV.

PETITIONS.

For Initiation, Membership, Advancement, Demit, Diploma, Charity, Appeal, Action on Petitions.

SEC. 1.—*Petition for Initiation.*

An application for initiation into the Masonic Order through this Lodge, shall be made by a written petition, signed by the applicant's own hand, and in the following form:

To the Worshipful Master, Wardens and Brethren of ——— Lodge, No. ——.

The undersigned respectfully petitions, that having long entertained a favorable opinion of your ancient and honorable institution, he is desirous of being admitted a member thereof, if found worthy. He pledges himself to a cheerful obedience to all the requirements of the institution. His age is — years; his avocation is that of ———; his residence is ———.

(Date.) A—— B——.

This petition shall be recommended by at least two members, Master Masons, and delivered to the Secretary, with the sum of — dollars accompanying it. If the Lodge consent to receive it, it shall be referred to a Committee of three members, Master Masons, who shall diligently investigate the character and standing of the applicant, and make a report to the Lodge at its stated meeting one month thereafter.

The qualification for an initiate are faith in God, hope in immortality, and charity (love) toward all mankind. An applicant shall furthermore have attained to the age of twenty-one years and be under the tongue of good report.

Before a candidate shall enter the Lodge for initiation, he shall plainly declare his assent to the three following interrogations:

1. Do you seriously declare upon your honor before these gentlemen, that unbiased by friends and uninfluenced by mercenary motives, you freely and voluntarily offer yourself a candidate for the mysteries of Masonry.

2. Do you seriously declare upon your honor before these gentlemen, that you are prompted to solicit the privileges of Masonry by a favorable opinion conceived of the institution, a desire of knowledge, and a sincere wish of being serviceable to your fellow-creatures?

3. Do you sincerely declare upon your honor before these gentlemen, that you will cheerfully conform to all the ancient established usages and customs of the fraternity?

Should the applicant be rejected, the deposit fee shall be returned to him. Should he be elected, and fail to come forward for initiation within six months, his fee shall be declared forfeited, and the whole proceedings in his case null and void.

SEC. 2.—*Petition for Membership.*

An application for membership into this Lodge by a Mason regularly demitted from some other Lodge of Free and Accepted Masons, shall be made by a written petition, signed by the applicant's own hand, and in the following form:

To the Worshipful Master, Wardens and Brethren of ——— . Lodge, No. ——.

The undersigned, a ——— Mason, late a member of ——— —— Lodge, No. —, under the jurisdiction of the Grand Lodge of ———, respectfully petitions for membership into your Lodge, if found worthy. He pledges himself to a cheerful obedience to all the requirements of your By-Laws, and to the ancient usages of Masonry as admitted among you. His age is — years; his avocation is that of a ———; his residence is ———.

(Date.)

This petition shall be recommended by at least two members, Master Masons, and delivered to the Secretary, with the sum of — dollars accompanying it. If the Lodge consent to receive it, it shall be referred, lie over and be reported upon, as in the case of a petition for initiation.

No person shall be considered a member of this Lodge until he shall have subscribed his name to the By-Laws.

Sec. 3.—*Petition for Advancement.*

An application by an Entered Apprentice or Fellow-craft, a member of this Lodge, for advancement to a higher degree, shall be made verbally through a member, a Master Mason.

The qualifications for an applicant for a higher degree are thorough proficiency in the preceding degrees, and satisfactory evidences that he possesses the genuine spirit of a Freemason.

No petition for advancement shall be entertained until a public examination has been had, in open Lodge, as to the petitioner's qualifications, and an interval of at least one lunar month occur from the reception of the preceding degree.

Sec. 4.—*Petition for Demit.*

An application for a demit (withdrawal), from this Lodge by a member hereof, in either degree, shall be made by a written petition, signed by the applicant's own hand, and in the following form:

To the Worshipful Master, Wardens and Brethren of ——— Lodge, No. ——.

The undersigned, a ——— Mason, respectfully prays to withdraw from the membership of your Lodge, and asks for a certificate to that effect. His motives for this request are ——— ———. A—— B——.

(Date.)

This petition shall be accompanied by a certificate from the Secretary of the payment of the applicant's quarterage, and all other dues, up to the end of the quarter in which the petition dates.

No petition for a demit shall be entertained by this Lodge if the petitioner is under charges for unmasonic conduct of any sort.

Sec. 5.—*Petition for Diploma.*

An application for a diploma or certificate of present good standing, by a Master Mason, a member of this Lodge, shall be made verbally, and be accompanied by a certificate from the Secretary of the payment of quarterage and all other dues up to the end of the quarter in which the application dates.

No petition for a diploma shall be entertained by this Lodge, if the petitioner is under charges for unmasonic conduct of any sort.

Sec. 6.—*Petition for Charity.*

Applications for relief from persons in distress, whether Masons or otherwise, must be made through some member or members of the standing Committee of Charity, either verbally or in writing.

Sec. 7.—*Petition for Appeal.*

An application for an appeal to the Grand Lodge, by a member of this Lodge (or by a non-affiliated Mason under the jurisdiction of this Lodge) under sentence for unmasonic conduct, must be in writing, directed to the "Worshipful Master, Wardens and Brethren," and deposited with the Secretary.

Sec. 8.—*Action on Petitions.*

All applications and petitions of every sort, except for charity, must be presented at the stated meetings of the Lodge.

Applications for initiation or for membership, must lie over at least one lunar month from the date of their reception; all others may be acted upon at the same meeting at which they were received.

The vote upon applications for diplomas, charity or appeals to the Grand Lodge, may be taken either *viva voce*, or by a show of hands, or by secret ballot, and a majority of votes shall decide all such questions.

The vote upon applications for initiation, advancement or membership, or demits, must be by secret ballot, and one negative vote shall reject.

Every member of the Lodge present when a motion is put or a question stated, shall be bound to vote, unless excused by action of the Lodge.

In balloting, if more than one negative vote appear, the balloting shall cease, and the candidate be declared rejected; but if, on the first ballot, one negative only appear, a second ballot shall immediately take place; and if, on the second ballot, a negative still appear. no further ballot shall be taken for one year thereafter, unless by the second regular meeting thereafter the member opposing shall voluntarily withdraw his objections in open Lodge.

No one shall inspect the ballot save the Master and Wardens, and no Brother shall be permitted to make known to another, or to the Lodge, what manner of vote he cast.

No restriction of any sort shall be placed upon a Brother in the matter of voting, nor shall he be questioned as to how he exercised that right.

A rejected applicant for initiation, advancement, or membership, can not again present his petition to the Lodge within the space of —— months from the date of his rejection.

CHAPTER V.

FINANCIALS.

Fees, Charity, Wages, Management of the Funds.

SEC. 1.—*Fees.*

The fees are for degrees, membership, for quarterage, and for extraordinary contributions.

Fees for Degrees.—The fee for the first degree (or that of E. A.) shall be — dollars, to accompany the petition.

The fee for the second degree (or that of F. C.) shall be — dollars, to be paid before the degree is conferred.

The fee for the third degree (or that of M. M.) shall be — dollars, to be paid before the degree is conferred.

No candidate shall be initiated, passed and raised in this Lodge for a less sum, in the aggregate, than — dollars.

When a degree is conferred upon a candidate at a meeting called for the purpose, by request of said candidate, he shall pay all the expenses of the meeting.

Fees for Membership.—The fee for membership shall be — dollars, to accompany the petition.

Fees for Quarterage.—The fee for quarterage shall be one dollar and fifty cents, to be demanded of each member by the Secretary at the close of each quarter. The first quarter shall commence on the first Monday in November.

Fee for Extraordinary Contributions.—A fee for extraordinary purposes may be levied by a majority at any stated meeting at the discretion of the Lodge.

SEC. 2.—*Charity.*

The virtue of practical charity or alms-giving is recognized by this Lodge as one of the primary principles of the Masonic institution.

The Standing Committee of Charity shall have the power, at any time, to draw upon the Treasurer, through its Chairman, the Worshipful Master, for any sum, not exceeding — dollars, in the discretion of the Committee, to bestow upon a distressed worthy Master Mason, his wife, widow or orphan child, or any other distressed worthy applicant for aid.

SEC. 3.—*Wages.*

Pecuniary wages shall be paid to the Treasurer, Secretary, Steward and Tyler.

Wages of the Treasurer.—The Treasurer, for his services as heretofore specified, shall receive the amount of his quarterage.

Wages of the Secretary.—The Secretary for his services as heretofore specified, shall receive the amount of his quarterage.

Wages of the Steward.—The Steward, for his services as heretofore specified, shall receive the sum of ———— for each meeting at which he performs the duties of his office.

Wages of the Tyler.—The Tyler, for his services as heretofore specified, shall receive ———— for each meeting at which he performs the duties of his office; or, if he performs the duties of Steward in addition to those of Tyler, he shall receive, in addition thereto, the amount of his quarterage.

The Lodge may make such further appropriations for special purposes, as Masonic law and usage justify.

SEC. 4.—*Management of Funds.*

All moneys received by the Secretary on behalf of the Lodge, shall be handed over to the Treasurer, at or before the next meeting subsequent to its reception.

All moneys received by the Treasurer, on behalf of the Lodge, shall be kept by him as a separate fund from his private-hoard, and be at the command of the Lodge at any moment when drawn upon or called for.

The Lodge, at its discretion, may loan out its funds at lawful interest, under the supervision of the Treasurer, he taking good and sufficient security therefor.

CHAPTER VI.

COMMITTEES.—*Standing, Special.*

SEC. 1.—*Standing Committees.*

There shall be two Standing Committees of the Lodge, viz.: A Committee of *Charity* and a Committee of *Finance.*

Committee of Charity.—The Committee of Charity shall consist of the Worshipful Master and the Wardens.

The duties of the Committee of Charity shall be, to dispense the benevolence of the Lodge so as to relieve human distress in the most speedy and practicable manner.

The Committee of Charity shall have power at any time to draw upon the Treasurer, through its Chairman, the Worshipful Master, for a sum not exceeding — dollars at a draft, to be bestowed upon a distressed worthy Master Mason, his wife, widow or orphan child, or upon any other distressed worthy applicant for aid.

The Committee of Charity may take such measures in employing nurses to wait upon the sick, engaging the burial of the dead, etc., as any sudden contingency may demand, and present the bills through the Finance Committee for settlement.

Committee of Finance.—The Committee of Finance shall consist of three members, Master Masons, to be appointed by the Worshipful Master on the day of his installation.

The duties of the Committee of Finance shall be to examine the books, vouchers, etc., of the Treasurer and Secretary from time to time, and to make a detailed report, in writing, at the stated meeting preceding the next St. John's day subsequent to their appointment. Likewise, to examine and audit all bills, accounts and claims that may be presented to the Lodge for payment, and report upon the same in writing. Nor shall any account be allowed by the Lodge until it shall have been examined and reported upon by the Finance Committee.

SEC. 2.—*Special Committees.*

Special Committees shall be appointed upon all applications for initiation or membership, and upon other items of business, at the discretion of the Lodge.

Special Committees upon applications for initiation or membership, shall consist of three members; but upon other items of business of such number as the Lodge in its discretion may decide upon.

Special Committees upon application for initiation or membership shall report at the stated meeting one month subsequent to their appointment; all other special committees shall report at the meeting at which they were appointed, or at the next stated meeting after their appointment, unless the Lodge shall otherwise order.

All reports of Committees shall be in writing unless otherwise ordered by the Lodge.

All Committees, whether standing or special (except the Committees of Charity), shall be appointed by the Worshipful Master; and all Committees shall be composed of Master Masons.

Members who are appointed to serve upon Committees shall feel bound in Masonic honor to give patient and diligent attention to the business of their appointment, and report their conclusions to the Lodge without fear or favor.

CHAPTER VII.

DISCIPLINE.

Offenses, Trials, Penalties, Appeals.

SEC. 1.—*Offenses.*

An offense in Masonry is hereby defined to be an act which contravenes any clause of these By-Laws; any constitutional rule or edict of the Grand Lodge; any requisition of the unwritten law of Masonry; any law of the land, or any law of God. The ten commandments (Exodus, Chapter 20) constitute the Divine law to which Freemasons are particularly subject. The popular vices of intemperance, profanity, Sabbath-breaking, evil speaking, licentiousness and gambling, are, in a special manner, interdicted as unmasonic.

Non-payment of dues; divulging the transactions of the Lodge to any but a member thereof; violating the secresy of the ballot-box or of the Lodge; rude behavior within the Lodge; neglect of family and neighborhood duties; contumacy in refusing obedience to a Lodge summons, etc., are specially declared unmasonic.

Reporting Offenses.—The members of the Lodge while at *labor* (the space of time occupied by the meetings of the Lodge) are under charge of the Senior Warden, who will report to the Lodge all offenses that occur during his administration.

The members of the Lodge while at *refreshment* (the interval between one stated meeting and another), are under charge of the Junior Warden, who will report to the Lodge all offenses that occur during his administration.

But the Wardens, respectively, shall be allowed their discretion whether to report trivial offenses to the Lodge or make them the subject of private counsel, caution and reprimand.

The report shall be in writing, and in the form of charges and specifications, which the Warden who presents them shall personally prosecute before the Lodge.

Non-affiliating (demitted) Masons living within the jurisdiction of this Lodge are under its cognizance, and shall be reported for unmasonic behavior in the same manner as the members of the Lodge.

Sec. 2.—*Trials of Offenses.*

No penalty shall be inflicted by the Lodge until after a fair trial and examination of evidence or confession of the fact of guilt shall be manifest. The *manner of trial* shall be as follows: The written charges and specifications shall be filed with the Secretary of the Lodge whose duty it shall be to have a copy thereof duly delivered to the accused, as also a notice which shall give a reasonable time for the taking of proof to sustain the charges and specifications; also to inform the accused that he may at the same time and place offer proof to exculpate himself from such charges, and that the accused may also have leave to take proof at such other time and place as he may designate upon giving seasonable notice to the Master or presiding officer of said Lodge, for which purpose the Lodge shall allow a reasonable time if asked for. And in all cases the whole of the testimony shall be reduced to writing if not improper to be written, and shall be carefully preserved by the Secretary of the Lodge.

Every member shall be duly tried in the Lodge opened in the highest degree which he has attained; and he shall be allowed to remain in the Lodge during the trial and until the summing up of the evidence is completed.

If the accused member has absconded, so that notice can not be served upon him, charges may be preferred against him which shall lie over —— months, and if the Secretary shall then report he can not serve notice upon him he shall enter a denial of the charges upon the record, and some Brother shall be appointed to defend him and proof may be taken and the case tried as if he were present.

SEC. 3.—*Penalties for Offenses.*

The object of all Masonic penalties is declared to be twofold—to vindicate the honor of Masonry and to reform the erring Brother.

The only penalties recognized by this Lodge or known to Freemasonry, are expulsions, suspensions and reprimands.

Expulsions.—The highest grade of Masonic punishment is expulsion. It is only to be inflicted for aggravated offenses, or for contumacy in refusing to acknowledge subjection to the Lodge, or for such offenses as are notoriously subversive of the foundations of virtue and morality, and would therefore be calculated to render the Masonic institution contemptible in the eyes of the community.

The Secretary shall immediately report to the Grand Secretary the names of all members expelled from this Lodge, and of all non-affiliated Masons expelled by this Lodge from the privileges of Masonry.

Suspension.—Suspensions may be either definite, as for a

certain period; or indefinite, as contingent upon some subsequent act of the individual thus suspended.

It shall require a unanimous vote to reinstate a suspended or expelled member.

The Secretary shall note in the annual report to the Grand Lodge, the names of all persons suspended or expelled by this Lodge.

Reprimands.—The lowest grade of Masonic punishment is public reprimand, in open Lodge. This shall be done by the Worshipful Master, in a manner which, while it conveys a clear idea of the offense thus reprehended, holds out a full measure of love and pardon to the repentant Brother.

SEC. 4.—*Appeals.*

Any Brother who feels himself aggrieved by the action of this Lodge in the infliction of a Masonic penalty may take an appeal to the Grand Lodge.

When an appeal has been granted by the Lodge the Secretary shall prepare exact copies of all the proceedings of the Lodge, the evidence taken on both sides, and all documents used on the trial, and send said copies to the Grand Secretary to be used before the Grand Lodge in the investigation of the case.

A Brother suspended or expelled by this Lodge, but restored by the Grand Lodge on appeal, is not thereby restored to membership in this Lodge, until after petition, reference and clear ballot, as is the case of a demitted Mason.

CHAPTER EIGHTH.

AMENDMENTS.

Amendments to these By-Laws may be made either by action of the Grand Lodge or of this Lodge.

Amendments by the Grand Lodge.—Any amendments that may be made by the Most Worshipful Grand Lodge of ——, in her own constitutional rules or in these By-Laws, and any edicts or resolutions of a general character, promulgated by the Grand Lodge, which affect any subject embraced in these By-Laws, shall be considered as so many amendments to these By-Laws, from the date thereof, without any formal action on the part of this Lodge.

Amendments by this Lodge.—Any portion or the whole of

these By-Laws may be amended or others substituted in their stead, at the will of the Lodge, provided the general principles of Freemasonry, and the constitutional rules and edicts of the Most Worshipful Grand Lodge of —— are carefully maintained. But all amendments, substitutions, etc., shall be proposed in writing, read before the Lodge, and laid over for one month before the vote of the Lodge shall be taken; and a majority of two-thirds of the members present shall be essential to the adoption of said proposition.

No By-Law, or any portion thereof, can be temporarily dispensed with except the clause relative to the order of business, and such others as are especially excepted in the body of these By-Laws.

CERTIFICATE.

(See Diploma.)

CHAPLAIN.

(See Religion; Scriptures.)

The Master of the Lodge is its priest, and the director of its religious ceremonies. His duty is to select the scriptures, prayers, etc., and he should be present at the burial of the dead. A meeting of a Masonic Lodge is a religious ceremony. Those who take part in it have come "to learn to subdue their passions and improve themselves in Masonry;" and Masonry, in many features, is a religious as well as moral institution. But for convenience sake, the Master may depute the religious portion of his duties to one assistant, who is termed the *Chaplain*.

The Chaplain has no privilege as an officer of the Lodge. He is not installed, but performs whatever duties are, from time to time, devolved upon him by the Master. (*See Religion.*) He should, of course, be a pious man. A professional minister of religion is usually appointed to this office.

CHARITY.

(See also Almsgiving; Assistance; Benevolence; Relief.)

Charity or Benevolence is one of the leading purposes of the Masonic Institution. It is for this, in a large part, that

Lodges are built up and sustained. In foreign countries even more than this, charity is the chief purpose of Masonry.

It is a covenanted duty of the members of a Lodge, both in their individual and associated capacity, to aid and assist distressed worthy Brothers (Master Masons) their widows and orphans. A Lodge neglecting this, incurs the censure of the Craft in general, and the discipline of the Grand Lodge in particular. A Brother (Master Mason) neglecting this, incurs the discipline of his Lodge. The amount to be bestowed is left to the conscience of the giver; the rule is, "as much as the necessity of the applicant demands and the means of the giver justify."

An affiliated Master Mason traveling and falling into distress, proving himself by indubitable tokens to be worthy, skillful in the Masonic Art, and in real need, may claim from any Lodge a measure of relief as above. This relief may be bestowed either in money, or by procuring employment for the Brother, whereby he may earn it; at the option of the giver. If in money, it may be made either as a loan or gift. The amount to be advanced need not exceed a sum sufficient to carry the Brother as far as the next Lodge.

It is not a judicious arrangement, in the dispensation of charity, to have a regular fund set apart for that purpose; the hearts and purses of worthy brethren form an inexhaustible fund for this purpose.

The Master and Wardens form the usual and most appropriate *Committee on Charity* of the Lodge. (*See By-Laws.*) To them the By-Laws should grant power to draw upon the Treasurer for a maximum sum at discretion ($3, $5, $10, or $20), for the relief of each applicant. The amount may be proportioned to the expensiveness of living.

In the cities of New Orleans, New York, San Francisco, and St. Louis, there are *Relief* Lodges severally, to whom the whole subject of dispensing Masonic charities is referred. The plan has proved successful, and might, with propriety, be extended to embrace every large city in the Union.

Impostors and vile marauders upon the charitable sentiments of the Masonic Fraternity abound. This is due to the ignorance of the officers of Lodges; carelessness in examinations; a reprehensible looseness in voting away the funds of the Lodge; a want of proper Masonic documents, and other equally disgraceful or unfortunate causes. Owing to these, the means which belong to the worthy distressed, and which should be sacred to honest grief, have been squandered upon the basest crime and the gratification of the most disgraceful lusts. The remedy is in the dissemination of knowledge—knowledge, firmness and decision in examinations, and devotion to official and associated duty.

Any system of benevolence by which the dispensation of charity shall be *equal in amount* among the applicants, is unmasonic. Human distress does not submit to arithmetic, nor should its relief be placed to such a standard. Whatever amount "the necessity demands and the giver can afford," must be given, or the Masonic covenant is violated.

The funds of the Lodge should not, except in extraordinary cases, be bestowed upon applicants other than the classes mentioned.

CHARTER.

(See Warrant.)

A traveling Brother being informed of the time and place of the meeting of a Lodge, applies for admission as a visitor. His request being favorably listened to, he asks for the perusal of the By-Laws and to examine the *Charter* or Warrant of the Lodge, knowing that without a document of this kind the Lodge is but bogus or clandestine. The Charter being exhibited to him, he estimates its authenticity by the manner of its getting up, its form and style, the signatures and the seal. (*See Warrant.*) All these appearing regular and authentic, he cheerfully submits to the rigid questioning and examination proper to him as a visitor. He has proposed to endure every means of trial *on his part*, and he claims the right to examine those things which will assure him of the legitimacy of the Lodge *on their part*.

The loss of the Charter, or its being even temporarily mislaid and not in the Lodge, is an insuperable obstacle to further meetings. Any act of the Lodge under such circumstances would be clandestine or unlawful.

A Lodge refusing to exhibit its Charter, when properly asked for by a visiting Brother, subjects itself to discipline from the Grand Lodge.

The Charter (or Dispensation) of the Lodge must be open and visible to every member during the sessions thereof. It is best kept in a tin case, from which at such times it may be unrolled; to frame and suspend it from the walls is particularly improper.

The Charter (or Dispensation) is in the keeping of the Master, who may, at discretion, intrust it to the custody of the Wardens or the Secretary.

Upon the forfeiture of a Charter, it is returned to the Grand Lodge and filed among the archives. At a future period it may be restored by the will of the Grand Lodge, upon application of a due portion of the original members.

CLANDESTINE.

(See Charter; Discipline; Materials.)

A Lodge working without possessing a regular Charter (or Dispensation) is styled a Clandestine Lodge. This document issued by the Grand Lodge, having jurisdiction, and unforfeited, must be visible to each member present, or the Master can claim no obedience or respect from the Craft.

A Lodge made up of persons of African descent, according to American usage, is Clandestine, as regular Charters are not granted to such.

A Mason made in a Clandestine Lodge, or living in affiliation with one, is Clandestine.

A Lodge working after the loss or forfeiture of its Charter, is a Clandestine Lodge.

A Grand Lodge formed within the jurisdiction of another Grand Lodge, is Clandestine, with all its Subordinates and their members, individually and collectively.

To communicate Masonically with a Clandestine Lodge or Mason, is a positive violation of the Masonic covenant, and becomes, therefore, an extraordinary case of discipline.

COLLEGIATE.

Two or more Lodges at work in the same town or city, constitute for some highly important purposes a *Collegiate* Lodge, possessing Charters, etc., as independent bodies (so far as

Masonic Lodges can be termed independent), but sharing the local privileges and burdens of the Fraternity in an amicable co-partnership with each other. This theory requires that there should be a distinct understanding among Lodges so situated, both as to duty and to privilege.

The materials of Masonry in a Collegiate Lodge, should be shared strictly in common. An applicant may prefix his petition to either Lodge in the Collegiate body without constraint from the others. Visitors from either Lodge should be admitted into the others with a peculiar fervency of welcome; and officers so visiting, be received with the honors due their station. The Masters and officers of the various Lodges should confer frequently together upon the details of their respective offices, rendered more complex by being shared among so many. Violation of Masonic law, on the part of non-affiliating Masons, should be dealt with by some one of the Lodges designated for that purpose by joint agreement and consent. A general Board of Relief (or Relief Lodge) should have in charge all cases demanding charity; thus avoiding imposition and dispensing prompt assistance where needed.

COMMANDMENTS.

(See also Discipline; Blasphemy; etc.)

The Ten Commandments enunciated by Moses, and recorded in the Pentateuch, constitute the chief basis of Masonic Discipline. They are considered as the essence of its code of morality, and being accounted of divine origin, bear a relation to the Masonic covenant, which no other system of morality can do.

They forbid: 1. Paganism.
" " 2. Image Worship.
" " 3. Blasphemy.
" " 6. Murder.
" " 7. Adultery.
" " 8. Theft.
" " 9. Perjury—False Witness.
" " 10. Covetousness.
They enjoin: 4. Respect to Parents.
" " 5. Sabbath Keeping.

COMMITTEES.

(See also By-Laws; Charity; Library.)

The Stated Committees of a Lodge are usually those upon Charity, Finance, and the Library. That upon Charity is best formed of the Master and Wardens. That upon Finance is elected at the time of the annual election of officers. That upon the Library is made up of the three higher officers, together with the Treasurer and Secretary.

Special Committees are appointed by the Master, at the instance of the Lodge, in all the workings and details of its business. The ordinary rules that govern deliberate bodies in relation to this subject, equally prevail in Masonry. Committees usually consist of three, all Master Masons, but may be made up of a larger number.

A Special Committee is bound to report at every stated meeting of the Lodge. They may, if necessary, ask further time for the preparation of a final report. This, when received, discharges the committee.

The first person named in the appointment of a committee, is the Chairman, unless otherwise designated. As such he sets the time of the committee's meeting, and gives order to the business. If a clerk is needed, he appoints one, and sees to it that due reports are made to the Lodge.

The trial of an Entered Apprentice or Fellow-craft, for breach of discipline, is best performed before a committee. (See those captions.)

CONSTITUTIONS.

(See By-Laws; Edicts; Rules.)

The Ancient Constitutions and Charges, compiled by Payne, Anderson, and Desagulers, and first published in 1723, in conjunction with those fragments of Masonic law still older, form the basis of the universal jurisprudence of Masonry. They are acknowledged as such in the legislation of all Grand Lodges, and usually in so many words in their own Constitutions. The Ancient Charges are inserted in preceding pages of this volume.

The Constitution of a Grand Lodge, however, is the working model upon which every design upon the trestle-board of its Subordinates must be drawn. It is supposed to embrace many details of a local character, as well as the general landmarks of the institution. The Constitution of a Grand Lodge bears the same relationship to that body which the By-Laws of a Subordinate Lodge do to that.

CONTUMACY.

(See also Discipline; Disobedience; Penalties; Summonses.)

The offense of Contumacy or disobedience to the due summons of a Lodge, is one of the highest misdemeanors in Masonry. It is a direct violation of its covenant, and a fatal blow at its Discipline. There is therefore, no recourse but the peremptory infliction of our highest penalty upon a Brother who is contumacious.

A Brother refusing or neglecting to obey a due summons, must be cited again, and a third time. The summons in the last two citations, requiring him to show cause why he should not be summarily dealt with for disobedience. Upon his failure to come forward, the Lodge may proceed without delay, and by the proper majority, expel him without further trial.

CONVOCATIONS.

(See Assemblages.)

CORRESPONDENCE.

(See also Secretary; Archives, etc.)

The regular correspondence of the Lodge is with the Grand Lodge, represented by the Grand Secretary. It demands an annual report, according to forms prescribed by the Grand Lodge, of all work performed, discipline executed, the roll of officers, and other details. In this the Lodge is represented by its Secretary.

A correspondence by circulars and special letters with other Lodges, at home or abroad, in which the progress of the Lodge is announced, and its good will toward the Craft in general declared, will conduce immensely to the general good of Masonry. Such a practice prevails in many jurisdictions.

A stated correspondence between the honorary members of the Lodge and the Lodge, in which the former recite from time to time their fraternal sentiments, and bid the latter God speed, forms one of the most delightful features in the Masonic system.

A correspondence between the Lodge and some Masonic periodical, in which the world of readers is informed of the general progress of the former, and of any important episodes in its history, is greatly to be commended.

All this and other correspondence is performed by the Secretary, under the direction of the Lodge, and return communications must be carefully preserved by him in its archives.

The Secretary must be a man of intelligence, and of good attainments, to give tone to the correspondence of his Lodge. The symbol of the Lodge is its Secretary.

CRAFTS.

(See also, Apprentices; Fellow-crafts; Materials; Religion.)

A Brother having been initiated regularly into the first degree of Masonry, and as regularly passed to the second degree, is styled a *Craft* or *Fellow-craft*. By the philosophy of the Institution he is covenanted to preserve its secrets, to be honest, obedient and charitable. He is charged to be a lover of the liberal arts and sciences (Grammar, Rhetoric, Logic, Arithmetic, Geometry, Music and Astronomy), and in a peculiarly impressive manner is taught to respect the name of Deity.

A Fellow-craft is encouraged to attend his Lodge at every meeting, it being understood that it shall be opened on the second degree for his accommodation. He can not travel as such, nor visit other Lodges than his own, except by special courtesy, and then avouched by some one who has sat with him in his own.

A Fellow-craft is not allowed the benefits of the Masonic treasury; nor to be interred with the honors of the Order. Neither can he take any part in the ceremonials of Masonic interment, the Funeral Lodge and procession being opened in the third degree. The female relatives of a Fellow-craft have no claim as such to the protection and aid of the fraternity. He has no vote in the proceedings of the Lodge, but may take a part in debate, if conducted in his degree. An exception to this rule of exclusion, however, as also to his exemption from dues, is found in various Lodges in Canada and Kentucky.

No dues are charged to Fellow-crafts, nor are the dues, ordinary or extraordinary, of the Lodge, exacted from them. See the exception cited above.

A Fellow-craft may be tried upon regular charges for any offense against law, morals, or good behavior, and punished accordingly. The trial in such a case will be had before a committee of the Lodge, the evidence, etc., being taken in the presence of the accused, or it may be conducted in a Lodge of Fellow-crafts, if preferred, but the final decision had in the Master's Lodge, where he can not enter. The offenses of divulging Masonic secrets. dishonesty, disobedience, and the want of benevolence, are peculiarly heinous in a Fellow-craft.

A Fellow-craft changing his residence, and desiring to attach himself to a Lodge contiguous, may, by order of his former Lodge, have a certificate of his standing and good conduct, with a recommendation.

(See *Non-affiliation* for form of certificate.)

A Fellow-craft can not hold office in the Lodge, nor serve upon a committee, nor even fill an official station temporarily.

No person can lawfully receive the degree of Fellow-craft save an Entered Apprentice who has become suitably proficient in, and exemplified the virtues and merits of that degree. (See *Materials.*) That proficiency, rightly understood, embraces the three sections of the "Webb" lectures of the first degree corresponding with the monitorial portions of this book. At least one month is requisite before the initiate can be passed to this degree.

The theory of the second degree is *Science.*

CROTONA, SCHOOL OF.

(See Knowledge; Libraries; Statistics.)

This is a society organized in 1856, for the purpose of disseminating Masonic literature by exchanges among its members. Prior to that period it was known that vast amounts of Masonic matter, much of it antique and of a highly important character, were lying in disuse and neglect anong the Lodges, and on the shelves of individual Masons. By the operations of this system, much of these accumulations has been distributed from hand to hand, and now properly separated and made up into volumes, forms material for the *History of American Masonry* yet to be written.

The plan of *The School of Crotona* is perfectly simple. The presentation of a Masonic work of any kind, a book, pamphlet, etc., is the fee for membership. A full equivalent is given in exchange for all Masonic objects furnished *the school.* Thus, a Lodge sending a number of its By-laws, receives an equal number of the By-laws of other Lodges (but no two of the same Lodge) in exchange. A Brother forwarding a number of addresses, receives an equal number of addresses (but no two of the same sort) in exchange. The plan extends to all objects of Masonic interest: medals, impressions of seals, engravings, etc., etc. Many of the most zealous and intelligent Masons of the day are among its members and officers.

COVENANTS.

(See also, Discipline, Obligation.)

The Covenants of Masonry are those pledges or engagements which being voluntarily taken, agreeable to the Holy Scriptures, equitable, ancient and irrevocable, are well styled *the cement of its walls.* It is the covenant which makes the Mason. It is the line between his darkness and his light. *Previous to its reception*, he may refuse to proceed, or be rejected by any member of the Lodge, without reason asked or given; *after its reception*, he is entitled at once to all the light of the degree to which the covenant appertains.

The covenant is irrevocable. Even though a Mason may be suspended or expelled, though he may withdraw from the Lodge, journey into countries where Masons can not be found, or become a subject of despotic governments that persecute, or a communicant of bigoted churches that denounce Masonry, he can not cast off or nullify his Masonic covenant. No law of the land can affect it—no anathema of the church weaken it. It is irrevocable.

DEACONS.

(See Officers.)

The Deacons of a Lodge are two in number, styled respectively the Senior and Junior Deacons. The former is appointed by the Master, the latter by the Senior Warden. They are considered as the proxies of those officers respectively in the active duties of the Lodge. They may be dismissed at pleasure by the officers who appoint them.

The duties of Senior Deacon are of very great consequence to the dignified and successful workings of the Lodge. This will plainly appear under other captions.

DEGREES.

(See also, Honorary.)

There are two general classes of degrees in Masonry—*regular* and *honorary*. So far as the first nine extend (the E A. P., F. C., M. M., Mrk. M., P. M., M. E. M., R. A. M., R. M., and S. M.), only the first three are *regular*. The orders of Chivalry form a third branch, being *mixed* degrees, or those which add the element of Christianity to Freemasonry.

All the degrees cited above in the parenthesis, are contained in spirit and purpose in the first three. It is by those of the E. A. P., F. C. and M. M., that a traveling Mason is avouched for and welcomed. He is aided in his distress, disciplined for malconduct, and Masonically interred, as an M. M. The Grand Lodges are composed of Master Masons. It is, in brief, to the *regular* degrees that the Masonic philosophy, history and jurisprudence are to be referred.

DEMITTING.

(See Withdrawing.)

DIPLOMA.

(See also Certificate, Travel, etc.)

The certificate which a Brother receives from his Lodge, attesting the fact that he has received the several degrees of Masonry, and of his good Masonic standing at a certain date, is called a Diploma or Certificate. Any member of the Lodge, being a Master Mason in good standing, may petition his

Lodge for a Diploma. If granted, he receives one of the Secretary by paying the usual fee. Brethren preparing to travel abroad will find it to their interest to secure Diplomas, and these, if possible, on parchment.

A Diploma, to be valid outside of the Grand Lodge jurisdiction where issued, must have the certificate of the Grand Secretary, authenticated by the seal of the Grand Lodge, that the Lodge which issued it is itself in good standing upon the roll of the Grand Lodge, and consequently all its Masonic acts entitled to faith and respect.

The best forms of Masonic Diplomas are here given.

To all Free and Accepted Ancient Masons on the Face of the Globe:

WE, the Worshipful Master, Senior and Junior Wardens of *Lodge No.* of the Most Ancient and Honorable Fraternity of *Free and Accepted Masons*, held in and working under the authority of a Charter from the *Most Worshipful Grand Lodge of* do hereby certify that our worthy Brother who has signed his name on the margin hereof, has been regularly Entered, Passed and Raised to the Sublime Degree of *Master Mason*, and during his continuance with us, has behaved himself as an honest, faithful Brother, and, as such, we recommend him to the fraternity around the Globe.

In Testimony Whereof, We have subscribed our names, and caused the Seal of our said Lodge to be hereunto affixed, this day of A. D. 18 A. L. 58

——————— W. M.

——————— S. W.

——————— J. W.

——————— Secretary.

To all Royal Arch Masons under the Canopy of Heaven, Greeting:

WE, the Officers of *Royal Arch Chapter*, No. working under the authority of the *Grand Chapter of the State of* and within the jurisdiction of the *General Grand Chapter* of the United States of America, Do certify that our Worthy Companion, has been duly advanced to the honorable degree of *Mark Master*, seated in the *Oriental Chair*, received and acknowledged as a *Most Excellent Master* and exalted to the Most Sublime degree of *Royal Arch Mason.*

We, therefore, recommend him as a true and faithful companion to all Royal Arch Masons on the Globe.

In Testimony Whereof the Seal of our Chapter is affixed.

A. D., 18— A. L., 58— ———————— H. P.
———————— K.
———————— S.

To all Sir Knights of the Illustrious Order of the Red Cross, and of the Valiant and Magnanimous Orders of Knights Templar and Knights of Malta around the Globe, to whom these presents may come, Greeting:

WE, the presiding Officers of Encampment of Knights Templar, No. held at in the State of Do hereby certify and make known that our Illustrious Sir Knight, having previously received the necessary degrees, has been regularly dubbed and created in this Encampment, a Knight of the Illustrious order of the Red Cross, and of the Valiant and Magnanimous order of Knight Templar, and Knight of Malta, or order of St. John, of Jerusalem.

We do therefore cordially recommend him to the Friendship, Assistance and protection of all Valiant and Magnanimous Sir Knights, in all parts of the Globe, wherever he may go.

In Testimony whereof, having previously caused our Illustrious Sir Knight to sign his name on the margin, We have hereunto set our hands and caused the seal of our Encampment to be affixed, the day of A. D. 18 and of the order of Knights Templar.

M. E.———————— G. C.
E.———————— G.
E.———————— C. G.
E.———————— P.
Recorder.

The difference between a *Demit* and a *Diploma* is that the former shows the Brother *not* a member of the Lodge, the latter that he *is* one. Neither document proves its possessor a worthy Mason at any period subsequent to that of its issuance.

In some jurisdictions the Grand Lodge provides, for a small

fee, a Diploma for every Master Mason upon his being registered in the Grand Lodge Registry.

Many Brethren apply for Diplomas for the purpose of having them framed as parlor or office ornaments. For this purpose beautiful and costly Diplomas have been prepared on copper, wood and stone.

The possessor of a Diploma being convicted of an unmasonic act, and suspended or expelled for the same, the Lodge has the right to demand the Diploma from him, and upon his refusal to give it up, to warn the surrounding Lodges (through the Grand Secretary) of their liability to imposition through the forfeited but unreclaimed certificate.

DISCIPLINE.

(See also Appeal; Discipline; Commandments; Trial, etc.)

No Brother can lawfully take the punishment for offenses into his own hands, no matter what may be the provocation. He may *defend* himself, his family and his property against all attacks; the law of nature, as well as the usages of society, justify and require this. But all the the machinery of punishment, whether considered as a means of restraining evil, or as a return for the act committed, is in the command of the Lodge; no amount of harsh and abusive epithets from a Brother will justify a blow.

The exercise of discipline is the highest duty of a Lodge. To build up the mystic Temple by the addition of new members may appear more pleasing and profitable to the Craft, but to bind the brotherhood together, secure peace and harmony, and present the institution in a dignified attitude before the world, is a more sacred duty, and this requires the exercise of Masonic discipline, according to ancient rules.

The offenses which demand Masonic notice are any acts that contravene the By-laws of the Lodge; the constitutional requisitions of the Grand Lodge; the unwritten laws of Masonry; the laws of the land, or the laws of God. The latter are referred by Masons chiefly to the Ten Commandments. The popular vices of profanity, intemperance, evil-speaking, Sabbath-breaking, gambling and licentiousness, are marked as specially contravening the principles of Masonry. Contumacy in refusing to obey a summons is one of the most serious offenses in Masonry.

The junior Warden is by office the proper officer to observe unmasonic acts committed during the intervals between the Lodge meetings, and, if in his opinion, the cause of justice demands it, to present charges before the Lodge. But it is a part of the covenant of every member to observe and rebuke unmasonic conduct, and give wholesome and affectionate counsel to the erring. A Lodge can not with propriety inflict severe punishment upon a Brother, unless its members have urgently and frequently warned him of his errors, and counseled amendment. It is also the privilege of any Brother to bring charges against another at his discretion.

The charges must be in writing and prepared with specifications. These must extend no further than the accuser, whose name is appended to them, is confident he can substantiate them. Vague and undefined accusation should be ruled out by the Master as unfraternal and unmasonic.

The charges being presented, the question is taken by the Lodge, at a stated meeting, "Will the Lodge proceed to trial?" A majority voting in the affirmative, the Master appoints a committee of three or more to represent the Lodge in taking evidence, etc. If a prosecutor is needed, the Junior Warden or the accuser may act, or still better, some member of the committee. The accused is to be notified of the time and place of taking evidence, and ample opportunities given him to hear and cross-examine witnesses. He may also specify a time and place to secure rebutting testimony, at which the committee may attend to cross-examine, etc. All the testimony proper to be written must be reduced to writing, for which purpose the Secretary of the Lodge must attend the various meetings of the committee. All testimony, so far as practicable, should be given under oath and preserved in the hands of the Secretary.

At each stated meeting of the Lodge subsequent to the appointment of the committee, a report of progress must be made to the Lodge, and further time asked until the committee deem the testimony complete. Then it is read to the Lodge, and the question put, "Shall the Report be received and the committee discharged?" A majority voting in the negative, the committee is placed under instructions and required to amend or enlarge their report. A majority voting in the affirmative, the committee is discharged and the report is considered to be fairly in possession of the Lodge.

Arguments may now be heard, objections made by the accused, protests entered, etc., but all in the most respectful and fraternal spirit. It must be held for granted that the defendant is innocent until proved guilty. It must equally be taken for granted that the prosecution was made from the purest motives, and that the brethren concerned in it, or who have given testimony as witnesses in the course of the trial, have acted conscientiously throughout. The accused may be represented, if he prefer it, by a Mason. The trial takes place in the Lodge opened in the highest degree the accused has received; but when the final vote is taken it must be done in the Master's Lodge.

The discussion being ended, the accused must retire. Then the question is taken: "Are the charges, as detailed in the *first* specification, sustained?" The vote is by secret ballot. A majority vote condemns. The same vote is taken upon each specification.

If the decision is in the affirmative, the question is taken: "Shall the accused be expelled?" The vote is taken by secret ballot. A majority specified in the By-Laws (usually two-thirds) expels. If the Lodge refuses to *expel*, the question is taken, as before: "Shall the accused be *suspended?*" If the decision is in the affirmative, the question is then taken for a suspension for twelve months. The Lodge refusing, the question is taken for eleven months; and so successively down to *one*, which is the shortest possible period.

Should the Lodge refuse to *suspend*, the next and lowest penalty is *reprimand*, administered by the Master in open Lodge. The sentence, of whatever nature it is, must be committed to record, and the papers collected in the course of the trial preserved in the archives. A sentence of expulsion or suspension must be promptly certified to the Grand Secretary, to be by him communicated to the Grand Lodge. Publications of Masonic punishments in newspapers is improper, save by dispensation of the Grand Master.

Upon the question of restoring a suspended or expelled Brother to Masonry, usage is divided. In a few jurisdictions none can restore but the Grand Lodge; in the most the Subordinate Lodges exercise the power. In the latter the question must be laid before the Lodge at least one month before final action; a unanimous vote is essential to restoration. The Grand Lodge in no case can restore to *membership*.

The accused is entitled upon any contingency to appeal to the Grand Lodge, and so is any Brother who may deem the punishment or acquittal of the accused to contravene the requirements of Masonry. In case an appeal is taken, a certified copy of all the papers used in the course of the trial must be forwarded to the Grand Lodge. The taking an appeal does not give the accused any standing as a Mason.

But three grades of punishment are known to Masonry:—1, Expulsion; 2, Suspension for a definite period; 3, Reprimand. Fines are particularly unmasonic.

No officer but the Master of the Lodge is exempt from the penalties alluded to; nor is he only during his official term. The *Tyler* is subject to discipline, if he performs his duties as sentinel unskillfully; the *Junior Deacon*, should he suffer the dignity of the Lodge to be infringed by neglect of his duty; the *Senior Deacon*, should visitors be neglected or insulted, candidates wrongly prepared, received, etc.; the *Secretary*, should he neglect to collect dues or pay them promptly over to the Treasurer, allow the records to be lost or defaced, or fail to keep the minutes accurately; the *Treasurer*, should he employ the funds of the Lodge in any manner save that ordered by the Lodge through the Master; the *Wardens*, should they neglect any part of their covenanted duties; while for a breach of the moral law either of these officers, except the Master, is directly responsible to the Lodge as private members.

DISHONESTY.

(See Discipline.)

Dishonesty to the brethren individually and to the Lodge is solemnly prohibited in the covenants of the institution. The smallest amount of dishonesty constitutes wrong and fraud among Masons, and is equally forbidden with the largest.

It is a fraud upon the Masonic relation to suffer a wrong of any kind done a Brother or a Lodge without warning him of the impending danger.

One frequent cause of dishonesty, disastrous to the successful workings of the institution, is non-payment of dues.

DISOBEDIENCE.

(See Contumacy; Discipline.)

DISPENSATION.

(See Charter; Warrant; Travel.)

The written authorization from the Grand Master to a certain number (usually seven or more) of Master Masons to form and open a Lodge, and make Masons therein, for a period to terminate on the first day of the ensuing Grand Annual Communication of the Grand Lodge, is styled a Dispensation. In some Grand Lodge jurisdictions the Deputy Grand Master is allowed the prerogative of issuing Dispensations to open Lodges, and, in one or two instances, it is even allowed to District Deputy Grand Masters and Grand Lecturers.

This document is commonly drafted on paper, as being of a temporary character, and must be countersigned by the Grand Secretary and attested by the seal of the Grand Lodge. It is a document of such vital importance to the Lodge, that its loss is an instantaneous forfeiture of all the privileges that have accrued under it.

At the termination of the *Dispensation* as above, all the books, papers and property of every sort which have accumulated through the workings of the *Lodge U. D.*, become the property of the Grand Lodge. Should a *Charter* be granted, they are returned to the Lodge for its use so long as it maintains a constitutional existence.

The following is the usual form of a petition for a Dispensation:

FORMS.

A Petition to the Grand Master (or Grand Lodge) for authority to open a Lodge, U. D.

To the Grand Master of Masons in the State of ——.

The undersigned respectfully represent, that we are Free and Accepted Master Masons; that we are at present or have been, members of regular Lodges; that having the prosperity of the fraternity at heart, we are willing to exert our best endeavors to promote and diffuse the genuine principles of Masonry; that for the convenience of our respective dwellings, and for other good reasons, we are desirous of forming a new Lodge in the town of ——, to be named ——; that, in consequence of this desire, we pray for Letters of Dispensation, or Warrant of Constitution, to empower us to assemble as a legal Lodge, to discharge the duties of Masonry, in a regular and constitutional manner, according to the original forms of the Order and the Regulations of the Grand Lodge. That we have nominated and do recommend —— —— to be the first Master; —— —— to be the first Senior Warden; and —— —— to be the first Junior Warden, of the said Lodge; and that, if the prayer of the petition should be granted, we promise a strict conformity to all the Constitutional Laws and Regulations of the Grand Lodge. *

(Signed by at least Seven Master Masons, each giving the name and locality of the Lodge of which he is or was last a member.)

The following is the usual form of a Dispensation to open and work a Lodge, U. D.

The Grand Lodge of ——, By —— —— Grand Master. To all to whom these presents may come, Greeting: Whereas, it has been duly represented to me, that in the Town of ——, County of ——, and State of ——, there reside a number of Worthy Brethren of the Most Ancient and Honorable Fraternity of Free and Accepted Masons, who are desirous of being authorized to proceed forthwith to work as a Regular Lodge; and it appearing to be for the benefit of the Craft in general, as well as the aforesaid brethren in particular, that they should be encouraged in their laudable endeavors and design; and it further appearing to my satisfaction, that the petitioners have complied with the Laws and Regulations on this subject, enacted by the Grand Lodge: Therefore, be it known, that I, —— ——, Grand Master of Masons, in and for the State of ——, by

(*) This form, with a few modifications, will equally serve for the other Masonic bodies as the Chapter, Council and Commandery.

virtue of the power and authority in me vested, during the recess of the Grand Lodge, do hereby appoint our trusty and well beloved Brother, ——— ———, as Master; Brother ——— ———, as Senior Warden; and Brother ——— ———, Junior Warden, together with their associates, Brothers ——— ——— ——— ——— ———, to assemble and work as a regular Lodge in the Town and County aforesaid, in our jurisdiction, by the designation of ——— Lodge, U. D., and there to Enter Apprentices, pass Fellow-crafts, and raise Master Masons, agreeably to the usages and customs of Ancient Free and Accepted Masons, and the Laws and Regulations of the Grand Lodge of ———, but not otherwise.

And I do hereby require and enjoin the said ——— Master and his Wardens, aforesaid, to make due return of this Dispensation, and returns and transcript of the work at the next Grand Annual Communication of ———, to be holden in the Town of ———, on the ——— next, until which time, unless sooner revoked, this Dispensation shall continue in full force and effect.

Given under the hand of the Grand Master and Grand Secretary, with the Seal of the Grand Lodge affixed, this ———.

——— Grand Secretary. ——— Grand Master.

DISPENSATIONS.

(See Grand Master.)

The Grand Master as the executive of the Grand Lodge, may, during the intermission between its Communications, grant Dispensations for various purposes. Among the more common and important of them, are the following:

1. To a Past Master to install the officers of a new Lodge.
2. To the members of a Lodge to hold a public festival, lay corner-stones, dedicate Masonic Halls, perform funeral obsequies of Masons, etc., etc. These privileges, however, are granted by most Grand Lodges to their Subordinates as a general favor, without Dispensations.
3. To the members of a Lodge to hold their annual elections, at other than the constitutional period.
4. To the same, permitting them to act upon the petition of a rejected applicant, waiving the constitutional period.

5. Letters deposing the Master or other officers of a Lodge for malfeasance in office.

6. Authority to Lodges for constitutional reasons stated, to remove their places of meeting respectively.

7. Authority to a Lodge to waive the constitutional period of delay between the several degrees in particular cases cited, and for special reasons advanced.

8. Summoning the Grand Lodge to assemble in emergent communication.

9. Summoning a Subordinate Lodge to assemble in special session.

The following is the form of a Dispensatory Letter to a Past Master to constitute a new Lodge and install its officers. *

OFFICE OF THE GRAND MASTER OF MASONS IN THE STATE OF ——— }

Whereas a Charter has been issued by our Most Worshipful Grand Lodge, dated the —— day of ———, A. H. ——— A. D. ———, for the permanent establishment of a Lodge at ———, in the County of ———, and State of ———, by the name title and designation of ——— Lodge No. ——; These are, therefore, to all Worthy Brothers, Greeting:

Know ye that reposing special confidence in the integrity and Masonic ability of our Worthy Brother ——— ———, I do by these presents constitute and appoint him my Proxy for me and in my name, as Grand Master of Masons in the State of ———, to summons or otherwise meet the present officers and members of ——— Lodge No. ——, aforesaid, at their hall in the Town aforesaid, at such time as may be convenient, and then and there to organize the said Lodge, preside at the election of and install the officers thereof, according to the ancient usages and ritual of the Order, making due return to me of this proxy and his proceedings in the premises indorsed thereon.

Given under my hand and private seal at ——— ———, this —— day of ———, A. D., ——— A. L., ———.

Seal. ——— ——— Grand Master.

It is usual to insert two or more names in the body of a

(*) This form, slightly modified, will serve equally well for other Masonic bodies.

Dispensatory Letter, so that the assembled Craft may not be disappointed by a failure in attendance. In this case, read "or —— —— his alternate," etc.

It is in the power of any Subordinate Lodge to grant a Dispensation to a neighboring Lodge by its request regularly preferred, to act upon a petition for initiation or membership, even though the applicant lives nearest the former Lodge. Also to allow a trial for breach of Masonic Discipline to be conducted in another Lodge, even though the accused be a member of its own body, provided both parties consent to the change of venue. The comity between neighboring Lodges justifies such acts of a fraternal character, where the Constitution of the Grand Lodge do not interpose objections.

DUE.

(See also Summonses; Signs; etc.)

This term denotes fit, proper, regular, legal, constitutional or full. No sign or summons is obligatory upon a Mason, unless it may be explained by one of these words, as a *due* sign or summons.

A summons from the Lodge not regularly certified by the Secretary, under his official seal, if any, would not be a *due* summons.

A Masonic sign made by a Mason engaged in an unlawful act, or made by one not a regular Mason, would not be a *due* sign.

DUES.

(See also Discipline; Fees; Fines.)

Regular contributions by the members (Master Masons) to the treasury of the Lodge, are lawful and necessary. They enable the Lodge to maintain the honor and dignity of the Institution, pay the current expenses of meetings, etc., support the Grand Lodge, and afford the means of charity to the distressed. These demands are proportioned to the expensiveness of the locality. In small and remote country Lodges an annual contribution of two dollars by each member, usually suffices both for the Grand Lodge quota and all other outlays. In cities the average demands upon the membership are five dollars per annum—sometimes much higher; while the occasional calls for charity, etc., met by voluntary contributions, exceed that sum two fold.

It is not lawful for a Lodge to demand contributions from members, except for the regular purposes of the Masonic Institution. The building of monuments, granting Honorariums, subscriptions to national enterprises, etc., so common among our zealous Fraternity, are undertakings purely voluntary and must be treated as such. Lodges misuse their revenues and defraud their own treasuries in expending their regular funds for such purposes, however creditable in themselves the schemes may be.

No dues from Entered Apprentices and Fellow-crafts are proper; they simply pay the fees demanded at their reception. An exception to this rule exists, however, in Kentucky, where Masons of every degree contribute alike to the revenues of the Order.

Fines are improper in Masonry. All demands must be equal upon the members (Master Masons), and offenses against the rules are provided for in the discipline of the Institution. The Grand Lodge, on appeal, would remit a fine charged upon a member, and censure the body that exacted it. All clauses establishing fines as a means of discipline, should be stricken from the By-Laws of Lodges.

Contributions may be extraordinary in their nature, as for the erection of a new Hall, or some other strictly Masonic purpose. But the vote, in such a case, must not be taken until the matter has been thoroughly discussed, ample time allowed for its consideration, and every member of the Lodge notified of the proposed action.

No dues are exacted of Honorary members.

Members in indigent circumstances may (and ought to) be exempted from dues, but only by vote of the Lodge. The neglect of this most reasonable lenity has driven many of the truest Masons from their affiliations.

The Secretary and Tyler, as a portion of their wages (compensation), are usually exempted from the regular dues of the Lodge.

The regular collection of the Lodge dues from the members, forms a part of the covenanted duties of the Secretary. Neglect on his part is usually followed by indifference on theirs. The neglect to pay dues, which creates so much embarrassment to Lodges and compels discipline (suspension) upon hundreds every year, is more the fault of the Secretary, who neglects to collect them of the members who neglect to pay. By-Laws should demand payments *quarterly;* Secretaries should present accounts *quarterly;* brethren will then pay *quarterly*. So says all experience.

All moneys collected for dues, etc., must be paid by the Secretary to the Treasurer before the conclusion of the Session of the Lodge next succeeding such collection. Failure in this subjects the Secretary to discipline.

It is the common usage to excuse clergymen from paying dues to the Lodge.

EASTERN STAR.

(See also, Androgynous; Adoption; Females; Good Samaritan; Heroine of Jericho; Holy Virgin; Mason's Daughter.)

An Order of Adoptive Masonry in considerable repute in the United States. It consists of four points or degrees, termed Jephthah's Daughter, Ruth, Esther, Martha, and Electa, and is communicated in the form of a lecture, after an honorable pledge of secresy, by any Master Mason possessing it, to the worthy wives, widows, sisters, and daughters of Master Masons, being eighteen years of age and upward. Not less than five females must be present at its communication. Certificates of their having received the degree are furnished them, signed by any five of the brethren present. There is, likewise, an emblem peculiar to this Order, which is worn by the Sisters as a decoration. The Eastern Star is by far the most popular of all the Orders of Adoptive Masonry in use in this country, and approaches nearest to a uniform system.

In the year 1855, a regular system of degrees styled "The American Adoptive Rite," was framed by Rob Morris and others, upon the *Eastern Star* as a basis, societies of which styled *Constellations*, have been established in most of the States and Territories with great success. The peculiarities of the "Rite" are, that an impressive ceremonial, founded upon Scriptural history, is performed; a semi-annual password styled a *Memorial*, is communicated, and regular rules of discipline adopted, as in all Masonic societies. To prevent a mercenary use of this system, it is expressly forbidden that any lecturer should receive a fee for communicating it.

EDICTS.

(See also, By-Laws; Constitutions; Rules.)

An Edict differs in no respect from a Rule, By-Law, or Standard Regulation, except as it is more limited in character, and issued by the Grand Lodge alone. It is usually directed to a specific act; as an Edict requiring every Mason to be registered; an Edict forbidding communication with the Masons under the jurisdiction of the Grand Lodge of ———, etc. Even then the word *Regulation* expresses almost precisely the same order.

Edicts of Grand Lodges may be, and sometimes are, oral and unwritten. In such cases, the representatives present at Grand Lodge bear home the edict to their constituents.

All utterances of Grand Lodges partake of the character of edicts, being authoritative in the highest degree. Mere recommendations and advice are unsuitable to the sovereignty they exercise over their Subordinates.

All Edicts must be in accordance with the ancient landmarks of Masonry, as conveyed in the Constitution of the Grand Lodge and the Ancient Constitutions of Masonry, else they are not binding upon the Fraternity to whom they are directed.

The Edicts of Grand Lodges, so far as they can be committed to writing, are found in the printed proceedings of those bodies respectively.

ELECTION.

(See Balloting; Installation; Voting.)

Elections are usually held annually. They come off upon some day designated by the By-Laws of the Lodge, or the Rules of the Grand Lodge. Members in arrears for a considerable period, should be debarred from holding office or taking part in the election. Elections are held in the third degree. Nominations to office are both common and proper.

The officers elected are the Master, two Wardens, Treasurer, and Secretary, and in many Lodges the Tyler. They are elected in the order designated. The Senior Deacon is then *appointed* by the Master elect, the Junior Deacon by the Senior Warden elect; the Stewards, if any, by the Junior

Warden elect; other officers, if any, are appointed by the Master. The installation should succeed the election at as brief an interval as convenient. (*See Installation.*)

By a common usage the Master is considered always in nomination for re-election to office, and the Wardens his competitors. Frequent changes in such offices as that of the Master, the Secretary, and the Tyler, are opposed to good Masonic policy, and entail serious evils upon the Lodge.

No caucusing or arts of any kind to secure the election of favorite persons, are lawful. Officers must not be elected for seniority but for merit. Brethren elected to office, unless excused by the Lodge for reasons presented, are bound in Masonic reason to accept and act; an exception, however, may be made in behalf of one who has already filled an office to which the Lodge desire against his will to re-elect him.

The election should be by ballot and secret, each voter marking upon a slip of paper the name of one of the members in nomination, and depositing the slip as a ballot.

Officers hold over until their successors are elected and installed. If, therefore, for any cause, the period prescribed for holding the election should pass without it, the officers of the preceding term will act for another year, unless the Grand Lodge or Grand Master grant a Dispensation to supply the omission.

The death or removal of an officer after his installation, does not authorize a new election to fill the vacancy. If the vacant office be that of Master, the Wardens fill it by that of seniority; if that of any other, the place is filled by appointment of the Master until the next election.

The results of an election should be immediately communicated by the Secretary, under his official seal, to the Grand Secretary.

Immediately following the installation, the retiring officers give to the officers installed the badges of offices, records, moneys, etc., pertaining to their offices respectively.

ENTERED APPRENTICES.

(See Apprentices.)

These are Masons whose progress has brought them upon the Checkered Pavement of the Mystic Temple whose covenants impel them to secresy; who are enjoined to hold the tenets of Brotherly Love, Relief and Truth, to practice the cardinal virtues of Temperance, Fortitude, Prudence and Justice, and to revere those of Faith, Hope and Charity; to serve their Master with Freedom, Fervency and Zeal; and to practice charity, and whose working tools are the Gauge and Gavel.

By American usage, one month's service upon the checkered pavement entitles the Entered Apprentice, due proficiency having been made, and his character remaining unimpeached, to be passed to the degree of Fellow-craft.

EXPULSION.

(See also Discipline, etc.)

The highest grade of punishment known to Freemasonry. Its equivalent in the symbolic expressions of our fathers is "casting away among the rubbish as unworthy for the building." Unless for great criminality it should be inflicted only after faithful counsel and rebuke and a trial of the minor penalties of reprimand and suspension.

In the most of Masonic jurisdictions the Lodge which expels may restore; in a few, none but the Grand Lodge can restore. In the former case his proposal to restore must be made at a stated meeting, lie over at least one month, and receive a unanimous vote upon adoption. The Grand Lodge can in no case restore an expelled brother to membership.

The expulsion of a Mason while it deprives him of every privilege with which his Masonic attachment endowed him, leaves him bound by every part and point of his Masonic covenant. Of this no act of his own or of the Lodge can ever divest him. The tie of Masonry is perpetual.

The *second* penalty in Masony is *suspension;* the *third* and lowest *reprimand.*

FEES.

(See Dues.)

The sums exacted from the candidate prior to the conferring of the degrees respectively are termed fees. They vary in the different sections of the United States and Canada from fifteen dollars (for the three degrees) to one hundred dollars. They are in general set too low for the best results.

Clergymen are usually excused from the payment of fees.

FELLOW CRAFTS.

(See Crafts.)

These are Masons whose progress has brought them to the Middle Chamber of the Mystic Temple; whose covenants impel them to be secret, honest, obedient and charitable; and whose working tools are the Plumb, Square, and Level.

By American usage one month's service in the middle chamber entitles the Fellow-craft, due proficiency having been made, and his character remaining unimpeached, to be raised to the degree of Master Mason.

FEMALES.

(See also Adoption; Androgynous; Eastern Star; Good Samaritan; Heroine of Jericho; Holy Virgin; Mason's Daughter.)

According to the solemn covenants considered in symbolical Masonry, the cement of the Order, certain classes of females possess from their relationship to Master Masons peculiar claims to countenance and support. The worthy wife and daughter during the lifetime of their family head, share with him in many of the benefits and honors of this noble and world-wide institution. Their position in society is thus enhanced; their protection from insult secured; their honor shielded from scandalous breath; their wants relieved. They have good reason therefore to feel that it is well for a worthy man to be a Freemason.

But when the hand of death falls upon the happy and fortunate group, and the family head is snatched from them, consigning to widowhood and orphanage, perhaps to poverty and friendlessness, those tender ones, the glory and beauty of Freemasonry shines forth even more conspicuously. Then the tearful widow, then the pale orphan assume that place in the affections of the brethren which late the husband and father occupied. All the good will he had secured to himself by long and faithful Masonic services and contributions to the Masonic treasury, inures to them. The gratitude due to him is cheerfully paid to them; and counsel, sympathy, aid and protection are abundantly tendered to those whom God has thus severely bereaved. Such is the theory of Masonry in its relation to wife and daughter.

A relationship less intimate but yet tender and important also exists between the fraternity and the mother and sister of the Master Mason. By this tie their virtue is shielded and they defended from those lawless attacks to which unsuspecting woman so often falls a prey.

No general decision has ever been made of the questions whether a Mason, by non-affiliating, deprives his female relatives of the privileges alluded to; or what amount of improper conduct, opposition to Masonry, etc., would forfeit their claims to Masonic protection and aid. Our opinion is that a demitted Mason has no Masonic privileges that can inure to his family, and that females themselves may forfeit their inherent claims by bad conduct and opposition to the institution.

The widow of a Master Mason marrying again resigns her claims upon the Masonic Order. Several Grand Lodges have ordered their Subordinates to furnish the widows and orphan daughters of Master Masons with certificates avouching their claims to Masonic benevolence. This is a laudable custom and should be made general.

To give to females an easy and reliable method of proving their Masonic relationship as above described, when among strangers, various orders or degrees enumerated in the caption, have been invented and communicated to them. These form what is styled Adoptive Masonry. Thus far, however, the system has not met with general success.

If by accident or improper conduct on the part of Masons, a female comes to the knowledge of any Masonic secrets she is not thereby to be admitted into the Lodge nor can the brethren communicate with her upon Masonic subjects. Any Lodge violating this rule would forfeit its charter; any brother infringing upon it would subject himself to certain expulsion.

FINES.

(See also Dues.)

Fines in Masonry are improper and unlawful. As a means of discipline, they are absurd; as a method of replenishing the treasury of the Lodge, unequal and unjust. They have been employed in foreign Lodges where charity (alms-giving) was the greatest, almost the only object, of the Institution; but here, where morality is pursued as the chief end of Masonry, they are almost universally discarded. They are unequal, because the infliction of fines is never proportioned to the pecuniary ability of members. They produce nothing but heart-burnings or indifference, and no moral effect follows. Experience, therefore, as well as theory, denounce their use.

FORNICATION.

(See also Adultery; Discipline; Females.)

Among the numerous instances of violations of Masonic laws committed among the widely-extended Masonic Fraternity, and made the subjects of Masonic penalties, few indeed partake of the nature of carnal intercourse committed with the female relatives of Master Masons.

FUNDS.

(See also Treasury.)

The funds of the Lodge are made up by regular contributions from the members, and fees for conferring the degrees. Donations, legacies, etc., are often made to Lodges by members who have greatly experienced the benefits and pleasures of Masonry. Of this sort was the large legacy by Stephen Girard to the Craft in Pennsylvania.

An accumulation of funds through fines is not in accordance with Masonic principles.

It is not politic for a Lodge to swell its funds at the expense of charity, or of such objects of a literary character as the well-working of the Institution demands. Each Masonic generation is best able to provide for itself the resources necessary to perpetuate the Order.

FUNERALS.

(See also Interment.)

Every Worthy Master Mason, affiliated at the period of his death, is entitled to, and should receive a Masonic Funeral.

The Lodge of which the deceased was a member is the proper body at whose expense and under whose direction the funeral rites should be conducted, unless owing to his high official position, or singular great merit, the Grand Lodge assumes its prerogative. If the deceased die when absent from home, the Lodge nearest the place of his death, aware of his character and Masonic connection, will perform these duties, and all expense will be refunded to them by the Lodge to which he actually belonged. A full course of instruction is given for Masonic funerals under the head of Past Master, in an earlier part of this volume.

GOOD SAMARITAN.

(See also Adoption; Androgynous; Eastern Star; Females; Heroine of Jericho; Holy Virgin; Masons' Daughter.)

A form of Adoptive Masonry highly valued in the United States. It is usually confined to Royal Arch Masons, and their wives and widows; but owing to the want of a general head or standard, we have found the degree in at least one section of the country in the hands of Master Masons, and their wives and daughters. It is founded upon the story of the Good Samaritan, and displays by an elegant ceremonial the virtue of charity, prompt and decisive in a most impressive and solemn manner. Its medal is contrived with remarkable ingenuity, but its means of recognition are meager. In Missouri, a system of Adoptive Masonry has been devised, based upon The Good Samaritan. Societies working by this system are styled *Circles*.

The Medal of The Good Samaritan is thus described: A circle having in the center G. S. Around the border EFIW. STOL. Upon curved lines through the area, the following: LTTN. ONAO. TIMITW. SIITC. WIIC. ITMTSAIWGIU. FWNOWITSD. EWAFL.

GRAND MASTER.

(See Dispensation; Dispensations; Officers.)

The executive of the Grand Lodge, and the highest dignitary known to the Masonic Order is styled the Grand Master. In him, during the intermissions between the Grand Communications, is vested the government of the Craft in all its departments. He is not so much the Grand Master of the Grand Lodge as of the Masonic Fraternity in his jurisdiction; his duties as President of the Grand Lodge being but subordinate to his higher and broader duties as the head of the Order.

The Grand Master is elected for one year, or until his successor is constitutionally elected and installed. He must be a Past Master to be eligible to this office, and his covenant as Grand Master is an extension of that of a Past Master.

So numerous are the duties, so arduous the responsibilities of the Grand Master, that few attempts have been made by the Masonic legislatures to define or confine them. It has been thought safer thus far to select worthy and competent men for the charge, than to hedge in and embarrass the Grand Master by drawing the outlines of his duties. In general, whatever the Grand Lodge can do, or should do, in accordance with their own Constitutions, the Grand Master, if in his own discretion called upon to perform it, can and should do likewise.

The Grand Master may grant Dispensations for many purposes. See those heads.

The instruction and illumination of the Craft being the Grand Master's special prerogative; the lectures, rituals, and those who impart them, are subject to his orders. He is expected, during his continuance in office to visit many Lodges for the purposes of illumination, as well as to exercise discipline, inspect the work and records, and keep the Fraternity generally within the ancient landmarks.

The title of the Grand Master is Most Worshipful. No emoluments are attached to the office, "the approbation of the Craft and the approval of God" being a richer reward.

HAND BOOKS.

(See Monitor.)

HARODIM, COLLEGE OF.

(See also, Instruction; Knowledge, etc.)

HEROINE OF JERICHO.

(See Adoption; Androgynous; Eastern Star; Females; Good Samaritan; Holy Virgin; Mason's Daughter.)

A form of Adoptive Masonry, formerly in extensive use in the United States. It is properly confined to Royal Arch Masons and their wives and widows, but, like the *Good Samaritan* (which see) it has to a small extent, fallen into the possession of Master Masons. It is founded upon the history of Rahab, and her rescue of the spies from the hands of the king of Jericho. There is no ceremonial attached to it, but its means of recognition are full and ingenious.

The medal of the Heroine of Jericho is usually heart-shaped, with the letters ARHAB in the center, and around it the letters BFRPNWTTBN. On some medals may be seen in addition the letters ML. FY. IYUN. TOB.

HISTORY.

(See Archives; Secretary.)

HOLY VIRGIN.

(See also, Adoption; Androgynous: Eastern Star; Females; Good Samaritan; Heroine of Jericho; Mason's Daughter.)

A form of Adoptive Masonry but partially disseminated in this country. A little work, styled "Ladies' Masonry," published in 1851, by Wm. Leigh, Past Grand Master of Alabama, gives detailed accounts of it. The sentiments, etc., are beautiful.

HONORARY.

(See also, Degrees; Membership, etc.)

Those degrees of Masonry are styled *honorary* which are given in due course, and as a matter of course to Master Masons; which require no covenant more binding than that of a Master Mason; which are in some degree explanatory of symbolical Masonry, or wanting to the system. Of this sort are the *Mark Masters*, the *Royal Masters*, and *Select Masters*, which are complementary to the *Fellow-craft*; the *Most Ex-*

cellent and *Royal Arch*, which seem necessary to the *Master Mason;* the *Red Cross*, which is the complement of the *Royal Arch.* Also, the whole array of *Side Degrees*, also termed *Honorary Degrees*, which are used to illustrate or impress Masonic virtues, and increase the means of Masonic recognition.

That kind of membership based upon meritorious services alone, and not contingent upon fees or residence is styled *honorary*.

IMPOSITION.

(See Charity; Travel, etc.)

That the Masonic Order at the present time abounds with impostors, through whose impositions the Craft are great sufferers, is but saying that due care in examination is not exercised. If Lodges and Masons will take the assertions of every stroller for truth, counsel is but wasted upon them.

The principles and technicalities of Masonry afford an infallible test whereby impostors may be detected, and charity prudently and worthily bestowed.

INITIATION.

(See Entered Apprentice.)

The ceremony of introduction into the first degree of Masonry, symbolically expressed as "introducing the candidate to the Checkered Pavement of King Solomon's Temple," is properly styled *Initiation;* although many writers use the term indiscriminately in reference to all Masonic degrees. The conductor is the Senior Deacon. The instructors are the Master and Wardens.

The ceremony of initiation is exceedingly instructive and beautiful. Performed with the necessary machinery, each assistant having his part perfectly clear in his memory, and with a tongue fluent to express his part, and followed up by the lectures in three sections appropriate to the degree, it never fails to gratify and satisfy the initiate, and to improve the mind and morals of the brethren present.

A Brother long absent from his Lodge, having no vouchers, and being totally unable to prove himself a Mason, may lawfully be initiated a second time.

INSTALLATION.

(See Election; Officers, etc.)

The act of qualifying officers elect for their respective duties is styled installation. It is performed in open Lodge, opened in either degree, or after a slight preparation, it may be done in public. It consists, 1st, In an acknowledgment by the brethren present that the persons named have been truly elected by them for the offices respectively. 2d, In a further acknowledgment by the brethren present that they yet adhere to their choice. 3d, In a covenant by the parties elect faithfully to perform their respective trusts until their successors are duly elected and installed. 4th, In an enumeration and acceptance of the various duties. 5th, Rendering due homage and respect to the new officers. All these, except the third specification, may be performed in public.

The retiring Master installs the Master elect, who then installs the remaining officers.

After an officer is installed, he can not honorably resign the office, or neglect the duties involved in it. In case of death or absence, no new election is held; the office is supplied by brethren appointed temporarily by the Master.

In case of public installation, an address to the audience should follow, in which the purposes and theory of Masonry, and the vital relation in which the newly-installed officers stand toward the Lodge may be rehearsed.

INSTRUCTION, LODGES OF.

(See also, Harodim; Knowledge.)

These are moot Lodges, in which the ceremonies of Masonry are performed, their technicalities rehearsed, etc., for the purpose of perfecting the attendant brethren therein. When conducted with dignity, and the ancient rituals rigidly followed, they are productive of much benefit to the fraternity.

INTERMENT.

(See also, Funeral.)

None are entitled to the honors of a Masonic interment save Master Masons, and those only who are in good standing at the time of their death, and affiliated in a regular Lodge. It is to be understood, also, that the deceased had expressed his desire for Masonic interment. The consent of his surviving family, or those having the immediate charge of his remains, must likewise be had. It is well for Lodges to keep a "Book of Memory," in which members may record their wishes as to the disposition of their remains after death. This will often obviate an unpleasant altercation between the Lodge and the family of the deceased.

An Entered Apprentice or Fellow-craft, however distinguished socially or politically, can not have a Masonic burial. The reason of this is found in the peculiar philosophy of Masonry, which has appropriated all questions relative to death and the resurrection to the Master's degree.

A Mason who has taken his own life, or perished in a duel or any unlawful brawl, or has suffered death at the hands of justice, or died from the effects of dissipation in any evil course, can not have the honors of Masonic interment.

Assemblages for funeral purposes, if met within a reasonable distance, must be controlled as other Lodge meetings—a Master, the Warden, a Secretary for recording, and an open Lodge. But in the absence of a Lodge organization, or at a distance too great for such formality, a proper number of brethren working in the spirit of seriousness and prudence, may convene, and with the solemn rites of Masonry lay "dust to dust."

JURISDICTION.

The jurisdiction of a Grand Lodge extends to the boundary of the State, Province, or Territory in which it is found. Over all Lodges and individual Masons therein it has primary and exclusive rule. But this is not all. Any State, Province, etc., in which no Grand Lodge exists, is subject to the joint occupation and rule of all the Grand Lodges in the world. Such at the present time (1858) are New Mexico, Washington Territory, Utah, etc., in the United States and Mexico; Central America, the greater part of Africa and Asia, the Sandwich Islands, etc., etc., elsewhere, in each of which any Grand Lodge acknowledged to be regular, may establish Lodges in accordance with their own constitution.

By a reciprocal and beautiful courtesy, many Grand Lodges waive jurisdiction to the Subordinates, working under contiguous Grand Lodges, and authorize them to admit members whose residences are nearer those Lodges than any under their own government.

The jurisdiction of every Subordinate Lodge extends to those points on every side which are midway to contiguous Lodges respectively. But the same principle of reciprocal courtesy will justify the waiving of Jurisdiction to neighboring Lodges by special order. The Lodge situated nearest the boundary line of the State has exclusive jurisdiction to that line, subject only to such international courtesy as may be allowed by the Grand Lodges respectively.

The violation of Masonic jurisdiction is a high misdemeanor in Masonry, and has led to many and serious altercations between brethren.

JURISPRUDENCE.

There are seventeen rules of Masonic jurisprudence, which may well be styled Landmarks, which embrace its entire code. They are deduced from the Ancient Charges compiled by Payne, Anderson and Desagulers, and first published in 1723.

LANDMARK I. The Masonic Landmarks are unchangeable and imperative.

LANDMARK II. Freemasonry is a system teaching symbolically, piety, morality, science, Charity and self-discipline.

LANDMARK III. The Law of God is the rule and limit of Masonry.

LANDMARK IV. The civil law, so far as it accords with the Divine, is obligatory upon Masons.

LANDMARK V. The Masonic Lodge and the Masonic Institution are one and indivisible.

LANDMARK VI. Masonic qualifications regard the mental, moral and physical nature of man.

LANDMARK VII. Personal worth and merit are the only basis of official worth and merit.

LANDMARK VIII. The official duties of Masonry are esoteric.

LANDMARK IX. The selection of Masonic material and the general labors of the Masonic Craft, are exoteric.

LANDMARK X. The honors of Masonry are the gratitude of the Craft and the approval of God.

LANDMARK XI. Masonic promotion both private and official, is by grades.

LANDMARK XII. The Grand Master may have a Deputy.

LANDMARK XIII. The head of the Lodge is the Master, duly elected by the Craft.

LANDMARK XIV. The medium of communication between the head and the body of the Lodge is the Wardens.

LANDMARK XV. Obedience to the Master and Wardens is obligatory upon the members.

LANDMARK XVI. Secresy is an indispensable element in Masonry.

LANDMARK XVII. The Grand Lodge is supreme in its sphere of jurisdiction, and controls both the Subordinate Lodges and individual Masons, but always subject to the Ancient Landmarks.

KNOWLEDGE.

(See Discipline; Harodim; Instruction.)

The advantages of Masonic knowledge to the brethren are, *First*, To afford them the means of communication with the Craft wherever met, thus enabling them to enjoy the social, honorary and pecuniary privileges of the Institution. *Second*, To expand the mind and improve the morals. A Lodge which does not afford to its members these classes of advantages is not doing its part in the work of Masonry, and upon proper charges before the Grand Lodge, may be reprimanded or deprived of its charter.

It is the duty of the Master of the Lodge to communicate Masonic knowledge to his members at every meeting of the Lodge. Upon his failure to do so, should dissatisfaction arise, it is quieted by the ability and readiness of the Senior Warden, who performs the duty thus slighted by the Master. A Lodge can not lawfully be opened or closed without this communication of Masonic knowledge. Upon the failure of the Master (or Senior Warden) to perform this duty, upon proper charges being made to the Grand Master, he may be reprimanded, or even deposed from office by that high official.

No Brother, not properly identified and vouched for as a Masonic acquaintance, can be admitted as a visitor into a Lodge, until by the communication of his Masonic knowledge he satisfies them of his legitimacy as a Mason.

Should an applicant as aforesaid fail in his attempt to visit, by the want of Masonic knowledge, a notification should be promptly made to the Lodge of which he claims to be a member, that the imposition, if any, may be detected.

Honorariums and testimonials of various sorts are made by a grateful fraternity to those brethren who through much travel, reading and study become conspicuous for their Masonic knowledge.

The officers of Lodges, Grand and Subordinate, are properly selected on account of their knowledge, as well as their zeal and moral worth.

LABOR.

(See Refreshment.)

The work of Masonry, including the opening and closing of Lodges, and all that is done in them, also the public exercises of the Craft, as seen in the burial of the dead, laying corner-stones, dedicating Masonic Halls, public installation of officers, etc., is styled *Labor*. The behavior of the Fraternity at other periods is said to be *while at Refreshment*. During the period of *Labor* the Senior Warden has direct charge of the laborers, the elevation of his column implying so much. During that of *Refreshment* the charge is in the Junior Warden, and his column should be erected accordingly.

The ancient practice of the Fraternity required actual *Re-*

freshment of food and drink, typified by the other, to be dispensed to the brethren before they dispersed after *Labor*.

The whole purposes of Masonic *Labor* may be embraced in the divine sentence, "Glory to God in the Highest! on earth peace: good will to men!"

LIBRARY.

(See also Secretary, Archives, etc.)

Every well-working Lodge should be possessed of a Library to contain all the proceedings and printed documents emanating from the Grand Lodge by whose authority it works; a good supply of manuals or hand-books for convenient use; one or more of the Masonic periodicals of the day; all the standard and approved works upon Masonic History, Philosophy, Jurisprudence, and Belles-lettres extant; and such other publications of a Masonic or more general nature, as the taste and wants of the Lodge may dictate.

The Librarian of the Lodge is the Secretary. Regulations for the preservation of the Library and the loaning of the books to members, should be attached to the By-laws of the Lodge.

A fund, consisting of a regular per cent. on all collections, should be annually appropriated to the increase of the Library. This may be expended under the directions of the *Committee on the Library*, who consist, usually, of the three higher officers of the Lodge, together with the Treasurer and Secretary.

The only complete Masonic Library or collection of works upon the History, Philosophy, Jurisprudence, and Belles-lettres of the Institution ever prepared for general use, is that styled "The Universal Masonic Library," of which the Catalogue is presented at the end of this volume."

LIGHT.

(See Knowledge.)

By the term *Light* is implied in Masonry, all that knowledge esoteric or exoteric peculiar to the Institution. The covenant is the boundary line between Masonic light and darkness.

There is no Masonic light as such in any degree beyond that of the three symbolic grades.

The possession of Masonic light entitles a Brother to all the privileges and honors of Masonry, so long as he possesses the mental, moral and physical means of establishing his claim to them.

MANUALS.

(See Monitor.)

MASON'S WIFE OR DAUGHTER.

(See also Adoption; Androgynous; Eastern Star; Females; Good Samaritan; Heroine of Jericho; Holy Virgin.)

A form of Adoptive Masonry very extensively diffused in this country. Its popularity is owing, we apprehend, to the ease with which the most unintelligent persons can communicate it, as it requires neither eloquence, memory, nor Scriptural knowledge to display its full merits.

It is usually confined to Master Masons and their wives, widows, sisters and daughters; but in some localities it is communicated to the *mothers* of such. There is no incident of Scripture particularly illustrated by it, nor are its means of recognition sufficiently uniform or complete to render it a matter worthy of much attention. Its jewel is a circle with the letters AMRY; in the center and around it, the letters FNDOS BTKC.

MASTER.

(See Officers, etc.)

The Master of the Lodge is elected by those members eligible by the By-Laws, and upon a day specified either in the By-Laws or in the Constitutional regulations of the Grand Lodge. He is elected annually, and holds office until his successor is duly elected and installed. He is installed by the retiring Master, or some other Past Master. It is essential that he should first receive the degree (or Order) of Past Master before he can be installed. He is elected not for his seniority, but according to his merit. If re-elected without an interval, he need not be re-installed.

All matters relative to the progress, discipline, cementing

and good order of the Lodge, devolve in general upon the Master. He appoints all committees, is custodian of the Charter, summons the Lodge at discretion, admits and rejects visitors at pleasure, appoints the Senior Deacon and performs the work. The Wardens are his assistants, the Past Masters his counselors and aids, the members his co-laborers in the glorious work of Masonry.

The Master is responsible for his official acts not to his Lodge, but to the Grand Lodge, or (which is the same thing) to the Grand Master for the time being. Therefore, he will put no question to his Lodge that he deems contrary to the Constitution and By-Laws, or subversive of the true spirit and intention of the ancient landmarks. This is the spirit of his installation covenant.

MASTER MASON.

(See also Apprentices; Crafts; Materials; Religion.)

A Brother having been initiated regularly into the first degree of Masonry, as regularly passed to the second degree, and as regularly raised to the third degree, is styled a Master Mason. He is a completed edifice, prepared for the reception of all Masonic knowledge, and the exemplification of every virtue. To him all the ancient landmarks may and should be entrusted; upon him are laid all the burdens of the Institution—he is authorized to use and enjoy every privilege, honor and pleasure of which Freemasonry is susceptible. By the philosophy of the Institution he is covenanted to preserve its secrets, to be honest, obedient and charitable, to avoid slander, violence and licentiousness, to have no Masonic communication with clandestine Lodges or Masons, and to reject in the quarry all improper materials. (See *Materials.*) As *morality* is the great doctrine of an apprentice, and *science* the great purpose of a Craft, so *religion* of a broad and universal character is the prime inculcation of the *Master's* degree.

The Master Mason is the teacher of all Masons of inferior grades, and must ever be found as ready to communicate knowledge as they to receive it. No Master Mason should content himself with less than the seven sections of the lectures in the first, second and third Degrees, as these, or large parts of these, form the necessary means of recognition between the brethren the world over.

The Treasury of the Lodge belongs to the Master Masons, who are its members (see Treasury), and its benefits accrue only to them, their widows, and orphan children.

Only Master Masons can be interred with Masonic honors, or unite in the solemn ceremonies appropriate to that act. The symbols of Masonry are elucidated to Master Masons chiefly; its grand and sublime traditions which give dignity and permanency to the Order, are unfolded only in this degree.

The preparation of By-Laws, their amendment, etc.; service on committees; the official stations; all voting, balloting and debating; attendance either as representatives or visitors at the Grand Lodge; all these are the prerogatives of Master Masons.

Only Master Masons are required to pay the contributions, ordinary or extraordinary ordered by the Lodge and Grand Lodge. An exception to this rule is found in Kentucky, where dues, etc., are required of all grades of Masons.

A Master Mason as such may travel, visit Lodges upon lawful examination, and disseminate the light and knowledge of the Order around the world.

Only Master Masons can unite in the organization of new Lodges, or the revival of old Lodges. Charters and Dispensations are granted to Master Masons exclusively.

MATERIALS.

(See Master Mason; Crafts; Apprentices.)

This topic is conveniently subdivided into 1. Lawful. 2. Unlawful.

Lawful Material to the mystic temple of Masonry consists of men free born, of lawful age (twenty-one years and upward is the American usage); mentally, morally, and physically perfect (according to the ancient standard), well recommended, and presenting, unsolicited, a request to the Lodge for initiation.

Such an applicant as this is scrutinized by each member of the Lodge by every light presented in the Masonic system. A committee is appointed on behalf of the Lodge, with ample powers and ample time (one month or longer if any ask it), to make inquiry into his qualifications in the three particulars of mind, heart, and body. Their report being delivered and accepted, a ballot is spread (secret in the strictest acceptation of the term), and upon the unanimous consent of the brethren assembled (one objection being fatal), the applicant, with every caution that the time-honored principles of Masonry inculcate, and the experience of brethren suggests, is entrusted with a portion of the secrets of the Fraternity, bound by a link of its mystic covenant, and endowed with a little part of its privileges.

But this, by no means, ends the scrutiny with which he is viewed by those to whom is entrusted the building up of the ancient walls. It is not alone in selecting and breaking the stone in the quarry, that skill and caution are necessary, but in every step from its choice to its elevation to place in the walls. The candidate having worked awhile (not less than a month by American usage) as an Entered Apprentice, the brethren have been enabled to view him more closely, and to criticise his qualifications for Masonry more accurately than before he came among them. He now undergoes a second ordeal by secret ballot, and if a single objection is found he must remain awhile longer to wield the Gauge and Gavel, the instruments of his vocation upon the checkered pavement.

Having, however, by unanimous consent *passed* to the degree of Fellow-craft, and assumed an enlarged and solemn covenant, the *materials* begin to assume a shape pleasing to the Masonic eye. An intimacy, tender and delightful, is formed between the Fellow-craft and his brethren. It becomes good and pleasant to dwell with him in unity. The task of scrutinizing the mental, moral, and physical character of the Brother is easy and agreeable. The weeks pass swiftly by (not less than four by American usage), and the plumb, square, and level may be laid aside, the Middle Chamber vacated, the apron turned to represent a mystic form, and the Brother *raised* to the sublime degree of a Master Mason. This is equivalent to laying the block upon the wall and cementing it there, never, it is hoped, to be removed. The Trowel placed in the Brother's hands, indicates a duty the most sacred of all Masonic inculcations, and his future place as a Mason, the Sanctum Sanctorum of the Temple. Such are the materials of Masonry; such the working up taught by its founder.

Unlawful Material consists of females; minors; slave-born persons; those whose minds are impaired by age; irreligious libertines (scoffers at religious sentiment); atheists; idots and deranged persons. To these are added the immoral; the lecherous; the disobedient to law, human and divine; the indiscreet in confidential communications; the halt, maim, and blind; the eunuch; the parsimonious; the contumacious; the unintelligent; the brawler, and the violent. Such persons are not alone debarred by ancient law, but by the very nature of Masonic attachments which present no permanent allurement or reward for them.

The standard of *perfection* in Masonic material requires that the applicant for Masonic light shall have such senses, members, and powers as will enable him to give and to receive all the means of Masonic recognition, according to the strictest Masonic forms. This standard applies to various parts of the *body*, from sole to crown; to the *mind*, and to the *heart*.

MEETINGS.

(See Assemblages.)

MEMBERSHIP.

(See also, Honorary.)

The members of the Lodge are those Master Masons who were concerned in its organization and named in the charter; or those who have been regularly raised to the sublime degree of a Master Mason therein; or those who have been affiliated by unanimous vote, and signed the By-Laws, having first received the degree of a Master Mason in another Lodge.

The membership of a Lodge should not, in general, exceed fifty or sixty: it will be found, indeed, that a smaller number than fifty suffices for all the proper purposes of the Craft. The best working Lodges in the land are rarely found to exceed thirty-five members each. The average of the entire catalogue of Lodges in the United States, is less than thirty-four. Whenever the membership of the Lodge becomes so extended that the Secretary can not regularly serve notices and collect dues from them; the Junior Warden supervise their conduct at refreshment; and the Master maintain a fatherly care over them, and dispense sympathy, counsel, praise, and blame in due proportions, the Lodge is too large, and there is space for another. Those Lodges, of which there are many, whose rolls exceed one hundred, and even one hundred and fifty members each, however they may accumulate funds, build splendid halls, and make a magnificent display in public, are actually accomplishing but a small and inferior part of the genuine purposes of Masonry.

The membership of the Lodges (4600) in the United States and Canada, forms an aggregate approximating to 160,000 Master Masons, divided into thirty-seven Grand Lodge jurisdictions.

No Mason can be regularly a member of more than one Lodge at a time. It is, therefore, necessary, before he can change his affiliation, that he shall produce evidences in the form of a demit, of his having honorably withdrawn from a former Lodge, having first paid up all dues, and standing in good repute with the brethren. But it will not be improper for a Lodge to elect the Brother as a member, conditioned upon his producing his demit and signing the By-Laws. This plan is recommended as requiring not a moment's severance from the former Lodge.

To perfect the contract of affiliation requires four acts. 1. The Brother petitions the Lodge for affiliation, accompanying the petition by the requisite fee. 2. The Lodge refers the request to a Committee, with ample time and powers to make thorough inquiry into the applicant's character and standing. 3. The Lodge, at a stated meeting, elects him by secret, unanimous ballot. 4. The Brother signs the By-Laws of the Lodge. Many Lodges omit the fourth link in this chain, but it is best maintained entire.

The system of Honorary membership, prevalent in foreign countries, is being extensively introduced into this country with most favorable results. It differs from ordinary membership in these points: 1. The application is made by some Brother of the Lodge and not by the member to be affiliated. 2. The grounds of affiliation are not a residence within the jurisdiction, but honorable, zealous, and devoted services to the Masonic Order at large. 3. No fee accompanies the application, nor are any charges made upon an Honorary member. 4. It is not necessary he should sign the By-Laws of the Lodge. 5. An Honorary member is not under the discipline of the Lodge for misconduct. 6. The connection of an Honorary member with the Lodge may be severed by a majority vote of the Lodge, or by the expressed wish of the member himself.

MINUTE-BOOK.

(See Secretary.)

MONITOR.

(See also Hand-Books; Manuals.)

A publication in which the exoteric doctrines and practices of Masonry are arranged to accord with the esoteric portions styled the *Ritual*, is termed a *Monitor* or *Hand-Book*.

All the Charts, Hand-Books, Monitors, etc., are derived from the first or Webb's *Monitor* (1797), and exhibit such resemblances to that and to one another as to be used interchangeably in the Lodges. (*See Ritual.*)

An expert Master will never *exhibit* his Monitor while instructing the younger brethren or the Lodge. All the monitorial passages will be carefully committed to memory and fitted properly, each to each, with the corresponding portions of the *Ritual*, and so delivered with the impressiveness of an extemporaneous oration. The same injunction is given as to the public ceremonies of the Order.

MUSIC.

The use of odes and instrumental music in the work of Masonry, formerly so prevalent in the Lodges of America, is being resumed with the best results. A good collection of Odes for this purpose is offered in the present volume.

NON-AFFILIATION.

(See also Affiliation; Discipline; and Withdrawal.)

The severance of the connection between the Master Mason and his Lodge, a connection vitally important to his Masonic character and usefulness, and urgently required by the "Ancient Charges," is denominated *non-affiliation.* It is a great evil, and has done more in modern times to dishonor the Masonic institution and weaken the bonds of the Masonic covenant than any other innovation known to us. In many places, the numbers of non-affiliating Masons equal those of the affiliated, thus crushing the latter under such dead weights as to render it morally impossible for them to carry on the Masonic building with success.

Non-affiliation should be discouraged by every means at the command of the Order. Grand Lodges should fulminate decrees against it, forbidding any Masonic benefits or attentions being bestowed on non-affiliating Masons living, and any Masonic honors when dead. The By-Laws and usages of Subordinate Lodges should pointedly discountenance them while in that condition, at the same time presenting every allurement to them to re-affiliate. They should be forbidden to visit the Lodge more than once or twice. They should not be admitted to the public demonstrations of the Order, its festivals, funerals, etc., under any circumstances, or aided from the Lodge funds, or introduced to Masons as brethren. They are Masonically outlaws while in their voluntary condition of estrangement, and should be treated as such.

It is lawful and proper to solicit them to affiliate with the Lodge.

A fee of $5, or $10 might with propriety be charged for a Demit.

There is no lawful reason for a Brother demitting from the Lodge except to unite himself immediately with another.

A Brother removing his residence to another jurisdiction should not withdraw from his former Lodge until he has discovered that there is a Lodge at a convenient distance from his new residence, and that it is composed of such materials as he can with pleasure associate with. It would be well even then to defer demitting until he has petitioned and been elected by the Lodge as a member. A Lodge may elect an applicant under those circumstances to membership, contingent upon his afterward producing a Demit from his former Lodge.

Thus a zealous, intelligent Brother will never *for a single moment* be in a state of withdrawal from a Lodge; but from the evening of his initiation to the day of death, be in the full enjoyment of the privileges, pleasures and honors of the Royal Craft.

A Demit should only be granted by the Lodge, and in the form of a regular action upon the following petition:

Date.

"To the Master, Warden and Brethren of Lodge, No.

The undersigned respectfully asks leave to withdraw from the membership of this Lodge. His reasons for this request are

Signed

This paper should be carefully preserved by the Secretary, and filed in the Archives of the Lodge. It need not be referred to a committee, but may be acted upon peremptorily by the Lodge. A majority vote would suffice to grant the request.

If granted, *the entry of the fact constitutes the Demit*, and from that meeting the tie of affiliation is severed. Should the Brother afterward desire to return, he can only do so as any other applicant, viz., by regular petition, to be referred to a committee, to lie over a certain period, and be granted only by secret and unanimous ballot.

If the Brother asks for a copy of the record of Demit, the Secretary grants one in the following form:

"HALL OF LODGE, No.

Date.

This is to certify that Brother A—— B——, a Master Mason, and a member of this Lodge, having paid up all dues and charges against him, and being in good standing in the Lodge, has this day, by order of the Lodge, been permitted to withdraw from the same.

By order,

(Seal.) C—— D——, Secretary."

If the Lodge has no seal, the Secretary may authenticate the document by his private seal.

An Entered Apprentice or Fellow-craft, changing his residence as aforesaid, may, by his own and the consent of his former Lodge, be transferred to the care, good will and government of the Lodge nearest his new home. A certificate may be granted him in the following form:

"HALL OF LODGE, No.
Date.

By order of the Lodge, and at the his own request, Brother A—— B——, an Entered Apprentice (or Fellow-craft), has this day been transferred to the care, good will and government of Lodge, No. at he having made good proficiency in his degree (or degrees), and exemplified the exalted virtues of the Royal Art during the period of his connection with us.

By order of the Lodge,
(Seal.) C—— D——, Secretary."

A non-affiliating Mason is as much under the control of the Lodge in whose jurisdiction he resides or sojourns, as to moral conduct and behavior, as though he were affiliated; while he is in effect deprived of all its privileges. All the offenses enumerated in the disciplinary code of the institution are doubly offenses in him, because he evinces none of the virtues of obedience, industry and charity, which are exemplified in the conduct of affiliating Masons. Upon trial for unmasonic conduct, therefore, he labors under a peculiar disability. This is one of the penalties of his withdrawal. In practice, it is found, therefore, that the forgiving spirit of the fraternity which pardons almost every offense in a repentant, humbled Brother has but little exercise in the case of non-affiliating Masons.

The condition of protracted non-affiliation, in its results, is nearly equivalent to a total severance from Freemasonry. It being impossible for a Mason to display the virtues and merits of the Order when forbidden to share in its privileges, such an one becomes in process of time indifferent. He violates the secresy of Masonry because he has forgotten what portions of Masonry are secret. He passes the distressed Mason without recognition, for his memory has lost the means of recognition; even those signs and words, so solemnly interwoven into his covenant, have lost their force to him. He fails to rebuke an erring Brother, or to give to a Brother in danger a timely warning. His evil inclinations spare not those who are bound to him by indissoluble ties; nor is the helpless widow and orphan daughter, who trusted in him for his Masonry's sake, preserved from the curse of his lusts. As years pass, the memory of his Masonic connection fades away from his mind; the new generation of Masons entirely forgets that he was ever a Brother among them, and he goes to his grave as one freed from the ties of brotherhood. None but God and the Recording Angel remember that he was ever bound in a covenant stronger to an honorable mind than chains of brass and fetters of iron! To the Great Tribunal above will he respond to the inquiry, Who dissolved for thee this indissoluble bond?

NOTICES.

(See Summons.)

OBLIGATION.

(See Covenant.)

The spirit of all Masonic obligations or covenants may be found in the ancient fragments of Masonic law and usage, anterior to or included in the Ancient Charges, published by the Grand Lodge of England, in 1723. The applicant for Masonic light may safely believe that he will never be required to assume any covenant whose spirit and intention can not be found in those publications, open to all.

OFFICERS.

(See Grand Master; Master, etc.)

Freemasonry is, to some extent, a system of offices. There is a regular chain of authority and responsibility stretching from the Grand Master in the Grand Lodge, down to the Tyler of a Subordinate Lodge.

The *Tyler* is responsible that none enter unless in due garb and with the Master's permission. The *Junior Deacon* that none retire without due permission and salutation. The *Senior Deacon* that candidates be duly prepared, received and conducted, visiting brethren duly welcomed, etc., and the Master's will in general obeyed. The *Secretary* that the records be faithfully kept, and the income of the Lodge promptly collected. The *Treasurer* that the Lodge funds be securely preserved according to its will. The *Junior Warden* that the moral and social laws of Masonry be duly regarded by the brethren, when *out of* the Lodge. The *Senior Warden* that the Master have ample aid and counsel when required, and the Lodge be governed in his absence. The *Master* that the By-Laws of the Lodge and the Constitutions of the Grand Lodge be strictly obeyed, the work correctly and impressively performed, the charter, records, and property of the Lodge preserved, a due representation of the Lodge had at every Communication of the Grand Lodge, discipline exercised upon erring members, due honors paid the faithful deceased Brothers, and the peace and harmony of the mystic work maintained. Over all this, in ten, a hundred, or five hundred Lodges, as the case may be, stands the *Grand Master*.

OUTLAWED.

(See Materials.)

PARSIMONY.

(See Benevolence; Discipline.)

PASSING.

(See Fellow Craft.)

The ceremony of induction into the second degree of Masonry, symbolically expressed as "conducting the candidate into the middle chamber of King Solomon's Temple," is styled *passing*. The conductor is the Senior Deacon. The instructors, the Master and Wardens.

The ceremony of passing is highly instructive, as a perusal of the monitorial passages under the head of Fellow-craft, in the earlier part of this volume, will show.

PAST MASTERS.

(See Membership.)

A Brother elected by his Lodge to preside over them as Master, is required by those who are serving or who have heretofore served in that capacity, to enter into peculiar covenants and engagements before his installation. The whole is styled the Degree or Order of Past Master, which is fully described under that head in an early part of this volume.

PROCESSION.

(See also, Labor.)

The public appearance of the fraternity in Masonic clothing and emblems is described under this head. It is lawful for a Lodge, by Dispensation from the Grand Master (or without it, if the usage of the jurisdiction allows), to appear in public at the burial of worthy deceased Master Masons, at the laying of corner-stones of Masonic edifices, at the dedication of Masonic edifices, and at the installation of the officers of the Lodge or Grand Lodge.

A public procession must be conducted with all the decorum and strictness of a tyled Lodge. A marshal specially appointed by the Master to preserve order, is the medium of communication between that officer and his members, and takes public control of the proceedings. None but Masons can enter a procession as such. The admission of other societies, by whatever name distinguished, is a gross infraction of Masonic principle. A place is found at the laying of corner-stones for the chief magistrates, etc., but not as associates in an affiliated institution.

None can enter a procession when formed, except by permission from the Master, demanded with the same formality as in a tyled Lodge; and none retire without the same formality of asking and receiving.

RAISING.

(See Master Mason.)

The ceremony of induction into the third degree of Masonry, symbolically expressed as "introducing the candidate into the sanctum sanctorum of King Solomon's Temple," is styled *Raising*. The conductor is the Senior Deacon. The instructors are the Master and Wardens.

The ceremony of raising is solemn, and rightly appreciated, sublime. The most important problems of human destiny are considered; death, interment, the resurrection of the body, and the immortality of the soul arrest by turns the attention, and are rationally applied to the present improvement of the heart.

RECOGNITION.

(See Signs; Words.)

Freemasons possess in their ancient mysteries infallible means of recognition. These consist of signs, tokens, words, and points of entrance. They are unchangeable, consistent with each other and with a general plan, and form a part of the nstruction communicated to every Brother upon his reception into the several degrees. A visitor endeavoring to enter a Lodge without a competent knowledge of these, must be viewed as an impostor. A visitor possessing them in perfection, must be hailed as a Brother, and welcomed accordingly.

REFRESHMENT.

(See Labor.)

The term *Refreshment* in Masonry implies cessation from *Labor*. The *Labor* of the Fraternity is all that is done strictly as Masons, whether in or out of the hall, and includes the opening and closing of Lodges. conferring degrees, exercising discipline, burying the dead, laying corner-stones, dedicating Masonic edifices, public installation of officers, etc. *Refreshment* refers to the conduct of the brethren at other periods.

The behavior of Masons while at *Refreshment* is under the special supervision of the Junior Warden, who is required to counsel, direct, rebuke and prefer charges, as necessity may demand. The elevation of his official column during the period of *Refreshment*, indicates to the Craft his duty.

A revival of the time-honored practice of dispensing the

tangible refreshments of food and drink to the Brethren after labor, of which the other is typical, is happily on foot in the United States.

REGULATIONS.

(See By-Laws; Edicts; Rules.)

Such Masonic rules as are of a standing and general character, are usually denominated *regulations;* but there is little difference in the Masonic meaning of the various terms, rules, edicts, regulations and commands.

No regulation of a Grand or Subordinate Lodge is binding upon a Brother, unless it be accordant with the ancient landmarks, as presented in the Constitution of his Grand Lodge, and the old charges, Constitutions, etc., of the Order.

The regulations of Subordinate Lodges, so far as they can be prudently committed to writing, are found in the By-Laws, which are usually printed and published for general distribution.

RELIEF.

(See Charity, etc.)

This is one of the three principal tenets of Masonry, and beautifully illustrated in the history of every true Mason. The measure of relief to be bestowed is, "the necessity of the applicant and the ability of the giver."

RELIGION.

(See Chaplain; Blasphemy; Discipline; Scriptures.)

The meeting of a Masonic Lodge is strictly a religious ceremony. The religious tenets of Masonry are few, simple, but fundamental. The candidate must profess a belief in Deity before initiation. The intimate and continued use of the Holy Scriptures, which are described in the lectures of the Apprentice, as "the rule of faith," "the inestimable gift of God to man," "the vertex of the circle," etc., demands faith in their Divine authenticity. Reverence to the name of Deity is taught in the lecture to the Fellow-craft, by the most impressive ceremonial, and the Apprentice is charged never to utter that name "but with that reverence due from the creature to the Creator."

No Lodge or Masonic assembly can be regularly opened or closed without prayer. The Holy Scriptures is an essential part of the furniture of the Lodge, without which no work can be done or instruction imparted. A copy of the Scriptures is symbolically held between or under a Mason's hands at all times.

Blasphemy ranks among the most heinous offenses in the disciplinary code of Freemasonry. While in itself inexcusable, being performed without temptation, profit or pleasure, it strikes directly at the root of all religion, and is fatal to all.

So broad is the religion of Masonry, and so carefully are all sectarian tenets excluded from the system, that the Christian, the Jew, and the Mohammedan, in all their numberless sects and divisions, may and do harmoniously combine in its moral and intellectual work with the Buddhist, the Parsee, the Confucian, and the worshiper of Deity under every form. The ten commandments, or their equivalent, embrace the gist of the Masonic religion, and whatever system of faith contains them, without any thing that contravenes them, accords with the Masonic.

The dedication of Lodges in a large part of the Masonic world, is to the Saints John, not in their Christian so much as in their Masonic and moral character; in another large part, Lodges are dedicated to King Solomon, not in honor to his Jewish fame, but as the great founder of symbolical Masonry.

Prayers in Masonic Lodges should be of a general character, containing nothing offensive to any class of conscientious Brethren. In theory, the whole world of Masons is supposed to be present at every meeting of every Lodge, and the instruction, moral and religious, should be directed accordingly.

Passages of Scripture are read, or paraphrases sung during the conferring of the several degrees. The selections usually made (although this matter is in the province of the Master), are, for the first degree, Psalm 133d; for the second, a portion of Amos, 7th chapter; for the third, a portion of Ecclesiastes, 12th chapter, and extracts from the Book of Job.

Forms of prayers are inserted in many of the handbooks, designed for the convenience of the Master. One founded upon passages in the Book of Job, and used in the ceremony of Raising, is peculiarly sublime. Another, prepared for the ceremony of Initiation, is highly appropriate. Others framed for funeral purposes, etc., may be found useful.

REPRIMAND.

(See also Discipline, etc.)

The third and lowest grade of punishment known to Freemasonry. It is inflicted after fair trial (see Discipline), by the Master in open Lodge. An appeal from the sentence of the Lodge will not release the accused from the penalty of reprimand, and should he refuse to appear and receive it, he must be expelled for contumacy, one of the highest offenses in the Masonic code.

RITUALS.

The *ritual* of esoteric Masonry in common use in the United States is that which was arranged by Thomas Smith Webb, (deceased July, 1819), from the formulas of Wm. Preston. It embraces, in the Blue Lodge degrees, a lecture for each. That of the APPRENTICE is in *three sections*, the *first* rehearsing the ceremonies of initiation; the *second* being rationally explanatory of the first; the *third* affording a description of the Lodge and its appendages and the principles and duties of Masons. That of the FELLOW CRAFT is in two sections. That of the Master Mason is likewise in two. The whole is given in 301 paragraphs or responses.

The language of the *Webb Ritual* is old and quaint, but exceedingly well chosen and beautiful. The various attempts to amend it have proved like "the putting of new cloth upon an old garment" whereby both are marred. The results of this tinkering have been confusion in the work, discouragement to learners, difficulty in recognizing and being recognized, and encouragement to mercenary illiterate men who have fattened upon the Fraternity. Every well-meaning Brother should set himself resolutely to the task of casting aside all local rituals as worse than useless and returning to that of Webb, while yet it may be had in pristine beauty and perfection.

The ritual of Pennsylvania differs essentially from that of Webb. The ritual of many of the Canadian Lodges is the arrangement of Dr. Henning and others, adopted in 1813, by the United Grand Lodge of England; it differs seriously from that of Preston and Webb.

A knowledge of the ritual of Masonry can only be acquired orally, no written exposition being made or allowed. Symbols, emblems and aids to the memory are however permitted in the cautious form invented by the old lecturers, and transmitted to the present day. An intelligent use of Masonic emblems alone will develop almost every esoteric lesson and tradition in Masonry. (See symbols). The monitors, manuals, etc., are arranged mnemonically, and afford to the expert Mason a great help in imparting instruction.

No Mason can with propriety apply to the door of a Lodge as a visitor, before acquainting himself with the whole or a considerable portion of the esoteric ritual of Masonry, as this embraces all the means of recognition and is the acknowledged passport of the Order wherever Masonry is practiced. A slight variation in language ought not to subject the visitor to dismission. The examining committee should let him proceed and when his proof is ended, judge of his examination as a *whole*.

RULES.

(See By-Laws; Constitutions; Edicts.)

The rules of Lodges, whether Grand or Subordinate, so far as they can be committed to writing are usually found in the By-Laws of Subordinates, and in the printed proceedings of Grand Lodges respectively.

No rule promulgated by a Masonic Lodge is obligatory upon the members unless it accords with the Constitution of the Grand Lodge and the Ancient Charges and Constitutions of the Fraternity.

SCRIPTURES.

(See Chaplain; Religion.)

Certain passages of Scripture are read or paraphrases sung during the ceremony of initiating, passing and raising. Those for initiation are the 133d Psalm. For passing, a portion of the 7th Chapter of Amos; for raising, a portion of the 12th Chapter of Ecclesiastes and passages from the Book of Job. Selections at the discretion of the Master may be used at opening and closing of the Lodge, and at the public and private demonstrations of the Order. The Sacred Record is so richly filled with appropriate gems for the moral and religious work of Masonry that the only embarrassment is that of selection. Mottoes from Scripture should adorn the walls of the Lodge on every side.

The following from the private manuscripts of Thomas Smith Webb, is a list of those quotations peculiarly suited to Masonic uses and has never before been published:

Genesis.—i: 1–3; ii: 7, 9; iii: 7, 22; iv: 22; xv: 17; xvii: 1; xviii: 19; xxviii: 3,12; xxix: 11; xxxviii: 29, 30; xlviii: 3, 4; xlix: 10, 28.

Exodus.—ii: 16, 18; iii: 1, 6, 14; iv: 1–9; vi: 2, 3; vii: 19, 20; xii: 6; xiv: 14–25; xv: 21; xviii: 5; xix: 9–21; xx: 18–26; xxiv: 12–18; xxviii: 1, 43; xxix: 5, 9; xxx: 1, 23, 38; xxxi: 1, 11; xxxiii: 9, 12; xxxv: 15, 23, 27, 38; xxxix: 1, 9, 14–43; xl: 14, 15, 35–38.

Leviticus.—vi: 10; viii: 7–10; x: 11, 16, 24; xix, 12, 13, 17; xxiii: 42, 43.

Numbers.—iii: 6–10; iv: 6; vi: 23, 24; viii: 7–9; x: 2; xi: 17, 25, 28; xii: 10; xxvii: 18, 23; xxix: 1.

Deuteronomy.—i: 30; iii: 28, 29; iv: 9–12, 36, 39; v: 5; xxiii: 3, 23; xxii: 9, 14, 15; xxvii: 4–6; xxviii: 22, 23; xxx: 4; xxxi: 6, 8; xxxiii: 8–10, 15, 16; xxxiv: 6, 9; xii: 5.

Joshua.—i: 5, 9; ii: 11, 12; iii: 18–24; v: 13, 15; ix: 20, 27; xxiv: 25–27.

Judges.—v: 4, 5, 23; vi: 24; xii: 5, 6; xxviii: 18.

1*st. Samuel.*—vi: 18, 19; x: 5, 10; xvi: 11, 13, 18.

2*d Samuel.*—vii: 1–7, 9, 29; xii: 24.

1st Kings.—ii: 4; iii: 11–13; iv: 1–12, 36; vi: 1–22; viii: 1, 13, 14; ix: 1–13, 27, 28; xix: 8.

2d Kings.—xiv: 13, 14; xxi: 12, 13; xxiii: 24, 25; xxiv: 13–15; xxv: 8–10, 17.

1st Chron.—iii: 17, 19; iv: 14; vi: 13, 22; viii: 12; ix: 11–44; xii: 18; xvi: 4–7; xxiii: 1–32; xxiv: 8, 9, 14; xxvi: 20–32.

2d Chron.—i: 1–17; ii: 1–18; iii: 1–17; iv: 1–22; v: 1–14; vi: 1–19; xxiii: 1, 15; xxiv: 1, 26; xxvi: 9, 10, 16, 19; xxvii: 1–4; xxix: 1–5; xxxiii: 4, 5, 11–13; xxxiv: 12.

Ezra.—i: 1–11; ii: 26–70; iii: 1–13; iv: 1–24; v: 1–17; vi: 1–28; vii: 1–28; viii: 1–36.

Esther.—i: 14; ix: 19, 22.

Job.—xx: 6; xxxiii: 25.

Nehemiah.—i: 1–11; ii: 1–20; iii: 1–30; iv: 1–23; v: 1–19; vii: 1–70; viii: 1–18; xi: 1–36; xii: 1–47; xiii: 1–73.

Psalms.—xxx; lxxiv: 9; lxxvii: 20; lxxviii: 4–6; lxxxvi: 8, 10; c: 4; cxviii: 22; cxxxii: 12; cxxxv: 13; cxxxix: 7, 8; lxix: 27, 28.

Ruth.—ii: 11, 12, 19; iv: 7–17.

Ecclesiastes.—x: 6.

Song of Solomon.—iii: 7–11; iv: 12–16; v: 12–16.

Lamentations.—ii: 7–10; iv: 20.

Isaiah.—i: 17; ii: 2, 3; iv: 1–9; vii: 14; viii, ix: 61; xi: 1–3, 9–12; xii: 1–6; xvi: 5; xix: 12; xxi: 8, 9: xxviii: 16, 17; xxix: 8–10; xxxiv: 11–14; xli: 1–10; xlv: 11–13, 21; xlvii: 12, 13; liii: 1–12; lv: 10, 11; —— 10, 14; lxiii: 9–19; lxvi: 1, 2, 5, 6.

Jeremiah.—i: 6–9; ii: 6; x: 6–9; xx: 11–13; xxiii: 5, 6, 24; xxxi: 12, 40; xxxii: 17, 21; xxxiii: 6, 7, 14–17; xlix: 16, 19, 30, 39; li: 53; lii: 20–24.

Ezekiel.—xix: 11; xxvi: 12–16; xliv: 1–19.

Daniel.—iv: 8; ix: 15, 22–27; x: 4, 5; xii: 1–10.

Obadiah.—i: 17–19.

Joel.—i: 13–16; ii: 1–3, 15–18, 20, 21.

Nahum.—i: 15.

Zephaniah.—i: 10; ii: 13, 14; iii: 2–4.

Hosea.—xii: 6–9; xiii: 4–9; xiv: 1.

Amos.—vii : 7, 8 ; viii : 1–3 ; ix : 2, 3.
Micah.—i : 1–4 ; ii : 7, 12, 13 ; iii : 10, 12 ; iv : 1, 2, 7, 8 ; v : 2–5, 7.
Habakkuk.—ii : 20 ; iii : 2–4.
Zachariah.—i : 13–21 ; ii : 1–13 ; iii : 1–10 ; iv : 9, 10, 14 ; vi : 9–15 ; viii : 1–12 ; ix : 9 ; xiv : 11, 12, 20, 21.
Malachi.—ii : 11, 12 ; iii : 1–6 ; iv : 4.
1*st Esdras.*—i : 1–5 ; ii : 1–30 ; iv : 42–63 ; v : 39–73 ; vi : 1–36 ; vii : 1–15 ; viii : 1–64.
Tobit.—i : 3, 4 ; iv : 13, 14 ; v : 1–16.
2*d Esdras.*—i : 38–40 ; ii : 38–40 ; vii : 36–38 ; viii : 52 ; x : 19–22 ; xiv : 1–9, 45–48.
Judith.—i : 1–4 ; viii : 24, 25 ; x : 20–22.
Wisdom.—ix : 7–9 ; x : 4 ; xi : 14.
Ecclesiastes.—iv : 9, 10–16 ; v : 1–22.
Baruch.—i : 1–8 ; ii : 34, 35 ; ii : 23, 24 ; iv : 14–16, 36–37 ; v : 5.
1*st Maccabees.*—vi : 62 ; vii : 33–38 ; xxiv : 25–29.
2*d Maccabees.*—ii : 8 ; x : 1–3.
Matthew.—i : 22, 23 ; iv : 2 ; v : 33–37 ; x : 26, 27 ; xi : 15 ; xiii : 9–13 ; xv : 14 ; xvi : 17–19 ; xviii : 15–20 ; xxi : 24, 42 ; xxii : 32 ; xxiii : 16–32 ; xxiv : 27 ; xxvii : 45–51.
Mark.—iv : 11, 12, 22 ; xii : 26, 27 ; xv : 37, 38.
Luke.—i : 17, 32, 33 ; viii : 10 ; xii : 2, 3 ; xvii : 3, 4 ; xx : 36, 37 ; xxiii : 44, 45 ; xxiv : 27.
John.—i : 1–45 ; v : 1, 2 ; xii : 38–41 ; xvii : 8–12 ; xxi : 1, 2.
Acts.—iv : 11 ; vii : 30–33, 48, 49 ; xvii : 24, 25 ; xx : 28 ; xxviii : 26, 27.
Romans.—ix : 31–33 ; x : 3 ; xi : 6–8 ; xv : 7–9.
1*st Corinthians.*—i : 30, 31 ; ii : 10, 17, to the end ; iii : 9–17 ; v : 2–12 ; ix : 15.
2*d Corinthians.*—i : 20 ; iii : 7 ; iv : 6 ; v : 1 ; vi : 10–15 ; viii : 22, 23.
Galatians.—iv : 23–27 ; v : 13 ; vi : 1–6.
Ephesians.—i : 6–10 ; ii : 8–10, 21, 22 ; v : 11.
Philippians.—iii : 3–7.
Colossians.—iv : 3–5.
1*st Thessalonians.*—iv : 9, 10.
2*d Thessalonians.*—iii : 5–10 ; v : 20–22.

1st Timothy.—iii : 5–10 ; v : 20–22.
2d Timothy.—ii : 4–6.
Titus.—i : 15.
Philemon.—i : 13–16.
Hebrews.—iii : 1–6 ; iv : 14–16 ; vi : 19, 20 ; vii : 20, 21 ; viii : 1–6 ; ix : 1–6, 11 ; xi : 16 ; xii : 18–26 ; xiii : 6–8.
1st Peter.—i : 19 ; ii : 4–9.
2d Peter.—i : 10, 11 ; ii : 10, 11.
Revelations.—i : 4, 5, 8, 12 ; ii : 7, 11, 17, 29 ; iii : 1, 6, 7, 12 ; iv : 5, 8 ; v : 6, 9 ; xi : 10, 17 ; xii : 7 ; xiii : 9, 22 ; xiv : 18 ; xviii : 2 ; xix : 12 ; xx : 14 ; xxi : 2, 6, 8, 10 ; xxii : 13, 14.
Leviticus.—xviii : 72.
Exodus.—iii : 5.

SEAL.

The official Seal of the Lodge should contain its name, date of organization, and some Masonic device. No Lodge document possesses any authority without a Seal; if taken into consideration by another Lodge, it can only be from an exaggerated sense of Masonic courtesy.

SECRET-BREAKING.

(See Discipline.)

SECRETARY.

(See Officers; Archives, etc.)

The office of Secretary is one of the most important in the Masonic system. He is the historian of the Order; what the Lodge *does* is nothing unless *recorded*. The Secretary perpetuates the proceedings of the Craft. In the financials of the Lodge, he bears an equally important part; what is *due* the Lodge is nothing unless *collected*; the Secretary is the collector. The Lodge that has secured a good Secretary, and retains him a term of years in office, until he is familiar with its finances and history, gains in every relation, whether to the community, the Grand Lodge, or the Craft universal.

The specific duties of the Secretary involve much labor in

the intermissions, such as the collection of dues, taking evidence in trials, managing the correspondence, etc. It is therefore proper that he should have a pecuniary compensation for his services, and this ranges in the various Lodges through the country, from six dollars per annum to sixty. But for the mere labor of keeping the minutes of stated meetings, no compensation ought to be allowed him.

The archives of the Lodge are in the keeping of the Secretary. He needs, therefore, a secure cabinet or chest. He is, *ex-officio*, its Librarian.

The following is a convenient form for a Minute Book:

Elephantus Lodge, No. 65, Valley Forge, Ky., met at the Masonic Hall, in Stated Communication, January 16, 1854, at 7 P. M. The Lodge was opened in the THIRD DEGREE of Masonry.

COMMENT.—1 If the meeting is not a stated one, say in the caption, "At a *called* Communication," etc., and specify the purpose of the call. If for a funeral celebration, it should read, "Called by the order of the Worshipful Master, for the purpose of paying the last tokens of respect to the memory of our deceased Brother, Charles Wellen," etc. The Master of the Lodge has the unrestricted privilege of calling his Lodge, at any time, when there shall appear to him an emergent occasion, but the purpose of the meeting must be stated in the summons and in the caption of the minutes, and no business must be done at said meeting, save that which was specified in the same. 2. Leave a line blank between each entry all through the record.

Officers present. A—— B——, W. M.; C—— D——, S. W.; E—— F——, J. W.; G—— H——, Tr.; I—— J——, Sec'y; K—— L——, S. D.; M—— N——, J. D.; O—— P——, S. and T.

COMMENT.—1. Underscore the words THIRD DEGREE, or whatever degree you are opening in, so as to be able to find those words easily in looking over your records at some future time. 2. Leave a margin on the inner side of each page in the record, of about an inch and a half, in which insert, in brief words, *index notes* or synopses of paragraphs, on the plan of Law Books, which see. This greatly facilitates the after examination of a record, and more than doubles its value. 3. If any regular officer is absent, write the letters P. T. (*pro tempore*), in capital letters, after the name of the temporary appointee. 4. If your Lodge has a *Steward*, independently of the Tyler, add his name to the list of officers—so of the Master of Ceremonies, Chaplain, Organist, Architect, Orator, etc., if there are any. 5. Always write the Treasurer's name before the Secretary's. He is installed first, ranked first in all processions, and occupies a higher station relative to the East.

Members. Q—— R——, S—— T——, U—— V——, W—— X——, Y—— Z.

Visitors.—Jno. Smith, of Hover Lodge, No. 72, Hover, Ia.; William Jones, of Carlotte Lodge, No. 240, Carlotte, Ky.; Alex. Brown, of Morgan Lodge, No. 117, Elkton, Tenn.; Chas. Lott, *late* of Lott Lodge, No. 35, Iverton, Ky.

COMMENT.—1. In recording names of members present, commence with the (Masonically) oldest, and come down to the (Masonically) youngest. 2. In recording names of visiting brethren, require them to pencil their addresses (name and locality of Lodge, etc., etc.) and hand to you in writing. If non-affiliating (demitted) they will name the Lodge to which they were last attached, and you will append the word "late" to their names, as in the form above. As brethren enter, after the Lodge is open, enter their names. 3. Many Lodges have a "Visitor's Book," in the Tyler's room, in which all these things are entered. In this case the Secretary need not notice them. In these little duties the Secretary may have the aid of the Tyler, or some other Brother, if he desires it.

The minutes of the last stated and the intermediate called meetings were read, approved by the Lodge, and signed by the W. M.

COMMENT. 1. This is the first business of every stated meeting; required, usually, in the code of By-Laws, and essential to the good management of the affairs of the Lodge. No vote to dispense with this reading can be allowed. 2. The minutes must be amended, if erroneous, and then adopted, by majority vote, of members present. 3. They must be signed as well by the W. M. as by the Secretary. The Constitution of the Grand Lodge of Kentucky, based upon the Constitution of the Grand Lodge of Maryland, positively requires that the W. M. should sign the proceedings before they can be considered valid. 4. If the meeting is a *called* one, it is not necessary to read the minutes of the last.

The unfinished business of the last stated Communication was called up. The Lecture on the Third Degree, postponed at the raising of Brother Benjamin Lam, at the last stated Communication, was given in public by the W. M.

COMMENT.—1. There are various forms of "Order of Business" in use. The following is convenient: *Unfinished Business*, *Reports of Committees*, *Balloting*, *Reception of Petitions*, *Motions*, *Work*. But the "Order of Business" may always be suspended by vote of the Lodge, and any portion omitted, renewed, etc., at pleasure. There is none of the sacredness about it that hangs around the By-Laws. 2. If the Secretary has been active, he has already made out and laid a slip upon the Master's pedestal, which contains a synopsis of all the unfinished business, from the records, with names of Committees, etc. This facilitates work in a remarkable degree.

The Committee on the petition of Bro. Leonard Harris, for membership in this Lodge, reported favorable to the prayer of the petition.

Resolved, That the Report be received and the Committee discharged.

The Committee on the petition of John Jackson, for initiation, reported unfavorably to the prayer of the petition.

Resolved, That the Report be received and the Committee discharged.

The Committee on the Treasurer's account, for the preceding term, reported said account correct.

Resolved, That the Report be received and the Committee discharged.

The Committee on the petition of Ebenezer Swift, for initiation, asked further time to make their Report.

Resolved, That one month further time be granted said Committee as requested.

The Committee on the account of Messrs. Landrum & Beers reported themselves as unable to agree as to its correctness, and asked to be discharged from further consideration of the same.

Resolved, That said Committee be discharged.

Resolved, That Bros. Lovell, Vineyard, and Carricks, be a Committee on the account of Messrs. Landrum & Beers.

COMMENT.—1. It is better to have all Committees report in writing; but this is a matter of local regulation, and the Secretary can not control it. 2. Every Committee must make a report, either complete or partial, at the time appointed. Any one or more of the Committee, the rest being absent, may legally offer the report in the name of the whole. 3. Reports should be as short and concise as possible. 4. Written reports must be labeled, filed, and preserved by the Secretary, among the archives of the Lodge.

The ballot was spread on the petition of Bro. Leonard Harris for membership in this Lodge, and he was declared duly elected.

The ballot was spread on the petition of John Jackson for initiation, and he was declared duly rejected.

COMMENT.—When the Master has inspected the ballot, he announces the result to the Lodge, and afterward to the Secretary, with a special order to him to make a record of it. Until this is done the Secretary should not enter it upon paper.

The petition of Constant Lane, for initiation, was read.

Resolved, That said petition be received and referred to the usual Committee.

Bros. Hope, Anderson, and Bentley, were appointed said Committee.

The petition of Bro. Seaver Owens, a Master Mason, late a member of Clarksville Lodge, No. 94, Missouri, for membership in this Lodge, was read.

Resolved, That said petition be received and referred to the usual Committee.

Bros. Oglethorpe, Tindall, and Orr, were appointed said Committee.

COMMENT.—1. The term "Usual Committee," refers to an injunction in the By-Laws, which requires, or ought to require, every petition, upon reception, to be referred to a Committee of three, who have a month to examine and report upon it.

2. Unless the money accompanies the petition, the Secretary should not present it to the Lodge. 3. Petitions should be read in the order they are handed to the Secretary. 4. No Lodge is obliged to receive a petition; and when one is offered that is highly objectionable (as from a person whose character is notoriously bad), it may be laid on the table or directly refused, in which case it should be returned, with the accompanying fee, to the petitioner. 5. Money received by the Secretary, as a depositing fee, should not be paid over to the Treasurer until after the candidate is initiated.

Motions on general topics of Masonry were then called up.

Resolved, That an appropriation of three dollars be made to the widow of our deceased Brother, Andrew Bell.

Resolved, That this Lodge will have its next installation a public one.

Resolved, That the Worshipful Master be requested to appoint a Committee to inquire into the out-standing difficulty between Brother Akers, of this Lodge, and a Brother of Troy Lodge, No. 63.

The Worshipful Master appointed Bros. Burk, Marks, and Leonard, said Committee.

COMMENT.—1. Any motion for the good of Masonry is in order at this stage of the proceedings. Each must be in writing, if required by the By-Laws, be seconded, and read either by the Master or Secretary. When the Master puts a question, he rises to his feet, all others being seated, declares the tenor of the question, and calls for an expression from the Lodge. The best mode of voting is by raising the hand—but taking the ayes and noes, *viva voce*, is most common in the West. 2. All who do not vote are counted in the affirmative. 3. The Master has only the casting vote, except when voting is done by ballot. This is general usage, though if the Master insists upon his vote, we know of no law that would deprive him of it. 4. The Master should not put a motion contrary to the By-Laws, to the Constitution of the Grand Lodge, or the body of Masonry. He must remember his pledge at installation: "It is not in the power of any man, or body of men, to make innovations in the body of Masonry." 5. Any motion may be re-considered after it has been passed, and then withdrawn, in which case a corresponding entry must be made on the Record. 6. As a general rule, motions that are voted down need not be noticed on the Record. This does not apply to rejections by ballot, which must be noted and reported to the Grand Lodge.

The Lodge of Master Masons was then called from labor to refreshment.

A Lodge of Entered Apprentices was opened for the dispatch of business.

Simon P. Garrard was introduced and initiated in due and ancient form; the Worshipful Master delivered the lecture in full.

COMMENT.—1. This latter clause is important. It is the Master's duty to give this lecture; and should he fail to do it at the meeting in which the degree was conferred, the omission should be entered on record, so that it can come up as "unfinished business" at a subsequent meeting.

Brother Constant White, on his application for the Fellow-craft's Degree, was examined as to his proficiency in the Degree of Entered Apprentice.

COMMENT.—1. Every member of the Order is styled *Brother* in the Minutes. 2. This examination *ought to* go through the three sections of the lecture—it *must go* as far as the usage of the Lodge, or the edict of the Grand Lodge may require.

The Lodge of Entered Apprentices was called from labor to refreshment.

COMMENT.—1. The Lodge may be called off, as ' ere indicated, or *closed*, just as the Master prefers. 2. No *motion* to close or call off is legal—when the work is done, or the hour arrives for closing, the Lodge is released.

The Lodge of Master Masons was called from refreshment to labor.

A Lodge of Fellow-crafts was opened for the dispatch of business.

Brother Constant White was introduced and passed in due and ancient form; the lecture on the Degree was postponed until the next stated meeting.

The Lodge of Fellow-crafts was called from labor to refreshment.

The Lodge of Master Masons was called from refreshment to labor.

Receipts of the meeting as follows:

Brother John Jones. dues - - - - - -	$0 50
" S. P. Farwell, dues, - - - - -	1 00
" C. White, fee for Fellow-craft Degree, -	5 00
" S. P. Garrard, fee for E. A. P. Degree, -	10 00
	$16 50

This amount paid to the Treasurer as per his receipt.

COMMENT.—1. Money must not be retained in the Secretary's hands beyond the hour of closing—it is sufficient grounds for a charge for unmasonic conduct against the Secretary if he does it. 2. The receipts should be entered as well in the Record as in the Dues Book of the Lodge.

The Minutes of the meeting were read by the Secretary.

No further business appearing, the Lodge of Master Masons, together with the two Subordinate Lodges, were closed at 10, P. M., in form, peace and harmony prevailing.

M. M. NORVELL, W. M.

V. WILLIAMSON, Sec'y.

COMMENT.—1. The hour of closing, as well as of opening, should always be specified. According to the ancient system, these hours were "from the vernal to the autumnal equinox, between the hours of seven and ten; and from the autumnal to the vernal, six to nine."

SIGNS.

(See Recognition.)

SLANDER.

(See Discipline.)

SOLICITATION.

(See Discipline.)

No solicitation to an outsider to become a Mason is lawful. Such an act is a breach of Masonic discipline. The applicant must declare in the ante-room before he can be initiated, that "he is unbiased by friends, and freely and voluntarily offers himself."

But it is proper and commendable to solicit a non-affiliating Mason to return to the Order and take an active, honored and profitable part in the institution whose covenants he is compelled all his life to bear.

STEWARDS.

(See Officers.)

In Lodges whose membership is large and whose trestle-board is rich with numerous and weighty designs, the duties of providing refreshments, preparing the candidates, cleansing the hall, furnishing fuel and lights, etc., which in general devolve upon the Tyler, are placed in the charge of two officers appointed by the Junior Warden, styled Stewards.

SUMMONSES.

(See also Signs, etc.)

All summonses whether of a general or special character ordered by the Lodge, must be certified under the hand and seal (if any) of the Secretary, and served by the Tyler or some other person selected for the purpose. Their tone must be peremptory. They must distinctly state the time and purpose of their issuance. Failure to obey a regular summons is a heinous offense in Masonry. (See Contumacy).

SUSPENSIONS.

(See also Discipline, etc.)

The second grade of punishment known to Freemasonry. It is always *definite*, that is for a stated period, and should be inflicted only after faithful counsel and rebuke. The limit of suspension as defined by general usage, is one year.

Use is often made of this grade of punishment to coerce the payment of Lodge dues. In such cases, after fair trial, as stated under the head of "Discipline" the accused may be suspended until he pays the debt. In such case the power of restoration is in his own hands. It is not lawful to expel for non-payment of dues, nor is there such a punishment known to Masonry as *indefinite suspension*.

The Lodge which suspends has it always in its power to restore. The proposal must be made at a stated meeting, lie over at least one month and receive a unanimous vote upon adoption. The Grand Lodge in no case can restore a suspended Brother to membership.

The suspension of a Brother while it deprives him of every privilege with which his Masonic attachments endowed him, leaves him bound by every part and point of his Masonic covenant. The tie of Masons is perpetual.

SYMBOLS.

Those devices which are of universal application in Masonry, ancient in date and expressive of the secret doctrines and ceremonies of Masonry, are styled symbols or emblems. Every part of the arcana may be and has been taught in this manner.

TITLES.

But one title is common to Masons, viz.: "Brother." A more formal epithet is applied to the Master of the Lodge, who is styled "Worshipful." The officers of the Grand Lodge are styled "Most Worshipful," "Right Worshipful," and "Worshipful" according to their grade.

TRAVEL.

(See also, Charter; By-Laws; Warrant, etc.)

A Master Mason on his travels, has a right to visit every regular Lodge in his way. It is indeed both a privilege and a duty for him to do so; for there is no other method of acquiring esoteric knowledge on a large scale but travel. Every well-regulated Lodge will have a seat and a welcome for him; every intelligent Brother a hand and words of greeting.

To secure this greeting and this welcome, the traveling Brother must have "the pass of King Solomon." He must be at least in outward semblance mentally, morally and physically perfect (See *Materials*). If his limbs are mutilated, or his senses deficient, *so that he can not give and receive all the Masonic means of recognition in the ancient Masonic manner*, he is *physically* imperfect, and can not visit the Lodge, because he has not "the pass of King Solomon." If he is in the violation of any moral law of Masonry, intoxicated, blasphemous, violent, etc., he is *morally* imperfect, and can not visit the Lodge, because he has not "the pass of King Solomon." If he is unable, from original ignorance or forgetfulness, to explain to the satisfaction of his examiners all the ceremonial of Blue Lodge Masonry, together with the rational intention of the same, and do it all *in the peculiar phraseology of York Masonry*, he is *mentally* imperfect, and can not visit the Lodge, because he has not "the pass of King Solomon." An exception may be made to the latter clause; the visiting Brother being a foreigner, or having received his degrees under another form of ritual, would receive allowance on the score of *phraseology*, but nothing else.

The traveling Brother, having first perfectly assured himself of the legitimacy of the Lodge he proposes to visit (see *Charter*), is made to undergo an examination, whose length and rigor are usually proportioned to the Masonic attainments of the examiners. Their report being made to the Lodge, and being favorably received, the Master gives order for him to enter, directing the Senior Deacon to give him the welcome of the Lodge.

At once he is made at ease. If a Mason, famed for attainments or for Masonic rank at home, honors proportioned to his dues are tendered him. If of peculiar intelligence, he is asked to address his brethren upon congenial themes. He shares in the work that may chance to be in progress, and in the after refreshments, if any. His name is entered upon the books as a visitor, and a welcome assured him at future visits. In all this he has realized one of the highest enjoyments growing out of the Masonic Institution.

A Lodge refusing to examine a visiting Brother, is liable to discipline from the Grand Lodge. But if business of a delicate character is in progress, as a trial, an election, etc.; or if the attendance is too scanty to spare members upon an examining committee, an excuse to that effect may be made to the applicant, and thus the Lodge acquitted of discourtesy.

Visitors should be at the Lodge a half-hour or more before the time of opening, that the examination may be completed in season so as not to interfere with the Lodge business.

A traveling Brother should carry with him a copy of the By-Laws of the Lodge of which he is a member, and, if convenient, a diploma or certificate of good standing and recommendation from the same. These he may exhibit to the examining committee. (See *Diploma.*) A non-affiliating Mason can not travel with credit to himself. He may visit each Lodge once or twice, but only on the theory that he is selecting from the various Lodges the one with which he desires to affiliate. Non-affiliating Masons receive but scant courtesy at the doors of intelligent Lodges. Entered Apprentices and Fellow-crafts can not travel as Masons.

TREASURER.

(See Officers.)

The office of Treasurer demands a person of marked integrity. In many Lodges, bonds with security are required of the Treasurer for the faithful performance of duty.

TREASURY.

(See Funds; Treasurer, etc.)

TRESTLE BOARD.

Every Lodge should at all times have designs of charity, piety, morality, science, and self-discipline upon its trestle-board. A Lodge *out of work* is a Lodge in great peril. While the world lasts, there will be distressed objects to relieve, the ignorant to instruct, the erring to advise, and the unrepentant to punish. The Divine "trestle board," upon which Deity has drawn his designs, will ever furnish a Lodge with infinite variety of subjects.

TRIALS.

(See Discipline.)

The rule for trials, given under the caption of By-Laws, is the best ever prepared for general use.

All trials for breach of Masonic discipline may conveniently be arranged thus:

Question 1. What offenses demand Masonic discipline?

Q. 2. Who should bring charges?

Q. 3. What form should the charges assume?

Q. 4. How and by whom should evidence be taken? How should evidence be substantiated?

Q. 5. Who should conduct the trial, and prosecute the case before the Lodge?

Q. 6. What penalty should be inflicted?

TYLER.

(See Officers.)

The duties of Tyler are usually blended with those of Steward. To him is entrusted *the security* of the Lodge. His place is beyond the door, and none of the labor of the Lodge, its arguments, its votes, its pleasant recitals, come to his ears. He has no part in what passes *within* the Lodge.

Should any difficulty arise in finding a Brother willing thus to forego the privileges and pleasures which other brethren enjoy, a Tyler may be made of a non-affiliating Mason, or of a member of some contiguous Lodge.

It is the Tyler's duty to serve all summonses, whether of a general or special character. For this, as well as the unpleasant duty of standing guard over the Lodge, he should receive a pecuniary compensation proportioned to his labor.

VIOLENCE.

(See Discipline.)

VISITATIONS.

Lodges should be frequently visited by the Grand Master and other officers of the Grand Lodge, and by Grand Lecturers. This is for the necessary purpose of inspecting and correcting their work, examining their records, quieting strife and discord, if any, communicating information, and cementing the entire fraternity as one man.

Visitations by the delegates of Lodges to those contiguous to them, is a pleasing feature of the ancient system, and produces good results.

VISITORS.

A Brother in good standing, a Master Mason, and member of a Lodge, properly vouched for or duly examined, may visit any Masonic Lodge by permission of the Master thereof. The latter extends to him a welcome, and assigns him a seat appropriate to his Masonic grade.

A Brother who has all the qualifications above named, but is non-affiliated, may visit any Lodge, as above, once or twice. This is for the purpose of enabling him to select with judgment the Lodge with which he will become affiliated.

The fact of a Brother having been rejected upon an application for affiliation, does not deprive him of the privilege last mentioned.

Visitors must furnish the Secretary with a memorandum of their present or late affiliations.

VOTING.

(See Balloting; Election.)

Questions in Lodges, not involving secresy, are decided according to the usual practice in deliberative assemblies. This is by *yeas and nays*, or by a *show of hands;* the latter is preferable, as according better with the gravity and decorum of a Masonic Lodge.

Each member must vote upon every question coming before the Lodge, unless excused by vote of the Lodge.

Elections of officers are best decided by written slips. (See *Election.*)

A majority vote of members present is sufficient to decide ordinary questions before the Lodge. In pronouncing the sentence of accused parties in cases of discipline, votes of *two-thirds*, *four-fifths*, etc., are often required by the By-Laws of the Lodge, or rule of the Grand Lodge. (See *Discipline.*)

All questions relating to financial matters, to amendments of By-Laws, of the acceptance of reports, petitions, etc., etc., are best taken by show of hands.

The count of hands or voices, after a vote, is the province of the Master.

WAGES.

The two officers who should receive pecuniary compensation for their Masonic services are the Secretary and Tyler. The propriety of this will readily be gathered by reference to those heads.

WARDENS.

(See Officers.)

There are two Wardens in the Lodge denominated severally the *Senior* and *Junior* Wardens. They are elected by the Lodge at the same meeting as the Master, and are installed by him. They serve for the same period as the Master. They are chosen, not for their seniority, but merit. The former sits in the West, the latter in the South. The Senior Deacon is the medium of communication between the Master and Senior Warden; the Junior Deacon between the Senior and Junior Wardens.

In the absence of the Master, the Senior Warden succeeds to every duty, privilege, honor and prerogative belonging to the Mastership. He *is* the Master for the time being. (See *Master.*) He governs the Lodge, confers degrees, presides upon trials, draws orders upon the Treasurer, controls the Secretary, directs the religious exercises, communicates Masonic instruction, expounds the Constitution and By-Laws, welcomes visitors, and appoints committees.

WARNINGS.

(See also Dishonesty.)

WARRANT.

(See Charter; Dispensation; Travel.)

The written authorization from a Grand Lodge to a certain number (usually seven, or more), of Master Masons, to form and open a Lodge and make Masons therein, is styled a *Warrant* or *Charter*. It is commonly drafted (or printed) on parchment, signed by the Grand Master, Deputy Grand Master, and Senior and Junior Grand Wardens; countersigned by the Grand Secretary, and authenticated by the seal of the Grand Lodge. It is a document of the highest possible importance to the Lodge, and its loss is equivalent to a forfeiture of all the privileges of the Lodge, and indeed to its very existence.

The *Warrant* or *Charter* is the successor and perfection of the *Dispensation*. The latter, granted (usually) by the Grand Master, terminates by its own terms, "on the first day of the annual session of the Grand Lodge next ensuing;" at which period the *Dispensation*, with all the books, papers and property that have accumulated through its use, is rendered up to the Grand Lodge. By a committee of that body the records are examined and passed upon. If found correct, and in the judgment of the Grand Lodge there are good and sufficient reasons for the permanent establishment of a Lodge, a *Charter* is granted, and the Lodge, usually with the same title as that mentioned in the Dispensation, is finally organized with the same powers, and under the same regulations as the other Lodges in that State jurisdiction. Its name and number are entered upon the rolls of the Grand Lodge, and announced to the world.

The following is the usual form of a charter:

IN THE NAME AND BY THE AUTHORITY OF THE GRAND LODGE OF ———.*

To all whom it may concern, Greeting:

Whereas, it has been duly represented to the undersigned, Grand Officers of the Grand Lodge of ———, by a competent number of brethren of the society of Ancient York Free and Accepted Masons, residing in the town of ———, and its vicinity, county of ———, and State of ———, praying that they be chartered and authorized to organize and proceed to work as a Lodge, and they having worked under Dispensation from this Grand Lodge, and their work and proceedings having been reported and confirmed, and it appearing to be for the benefit of the Craft in general, as well as for the aforesaid brethren, that their prayer should be granted; therefore,

Know ye, that we the undersigned, Grand Officers of the Grand Lodge of ———, by and with the consent of said Grand Lodge, do hereby constitute our trusty and well-beloved brethren, the Worshipful — —, to be the first Master, — — Senior Warden, and — —, Junior Warden, together with all such other true and lawful brethren as may be permitted to associate with them, to assemble and work as a regularly constituted Lodge of Free and Accepted Ancient York Masons, in the town of ———, county of ———, and State of ———, to be designated and known by the name and style of ——— Lodge No. ——; hereby requiring and enjoining all regular Lodges to hold, acknowledge and respect them as such.

And we do hereby grant and commit to the Master, Wardens and brethren aforesaid, full power and authority to receive members, to enter Apprentices, to pass Fellow-crafts, to raise Master Masons, and to perform all other work of the Craft, agreeably to the ancient customs and usages of Ancient York Freemasons, and the ordinances and regulations of the Grand Lodge of ———, and not otherwise. And also to choose a Master, Wardens, and other officers yearly, on the —— day of ——: and to exact from their members such fees as they shall judge necessary for the support of their said Lodge, the relief of their brethren in distress, and the

* This form, slightly modified, will serve for other Masonic bodies.

regular payment of their annual contributions toward the Grand Charity Fund.

And we do hereby require and command the Master, Wardens and brethren aforesaid, and their successors, to record in their books, along with this present Charter, their own Regulations and By-Laws, and their whole acts and proceedings, from time to time, as they may occur. And also to correspond with the Grand Lodge whenever occasion may require, and to attend the meetings thereof regularly, by their representatives or deputies, and also to pay due respect and obedience to all such ordinances and instructions as they may, from time to time, receive from the Grand Lodge, or from the Grand Master for the time being.

And lastly, the Master, Wardens and brethren aforesaid, in behalf of themselves and their successors, do, by accepting hereof, solemnly engage strictly to conform to all and every of the foregoing requisitions and commands, and at all times to acknowledge and recognize the Grand Lodge and Grand Master of ———, as their superiors, and as such to obey them, or either of them, in all things appertaining to the Craft.

Done in Grand Lodge at ———. *In testimony whereof*, we have hereunto affixed our names, and caused the seal of said Grand Lodge to be affixed, attested by the Grand Secretary, this ——— day of ———, A. L. ———, A. D. ———.

——— ——— Grand Master.
——— ——— Deputy Grand Master.
{SEAL.} ——— ——— Senior Grand Warden.
——— ——— Junior Grand Warden.
——— ——— Grand Secretary.

WITHDRAWALS.

(See also Demitting.)

A Brother, by consent of his Lodge, may *withdraw* or *demit* from its membership by a majority vote. That consent ought not, however, to be granted, save to give opportunity for the applicant to unite with another Lodge more contiguous or convenient. A regular petition for a demit is required, and it is not proper for the Lodge to act upon it unless all dues are paid by the applicant up to the end of the then present quarter. Every thing should be done by the officers of a Lodge to discourage withdrawals. Applications made in moments of passion, or to avoid further payments of dues, or on account of unfraternal feelings between members, should be peremptorily rejected. On the contrary, every allurement to reaffiliation should be held out, and none suffered to remain outside of membership whom kind words will tempt to enter.

WORDS.

(See Recognition.)

Form of Certificate of Demit; sometimes styled a Certificate of Withdrawal: (1)

HALL OF LODGE, No.

————, ———— ——, ——.

This is to certify that Bro. A—— B——, having paid all demands against him in this Lodge, and being in good Masonic standing, has been this day allowed to demit from the same. We fraternally recommend him to Lodges and brethren of the Masonic Order wherever he may sojourn.

By order of the Lodge,

[Seal.] (2) ————, Secretary.

---

(1) A Demit should only be granted upon a written application from the Brother himself, specifying the motives that induce him to ask it.

(2) Without an official seal this certificate will have no value.

MORRIS'S CHRONOLOGICAL TABLES

OF

MASONRY.

COMPILED FROM AUTHENTIC DATA EXISTING IN THE ARCHIVES OF GRAND AND SUBORDINATE LODGES, AND ELSEWHERE.

BY ROB MORRIS,

MASONIC AUTHOR AND LECTURER.

JANUARY.

First. 1787. Convention at Charleston to establish a Grand Lodge in South Carolina. 1851. The *Ancient Landmark* (journal) commenced at Mt. Clemens, Michigan. 1855. The *Acacia* (journal) commenced at Natchez, Mississippi. 1855. The *Signet and Journal* (journal) commenced at Marietta, Georgia. 1859. The *Voice of Masonry* commenced at Louisville, Kentucky.

Second. 1809. The Grand Lodge of Ohio was formed.* 1844. Convention at Iowa City to form a Grand Lodge in Iowa. 1844. Richard Ellis, Grand Treasurer of New York, died.

Third. 1855. National Masonic Convention at Washington, District of Columbia.

---

* I date the organization of a Grand Lodge upon the day its first Grand Officers were installed.

Fourth. 1808. Convention at Chillicothe to form a Grand Lodge in Ohio.

Seventh. 1852. *Masonic Mirror* (journal) commenced at Philadelphia.

Eighth. 1844. The Grand Lodge of Iowa formed.

Ninth. 1806. The second Convocation of the General Grand Royal Arch Chapter of the United States held at Middletown, Connecticut.

Tenth. 1740. First Lodge at Barbadoes, West Indies. 1821. Masonic Convention, Canandaigua, New York. 1822. Simon Greenleaf elected Grand Master of Maine.

Eleventh. 1800. Philip C. Tucker born.

Twelfth. 1818. The Grand Lodge of Indiana formed. 1828. Corner-stone of Charleston College, South Carolina, planted.

Thirteenth. 1780. The Grand Lodge of Pennsylvania proposed George Washington to be General Grand Master of the United States. 1858. Grand Council of Michigan formed. 1858. Grand Council of Florida formed.

Seventeenth. 1706. Benjamin Franklin born. 1822. Masonic Hall at Lexington, Kentucky, dedicated.

Eighteenth. 1836. Messrs. Chandler, Dallas, and others, appeared at the Bar of the Legislature of Pennsylvania, summoned to answer as to the Secrets of Masonry. 1855. Convention at San Antonio to form a Grand Encampment in Texas.

Nineteenth. 1855. The Grand Encampment of Texas formed. 1857. Convention at Hamilton to organize a Grand Chapter in Canada.

Twenty-First. 1831. Robert P. Dunlap elected Grand Master of Maine.

Twenty-Second. 1813. John Allen and John Simpson butchered at the river Raisin.

Twenty-Third. 1833. Andrew Jackson elected honorary member of the Grand Lodge of Florida.

Twenty-Fourth. 1712. Frederick the Great born. 1778. Funeral Oration of William St. Clair, G. M. of Scotland. 1852. Honorarium by Hiram Lodge, No. 4, Frankfort, Ky., to Henry Wingate.

Twenty-Fifth. 1759. Robert Burns born. 1820. Corner-stone of Monument to Burns, at Alloway, Scotland, planted.

1856. Corner-stone of Masonic Hall at Galveston, Texas, planted. 1859. Centennial of Burns' birth largely celebrated.

Twenty-Seventh. 1773. The Duke of Sussex born. 1813. Great Masonic Festival at London in honor of the Earl of Moira.

FEBRUARY.

Second. 1834. Lorenzo Dow died.

Third. 1728. Corner-stone of Parliament House, Dublin, Masonically laid. 1827. *Masonic Record* (journal) commenced at Albany, New York.

Seventh. 1778. Voltaire initiated in Lodge Neuf Seurs, Paris. 1827. *Masonic Intelligencer* (journal) commenced at Batavia, New York.

Eleventh. 1800. Grand Lodge of Massachusetts rendered funeral honors to Washington. 1828. De Witt Clinton, Past Grand Master of New York, died. 1847. Freemasons' Hall, Dublin, Ireland, dedicated. 1851. Masonic Missionary Station at Panama established.

Twelfth. 1744. The Lodge "Charles of the 3 Crowned Pillars" established. 1857. Union of Knights Templar in Pennsylvania.

Sixteenth. 1830. *Craftsman* (journal) commenced at Rochester, New York. 1856. The Grand Council of Louisiana was formed.

Eighteenth. 1843. *Masonic Mirror* (journal) commenced at Columbia, Tennessee.

Nineteenth. 1811. Grand Lodge of District Columbia formed.

Twentieth. 1776. American Union Lodge in the Connecticut Line Revolutionary Army was formed at Roxbury, Connecticut. 1788. Council of Princes of Jerusalem was formed at Charleston, South Carolina. 1856. Woodlawn, Masonic Institute, Camden, Arkansas, burnt.

Twenty-Second. 1732. Geo. Washington born. 1832. Grand Lodge of Arkansas formed. 1850. Corner-stone Washington Statue at Richmond, Virginia, planted. 1854. Masonic Temple at Wheeling, Virginia, dedicated. 1858. Washington Statue at Richmond, Virginia, dedicated.

Twenty-Third. 1853. The Grand Lodge of Minnesota was formed.

Twenty-Fifth. 1723. Sir Christopher Wren died.

MARCH.

First. 1848. Finlay M. King initiated.

Third. 1753. George Washington passed a Fellow-craft.

Fifth. 1855. Masonic Hall at Altoona, Pennsylvania, burnt.

Sixth. 1844. Earl of Zetland installed Grand Master of England.

Seventh. 1842. National Masonic Convention at Washington City, District Columbia.

Eighth. 1777. The Grand Lodge of Massachusetts formed on an independent basis. 1855. Masonic Hall at Weston, Missouri, burnt.

Ninth. 1819. Masonic Temple at Philadelphia, Pennsylvania, burnt.

Eleventh. 1313. Jacques de Molay burnt at Paris.

Fourteenth. 1838. T. S. Parvin initiated.

Fifteenth. 1767. Andrew Jackson born.

Sixteenth. 1857. Samuel Zimmerman killed near Hamilton, Canada West.

Seventeenth. 1822. Israel Israel, Past Grand Master of Pennsylvania, died. 1856. The Grand Lodge of Kansas was formed.

Twenty-First. 1825. Corner-stone of Monuments to Generals Green and Pulaski at Savannah, Georgia, planted.

Twenty-Second. 1312. Order of Knights Templar extinguished.

Twenty-Fourth. 1787. The Grand Lodge of South Carolina formed.

Twenty-Fifth. 1722. Ancient Charges ordered to be printed.

Twenty-Sixth. 1854. Samuel Harrington died at Lexington, Massachusetts. 1857. Masonic Cemetery, Lodgeton, Ky., dedicated.

Twenty-Ninth. 1801. Charles W. Moore born.

APRIL.

First. 1811. The *Freemasons' Monthly Magazine* (journal) commenced at Philadelphia, the first in America. 1828. The *Amaranth* (journal) commenced at Boston. 1834. The *Freemasons' Quarterly Review* (journal) commenced at London. 1855. The *Masonic Messenger* (journal) commenced at New York. 1857. The *Western Freemason* (journal) commenced at Iowa City, Iowa.

Third. 1842. Thaddeus Mason Harris died, aged 74 years. 1846. Col. C. K. K. Tynte installed Grand Master of Grand Conclave England and Wales.

Sixth. 1840. The Grand Lodge of Illinois, for a period dormant, reorganized.

Seventh. 1814. William Hutchinson died, aged 82 years. 1853. Corner-stone University of Nashville planted.

Twelfth. 1777. Henry Clay born. 1856. Corner-stone of Monument to Henry Clay at New Orleans planted. 1857. E. Smith Lee, Past Grand Master, Michigan, died, aged 62 years.

Thirteenth. 1853. Corner-stone Episcopal Church, Austin, Texas, planted.

Fifteenth. 1858. William R. Cannon, Past Grand Master Mississippi, died.

Sixteenth. 1821. Corner-stone of St. John's Chapel, Lexington, Kentucky, planted.

Seventeenth. 1790. Benjamin Franklin died, aged 84 years. 1809. Corner-stone Masonic Hall, Philadelphia, planted.

Nineteenth. 1850. Grand Lodge California formed. 1854. Corner-stone Mechanics' Hall, Toronto, Canada, planted.

Twenty-First. A. L. 2992. Corner-stone Temple on Mount Moriah at Jerusalem, planted. 1821. The Grand Lodge of Missouri was organized. 1843. Duke of Sussex, Grand Master of England, died, aged 70 years.

Twenty-Third. 1350. The Order of the Garter instituted. 1825. Lafayette visited the Grand Lodge of Louisiana.

Twenty-Fifth. 1748. First Temperance Society established. It was by Masons in Italy.

Twenty-Seventh. 1777. Monument to David Wooster at Danbury, Connecticut, dedicated. 1785. Prince Julian Maximilian of Brunswick, Germany, perished nobly.

Twenty-Eighth. 1738. First Papal Bull against Freemasonry fulminated. 1783. Charter of Alexandria Lodge, Virginia, granted. 1852. Magnificent Charity Ball (Masonic) at Dublin. 1855. Masonic Hall at Clinton, Kentucky, dedicated.

Twenty-Ninth. 1856. Masonic Hall at Benton, Arkansas, destroyed by tornado.

Thirtieth. 1733. Grand Lodge of England granted warrant for Provincial Grand Lodge at Boston.

MAY.

First. 1769. Duke of Wellington born. 1775. Corner-stone of Freemasons' Hall, London, planted. 1808. Grand Chapter of Virginia organized. 1847. Corner-stone of Smithsonian Institute, Washington, District of Columbia, planted. 1848. *Masonic Signet* (journal) commenced at St. Louis, Missouri. 1854. Hall of Bristol Lodge, Bristol, Pennsylvania, dedicated.

Second. 1775. The Duchess of Bourbon installed *Grande Maitresse*, Adoptive Rite, France. 1777. David Wooster, Grand Master of Connecticut, slain at Danbury.

Third. 1806. Convention at Norfolk to organize a Grand Chapter in Virginia.

Fourth. 1825. Lafayette visited Grand Lodge of Tennessee.

Fifth. 1821. Emperor Napoleon died.

Sixth. 1777. Convention at Williamsburg to establish a Grand Lodge in Virginia.

Seventh. 1856. William C. Dawson, Grand Master of Georgia, died.

Ninth. 1822. First National Masonic Convention in the United States, at Washington, District of Columbia.

Eleventh. 1838. Grand Lodge of Texas formed. 1851. William Page, Deputy Grand Master of the District of Columbia, died. 1853. Masonic Celebration, Tippecanoe, Indiana.

Twelfth. 1822. James L. Orr born.

Fourteenth. 1801. Corner-stone, Wet Docks, Leith, Scotland, planted.

Fifteenth. 1854. Grand Encampment of Indiana organized.

Sixteenth. 1852. John Snow, Past Grand Master of Ohio, died.

Seventeenth. 1798. Grand Chapter of Connecticut organized.

Nineteenth. 1823. Convention at Mobile to form a Grand Chapter in Alabama.

Twentieth. 1780. Henry Price, Past Provincial Grand Master of Massachusetts, died. 1829. Eli Bruce incarcerated. 1834. Marquis Lafayette died, aged 76 years. 1858. Corner-stone of Arsenal, Dunkirk, New York, Masonically planted.

Twenty-Second. 1853. *American Freemason* (journal) commenced at Louisville, Kentucky.

Twenty-Third. 1776. Freemasons' Hall, London, dedicated.

Twenty-Fourth. 1854. Corner-stone of Masonic Hall, Gordonsville, Kentucky, planted.

Twenty-Sixth. 1858. Corner-stone of Custom House, Portsmouth, New Hampshire, Masonically planted.

Twenty-Eighth. 1850. J. Newland Moffit died.

Twenty-Ninth. 1812. Grand Chapter of South Carolina organized. 1851. Grand Hall, Indianapolis, Indiana, dedicated.

Thirtieth. 1810. William Ball, Past Grand Master of Pennsylvania, died. 1832. Masonic Temple, Boston, Massachusetts, dedicated.

Thirty-First. 1801. Supreme Council, Thirty-Third Degree, Ancient and Accepted Rite, Charleston, South Carolina, organized.

JUNE.

First. 1820. Grand Lodge of Maine organized. 1850. *Masonic Union* (journal) commenced at Port Byron, New York. 1851. *The Temple* (journal) commenced at Carlisle, Pennsylvania.

Second. 1796. Columbian Hall, Boston, Massachusetts, dedicated. 1827. Grand Chapter of Alabama organized. 1852. *Masonic Pioneer* (journal) at Montreal commenced. 1858. Wilkins Tannehill, Past Grand Master of Tennessee, died, aged 71 years.

Third. 1816. The Third Communication of General Grand Chapter at New York.

Fifth. 1249. Battle of Damietta, fought by the Crusaders. 1820. Masonic Hall, Newcastle, Kentucky, dedicated. 1857. Grand Lodge of New York celebrated obsequics of E. K. Kane.

Sixth. 1813. Brother Captain James Lawrence died. 1855. Nathan B. Haswell, Grand Master of Vermont, died. 1858. Wm. R. Lackey, Grand Lecturer of Mississippi, killed.

Eighth. 1825. Lafayette elected Honorary Member of Grand Lodge of New Hampshire. 1845. Andrew Jackson died. aged 78 years.

Tenth. 1819. Grand Chapter of New Hampshire organized.

Eleventh. 1818. Convention at Hopkinton to organize the Grand Chapter of New Hampshire. 1856. Corner-stone of Masonic Hall, Napanee, Canada, planted.

Twelfth. 1798. Island of Malta surrendered to the French. 1798. Grand Chapter of Massachusetts organized.

Fourteenth. 1821. Convention to organize the Grand Lodge of Alabama.

Sixteenth. 1795. St. John's Lodge, No. 1, Newark, New Jersey, established. 1817. Grand Lodge of Massachusetts incorporated. 1851. Corner-stone of Masonic Temple, Louisville, Kentucky, planted. 1858. Corner-stone of Court House, Vicksburg, Mississippi, planted.

Seventeenth. 1775. Joseph Warren, Grand Master of Provincial Grand Lodge of Massachusetts, slain. 1783. Convention at Talbot Court House to organize Grand Lodge of Maryland. 1825. Corner-stone of Bunker-Hill Monument planted. 1857. Statue of Joseph Warren on Bunker Hill dedicated.

Nineteenth. 1792. Union of Masons in Massachusetts.

Twentieth. 1764. Warrant to establish Provincial Grand Lodge of Pennsylvania. 1816. General Grand Encampment organized. 1851. Austin W. Morris, Grand Secretary of Indiana, died.

Twenty-Second. 1850. Dabney Lipscomb died, aged 55 years.

Twenty-Fourth. 1731. First Masonic book accepted for publication. 1744. Grand Lodge of Berlin, Prussia, organized. 1769. Joseph Warren installed Provincial Grand Master of Massachusetts. 1791. Grand Conclave of England and Wales organized. 1811. Masonic Temple, Philadelphia, dedicated. 1816. Corner-stone of St. Paul's Church, Providence, Rhode Island, planted. 1844. First Masonic Festival in Wisconsin (Plattsville). 1854. Corner-stone of Masonic Hall, Brandenburg, Kentucky, planted. 1854. Masonic Festival, Honolulu, Sandwich Islands. 1856. Grand Masonic Rally at Lodgeton, Kentucky. 1856. Masonic Temple, Chicago, Illinois, dedicated. 1857. St. John's Lodge, No. 2, Providence, Rhode Island, celebrated its Centennial. 1858. Commandery Knights Templar of Richmond, Virginia, visited Boston, Massachusetts.

Twenty-Fifth. 1791. Grand Lodge of Rhode Island formed. 1819. Corner-stone of Asylum, Coasters' Harbor, Rhode Island, planted. 1827. Corner-stone of Masonic Hall, Natches, Mississippi, planted.

Twenty-Sixth. 1827. Masonic Hall, Pawtucket, Rhode Island, dedicated.

Twenty-Seventh. 1098. Antioch taken by Crusaders. 1825. Lafayette elected Honorary Member by Grand Lodge of Delaware.

Twenty-Eighth. 1822. Corner-stone of Hospital, Louisville, Kentucky, planted. 1826. Grand Lodge of Michigan organized. 1845. Grand Lodge of Missouri celebrated obsequies of Andrew Jackson at St. Louis.

Twenty-Ninth. 1801. Corner-stone, Bridge over Spey, Scotland, planted. 1852. Henry Clay died.

JULY.

First. 1821. *Masonic Miscellany* (journal), at Lexington, Kentucky, commenced. 1847. *Port Folio* (journal), at Nashville, Tennessee, commenced. 1857. *American Quarterly Review of Freemasonry* (journal), at New York, commenced. 1858. Honorarium to John Fitz Henry Townsend, Deputy Grand Master of Ireland.

Third. 1840. Corner-stone Masonic Hall, Lexington, Ky., planted.

Fourth. 1795. Corner-stone State House, Boston, Massachusetts, planted. 1815. Corner-stone Washington Monument, Baltimore, Maryland, planted. 1848. Corner-stone National Washington Monument, Washington, District of Columbia, planted. 1850. Corner-stone Masonic Hall, Pittsburgh, Pennsylvania, planted. 1851. Corner-stone Capital Extension, Washington, District of Columbia, planted. 1856. Corner-stone Insane Hospital, Northampton, Massachusetts, planted. 1857. Corner-stone Monument to Henry Clay, Lexington, Kentucky, planted.

Fifth. 1830. Grand Lodge of Florida organized.

Sixth. 1812. Convention at New Orleans to organize the Grand Lodge of Louisiana.

Seventh. 1768. Thaddeus Mason Harris born.

Eighth. 1789. Grand Lodge of Connecticut formed. 1789. Convention at Portsmouth to organize the Grand Lodge of New Hampshire. 1818. Corner-stone Mechanics' Relief Society Hall, Washington, District of Columbia, planted.

Ninth. 1856. Masonic Hall, Nashville, Tennessee, burnt.

Eleventh. 1812. Grand Lodge of Louisiana organized.

Twelfth. 1191. St. Jean d'Acre taken by Crusaders.

Fourteenth. 1858. Union of Masons in Canada.

Fifteenth. 1099. Jerusalem taken by Crusaders. 1819. Thomas Smith Webb died.

Sixteenth. 1789. Grand Lodge of New Hampshire organized.

Seventeenth. 1858. John A. Quitman died.

Nineteenth. 1819. Masonic Board Relief, Boston, Massachusetts, instituted.

Twenty-First. 1796. Robert Burns died.

Twenty-Second. 1817. Masonic Hall in Exchange Coffee-house, Boston, Massachusetts, dedicated. 1827. Grand Lodge of Kentucky performed the Obsequies of Samuel K. Woodson, Past Grand Master. 1858. Corner-stone Masonic Temple, Cincinnati, Ohio, planted.

Twenty-Fifth. 1314. Battle of Bannockburn.

Twenty-Seventh. 1818. Convention at Natchez to organize the Grand Lodge of Mississippi.

Twenty-Eighth. 1853. Masonic Hall, Leesburg, Kentucky, dedicated. 1854. Grand Chapter of California organized.

Twenty-Ninth. 1820. Corner-stone Second Presbyterian Church, Washington, District of Columbia, planted.

Thirtieth. 1733. St. John's Provincial Grand Lodge, Boston, Massachusetts, formed. First Lodge opened same day.

Thirty-First. 1783. Grand Lodge of Maryland organized.

AUGUST.

First. 1785. Corner-stone South Bridge, Edinburgh, planted.

Fourth. 1753. George Washington raised Master Mason.

Fifth. 1813. Supreme Council 33° Ancient and Accepted Rite Jurisdiction organized at New York.

Sixth. 1812. Duke of Sussex installed Grand Master of Grand Conclave England and Wales.

Seventh. 1800. John B. Hammett initiated. 1850. Grand Chapter of Wisconsin formed.

Tenth. 1854. Grand Council of Vermont formed. 1858. rand Encampment of California formed.

Twelfth. 1750. First Lodge in Maryland chartered.

Fifteenth. 1738. Frederick the Great initiated. 1771. Walter Scott born.

Sixteenth. 1851. Convention at Oregon City to form a Grand Lodge in Oregon.

Twentieth. 1852. Grand Consistory of Kentucky formed.

Twenty-Second. 1820. Corner-stone City Hall Washington, District Columbia, planted.

Twenty-Third. 1845. B. D. Crookshanks died.

Twenty-Fifth. 1818. The Grand Lodge of Mississippi formed.

Twenty-Seventh. 1812. Grand Lodge of Kentucky paid funeral honors to its deceased Grand Master, Joseph H. Daviess. 1818. Provincial Grand Chapter of Upper Canada formed.

Twenty-Eighth. 1852. Masonic Hall Alexandria, Louisiana, burned.

Twenty-Ninth. 1820. Henry Clay elected Grand Master of Kentucky.

Thirtieth. 1835. William T. Barry died. 1854. First standard form of By-Laws adopted.

Thirty-First. 1845. Masonic Congress at Steinbach.

SEPTEMBER.

First. 1807. Corner-stone North Pier, Frazersburgh, Scotland, planted. 1819. Grand Lodge Kentucky paid funeral honors to Thomas Smith Webb. 1820. *American Masonic Register* (journal) commenced at New York. 1841. Grand Masonic Hall, Lexington Kentucky, dedicated. 1855. First work on Masonic Jurisprudence published. 1855. *Ashler* (journal) commenced at Detroit, Michigan.

Second. 1851. Corner-stone Masonic Hall Detroit, Michigan, planted.

Third. 1833. Corner-stone Jamaica S. Bridge, Glasgow, planted.

Fourth. 1809. Union in South Carolina. 1829. Fourth Communication General Grand Encampment, and Sixth of General Grand Council, at New York.

Fifth. 1781. Provincial Grand Lodge of New York established. 1851. Hiram Lodge No. 1. New Haven, Connecticut, celebrated its centennial.

Sixth. 1757. Lafayette born.

Seventh. 1857. Publication of Universal Masonic Library completed. 1858. Grand Consistory of Arkansas 32° formed.

Eighth. 1800. Convention at Lexington to form a Grand Lodge in Kentucky.

Ninth. 1854. Edmund P. Hunter, Grand Master of Virginia, died. 1856. Thirtieth Communication General Grand Encampment, and Fifteenth of General Grand Chapter at Hartford. 1857. Honorarium to Wm. B. Hubbard from General Grand Encampment.

Tenth. 1804. Grand Lodge, Mass., ceased the numbering of its Lodges. 1844. Ninth Communication of General Grand Encampment and Eleventh of General Grand Chapter at New Haven, 1850. Eleventh Communication of General Grand Encampment, and Thirteenth of General Grand Chapter at Boston.

Eleventh. 1826. Disappearance of William Morgan.

Thirteenth. 1753. Corner-stone new Exchange, Edinburgh, planted. 1853. Twelfth Communication of General Grand Encampment and Fourteenth of General Grand Chapter, at Lexington, Kentucky. 1858. The 600th anniversary of dedication Salisbury Cathedral, England.

Fourteenth. 1815. Corner-stone Episcopal Church, Washington, District of Columbia, planted. 1841. Eighth Communication General Grand Encampment, and Tenth of General Grand Chapter at New York.

Fifteenth. 1851. Grand Lodge of Oregon formed.

Sixteenth. 1819. Second Communication General Grand Encampment and Fourth of General Grand Chapter at New York.

Eighteenth. 1793. Corner-stone Capitol, Washington, District Columbia, planted. 1826. Third Communication General Grand Encampment, and Fifth General Grand Chapter at New York. 1852. Duke of Wellington died, aged 83 years. 1856. J. Worthington Smith, Past Grand Master of Virginia, died.

Nineteenth. 1826. Corner-stone Masonic Hall, Washington, District Columbia, planted.

Twenty-First. 1832. Walter Scott died, aged 61 years.

Twenty-Third. 1857. Convention at Omaha City, to form a Grand Lodge in Nebraska.

Twenty-Fourth. 1858. Corner-stone State Inebriate Asylum, Binghampton, New York, planted.

Twenty-Fifth. 1786. Grand Lodge of Pennsylvania, formed.

Twenty-Sixth. 1853. Grand Lodge of New York donated $1,000 to suffering Brethren in New Orleans, and $500 to Mobile. 1854. Masonic Temple Philadelphia dedicated.

Twenty-Ninth. 1853. Masonic Cemetery Santa Fe, New Mexico, dedicated. 1858. Stephen Lovell died, aged 59 years.

Thirtieth. 1826. Corner-stone Methodist Church, Port Gibson, Mississippi, planted. 1851. Remains of Stephen Girard re-interred.

OCTOBER.

First. 1755. Jeremy Gridley installed Provincial Grand Master of Massachusetts. 1845. *Masonic Review* (journal) commenced at Cincinnati.

Second. 1824. Lafayette visited Grand Lodge of Louisiana, and was elected Honorary Member.

Third. 1814. Grand Lodge of Rhode Island built Ft. Hiram, at Providence.

Fifth. 1847. Grand Encampment of Kentucky formed.

Sixth. 1806. Convention at Lexington, Kentucky, to revise Constitution of Grand Lodge. 1853. Simeon Greenleaf, Past Grand Master of Maine, died. 1858. Corner-stone, Masonic Temple, Nashville, Tennessee, planted.

Seventh. 1822. Andrew Jackson installed Grand Master of Tennessee.

Ninth. 1782. Lewis Cass born.

Tenth. 1825. Lafayette elected Honorary Member of Grand Lodge of Tennessee. 1830. Grand Masonic and Patriotic Feast to Lafayette, at Paris.

Thirteenth. 1778. Grand Lodge of Virginia was formed. 1853. Masonic Hall, Hong Kong, China, dedicated.

Fourteenth. 1819. Convention to organize a Grand Lodge of Maine. 1830. Corner-stone of Masonic Temple, Boston, Massachusetts, planted. 1858. Grand Lodge of Kentucky received from Levi L. Todd, the Sword of Daviess.

Sixteenth. 1754. Morgan Lewis born. 1800. Grand Lodge of Kentucky formed.

Eighteenth. 1841. Corner-stone Grand Hall, Lancaster, Ohio, planted.

Nineteenth. 1794. Grand Lodge of Vermont formed.

Twenty-Third. 1667. Corner-stone New Exchange, London, planted. 1820. Masonic Convention, Batavia, New York.

Twenty-Fourth. 1797. Convention at Boston, Massachusetts, to organize General Grand Chapter, Northern States.

Twenty-Fifth. 1762. Grand Masonic Constitutions, Scotch Rite, ratified. 1826. Grand Hall, Lexington, Kentucky, dedicated. 1848. Corner-stone Grand Hall, Indianapolis, Indiana, planted.

Twenty-Sixth. 1789. Reuben N. Walworth born. 1858. Marcus M. Tyler, Past Grand Master, Kentucky, died.

Twenty-Eighth. 1813. Joseph R. Chandler initiated.

Thirtieth. 1858. National Masonic School Instruction formed at Louisville, Kentucky.

NOVEMBER.

First. 1820. Masonic Temple, Philadelphia, dedicated. 1841. *Freemasons' Monthly Magazine* (journal) commenced at Boston. 1849. *Southern and Western Masonic Miscellany* (journal) commenced at Charleston, South Carolina. 1856. James Webb, Past Grand Master, Texas, died.

Third. 1818. Exchange Coffee House, Boston, burnt. 1830. Winslow Lewis initiated.

Fourth. 1736. Grand Lodge Scotland, formed. 1752. George Washington initiated. 1852. Centennial Washington's initiation largely celebrated. 1854. Grand Lodge of Virginia performed funeral ceremonies in honor of deceased Grand Master, Ed. P. Hunter.

Seventh. 1811. J. H. Daviess, Grand Master of Kentucky, slain at Tippecanoe.

Eighth. 1781. Charter to first Lodge in Vermont. 1821. Philip C. Tucker initiated. 1855. Course of Scientific Lectures on Masonry commenced at New York by A. G. Mackey.

Tenth. 1857. Masonic Biographical Work published by Rob Morris—the first on record.

Thirteenth. 1756. Charter to St. Andrew's Lodge, Boston. 1856. Willis Stewart, Past Grand Master of Kentucky, died.

Fourteenth. 1855. Convention at Leavenworth to form Grand Lodge of Kansas.

Sixteenth. 1789. Corner-stone New College, Edinburgh, planted.

Eighteenth. 1855. Joseph C. Harrison, Grand High Priest, Texas died.

Twentieth. 1827. Corner-stone Monument to Wolfe and Montcalm, at Quebec, planted.

Twenty-First. 1838. Grand Lodge Arkansas formed.

Twenty-Second. 1815. Henry Wingate initiated.

Twenty-Fourth. 1836. Frederick Dalcho died.

Twenty-Fifth. 1851. John Posey died, aged 78 years. 1857. Monument to Gen. Worth, New York, dedicated.

Twenty-Eighth. 1794. Baron Steuben died. 1849. John Q. A. Fellows initiated.

Twenty-Ninth. 1822. Grand Hall, Baltimore, dedicated. 1832. Fifth Communication General Grand Encampment, and Seventh General Grand Chapter at Baltimore.

Thirtieth. 1737. Grand Lodge Scotland adopted this day (St. Andrews) for its Grand Arch Chapter. 1820. Grand Lodge "Espagnola" formed at Havana, Cuba.

DECEMBER.

First. 1806. Grand Lodge of Delaware formed.

Second. 1813. Convention at Knoxville to form Grand Lodge of Tennessee.

Fourth. 1817. Grand Chapter of Kentucky formed.

Seventh. 1790. Duke of Wellington initiated. 1835. Sixth Communication of General Grand Encampment and Eighth General Grand Chapter at Washington, District of Columbia.

Eighth. 1816. Geo. A. Baker, Grand Secretary of Pennsylvania, died.

Tenth. 1827. Grand Council of Kentucky formed.

Eleventh. 1809. Final Union of Masons in Massachusetts. 1810. Convention at Washington to form Grand Lodge of the District of Columbia. 1821. Grand Lodge of Alabama formed.

Thirteenth. 1838. Grand Council of Alabama formed.

Fourteenth. 1799. George Washington died, aged 67 years. 1805. Western Star Lodge, No. 107, formed at Kaskaskia.

Fifteenth. 1856. Corner-stone of Masonic Hall, Woburn, Massachusetts, planted.

Sixteenth. 1799. Washington Masonically interred.

Seventeenth. 1825. Corner-stone of Monument to Jonathan Maxcy, at Columbia, South Carolina, laid.

Eighteenth. 1786. Grand Lodge of New Jersey formed. 1843. Grand Lodge of Wisconsin formed.

Twentieth. 1804. Grand Chapter of Vermont formed. 1837. Convention at Houston to form Grand Lodge of Texas. 1855. Grand Council of Indiana formed.

Twenty-Second. 1820. Grand Lodge of North Carolina paid funeral honors to Grand Secretary A. Lucas.

Twenty-Fourth. 1746. Charter to first Lodge in Newfoundland. 1754. Provincial Grand Lodge of South Carolina formed. 1793. De Witt Clinton addressed Holland Lodge, New York.

Twenty-Fifth. 1522. Turks captured Rhodes.

Twenty-sixth. 1799. Grand Lodge of Pennsylvania paid funeral honors to Washington. 1831. Stephen Girard died.

Twenty-Seventh. 1749. Charter to first Lodge in Rhode Island. 1802. Henry Clay addressed Lodge No. 1. Lexington, Kentucky. 1813. Final Union of Masons in England. 1813. Grand Lodge of Tennessee formed. 1817. Final Union of Masons in South Carolina. 1835. Masonic Temple, Philadelphia, dedicated. 1854. Grand Lodge South Carolina celebrated its centennial.

Twenty-Eighth. 1778. Washington attended Grand Lodge of Pennsylvania. 1778. Charity Sermon by Wm. Smith at Philadelphia. 1778. Gen. Varnum addressed Grand Lodge Rhode Island, at Providence.

Thirty-First. 1809. Corner-stone Covent Garden Theater, London, planted. 1831. Declaration by 1500 Masons of Massachusetts, in behalf of Masonry.

ODES

FOR

MASONIC OCCASIONS.

BY ROB MORRIS AND OTHERS.

ODES

FOR

MASONIC OCCASIONS.

SECTION FIRST.

OPENING THE LODGE.

1. COME, BROTHERS.

BY THOMAS POWERS.

Air—*See Manual Masonic Music, page* 14.*

Come, Brothers of the Craft, unite,
In generous purpose bound;
Let holy love and radiant light
In all our works be found.
Where columns rise in beauteous form,
Untouched by time's decay,
We'll fear no dark or threat'ning storm,
To cloud our passing day.

And as we pass life's journey o'er,
Though trouble's waves may rise,
Our faith shall rest on that bright shore,
Beyond the changing skies,
Where columns rise in beauteous form,
Untouched by time's decay,
We'll fear no dark or threat'ning storm,
To cloud our passing day.

* The *Manual of Masonic Music* constitutes the XXIVth Volume of the Universal Masonic Library. It contains 121 Masonic Odes set to music; also a number of Marches and Voluntaries, and 126 Odes unaccompanied with notes.

2. THE MASONS' HOME.

BY ROB MORRIS.

Air—"*Bonny Doon.*"

Where hearts are warm with kindred fire,
  And love beams free from answering eyes,
Bright spirits hover always there,
  And that's the home the Masons prize.
    The Masons' Home! Ah, peaceful home,
      The home of love and light and joy:—
    How gladly does the Mason come
      To share his tender, sweet employ.

All round the world, by land, by sea,
  Where Summers burn or Winters chill,
The exiled Mason turns to thee,
  And yearns to share the joys we feel.
    The Masons' Home! Ah, happy home,
      The home of light and love and joy:—
    There's not an hour but I would come
      And share this tender, sweet employ.

A weary task, a dreary round,
  Is all benighted man may know,
But here a brighter scene is found,
  The brightest scene that's found below.
    The Masons' Home! Ah, blissful home,
      Glad center of unmingled joy:—
    Long as I live I'll gladly come
      And share this tender, sweet employ.

And when the hour of death shall come,
  And darkness seal my closing eye,
May hands fraternal bear me home,
  The home where weary Masons' lie.
    The Masons' Home! Ah, heavenly home,
      To faithful hearts eternal joy:—
    How blest to find beyond the tomb
      The end of all our sweet employ!

3. UNIVERSALITY OF FREEMASONRY.

BY ROB MORRIS.

Air—"*Feast of Roses.*"

Wherever man is tracing
  The weary ways of care,
Midst wild and desert pacing
  Or land of softer air,
We surely know each other,
  And with good words of cheer,
Each Brother hails his Brother,
  And hope wings lightly there.

Wherever tears are falling,
  The soul's dark wint'ry rain,
And human sighs are calling,
  To human hearts in vain,
We surely know each other, etc.

Wherever prayer is spoken
  In earnestness of faith,
We're minded of the token
  That tells our Master's death
We pray, then, for each other, etc.

Wherever man is lying,
  Unknowing and unknown,
There's one yet by the dying,
  He shall not die alone;
For then we know each other,
  And with good words of cheer,
Each Brother hails his Brother,
  And Hope wings lightly there.

4. YE HAPPY FEW.

Air—*See Chase's Masonic Harp, p.* 22.

Ye happy few who here extend
  In peaceful lines, from East to West,
With fervent zeal the Lodge defend,
  And lock its secrets in your breast.

Since ye are met upon the Square,
  Bid Love and Friendship jointly reign,
Be Peace and Harmony your care,—
  They form an adamantine chain.

SECTION SECOND.

INITIATION.

1. BEHOLD HOW PLEASANT.

BY GILES F. YATES.

Air—"*Auld Lang Syne.*"

Behold how pleasant and how good
For Brethren such as we,
Of the united Brotherhood,
To dwell in unity.
'Tis like the oil on Aaron's head,
Which to his feet distills,
Like Hermon's dew so richly shed
On Sion's sacred hills.

For there the Lord of Light and Love
A blessing sent with power:—
Oh may we all this blessing prove
Even life forever more.
On Friendship's altar, rising here,
Our hands now plighted be,
To live in love with hearts sincere,
In peace and unity.

2. WHILE JOURNEYING.

Air—*Masonic Musical Manual*, p. 6.

BY THOMAS POWERS.

While journeying on our darksome way,
By love fraternal led,
Supreme Conductor, Thee we pray,
To smooth the path we tread;
No fear shall cross the trusting heart,
In faith reposed above,
No dearer joy can life impart,
Than breathes in words of Love.

SECTION THIRD.

PASSING.

1. BROTHERS FAITHFUL.

BY HERCULES ELLIS.

Air—*Masonic Musical Manual*, p. 8.

Brothers faithful and deserving
 Now the second rank you fill,
Purchased by your faultless serving,
 Leading to a higher still.

Thus from rank to rank ascending,
 Mounts the Mason's path of love,
Bright its earthly course, and ending
 In the glorious Lodge above.

SECTION FOURTH.

RAISING.

1. LET US REMEMBER.

BY THOMAS POWERS.

Air—*See Manual of Masonic Music*, p. 10.

Let us remember in our youth,
 Before the evil days draw nigh,
Our GREAT CREATOR, and his TRUTH,
 Ere memory fail, and pleasures fly;
Or sun, or moon, or planet's light
 Grow dark, or clouds return in gloom;
Ere vital spark no more incite;
 When strength shall bow and years consume.

Let us in youth remember HIM!
 Who formed our frame, and spirits gave,
Ere windows of the mind grow dim,
 Or door of speech obstructed wave;
When voice of bird fresh terrors wake,
 And music's daughters charm no more,
Or fear to rise with trembling shake,
 Along the path we travel o'er.

In youth, to God let memory cling,
  Before desire shall fail or wane,
Or e'er be loosed life's silver string,
  Or bowl at fountain rent in twain;
For man to his long home doth go,
  And mourners group around his urn!
Our dust to dust again must flow,
  And spirits unto God return.

2. SOLEMN STRIKES.

BY DAVID VINTON.

Air—*Manual of Masonic Music, p.* 18.

Solemn strikes the funeral chime,
Notes of our departing time;
As we journey here below,
Thro' a pilgrimage of wo.

Mortals now indulge a tear,
For Mortality is here;
See how wide her trophies wave,
O'er the slumbers of the grave.

Here another Guest we bring!
Seraphs of celestial wing,
To our funeral altar come,
Waft a Friend and Brother home.

Lord of all below, above,
Fill our souls with Truth and Love;
As dissolves our earthly tie,
Take us to thy Lodge on high.

SECTION FIFTH.

CLOSING.

1. ONE HOUR WITH YOU.

BY ROB MORRIS.

Air—"*Auld Lang Syne.*"

One hour with you, one hour with you,
  No doubt, nor care, nor strife,
Is worth a weary year of wo,
  In all that lightens life.
One hour with you, and you, and you,
  Bright links in mystic chain—
Oh may we oft these joys renew,
  And often meet again.

Your eyes with love's own language free,
  Your hand-grips, strong and true,
Your voice, your heart, do welcome me
  To spend an hour with you, etc.

I come when morning skies are bright,
  To work my Mason's due—
To labor is my chief delight,
  And spend an hour with you, etc.

I go when evening gilds the west
  I breathe the fond adieu,
But hope again, by fortune blest,
  To spend an hour with you.
One hour with you, and you, and you,
  Bright links in mystic chain—
Oh may we oft these joys renew,
  And often meet again.

BROTHERS, ERE TO-NIGHT.

BY G. W. CHASE.

Air—*Chase's Masonic Harp*, *p.* 62.

Brothers, ere to-night we part,
Every voice and every heart,
Grateful souls to Heaven raise,
Hymning forth your songs of praise.

Brothers, we may meet no more;
Yet there is a happier shore,
Where, released from toil and pain,
Brothers, we shall meet again.

3. THE LEVEL AND THE SQUARE.

BY ROB MORRIS.

We meet upon *the Level* and we part upon *the Square*,
What words of precious meaning those words Masonic are!
Come, let us contemplate them, they are worthy of a thought,
With the highest, and the lowest, and the rarest they are fraught.

We meet upon *the Level*, though from every station come;
The monarch from his palace, and the poor man from his home;
For the one must leave his diadem outside the Mason's door,
And the other finds his true respect upon the checkered floor.

We part upon *the Square*, for the world must have its due;
We mingle with the multitude, a cold, unfriendly crew,
But the influence of our gatherings in memory is green,
And we long upon *the Level* to renew the happy scene.

* * * * * * * *

There's a world where all are equal,—we are hurrying toward it fast;
We shall meet upon *the Level* there, when the gates of death are past;
We shall stand before the Orient, and our Master will be there
To try the blocks we offer by his own unerring *Square*.

We shall meet upon *the Level* there, but never thence depart;
There's a *Mansion*—'tis all ready for each trusting, faithful heart—
There's a *Mansion* and a welcome and a multitude is there
Who have met upon *the Level*, and been tried upon *the Square*.

Let us meet upon *the Level* then, while laboring patient here;
Let us meet and let us labor, tho' the labor be severe;
Already in the Western Sky the signs bid us prepare
To gather up our Working tools and part upon *the Square*

Hands round ye faithful Masons, form the bright, fraternal chain,
We part upon *the Square* below, to meet in heaven again.
Oh what words of precious meaning those words Masonic are,
We meet upon the Level and we part upon the Square!

4. ADIEU! A HEART-WARM.

BY ROBERT BURNS.

Adieu! a heart-warm, fond adieu,
  Dear brothers of the MYSTIC TIE!
Ye favored, ye enlightened few,
  Companions of my social joy!
Tho' I to foreign lands must hie,
  Pursuing fortune's sliddry ba',
With melting heart, and brimful eye,
  I'll mind you still, tho' far awa'.

Oft have I met your social band,
  And spent the cheerful festive night;
Oft honored with supreme command,
  Presided o'er the SONS OF LIGHT:
And by that HIEROGLYPHIC bright,
  Which none but CRAFTSMEN ever saw!
Strong mem'ry on my heart shall write
  Those happy scenes when far awa'.

May freedom, harmony and love,
  Unite you in the GRAND DESIGN,
Beneath th' Omniscient Eye above,
  The glorious ARCHITECT divine!
That you may keep th' UNERRING LINE,
  Still rising by the PLUMMET'S LAW,
Till order bright completely shine,
  Shall be my pray'r when far awa'.

And YOU, farewell! whose merits claim
  Justly, that HIGHEST BADGE to wear!
Heav'n bless your honor'd, noble name,
  To MASONRY and SCOTIA dear!
A last request permit me here,
  When yearly ye assemble a',
One round, I ask it with a tear,
  To him, the BARD that's far awa'.

5. AULD LANG SYNE.

BY ROBERT BURNS.

Should auld acquaintance be forgot,
  And never brought to min'?
Should auld acquaintance be forgot,
  And days of Auld Lang Syne?
For Auld Lang Syne, my dear,
  For Auld Lang Syne;
We'll take a cup of kindness yet,
  For Auld Lang Syne.

An' here's a hand, my trusty fier,
  An' gie's a hand of thine;
An' we'll toom the stowp to friendship's growth,
  And days of Auld Lang Syne.
    For Auld Lang Syne, etc.

An' surely ye'll be your pint stowp,
  An' surely I'll be mine;
An' we'll take a right good willywaught,
  For Auld Lang Syne.
    For Auld Lang Syne, etc.

SECTION SIXTH.

FUNERAL RITES.

1. WREATHE THE MOURNING BADGE AROUND.

BY ROB MORRIS.

Air—"*Pleyel's Hymn.*"

Wreathe the mourning badge around—
Brothers hark! a funeral sound!
Where the parted had his home,
Meet and bear him to the tomb.

While *they* journey, weeping, slow
Silent, thoughtful let us go;
Silent—life to him is sealed:
Thoughtful—death to him's revealed.

How his life path has been trod,
Brothers, leave we unto God!
Friendship's mantle, love and faith,
Lend sweet fragrance e'en to death.

Here amidst the things that sleep.
Let him rest—his grave is deep;
Death has triumphed; loving hands
Can not raise him from his bands.

But the emblems that we shower,
Tell us there's a mightier power,—
O'er the strength of death and hell,
Judah's Lion shall prevail.

Dust to dust, the dark decree—
Soul to God, the soul is free:
Leave him with the lowly lain—
Brothers, we shall meet again.

2. PRECIOUS IN THE SIGHT.

BY ROB MORRIS.

Air—"*Mozart.*"

Precious in the sight of heaven
  Is the place where Christians die;
Souls with all their sins forgiven,
  To the courts of glory fly.
Every sorrow, every burden,
  Every CROSS they lay it down;
Jesus gives them richest guerdon
  In his own immortal CROWN.

Here, above our Brother weeping,
  Through our tears we seize this hope—
He in Jesus sweetly sleeping,
  Shall awake in glory up!
He has borne his CROSS in sorrow,
  Weary pilgrim, all forlorn,
When the sun shines bright to-morrow,
  'Twill reveal his sparkling CROWN.

Knights of Christ, your ranks are broken!
  Close your front! the foe is nigh!
Shield to Shield! behold the token
  As he saw it in the sky!
By that Sign so bright, so glorious,
  Ye shall conquer if ye strive,
And like him, though dead, victorious,
  In the courts of Jesus live.

3. UNVAIL THY BOSOM.

Air—*See Masonic Musical Manual, p.* 325.

Unvail thy bosom, faithful tomb;
  Take this new treasure to thy trust,
And give these sacred relics room
  To slumber in the silent dust.

Nor pain, nor grief, nor anxious fear,
  Invade thy bounds; no mortal woes
Can reach the silent sleepers here,
  While angels watch their soft repose.

Here, Brother, sleep, beneath the stone
  Which tells a mortal here is laid,
Rest, here, 'till God shall from his throne,
  The darkness break, and pierce the shade.

Break from his throne, illustrious morn!
  Attend, O earth! God's sov'reign word;
Restore thy trust—a glorious form—
  He must ascend to meet his Lord.

4. BEAR HIM HOME.

BY ROB MORRIS.

Bear him home, his bed is made
In the stillness, in the shade:
Day has parted, night has come,
Bear the Brother to his home.
                Bear him home.

Bear him home, no more to roam—
Bear the tired pilgrim home;
Forward! all his toils are o'er,
Home, where journeying is no more.
                Bear him home.

Lay him down—his bed is here—
See, the dead are resting near;
Brothers they their Brothers own,
Lay the wanderer gently down.
                Lay him down.

Lay him down; let nature spread
Starry curtains o'er the dead;
Lay him down; let angel eyes
View him kindly from the skies.
Lay him down.

Ah, not yet for us, the bed
Where the faithful pilgrim's laid;
Pilgrims weep! again to go
Through life's weariness and wo.
Ah, not yet!

Soon 'twill come, if faithful here,
Soon the end of all our care;
Strangers here, we seek a home,
Friends and Saviour, in the tomb.
Soon 'twill come!

Let us go, and on our way,
Faithful journey, faithful pray;
Through the sunshine, through the snow,
Boldly, Brother pilgrims go!
Let us go!

CPSIA information can be obtained
at www.ICGtesting.com
Printed in the USA
LVHW102315210123
737613LV00001B/193

9 783375 136420